# HIS UGL

Niko reached out till his fingertips touched Paige Conner's narrow chin. Gently, he turned her face until she was facing him. Eyes the shade of fine, rare amber, luminescent behind her ugly glasses, blinked quizzically.

"Ms. Conner," he said, his words barely audible even to him. "Paige."

He leaned forward, his fingertips tipping her chin so her mouth was the right angle. Her lips were soft and warm, and he made the kiss very gentle. That was all he meant to do—if he meant anything at all. But her mouth moved beneath his, and suddenly the kiss deepened. She tasted of the wine of dinner plus her very own special vintage, and he pressed his mouth hard against her.

His arms circled her, pulling her tightly to him. He felt her flail out, as though unsure what to do with her arms, but in a moment they wrapped about him. Her fingers dug into his hair, drawing him closer till he couldn't tell where his mouth ended and hers began.

His hands moved as though of their own accord. He reached out to her. As his fingertips grazed the base of her breast, she drew in her breath sharply.

The sound startled him, awakened him. He drew back. What had he been thinking of ?

He stood abruptly, looking down at Paige Conner. Her hair was pushed away from her face, emphasizing its heart shape and giving her a morning-after mussiness that made him throb despite himself. Her lips were drawn together as though she tried again to taste their kiss. Their eyes caught, and she immediately looked down at her lap. Her hair again half hid her face.

"Niko," she said, her soft voice wavering. "I don't think we should—"

"You are absolutely right, Ms. Conner. We should not." He turned and stomped away....

# LINDA O. JOHNSTON

## The Glass Slipper

LOVE SPELL  NEW YORK CITY

*Acknowledgment:*

*Special thanks to Joanna Cagan, my wonderful editor, who has shown me that fairy tales do come true.*

*Dedication:*

*For my sons Eric and Keith, with love, to embarrass them; For my parents, Estelle Richest Zangwill and Steve Osgood, in gratitude for the writing genes; And, as always, for Fred, my Prince Charming.*

LOVE SPELL®

July 1996

Published by

Dorchester Publishing Co., Inc.
276 Fifth Avenue
New York, NY 10001

The name "Love Spell" and its logo are trademarks of Dorchester Publishing Co., Inc.

Printed in the United States of America.

# The Glass Slipper

# Chapter One

The small, uniformed porter sagged beneath the weight of Paige Conner's two big suitcases and carry-on. Still, he managed to scuttle quickly through the unfinished airport terminal. Before she could help, he banged open the door with his backside. "Thanks," she said, squeezing around him.

The din outside was deafening; dozers and hammers and hollering workers were underscored by the distant roar of the departing jet that had brought her to Dargentia. This wasn't what she'd expected of an airport, even that of a newly emerging country. The crowd here was construction workers, not travelers. She'd been the only person to deplane.

There was nothing that should make her feel nervous. After all, the prince of Dargentia had invited her. Sort of.

The porter set down her bags. "*Ici*," he yelled above the chaos. Then, apparently assuming she didn't understand French, he pointed to where she stood and said in heavily accented English, "Here. You wait."

With her forefinger, she pushed her glasses up the bridge of her nose. Wasn't someone going to meet her? She saw no one but construction workers. Not even a taxi. Whom could she ask for help?

She felt sticky, uncomfortable. The navy blue suit she'd worn for travel was professional enough but much too warm for this damp, mild spring day.

A motor suddenly ground and growled, far louder than the rest of the noise. Startled, she turned to see its source.

A forklift was hurtling toward her. A huge crate bounced crazily atop its raised prongs.

"Hey!" Paige cried. She wasn't surprised the driver didn't hear. The monster didn't veer as it continued its collision course with her very vulnerable self.

Beside her, along the road, barreled a big black car. To step

7

off the curb would cast her to another equally gruesome fate. Her baggage blocked any quick retreat toward the airport building.

The car kept pace with the forklift as it gained on her, the box it held more tipsy than ever. With a small scream, she started running, her skirt swatting her legs. Her shoulder-length hair blew into her face.

She heard the squeal of tires. Suddenly she was shoved sideways and to the ground, a heavy weight crushing her, though something prevented her head from cracking against the sidewalk. "Hey!" she tried to say again—just as, from the corner of her eye, she saw the crate smash onto the pavement right where she'd been standing. The wood split open, loosing a melange of concrete chunks, splintering boards and a generally nasty conglomeration of debris in one enormous, dust-mushrooming crash.

Except for the plane in the distance, all other noise stopped. Her heart pounding, from fear as much as exertion, she tried to take a deep, calming breath, but the heaviness remained on her chest.

"Are you all right?" asked a deep voice in English, causing a reverberation throughout her body.

Startled, she looked up—into eyes the color of the rich, potent French coffee she'd sampled at Orly Airport. They belonged to the most gorgeous man Paige had ever seen.

She tried to nod but couldn't. Her head seemed caught in a vise, paralyzed. Maybe her spinal cord had snapped. Maybe . . .

"Here," the man said, causing a new vibration within her. Gently, he pulled away the hand that had been cradling her head, and she found her neck supported it just fine.

"Oh," she said. She thought about her own body for a moment. Everything seemed to be intact. "I'm fine," she said. She smiled. "Just great, in fact."

Only then did she become fully aware that the weight upon her was his. His chest was firmly atop hers, crushing her breasts most intimately. At least that explained the humming all through her each time he spoke. And then there was the feeling in the vicinity of her stomach, where something stirred and hardened and grew, instigating a strange, answering throb within her not far below.

The pace of her breathing quickened, and she moved a bit, unsure if she was trying to throw him off—or bring him closer.

He pulled away, not looking at all abashed as he stood and

held out his hand. His grip was firm as he helped her to her feet.

Her limbs were as stiff as steel. She ached everywhere. She knew she'd soon wear an assortment of bruises in odd locations. Still, she was alive. "Thanks," she said, holding on a moment longer than necessary. Realizing what she was doing, she let go as quickly as if the hand she held had bitten hers. Heat slunk from her neck to the crown of her head. Her skirt had ridden up her thighs, and she smoothed it down.

She couldn't help staring at him. Lord, was he handsome! His facial features were chiseled, full of angles and shadows, with a prominent bone structure framing the wonderful eyes she'd noticed before.

His brows slanted together in a frown as he looked her up and down, as though to assure himself she was unharmed. They were tawny blond in color and matched the wayward locks of long straight hair and the neatly trimmed beard that emphasized his mouth.

That mouth. It was incredible, with full, expressive lips that were open, enticing, moving. . . .

Only then did Paige realize that the man was talking to her. His frown deepened, though she couldn't tell if it was from anger or concern.

"You're sure you're all right?"

She nodded, suddenly finding a spot on the ground utterly fascinating. Why on earth was she doing such embarrassing things around this man? That wasn't like her at all.

Well, it wasn't like her, either, to be chased by a runaway forklift. Perhaps her strange behavior was some kind of internal celebration of survival.

"So," she began, searching for something suave to say to the man who'd just saved her life. But, fortunately, he wasn't looking at her as she began to shake in a delayed reaction to her close call. She compressed her lips tightly together, biting their insides. Maybe the pain would keep her from crying.

The man's attention was on the crowd of workmen now surrounding them. He began to speak in French so rapid that she picked out only a few words and phrases: *vide,* which meant empty; *personne,* which could mean a person, anybody or no one at all; *la machine folle,* which signified that the machine was either a runaway or stark raving mad. She was much more fluent in the written language than the spoken. A few men came forward, and the discussion was punctuated with eloquent shrugs and expansive gestures.

Her savior turned to her. "I'm sorry, miss." His voice was deep and rich, its English unaccented, but it seemed tinged with disgust. "No one knows what happened. It seems the forklift simply began running by itself. No one was driving it."

She tried to smile. "It doesn't matter. It was just an accident." It had to be. No one would purposely set things in motion to smash her with that slew of junk now spread harmlessly on the ground. But the sight of it made her shudder once more.

"Of course." The man sounded relieved at her reaction. He squared a pair of massive shoulders beneath an oversized natural-colored peasant shirt, gathered at the sleeves. Its v opening at the neck revealed a firm chest covered with a mat of hair a shade or two darker than that on his scalp and face. His brown trousers were tucked into a pair of laced boots. Paige felt surrounded by a wonderful aroma of autumn leaves and citrus.

She closed her eyes, taking a deep breath, trying to ignore that wonderful fragrance. The guy was good looking, in an earthy sort of way. He had sex appeal that wouldn't quit. And he'd done her a favor. But she couldn't stand around thanking him—or gawking at him—all day. Nor could she continue to rehash in her mind the way she'd almost been crushed.

"Well," she said, "now that's over, I have to get into the city." She turned to the crowd of workmen that still hovered about. In French, she said, "I'm here to do some work for Prince Nicholas. Would someone please tell me where to call a taxi?"

The men looked at one another and began to speak all at once, much too quickly for her to understand. They seemed upset, confused. What was the problem? Was the prince some kind of ogre?

"No need for a taxi. I've brought that." The man who'd saved her pointed to the large black car—a limousine, actually—that she'd seen careening forward when the forklift had followed her. It was now parked unevenly at the curb. He must have jumped from it to come to her rescue. "If you're the historian from the United States, I'm here to pick you up."

A thrill of excitement shot through Paige. She was to spend a while longer with this brave, gorgeous man who'd saved her. He must be the prince's chauffeur, an American like her, judging by his lack of accent and informal demeanor. "Great," she said in a cool and collected voice, determined to put her close call—and her reaction to this man—behind her. "My stuff's over there." She pointed toward her luggage.

With a smile barely curling the edges of those marvelous lips, he inclined his head slightly, then went to retrieve her things.

A short while later she was ensconced in the limo. She'd chosen the front seat; even if the guy was a chauffeur, she was American, too, and didn't want to seem like a snob. At least the prince hadn't insisted that his driver wear a conspicuous uniform. Actually, his peasant outfit appeared like something out of Robin Hood. And, boy, did it look good on him! Paige couldn't imagine anything that *wouldn't* look wonderful on him. She allowed herself just the tiniest speculation about his wearing nothing at all. . . .

*Cut it out,* she scolded herself. For someone who'd sworn off men nearly as soon as she'd first noticed them, she was certainly letting her mind veer in weird directions.

But here she was, being driven in a limousine by a perfectly gorgeous man, to meet a real prince.

As she'd done often in the past weeks, she wondered once more about this job that had fallen on her out of the blue. If she hadn't known better, she'd have thought the whole situation smacked of a hand wielding something a lot more potent than her brother Joe's minuscule influence over the U.S. Government. A genuine magic wand, perhaps?

Hardly!

Still, here she was, ordinary Paige Conner, about to go to work for the prince of a newly emerging country. The whole thing seemed just a bit too much like a fairy tale.

Thanks to her own futile but vivid fantasies, Paige had learned long ago not to believe in fairy tales. Although her ulterior motive for being here sure smacked of one.

But not for her.

As the car reached a stop sign at the end of the airport road, she turned to the driver and held out her hand. "By the way, my name is Paige. Paige Conner. I'm from near Washington, D.C. Thanks again for saving me."

His dark eyes sparkled as though he'd just heard a joke. Or maybe he was about to tell one. He took her proffered hand in

11

his strong, firm grasp and held on. "You're very welcome," he said. "My name is Nicholas, but you can call me Niko. I'm prince of Dargentia."

The woman called Paige inhaled sharply.

As Niko had lain atop her on the ground, he'd noticed a lot about her. She smelled soft and clean, like baby powder. Her body was curved in all the enticingly right places, though she'd hidden its soft roundness beneath a dark, stuffy suit. Her face was heart-shaped, her wide cheekbones emphasized by the awful glasses that sat upon them. Her chin was small and pointed and daunt-ingly determined.

Then there were her eyes. The large black rims of her glasses served to frame, not hide, their amazing amber shade. Now, the alluring amber deepened as those surprised eyes widened, then narrowed. Her well-defined but unadorned lips opened in apparent amazement, and she blushed quite attractively.

But then she began speaking, her accusatory tone not at all appealing. "Why didn't you tell me when you offered me a ride that you were the prince? Did you deliberately set out to humiliate me?"

He stiffened. "Not particularly. Did you deliberately set out to humiliate me by assuming I was not the prince?"

She stayed silent for a few moments. Her deep golden eyes studied him suspiciously. Then she gave a glimmer of a smile. "Touché," she said. "I guess we're even."

He relaxed, switched his foot from brake to accelerator, and turned the car onto one of Dargentia's main highways. It wasn't the fastest way to the capital, but he had a reason for using it.

"I'm sorry," she continued. "It never occurred to me that the prince might pick me up. I mean, I'm just a new employee. And you didn't act the way I expected a prince . . . I mean your clothes—"

"Perhaps I should have met you at the airport in a tuxedo. I've a collection, you know. Of course, then I might not have wanted to soil it by pushing you out of the way of the forklift."

He didn't try to stifle his sarcasm. Americans had such an of-fensive attitude toward royalty. He'd learned that during his child-hood and youth spent in exile in the exalted state of California. Even more while studying at Harvard, once some infernal news reporter ferreted out his true identity. American men wanted to be his buddy. Women wanted to marry him—or, rather, his title.

"I said I was sorry." After a moment's silence she continued, "Look, I didn't mean for us to start off on the wrong foot. Can we try again?"

Stealing his gaze from the road, he glanced at her. She stared at him intently. Her small hands clasped one another in her lap in seeming supplication. He'd no reason to be angry just because of where she was from. No need to make her worry about her job.

"Sure," he said. "No problem. Ms. Conner, I'm Prince Nicholas of Dargentia, and I'm pleased to meet you."

"I'm Paige Conner of the United States, Your Highness." She executed a small bow from her waist, no mean feat since she'd fastened her shoulder-strapped seat belt.

He smiled. Paige Conner and he would get along fine.

Paige was such a harsh, unfeminine name. She wasn't what he'd expected. Oh, he'd buy that a historical scholar might wear glasses, and wear her hair in a most unbecoming style—all bangs and straight length. But the color of that hair! It was beautiful, as black as the swans gracing the moat around his palace, but with highlights as deep and rich a red as his family's legendary rubies.

And the way she'd looked at him as she lay on the ground beneath him! The sultriness in those soft amber eyes had stirred him—they and the feel of her feminine curves. Oh, had they ever!

But things would go no further. They couldn't, no matter how she stoked his libido. American women's expectations soared after seduction by royalty. He had no reason to think this one was different. And he had obligations.

One of them, now, was to learn what had happened with that runaway forklift. He was sure the men were right; it had been an accident. But it could have had disastrous results.

Nothing like that could happen again. The cost to Dargentia for harming a visitor would be too high.

She was silent, staring out the window. He tried to imagine her thoughts. The place was full of rolling hills covered by farmland where newly sprouting crops had noticed it was spring. Here and there were farmhouses, many covered by scaffolding. Construction was not just afoot at the airport.

"Have you been to Dargentia before?" he asked to make conversation. The answer would be negative. Few strangers had ever been to Dargentia.

"This is my first time out of the United States." She didn't look at him as she replied. Her gaze was glued out the window. "There's a lot of building going on here."

"This country was neglected for a long time while it was a political football among Germany, France and Switzerland. The rebuilding is all part of my program to save Dargentia, the reason you're here."

He felt her eyes on him. "Why *am* I here?"

"To give Dargentia a history." He kept his tone carefully casual; no use shouting his usual anger about the tragedy of the past. His ancestral home had little recorded history. And if his plan to save it didn't work, it would not have a future, either.

"*Give* Dargentia a history? I'm not a fiction writer, Your Highness. I'm a historian."

"I know," he said. Again, he glanced at her. "Please call me Niko, and I'll call you Paige. All right?"

Looking startled and a little uncomfortable, she still nodded gamely. "Sure . . . Niko."

"Now, Paige, what were you told about your assignment?"

She shook her head. "Not much. My brother Joe's with the U.S. State Department, diplomatic support. He heard Dargentia needed a historian in a hurry and figured he could add a notch to his career belt if he recommended someone good and quick. His obvious choice was me."

"Obviously. But are you good?" He let his teasing show in his voice.

She took him seriously, though, sitting up straight. "Of course! I've written a textbook used at a lot of colleges. And you must know I turned down a job as curator of a museum to come here."

"I'm sorry."

She relaxed again. "It's okay. My decision. With luck, I'll make a name for myself here that'll open more doors."

"What museum?" he asked.

"A brand-new one in Miller's Mine, New Mexico."

Where in heaven's name was that? He tossed her a quizzical glance.

"It's a small town." Her tone was defensive. "But the museum would have been all mine to run."

He said nothing, but the worries on his shoulders increased by one. A lot rode on his plans for Dargentia. Now another person would be hurt if he failed.

But he would succeed. No matter what it took.

The road had started to climb into the mountains surrounding the capital, D'Argent City, changing from wide and straight to narrow and twisting. Oaks and beeches formed a thick, sheltering forest about them.

And then they rounded the bend he'd been waiting for.

Paige Conner reacted just as he had hoped she would. Staring in openmouthed wonder, she drew in her breath. "Oh, how beautiful!"

Not attempting to hide his wide grin, Niko settled back into his seat. Paige would surely be the first of many visitors to be impressed by the wondrous sight. Everything would work out fine.

Paige could hardly believe her eyes. The sight of D'Argent City could make her believe again in fairy tales. Almost.

They'd broken free of the woods, and her side of the road was now protected from a drop-off only by a lacy metal railing. And the view—it was magnificent!

Below was the coiling length of the majestic river that gave the country its name—the Argent. That meant silver. Paige could see where the name came from; the water shimmered, reflecting the town perched on the mountainside on the opposite bank.

Except for the ubiquitous scaffolding and construction, the town was picture-book perfect, a conglomeration of small, half-timbered buildings stretching along the riverbank near a bridge spanning the Argent. Houses sprouted up the mountainside, chaletlike and charming.

And above it all was the castle.

Proud and noble, it stood like a monarch surveying its subjects. The granite structure rose behind surrounding crenellated bulwarks. Its walls were interspersed with narrow, arched windows, its towers and turrets connected by parapets. It was more graceful, yet more forbidding, than anything Paige could have imagined, no matter how many castles she'd studied in her quest for her doctoral degree in history.

"Is that where you live?" she whispered.

"Sure." His deep baritone voice held a note of pride. "It's also where you'll live while you're in Dargentia."

"Really?"

She turned to him. He was watching her face, a smile stretching those wonderful, sensual lips. "Really!"

Unable to suppress an answering grin, she nestled back into the comfortable limousine seat, ignoring the soreness squeezing her muscles. She, ordinary Paige Conner, was going to live in a castle for—well, she didn't know how long. It didn't matter. She'd always dreamed. . . .

Forget that. That stupid dream evolved from her once-upon-a-time childish love of fairy tales. Now she was totally adult, totally logical.

But she was going to live in a castle!

She couldn't let Prince Niko see her excitement. He'd hired a historian, not an infantile dreamer. At least he neither heard the pounding of her heart nor sensed her urge, spreading from her toes all the way up her legs, to whirl and dance with joy. Nor did he know of her ulterior motive in accepting this assignment. No one did.

Keeping her voice calm, she asked, "Will I be researching the history of the castle?"

He nodded. "Yes, but there's more. I'll save my explanation for dinner tonight. Just be aware that your work is vital to Dargentia."

Paige smiled to herself. He'd confirmed what she'd been told before accepting this job: She would be doing something of national importance for this small, needy country. Impressive! If only her parents were impressed. . . . Her smile swiftly faded.

They drove past two large hotels. "They're opening in a week," Niko said. "They're luxury hotels, both of them, unaffiliated with any chain."

Again, Paige sensed pride. This time, though, it was tinged with something else. Concern? Worry? "Weren't there hotels here before?"

"Only small ones, and they were seldom filled. That's the root of my revitalization plan: tourists. I'll explain more tonight, when I fill you in about your job."

They headed over the bridge, passing into the old part of town. People were gathered in the central square, where a fountain spewed water into an oblong pool. A small flag in Dargentia's colors of crimson, silver and royal purple waved from a pole at the far end. In the center of the square was the statue of a stern-looking man, his chin raised proudly.

"An ancestor of yours?" Paige asked.

"Yes, Nicholas the First. He lived nearly three hundred years ago. I'm Nicholas the Second, and there weren't any ruling kings in between. A lot of wasted time separated him and me."

Paige noted the bitterness in his voice, his forbidding scowl. She hoped she'd learn about Niko's namesake—and why the long intervening gap. In all her studies she'd heard little about Dargentia. That revealed a lot about the tough times this tiny country must have undergone.

There had been that one small item, though—just a footnote in history, unimportant to anyone but her. But she could hardly wait to fill in the blank pages with what she could learn here.

As they passed through town, a lot of people waved, and Niko waved back. He used an automatic control to open the car windows, and calls of "Niko, Niko," soared in. No equivalent of Secret Service men ran nervously beside the car. No worries, Paige supposed, about violence.

But she couldn't help thinking about her own close call and shivering.

Eventually, the limo began the series of switchbacks up the mountain to the castle. In a short while they arrived at a filled moat that surrounded the outer castle wall, with attractive landscaping all about. Swans swam in the clear, green water, mostly black and all wonderfully graceful. The scene was lovely, the atmosphere peaceful—an anomalous impression, Paige thought, to be given by a former fortress and the moat that defended it.

The limo's tires made washboard noises as they drove over a wooden drawbridge. They had to stop at the lowered portcullis. Niko pressed a button on a control on his visor, and the gate drew upward.

"Bet invaders some time in this place's past would have loved to have done that," Paige commented.

"Bet you're right," Niko agreed with a laugh.

They drove through the narrow opening in the thick stone walls, beneath the pointed metal spikes of the raised portcullis and into a lushly landscaped courtyard. Willows and maples wore

# Linda O. Johnston

the pale green leaves of spring, and flowering bushes lent color along crisscrossed paths on the lawn.

And in the center was the castle, tall and towered and even more magnificent up close. From the peak of its foremost tower, an enormous Dargentian flag snapped in the breeze.

Niko parked before a huge, ancient wooden door and glanced at his watch. "Too late for a tour now. Dinner will be served in about an hour. I'll take you to your room, then leave you to freshen up, if you wish, though you look fine; we'll dine informally tonight."

As he glanced at her, she tried to stop the flush she felt creeping up her face, dipping her head in a motion she had perfected as a kid who'd tried to hide her ugly spectacles by the forward flow of her hair. She didn't believe she looked fine. Not with those dark, assessing eyes on her. She was rumpled from her trip, from being tackled to the ground for her own safety. But more than her clothing was at issue. She wanted, suddenly, to be beautiful, so this gorgeous prince would notice her as something other than his employee.

But Paige was nothing if not realistic. She was neither tall nor petite, svelte nor voluptuous, but just medium in height, perhaps on the curvy side but, well . . . simply ordinary. And she wore glasses, for heaven's sake.

She wasn't worthy of a prince's notice.

She leapt from the car, only to feel embarrassed that she hadn't waited, for Niko had come around to help her out. She lifted her carry-on, and he took her suitcases. She wondered why a retinue of servants hadn't rushed out to handle the luggage.

He pushed open the large wooden door. Not unexpectedly, it squealed as though its black iron hinges were antique. He led her inside.

The enormous entry hall felt surprisingly warm, though Paige smelled the mustiness of the ages. She vowed to return and take her time examining the many paintings and tapestries hung on the wood-paneled and stone walls they passed, to explore the myriad of sumptuous rooms she glimpsed. Niko led her up a wide stone stairway with a red plush runner, down one hall and then another, until she felt she ought to have dropped crumbs like Hansel and Gretel to find her way back.

Finally he stopped. "This will be your home while you're

here," he said, gesturing through an open door.

They were in one of the many towers, for the walls of the room she entered were curved. She gasped aloud in delight. The room was utterly charming. A surprisingly petite carved tester bed dominated the antique furnishings, and a painted scene that suggested Greek mythology graced the ceiling. "This is wonderful," Paige managed.

"I hope you'll be comfortable." Niko put down her bags and opened the wardrobe that matched the bed. "People who built castles didn't think about closet space," he explained.

They didn't know much about plumbing, either, so she was relieved when he showed her the place had been updated. In fact, her bathroom had nearly as much charm as the bedroom. Its fixtures were antique-looking but functional, all trimmed in gleaming brass.

"Someone will come to take you to supper." He turned to leave the room. Paige felt a momentary pang of abandonment, wishing he'd promised to come himself.

Ridiculous! He was the prince. Surely, he had a stable of servants who'd take care of her from now on. She was, she reminded herself, just an employee.

"Meantime," he continued, "if you need anything, just call." He gestured toward a dainty table beside the bed on which sat a many-buttoned telephone. It looked too modern for the quaint decor. "We've an updated phone system, though it doesn't always work the way it should." He explained how to use it.

"Thanks." Paige felt grateful for everything: Niko's hiring her, picking her up, bringing her to this fairy-tale setting—and saving her life.

The prince inclined his head, and his unruly blond hair swayed about his ears. She had an absurd urge to smooth it back.

Just because she was on a first-name basis with a prince . . . she, plain, ordinary Paige Conner was on a first-name basis with a prince! One more handsome than any she'd dreamed of even in her most imaginative fairy-tale days. Brave enough to leap in front of fire-breathing forklifts to save a life. And, of course, utterly charming.

Fortunately, he'd turned to leave, so he hadn't seen the scarlet color she felt creeping up her face. Prince Charming, indeed! "See you later, Niko," she said, too softly for him to hear.

Then he was gone.

Paige smiled as she began to unpack. This job was simply too good to be true. A gorgeous prince, a castle, the opportunity to pursue her own historical research—fantastic! She pulled a tailored blouse from her bag and unfolded it, laying it on the lacy bedspread.

"Isn't this wonderful?" A sweet, wavering voice from behind her echoed her thoughts.

"Oh, no!" whispered Paige.

# Chapter Two

Paige wasn't going to turn around. The voice was familiar. Too familiar.

A voice conjured up by her own overwrought imagination.

Well, she wasn't going to give in to it this time. "You're not there," she said aloud, staring at a row of wooden roses carved into the head of the tester bed.

"Don't be ridiculous, Eleanora," the voice demanded.

Paige whirled. "Don't call me that. My name is Paige."

An elderly woman sat on an upholstered wooden chair. She was short and plump, with a golden cap of hair growing from gray roots and skin as smooth and fragile as ancient parchment. She smiled beatifically and held out her arms as though soliciting a hug. "Dear Eleanora Paige Conner. How wonderful to see you."

Paige stepped back. "Go away, Millicent." Her voice was low and grumpy. "I don't need a fairy godmother right now. If anything, I need a reality check."

"Same difference." Dropping her arms, the woman rose. She wore blue jeans and a magenta sweat shirt emblazoned in gold letters, "FAIRY GODMOTHERS LOVE MAGIC WANDS."

Paige sighed. "What brings you here, Millicent?"

"You do, dear." Millicent came forward, and a cloud of something sparkling billowed behind her. Pixie dust, Paige supposed. It made as much sense as anything else about this situation. "Now, what can I do for you?" the woman asked.

Paige felt foolish for continuing a conversation with a creature she didn't believe in. Still, she said, "I don't imagine you could tell, with your purported magic, exactly what my job here will be."

"I can read your mind, dear, but no one else's."

"Then what good are you?" Paige felt ashamed of her peevishness but made no effort to hide it. She pulled off her suit jacket and tossed it on the bed. "Why don't you just go back where you came from?"

Millicent looked up into Paige's face. She smelled of lilacs. She had a long, thin nose and shiny, shoe-button eyes. Though the corners of her eyelids drooped, giving her a perpetually sympathetic expression, she always smiled.

Paige hated that most of all.

"I can't go till I've helped you, dear. You know the rules."

"I don't want your help, Millicent. It always turns into a disaster."

"Don't exaggerate, Eleanora. There was only that one time you considered the results a disaster."

Paige steeled herself against the painful recollection. "My junior prom. It was such a fiasco that I've hardly let you 'help' me since." She said *help* as though it were the ugliest swear word she could think of.

"That's true, poor dear. But you still haven't learned the secret of fairy tales." Her eyelids drooped even more sympathetically.

"Then why not just tell me and get on your way?"

"The rules, dear."

Paige turned her back and picked up a load of clothing from her suitcase. Stomping to the huge wardrobe, she began to hang pastel blouses, a blazer and a dress. Without speaking, she continued to unpack, trying to ignore her company who wasn't really there but feeling Millicent's kindly gaze on her all the while.

When she'd finished she went into the bathroom to wash her face, hoping her imagination would leave her alone on her return.

It didn't.

She grabbed a black skirt and a pale green blouse and began to change for dinner. Finally, she sighed, able to stand the silence no longer. "I suppose you're going to take credit for this assignment, even though my brother arranged it."

Hearing no reply, she whirled to face Millicent, who batted her skimpy eyelashes and beamed her nondenial.

That set Paige fuming. "And I suppose, since you want me to believe in fairy tales, that you're trying to set me up as the next princess of Dargentia."

"What do you think about that possibility, dear?"

Paige gnashed her teeth. "Ridiculous. I'm hardly the princess type, and I'm certainly not the kind of scintillating woman who'd attract a gorgeous hunk like Prince Niko.''

"Oh, you've noticed he's a gorgeous hunk?''

"I'd have to be dead and buried not to. And don't change the subject.''

"I didn't. What did you think of my little trick at the airport?''
Paige froze. "What do you mean?''

"The forklift. Wasn't that inspired?''

Paige took a step toward her tiny tormentor, one fist clenched about the comb she'd grabbed from her purse. "It was insane! Do you mean to tell me you set that thing after me——''

"So Prince Nicholas could save your life. And he did. Wasn't he marvelous?''

He was, but Paige wasn't about to admit it. She pulled the comb painfully through the snarls in her hair. "Millicent, I could have been hurt! Killed!''

"Not with me in control, dear.'' Millicent cocked her head for a moment, as though listening. Then she began to fade away.

"Now, wait!'' Paige demanded. "I don't want you to go till you promise you won't be back.''

"I'll return only when you need me.'' Millicent had become little more than a glittering shadow. There was a faint crackling and a whoosh of air, like dry leaves in a sudden breeze, then silence—but only for a moment. A knock sounded on Paige's door.

She stood still for an instant, staring after Millicent. The old woman hadn't been here. She'd never been anywhere. She had always been a result of Paige's imagination.

But why did Paige still smell lilacs?

Stomping her foot, she hurried to the door and opened it.

There stood Prince Niko. He'd changed into a white oxford shirt that did nothing to hide his broad shoulders. His sandy hair was combed back and slightly damp, as if he'd just showered. Though he stood tall and regally straight, his head was inclined. His coffee-brown eyes seemed to regard her warmly. And those sensual, expressive lips—they smiled at her from the frame of his neatly trimmed beard.

Paige suddenly felt shy. "Hi,'' she said softly.

"Hi.'' He tried to peer into the room over her shoulder. "Is someone else here? I thought I heard voices.''

Paige thought quickly. "That was just me. I . . . I've always

23

# Linda O. Johnston

loved acting, and when I'm alone I entertain myself by doing scenes from plays. All the roles.''

His golden eyebrows rose, and she could imagine what he was thinking of her: definitely *folle* in its craziest sense. ''What play?'' he asked.

Paige blurted the first one with fairies that she could think of. ''*A Midsummer Night's Dream.* I was doing Titania and Oberon.''

''I see.'' But those skeptical brows of his said he didn't see at all. Paige wished she could hide under the lovely Persian rug covering the floor. He asked, ''Ready for dinner?''

She was. All at once she was starving.

As she closed the door behind her, she glanced back inside. No wispy shade of Millicent hovering about, thank heavens. Not even a smell of lilacs.

Paige had to put a lid on her imagination, especially here. Besides, with a glance at Niko, she decided that around this place, reality wasn't so bad.

Niko led her through dank but stately corridors she hadn't seen before. ''There'll be other guests for dinner,'' he said. ''My aunt and cousin live here, though we don't always dine together. And a couple of friends asked to meet our new historian.''

As she walked, Paige glanced at the tall man striding beside her. His step never veered from the ubiquitous red runner rambling down each stone hall.

He didn't believe her story about solitary acting. Why should he? It was a silly lie, made up to hide an even more ridiculous reality.

But Millicent wasn't real.

If only she'd just stay away.

Paige was glad the prince had come himself, not sending a servant. She was delighted just to see him again. There was a rakish boldness in his step, a proud lift to his strong chin, firm beneath his beard. This was his domain, and he knew it.

The silence between them lengthened, broken only by the muffled sounds of their footfalls on the endless carpet. Paige struggled for something witty to say and settled on, ''I tried to research Dargentia before I came. I didn't find a lot''— though one lonely, intriguing reference had certainly gotten her adrenaline pumping—''but I know the kingdom only recently won its freedom.''

24

He glanced down without stopping, pride throwing a twinkle into his dark eyes. "That's right. For a long time my country was part of France."

She meant to ask the logical question—why France had liberated Dargentia—as they turned a corner and started down yet another totally unfamiliar hallway. She blurted, "I suppose you've only lived in this castle for a short while." At his nod, she continued, "Then how did you ever learn your way around?"

He chuckled. "Experience. How do you know your way around musty archives? Your résumé and references indicated that you're quite skilled at hunting down historical details."

She tossed her head forward so her hair sheltered her glasses— and her pleased smile. He seemed to wait for her response. Did the occasion call for modesty or the truth? Most likely the latter. "Well, yes, I've had a lot of experience."

"Thank heavens. If I'd brought you all the way here to learn I was the victim of a con job, I'd have had to order your head chopped off."

Paige nearly tripped on the edge of the runner. His deep voice was serious. He was a prince; was he obsessed with power? She ventured a look up at him just as he stopped outside a door. She blundered into him, and his large, firm hands steadied her as she peered anxiously into his face.

The twinkle still illuminating his eyes had been joined by a quirky smile.

She grinned back. The guy had a sense of humor about his position. She liked that. She liked *him*.

Of course she did; he was a handsome prince. But that didn't mean he had any interest in her other than as an employee skilled in historical research.

She placed her fingertips on her throat. "Well, Your Highness, I'm pleased to report that you've no reason to summon your chief executioner."

He laughed, then touched her shoulder lightly, guiding her into the room.

He'd mentioned other diners, so Paige had expected to eat in the Great Hall. Castles this age always had one, usually the size of a grand, old-fashioned movie theater or two. Instead, the dining room was small, as such things went—only about the size of her apartment. On its granite walls were wrought-iron sconces shaped like crossed torches that threw off a dim electric glow. The candelabra on the dark wood table held dozens of lighted tapers that cast eerie, dancing light around the windowless room. A mustiness pervaded the air, not quite disguised by the fragrances of fire and flowers from the scented candles.

Seated around the table were four people. Showing Paige to a chair, Niko introduced the others, who all stood. "This is my aunt Charlotte," he said, indicating the woman at Paige's right.

She was thin, with hair of an unnatural pumpkin shade. Her welcoming smile revealed a severe overbite. She held out a limp hand and barely touched Paige's fingertips. "Welcome, Mademoiselle Conner," she said, her voice low and warm, her French accent strong.

At her other side was her son Rudolf, Niko's cousin, who wore a starchy white shirt with a narrow pastel tie. His Ichabod Crane thinness emphasized the prominence of his angelfish nose—it looked narrow in front but stuck out like a sail from the side. His soft, "Yes, Ms. Conner, welcome," sounded as though it pained him to speak. "Please call me Rudy."

Then there was the tall, gray-haired gentleman across from Rudy, Edouard Campion. "Edouard's a distant relative," Niko explained, "and he and I have a business relationship as well." The silver fox's smile seemed sly.

There was no doubt in Paige's mind about the feelings of the fourth guest toward her: intense dislike. "This is Suzanne Pelletiere," Niko said. The stiff, disdainful woman was tall, slender and drop-dead beautiful, with high cheekbones many a model would envy. Her sloe eyes moved from Niko to Paige and back, a possessive pointedness in her gaze confirming to Paige that she had designs on the prince, so hands off.

Paige nearly laughed at the unnecessary warning. She, attract someone like Niko? Hardly.

"Suzanne's actually a distant relation, too," Niko added.

"*Very* distant. By marriage." Suzanne's low voice was filled with meaning: Her interest in Niko might be obvious, but it wasn't incestuous. Her silky, dove-gray dress clung becomingly to hourglass curves. The flowing waves of her platinum hair suggested she was a blonde who had a lot of fun.

Paige noted that everyone had spoken in English, though, unlike Niko, most had French accents. As the prince reached the head of the table, the others resumed their places, sitting only when he did. Well trained, Paige noted. Her seat was to Niko's right.

A young girl in a dirndl and frothy white cap served soup, a steaming, delicious consommé. The castle had servants after all, Paige thought.

"So you're here to help with this marmelade plan of Niko's," said his aunt Charlotte, her accent so thick that Paige was certain she'd heard wrong. She passed Paige a basket of warm brioches.

"That's 'marvelous,' Mother," Rudy corrected softly.

"What plan is that?" Paige hoped she'd find out at last why Prince Nicholas needed a historian in a hurry.

"Our dear Niko is on a course to turn Dargentia into a five-ring circus," said Edouard. "And I, for one, am all for it."

"Of course you are, Edouard," purred Suzanne. "But only if he trips off the tightrope onto his oh so handsome face." She turned to Paige. "Niko has cooked up the most delightful scheme to put Dargentia on the map, Ms. Conner." The name *Niko* tripped over her lips like a caress, but Paige's name seemed caught on broken glass.

"What's that?" Paige asked.

"He's spending millions of Dargentian francs to spruce the place up," Edouard replied.

"*Your* Dargentian francs," Suzanne said, then turned away from Edouard. "We're using them to develop our tourist industry."

"The place is certainly picturesque enough for that." Paige smiled at Niko. He acknowledged her comment by raising his golden brows.

"Scenery's the beans," Rudolf managed, his tone tiny and strangled. As everyone looked at him, he turned bright red and dropped his spoon into his soup bowl with a clatter. But he continued gamely, "As in 'Jack and the Beanstalk.' We sow the beans, and something big and bountiful will grow. That's where Suzanne comes in."

"Dear Suzanne is not a farmer, but she is expert in the travel industry." Charlotte beamed a rodent-toothed smile across the table. "She has her own agency with brunches—"

"That's 'branches,' Mother," Rudy whispered.

# Linda O. Johnston

"—in Paris and London, and now she is starting an office here."

Paige noted the small, feline smile Suzanne turned on Niko. This time the prince smiled back. A pang of something sharp shot through Paige. She couldn't actually be jealous of this lovely woman. Grow up, Conner, she thought. Of course the prince would flirt with someone as sexy as Suzanne without giving Paige a second glance.

As the meal progressed, she felt certain there was a gourmet chef behind the scenes. The food was superb: lamb cutlets, asparagus Bernaise, potatoes sautéd lightly in onion.

The discussion about Dargentia's future as a tourist haven continued. Everyone seemed excited, despite Paige's sense that Edouard's pleasure was hinged on something more basic than bolstering the small country's economic base. From what Paige could glean, the money to finance the tourist scheme had been a loan.

The beautiful Suzanne brimmed with ideas: castle tours, sightseeing walks, bicycle marathons, special attractions for conventions. Paige mostly listened, noting Niko's enthusiasm.

Over coffee and a delicious Sacher torte with whipped cream, she felt comfortable enough to ask, "How do I fit in? Why am I here, Niko?"

She felt Suzanne's cool gaze tell her exactly what *she* thought: no good reason.

But Niko said, "To turn Dargentia into a tourist mecca, it needs a history. I've a library full of old books and family papers, but there's no volume devoted strictly to Dargentia. That's your job."

Paige's pulse rate quickened. This was work she'd love! "Then I'm to research the country's past and write a book about it?"

"Exactly, and more: pamphlets, press releases, the works."

"While you're at it," Rudy whispered as he examined a spoon in front of his pink face, "maybe you'll find the Dargentian crown jewels."

"Really? Are there missing jewels?" Paige couldn't hide her delight.

Edouard grimaced. "Fabled, at least," he growled. "But so important to your plans, aren't they, Niko?"

Paige was surprised that Niko accepted Edouard's taunting tone without comment. "Maybe," he agreed, "but I'm going to ask a

28

different near-impossible feat: You're to write a glitzy promotional brochure in just two weeks. I need it to be ready for the ball.''

The others at the table all began speaking at once. They all asked the same questions. ''Ball?'' ''What ball?''

Niko's smile was more a grimace as he seemed to brace himself for expected reactions. ''A country promoting itself as a fairytale kingdom for tourists must have a ball given by its prince for his royal friends and neighbors.''

''Why?'' Suzanne's tone dripped suspicion.

''To find me a suitable princess to marry, of course.'' Niko nonchalantly took a bite of his torte.

''What are you talking about?'' Edouard demanded. He tensed one fist beside his empty plate. An enormous diamond glittered on his ring finger.

''Not a good idea, Niko,'' said Rudy. There was worry in his small, pale eyes.

Suzanne half rose from her chair, her gray dress gaping slightly to reveal more than a hint of cleavage. ''How could you?''

Charlotte frowned. ''Rudy's right, Niko. You know the townsfolk won't like it.''

''I can't run a country by superstitious silliness.''

Paige wondered what he meant.

As though she'd asked, Rudy glanced toward her, though he seemed incapable of looking her directly in the eye. ''Ms. Connor, you probably do not know about Dargentia's legends.''

''No,'' Paige said, ''though I hope to learn.''

''Rudy's our resident expert,'' his mother said, pride swelling in her voice.

Rudy went on, ''The entire time Dargentia remained part of France, its people clung to its old legends. The one given greatest credence was that, for freedom to be fully restored, the crown jewels, known as Les Fabuleux, had to be found. And then its king was to marry a commoner.''

''Not a princess,'' Suzanne stressed. Despite her family link with the prince, Paige imagined Suzanne must be distant enough to consider herself a commoner. Otherwise she wouldn't be so supportive of the legend.

''A royal bride will bring tourists,'' Niko said, ''not to mention an alliance that could provide economic aid. I've returned sovereignty to Dargentia already without finding Les Fabuleux. I can't govern this country based on the beliefs of my most naive subjects, and I'll wed whomever I must. Ironic, isn't it? For years I avoided anyone who chased me because of my title, and now I'm about to do the same to some poor princess.''

Paige didn't even know she'd reacted until Niko turned to her and said, ''You look shocked, Ms. Conner. Do I sound cold-blooded?''

She lifted her hand in protest, but he continued in a tone that invited no argument. ''A good monarch subordinates his own wishes for the good of his subjects—even when he must marry for their benefit without their blessings. And I intend to be a damned good monarch.''

''I'm sure you will be,'' she murmured. But not necessarily a happy one, she thought. Behind the strong resolve in his dark eyes, she believed she detected a hint of sorrow.

''Well,'' Charlotte said, patting her protruding mouth with her napkin, ''if you've made up your mind, I'd love to help with the guest list, Niko. Although I suppose Aldred will return soon for that.''

''Any day now,'' Niko confirmed.

Wondering who Aldred was, Paige asked, ''Does the name of the jewels mean they are extraordinary or only fabled?''

''Certainly the former,'' Rudy said softly. ''And some people think the latter as well.''

Thinking for a moment, Paige remained quiet, though she felt her insides tighten. Two weeks to put together enough history to prepare a glamorous brochure? She didn't know yet how monumental her task might be. But for Niko to take the time, money and trouble to import a historian—she suspected the job wouldn't be a piece of torte.

And how ridiculous that she should feel even a hint of dismay that Prince Nicholas of Dargentia was ready to select a bride. Of course he deserved a royal one, the legend notwithstanding.

A niggling nervousness teased her mind. Could Millicent have . . . ? Surely not.

At Charlotte's urging, Niko presented a few details he'd already worked out. ''The ball will be in five weeks, here in the castle. Everyone in Dargentia will be invited. We'll hire most to double as servants, though, for we'll also invite representatives of royal houses from all over the world. Tourists will be welcome, too, of course. Very welcome.''

"Of course," Edouard said. He sounded agitated. "But perhaps the royal guests will fill the hotels."

"We'll find them suitable lodgings elsewhere," Niko said. "Here at the castle, for one."

Paige wondered why Edouard's silver brows knit in a furious frown. "Your townsfolk will blow it," he growled. "They have no idea how to run hotels."

"They're already being trained, and they'll learn quickly enough," Niko said. "At least this way they'll have plenty of practice."

"Get them to practice right here," Edouard muttered. "You are in sad need of servants."

"There are more important things than seeing to our comfort," Charlotte said softly. "But, Niko, I'm afraid you'll have your work cut out to convince the townspeople to have anything to do with your ball."

"So our Prince Niko is setting out to find a Cinderella." Edouard sounded contemptuous. "How romantic."

"Not a Cinderella at all," said Rudy in his quiet voice. "Niko is inviting royalty, and he'll choose from them. Although I wish you'd reconsider. At least try to find Les Fabuleux first."

"I won't delay my ball for such nonsense," Niko said, "but I certainly wouldn't mind having the jewels available for paying off debts." He shot what appeared to be a telling glance at Edouard.

"Would you really dare sell them?" Edouard taunted.

"Could I really dare not?" responded Niko coolly.

Paige remained silent, staring at the congealing whipped cream over the remainder of her torte. With the mention of Cinderella, her nervousness had turned into a horrible certainty. Not only was her being in this newly restored fairy-tale monarchy a setup, but so was the whole idea of Niko's ball.

Paige didn't know how Millicent had done it. Magic, maybe, though Paige didn't believe in magic. She didn't even really believe in Millicent. Yet that syrupy sweet, inept fairy godmother was conniving to catch Paige a prince.

And that legend—no matter how ancient these people claimed it to be, Paige saw Millicent's phantasmic fingers all over it. Paige certainly was a commoner. But fortunately—maybe—Niko seemed determined to pick a princess.

Paige had experienced humiliation at Millicent's hands before. No way would she do it again.

And if Niko chose himself a royal bride . . . well, it was none of her business. No matter how much the idea stung.

Niko's voice broke into her thoughts. "I want Dargentia to have a history before the ball. Let's go, Paige. I'll introduce you to your work." He took a final sip of his coffee and set the cup back onto its saucer.

Paige eagerly excused herself from the table and followed him. She'd almost forgotten, for the moment, the incident at the airport, but her stiffness as she walked reminded her with a jolt. Could Millicent really have . . . ? Paige wouldn't put it past her!

The library was at the end of a nearby hall. Niko switched on the lights.

The library was even larger than the dining room. With its gleaming wood paneling and built-in shelves, its huge stone fireplace and plush sofas in deep, lush maroon, it appeared almost homey. As Paige and Niko entered, their footsteps echoed on the bare wood floor until they stepped onto one of several antique Oriental rugs. A dusty smell assailed Paige, unsurprisingly like the familiar odor of aging books.

The ample shelves were nearly empty. At one end of the room, though, next to an enormous worktable, were stacked dozens of boxes—filled, Paige assumed, with books.

Niko led her to the table, standing tall beside it. He looked regal in his white shirt and dark trousers. Or maybe his appearance had nothing to do with his clothes and everything to do with his demeanor. "These boxes contain all the European history volumes my family has gathered, plus our family papers. Some books mention Dargentia; many do not."

That didn't make him happy, Paige knew—not with that fierce lowering of his brow. She ventured, "I've studied history for a long time, but till I started looking for it, I don't think I'd read anything about Dargentia's past." Except, she thought, for one alluring tidbit.

"You and the rest of the world."

The prince pulled an ornately carved wooden chair from under the table and held it for her. Paige stifled her thrilled smile. She felt pampered, an odd, new sensation. To him, though, such an act must be an everyday courtesy. She smoothed her soft black skirt beneath her and sat.

He sat, too. "Let me give you some background." He stroked his beard pensively as he apparently decided how to start. There was pain in the set of his dark eyes. Paige wished she could soothe it away.

Such nonsense filling her thoughts again! She gave a tiny shake of her head. Where did these odd impulses come from? Was this an offshoot of Millicent's interference?

Well, Paige wouldn't give in to them. She had to act rational around Niko, no matter how impressive his looks—and no matter that he was a prince.

But he was a man, too, and he seemed to be hurting. She figured the best way to help was just to listen.

"You'll find Dargentia was independent until the seventeenth century. My namesake, Nicholas the First, was a strong leader. Some even considered him a tyrant. He apparently fought hard to keep Dargentia free, but France, after resolution of the Seven Years War, was stronger. After that, though those who remained kept the culture alive, Dargentia was a slave to whichever country was the better bully: mostly France, but also Germany and even Switzerland for a time."

"How did it gain independence?" Paige asked, resurrecting the question she'd intended to ask earlier. "I know it was recent. All I recall, though, is a short article in a news magazine—hardly anything compared with the coverage of the dissolution of the USSR and the reunification of Germany."

A smile curved Niko's wonderful full lips and sparked a light in his coffee-dark eyes, erasing the pain she'd seen. "Diplomacy," he said lightly. "Good timing mixed with careful negotiations, veiled threats and a large dollop of tact. And, voilà! A very old country emerges as one of the world's newest."

Paige joined in his joyous laughter. But in a moment their gazes caught and both fell silent. She felt suddenly shy. Intensity centered the prince's look, as though he sought something deep inside her. She was frightened that he'd find it, more terrified he wouldn't.

She wondered if he'd been the negotiator who'd set his country free. Probably. She believed he'd have stopped at nothing. But she felt too awkward to ask. Not then. She'd need to know, though, for the history.

She grabbed for a box on the floor, studiously staring at it to avoid looking at Niko, struggling for something conversational to say. "So I've only two weeks to gather information to write a historical pamphlet."

"Yes," he said. "And an outline a few days earlier for the illustrator. That way, the brochure will be ready for the ball."

The ball. The reminder splashed Paige with reality as fiercely as a dousing with ice water. She was imagining neediness in the man, when all he needed was for her to do her job. She imagined his interest in her, when his actions spoke only of common courtesy.

"When that's done," the prince continued, "I'll want you to keep digging up details. Eventually, I want to record Dargentia's past in all possible media. Maybe someday I'll even back a Hollywood movie."

"That's bound to attract tourists." Paige's voice was decisively professional, spiced with a suitable touch of enthusiasm.

"Of course. It's all in the marketing, and if there's anything I know, it's marketing."

Paige expected a prince to know leadership, protocol, diplomacy—but marketing? "Why is that?"

"By design," he answered. "I went to Harvard Business School, chose my major carefully."

"Marketing?"

"Sure. I had a feeling it might come in handy, and now it is." He stood suddenly. "Oh, blast!" He began to pace the room like a confined lion—an apt analogy, Paige thought, with his royal background and blond mane of hair. Obviously, he was annoyed.

With her? She glanced down at herself. Had she said something wrong? Done something unusually gauche, even for her?

But no—"I forgot something," he said.

Paige let her breath out slowly. At least he wasn't upset with her.

He stopped beside a pile of boxes and began stacking them on the table. They contained computer components, if their labels were correct.

"I'd intended to have this set up when you arrived. I'll get to it first thing in the morning."

Paige shook her head, unable suddenly to suppress a grin.

"What's that smile for?" asked Niko.

"My amazement. This place is such a mishmash of twelfth century combined with twentieth: a mechanized portcullis, indoor plumbing in a castle tower, a computer, telephones. . . ."

"You catch on quick! The atmosphere will attract tourists. That's the first thing. . . ." His voice trailed off, as though he was thinking; then he continued. "But they won't stay if they're not comfortable, so they'll find modern amenities here." He stopped stacking boxes. "Come on, Paige Conner. I'll show you back to your room. You must be exhausted, and you'll need to get to work first thing tomorrow. I'll give you a tour of the castle then, too."

She followed him to the library door, where he turned out the lights and locked the door behind them.

He led her through halls that, if not exactly familiar, at least contained paintings and other decorations she thought she'd seen before. Soon they stood before the door of her tower room.

"Thanks for everything," Paige said shyly.

He bent forward, lifting her hand and touching his lips to the back of it. A delicious shiver ran through her.

Forget it, Conner, she told herself. It's just part of Prince Charming's old-world charm.

Still, as she shut the door behind her, she couldn't help wishing, once again, that she scintillated just a little.

She suddenly sniffed a whiff of lilacs. Her hand still on the door, she turned her head ever so slowly.

Millicent sat smiling on the bed.

Paige closed her eyes. Oh, no! Not again!

When she looked once more Millicent was still there.

Without a word to her imaginary intruder, Paige threw open the door and fled down the hall.

# Chapter Three

The hall was empty, but Paige heard Niko's muffled footsteps on the runner along the stairs.

On impulse, she hurried after him.

Reaching the top of the narrow stairway, she saw him turn a corner at the bottom. She slid her hand along the cold wrought-iron railing as she sped down the steps.

He must have heard her, for he was waiting when she rounded the corner. "Is something wrong, Paige?"

Out of breath, she felt awkward. Stupid. Ridiculous. She couldn't exactly tell him she was fleeing a figment of her own imagination. Instead, she said, "Everything's fine. I just . . . well, I just wanted to ask your permission to look around the castle a little on my own."

He gave her an amused smile. "Of course. My house is your house."

The thought gave her a surge of pleasure that she quickly tamed. Hospitality was just part of his inherent charm.

"Tell you what," he continued. "I don't want to give you the grand tour at night, but I've something to show you."

"Great!" What if he thought she'd been hinting that she wanted to remain in his company? Well, she couldn't do anything about that now.

The halls through which he led her were brightly lit from iron sconces and were starting to look familiar—this was the same route they'd taken to dinner. Between the sconces were a myriad of oil paintings, most of pastoral or hunting scenes, many dark enough to indicate great age—and a great need for care. Paige had seen few portraits. When Niko gave her the tour she'd ask if there were any, since portraits in this ancestral home could be important in unraveling Dargentia's past.

They met no one else. Paige expected a place this size to overflow with servants, but she recalled Edouard's comment at dinner about the castle's lack of help. Surely Maibelle wasn't the only maid—was she?

Another matter puzzled her. "Niko, how did the castle survive all these centuries and come through in such wonderful condition?"

"Luck. And the foresight of my ancestors. The youngest sons of the would-be ruling family always returned here to live and keep an eye on things, whatever the political climate. They somehow always managed to convince whoever was in power to use the castle as a government house or museum."

Passing the dining room, they stopped in the castle's kitchen. Paige was impressed, but not surprised, to find the huge stone room filled with modern appliances: range, oven, refrigerator with ice maker, microwave oven. In contrast, a roasting spit hung in the large stone fireplace.

Reaching into the refrigerator, Niko extracted several extra dinner brioches. The hinges of a large wooden door in the outer kitchen wall squealed as he opened it. "After you."

She stepped outside onto a cobbled path.

Daylight had fled. A few bold stars were visible despite a scattering of clouds, the light from a nearly full moon and the rows of electric torches along the castle walls and driveway.

The evening was cool, and a spring dampness hung in the air. The breeze blew through Paige's silky blouse as though she wore nothing, and she wrapped her arms in front of herself for warmth.

"Cold?" Niko stopped beside her, his brow lowered in concern.

"No. It's bracing."

He smiled and continued on, leading her to a second cobbled path that seemed to circle the castle. There was a hush outside. Paige heard only the whisper of the wind and their footsteps. "It's so peaceful out here," she remarked, her voice almost reverent.

"Yes, especially now. It's my favorite time of the day. I usually come out here alone."

A thrilled tingle shot through Paige. Why was he sharing it with her?

Kindness, she thought, shrugging into the dimness. She would read nothing unintended into it.

As they strolled along, the scent of the shadowed spring flowers at the side of the walkway filled her senses. A few crickets started to chirp.

In a while, the path brought them near the outer bulwark. Spotting an intriguing iron gate in the thick wall, Paige was glad when Niko strode toward it. She followed. A stale mustiness from the ancient stone caught in her throat as she looked through the heavy grillwork. Beyond the iron bars was the shimmering water of the wide moat.

Niko pushed the gate. To her surprise, it opened easily; it hadn't been locked. They walked through.

The scene was lovely, almost pastoral, here outside the bulwark walls. The moon, and a few torchlights mounted on the outer wall, cast a glow on the sparkling surface of the moat. In the irregular illumination, Paige spotted a weatherworn statue of a swan on a thick pedestal. Near it, among sweet-smelling, flowering bushes, were a few stone benches. The grumping of a chorus of frogs filled the air.

"Over here." Sitting on the bench closest to the statue, Niko patted a spot beside him. Paige joined him, ignoring the hardness against her still-sore muscles. She guessed they were at the opposite side of the moat from where the bridge spanned it.

Following Niko's gaze, she saw five black swans sail gracefully through the water. "Oh!" Paige whispered, not wanting to startle them. Remaining aloof, none of the swans neared the bank. Soon they were joined by a family of white geese—mother and four babies, all in a row—plus several large males.

Paige laughed aloud. "They're adorable."

"They're greedy. Just watch."

Unlike the swans, the geese were not reticent; they honked as though demanding something. Food, of course. That was why Niko had stopped at the kitchen. He tossed out a few crumbs, causing a furor among the belligerent geese.

"Not exactly the most courteous animals, are they?" Paige asked.

"They remind me of my family at dinner." Niko handed her a few dry brioches.

"Oh, but your relatives don't fight over crumbs. They're much more subtle as they tell you what to do." Paige immediately bent her head forward, groaning inwardly. She had spoken without thinking. Would he be angry that she'd criticized his family? But he'd started it! ·

She could feel his eyes on her, and she ventured a look toward him.

His lips curved wryly. "More subtle? Well, maybe a little."

Straightening, she managed a return grin.

Together, they broke off pieces of bread and threw them toward the shore to the eager geese. Paige was glad the birds were so noisy. Otherwise, she'd have had to make conversation with Niko. Oh, she had plenty on her mind, mostly about how thrilled she was to have been chosen for the job, to be staying in the castle . . . to be out here, in this enchanted area, with Niko. But how unsophisticated she would sound if she spoke her mind. And she'd already stuck her foot in her mouth by insulting his relatives.

If only she scintillated. Where was Millicent when she needed her?

No! She didn't need Millicent. The contrary creature had to go away and leave her alone!

The swans remained disdainfully distant, but Niko began throwing them hunks of bread, too. They condescended to sweep their long necks forward so they could capture pieces of bread tossed into their paths.

"They're wonderful!" Paige exclaimed involuntarily, then wondered if she should take a lesson from the swans and remain aloof. Niko had already seen a sample of her incredible awkwardness. She cleared her throat. "I really appreciate your bringing me out here," she said stiffly. "But I think I'd better go to my room. I need to get up early to begin work."

"You *are* working," he said. "You need to develop a flavor for Dargentia. Knowing about our home should help you understand the royal family."

"Are you more like swans or geese?" Paige teased, then wished she could take back the words. He'd think her silly, totally unprofessional, as once again her toes seemed to levitate toward her mouth.

But he laughed. "Both. My family tends to demand a lot, like geese, but I'd like to think we've the grace of swans."

"Perhaps you're ugly goslings," Paige suggested, "who grew up into swans."

# Linda O. Johnston

He turned to her, his face shadowed in the dim light. The sudden dipping of his brow appeared angry, and Paige held herself taut to keep from flinching. Drat her gift of gauche gab! She'd somehow offended him.

"That's it exactly." His voice was low, but something in his tone sounded furious. "Like the story of the Ugly Duckling, never quite fitting in while growing up in a foreign country, adopting ways not our own. But now we can finally grow up into swans." He swept his arm expansively, as though to designate both the weathered statue behind their bench and the graceful black birds in the water.

"It must have been very hard," Paige murmured, upset that she'd stirred painful memories.

"Yes," he said, "it was."

Niko hadn't meant to mention his childhood. He seldom spoke of it.

But Paige Conner had made him remember.

"I'd like to hear about it, if you'll tell me," she said. Her voice was as soft as the wisps of clouds capturing the moonlight overhead. There was a huskiness to it, though.

He turned to stare at her. She wanted to hear about his pain? Was she no better than the media jackals who'd tried so hard to shred his dignity? Without looking, he slammed the remainder of the rolls down on the bench beside him.

But there was caring in her gaze, a compassion visible despite the dimness of the light. And behind those absurd black-rimmed glasses, her unusual amber eyes glittered with moistness.

He glanced back at the geese. He'd stopped tossing bread, and they scolded him from where they swam. "I suppose," he said coldly, "that you'll need to know all about me for the history of Dargentia."

"Only if you want me to be thorough." Her soft sarcasm suggested he'd hurt her feelings.

That didn't matter—did it? She was simply someone he'd hired to do a job. But he clenched his hands into fists. That was just what Americans seemed to think of royalty—stuck up, demanding, inhuman. But still worthy of attention. Lots of it.

"My childhood was all right," he said quietly, trying to relax the knot in his chest, "as long as kids didn't know I was supposed to be a prince. Once they found out, they teased.''

''Children can be cruel.'' There was a forcefulness in her voice that made him look at her again. Had she, too, experienced that kind of cruelty?

She was still in the soft green blouse and knee-length flowing skirt she'd worn to dinner. She'd looked childlike bending over to toss bread to the complaining geese. Now, as she stared at the leftover rolls in her lap, her dark hair that he'd compared to the black swans nearly hid her face, spilling over her cheeks.

Niko had forced himself, over years of fighting prejudice and animosity, of dreaming and planning for freedom, to think before he acted. He did nothing on impulse. But he hardly thought at all before he reached out till his fingertips touched Paige Conner's narrow chin. Gently, he turned her face until she was facing him. Eyes the shade of fine, rare amber, luminescent behind her ugly glasses, blinked quizzically.

He moved on the bench until his hip was against hers. The difference between the cold stone and her radiant heat was startling. ''Ms. Conner,'' he said, his words barely audible even to him. ''Paige.''

He leaned forward, his fingers tipping her chin so her mouth was held at the right angle. Her lips were soft and warm, and he made the kiss very gentle. That was all he meant to do—if he meant anything at all. But her mouth moved beneath his, and suddenly the kiss deepened. She tasted of the wine at dinner plus her very own special vintage, and he pressed his mouth hard against hers. His tongue forged a path till it teased hers in an erotic, pleasurable duet.

His arms circled her, pulling her tightly to him. He felt her flail out, as though unsure what to do with her arms, but in a moment they wrapped about him. Her fingers dug into his hair, drawing him closer till he couldn't tell where his mouth ended and hers began. The air he breathed belonged to her.

His hands moved, as though of their own accord. He reached between them. As his fingertips grazed the base of her breast, she drew in her breath sharply.

The sound startled him, awakened him. He drew back. For a moment he tugged away, for she seemed unwilling to release him. More forcefully, he pulled back, suddenly aware that his heart was racing as though he'd sprinted around the moat.

41

What had he been thinking of?

That kiss must have been his sense of isolation reacting to her sweetness.

But Paige Conner was his employee. A rather unpolished one at that, with those clothes, that hairstyle, those glasses.

Worst of all, she was an American, undoubtedly more than willing to leap into bed with a prince, then claim a permanent bond.

But that would not do. He had plans for Dargentia that did not include burdening himself, or his country, with scheming American women. He would find a royal consort whose presence would attract tourists from all over the world.

He stood abruptly, looking down at Paige Conner. Her hair was pushed away from her face, emphasizing its heart shape and giving her a morning-after mussiness that made him throb despite himself. Her lips were drawn together, as though she tried again to taste his kiss. Their eyes caught, and she immediately looked down at her lap. Again her hair half hid her face.

"Niko," she said, her soft voice wavering, "I don't think we should—"

"You are absolutely right, Ms. Conner. We should not." He turned his back and stomped away.

Paige sat still, staring at her skirt. Without looking up, she knew the exact moment when Prince Niko left.

She felt horrified. Mortified. Why had he kissed her? Had she somehow acted as though she craved his charity? There was nothing about her that would genuinely spark something in a prince.

And the kiss itself? She had never before felt anything like it. Every synapse of her being had been centered on the insistence of his lips, his strong embrace. The contact had instantly evoked dreams of strokes and touches and rhythms, heat, dampness and a myriad of other erotic sensations. She'd hungered for more. The memory still made her ravenous, and that was part of her embarrassment.

Well, she refused just to sit there blushing. She stood, grabbed from the bench what was left of the brioches and stalked toward the moat, where the geese still milled about on the bank.

"Here," she said, belligerently offering the bread to the honking birds. "Have some more."

## The Glass Slipper

Two of the geese must have taken offense. Or they were still awfully hungry. With a loud honk, the creatures spread their wings wide, enlarging themselves into angry white beasts. They lunged toward Paige.

She gasped, stepping back, but they were faster. One stretched and pecked at her extended hand. The other stabbed a beak at her nearly bare shin.

Pain shot through her fingers and leg. She felt her stockings run. *She* felt like running. "Stop it!" she hollered, throwing the bread to the ground.

Calmly, the geese dropped their wings and craned their necks. Their orange bills flitted over the remainder of the rolls. Their cronies, including the small goslings, waddled over to join the feast.

Paige was left to tend her wounds.

She sat back on the bench. What with the forklift at the airport and the hungry geese, she felt as if she'd had a bull's eye painted on her body.

She ached everywhere.

Especially inside, when she thought about Prince Niko's kiss.

She stayed there for a long while, watching the geese finish their food and meander back to the moat. She didn't blame them; she recalled hearing that startled geese weren't exactly gentle. Rubbing her bruised leg, she wished she'd remembered sooner.

At least there'd been sufficient time for the prince to return to the castle. She did not want to add to her shame by running into him again that night.

And tomorrow? She'd have to see him then, if only long enough for him to fire her. She sighed, rising slowly, inching into an aching walk. If she had to, she would beg Niko to forget what had happened, to give her another chance.

She wasn't a quitter. And this job was a historian's dream— an expedition through unexplored territory, offering as well the possibility of finding a missing piece to her own historical puzzle, an opportunity to help restore a small country's dignity.

And if her own dignity suffered in the process? She could deal with humiliation. She'd done it before.

On the other hand, she hadn't asked him to kiss her. He'd brought her out here to this romantic setting, to those nasty, ill-tempered geese . . .

Her mood turned abruptly brittle. Something to show her, indeed! This was all *his* fault. If he fired her, he'd darn well better give her adequate severance to get back home and find another job. Drat him anyway, his high-and-mighty highness, the prince of Dargentia!

With only a small limp, she stalked back toward the castle.

Paige was so lost in angry thoughts as she approached the castle that she nearly forgot her insecurity about how to find her way around.

Double drat the prince, for leaving her there alone!

She found the door they'd come out through and pulled on it. Fortunately, it opened, creaking as loudly as before. In the kitchen she switched on the lights, then carefully turned them off again when she exited into the hallway.

The lights in the sconces seemed dimmer than they had earlier. The hall was filled with shadows. How would she find her way to her room?

Don't be a wimp, Conner, she told herself. She'd gone this way before. She had a good sense of direction. She would be fine.

Her second turn put her into a passageway with two unfamiliar wooden benches. She retraced her route. Then she tried another hall. It looked familiar, though she didn't think it would lead her where she wanted to go.

No matter. She'd follow it for a while, then figure out what to do next.

She walked along the hallway till it emptied into the grand entry vestibule. She paused at the end of the hall, looking about while trying to decide where to go next.

The heavy front door suddenly swung open, startling her. She gasped, her hand rising to her throat.

An unfamiliar head was thrust inside. It turned, looking first one way, then another.

In a moment its owner crept inside the entry.

Whoever it was did not see Paige. That was fortunate, for she had no doubt that the elderly man was sneaking into the castle.

Her heartbeat had already been fast, from her uneasy blundering through the castle's passages. Now its cadence grew triphammer quick.

Should she go find Niko? Fat chance! She couldn't even find

her way back to the moat unless she located the kitchen. And she'd no idea where Niko's bedroom was. Or if that was where he'd gone.

Apparently satisfied that he was alone, the man tiptoed forward, and Paige shrank back against the wall, blessing the shadows beyond the reach of the wall sconces' lights.

What should she do?

The man moved closer. Should she step out, demand an explanation?

Or should she do the prudent thing and hightail it away from there? Sure, the guy looked slight, but she'd never studied self-defense in her life. And what if he were armed?

She decided to get the heck away. With luck, she'd run into someone who could handle the situation. Niko, maybe.

She turned—and stepped face-first into a stone-hard blockade. Someone grunted, ''Hey!'' A hand came down heavily on her shoulder.

She'd seen TV. She'd seen movies. Instinctively, she reacted as she'd seen hundreds of heroines do. Paige screamed—and brought her knee up sharply.

# *Chapter Four*

A quick hand caught her rising leg. Her own ears still reverberating from her scream, Paige tried to pull away—until she heard a voice saying, "What the hell?"

She recognized that deep voice, though not the anger in it. Prince Niko.

Paige stopped with her knee still in midair. She couldn't lower it even if she wanted to. Her leg, wrapped in her skirt, was still held aloft.

"You startled me," she whispered defiantly, looking up into dark eyes that simmered like hot oil. His jaw was clenched, and she swallowed as she tried to explain. "I was just coming to get you. Someone's sneaking in."

The fury in his gaze segued to surprise. "What!"

Her leg was abruptly dropped, and she cast herself against the wall for balance. The prince pushed past her.

"Aldred!" he exclaimed.

Oh, no! Paige thought. She'd heard that name before. She turned to see the large form of Prince Nicholas, still clad in the sports clothes he had worn earlier, bend to embrace the slight figure in a dark suit who'd so stealthily slipped into the entry.

How mortifying! She wanted more than anything to simply slide away, go up to her room and pack. And that was exactly what she would do—if she only knew her way.

Instead, she took a few steps forward. "I—I'm sorry," she stammered. "I thought—"

The little man stepped away from Niko's grasp. His shock of graying dark hair was thick and unruly, like a mottled mop stuck atop his head. "Miss Conner?" His voice held a question, so Paige nodded. He gazed at her steadily with bright blue eyes. "I'm Aldred, Prince Niko's majordomo," he continued, "and I'm the one who should apologize." His voice was cultured, though he sounded American. "I would imagine, from your vantage point, that I looked like an intruder.''

"Well . . . yes.''

"I simply didn't want to disturb anyone, with my coming in so late.''

"What he means,'' Niko said, "is that he was hoping not to run into me till tomorrow. You see, we had a little bet about when he'd actually get here. I believed he couldn't stay away from me any longer than three months, and I've won.''

Aldred looked at the large silver watch on his thin wrist. "Not at all, my boy. It *is* tomorrow.''

Paige found her grin turning into a yawn. This was her opportunity to leave, though she couldn't quite bring herself to ask how to find her room. "It is late. Good night.'' With a nervous glance about the entryway, she chose a hallway that surely led in the right direction.

"Paige!'' a deep voice called after her.

She stopped and turned.

"You're going the wrong way.'' At least Niko was smiling at her. But she'd never felt more humiliated in her life than she had that night.

"I'm lost,'' she admitted sorrowfully.

He pointed to a hallway in the far wall from the one down which she'd started. "That way,'' he said. "Pass two flights of stairs, then go up the third.''

Paige fled the way he'd directed.

The retreat to her room couldn't be quick enough for Paige. She desperately attempted to note landmarks for the next time—if there was a next time. She prayed that the multitude of fiascos that night hadn't convinced the prince to fire her.

His directions were impeccable; she found her room with no further trouble. But she felt like crying. First Prince Niko had apparently thought she'd coaxed him to kiss her. Then she'd nearly kneed him where it hurt. How could she even imagine he'd keep her around after that?

She wished she had a willing ear to bend for advice. Joe's? It would be hours earlier in Washington, D.C., but she didn't want to call her brother. What could he do, so far away? And he'd been kind enough to get her the job. He'd be utterly disappointed if he thought she hadn't the mettle to maintain it.

There was one person—or whatever—she could talk to now. Paige whispered, "Millicent? Can you hear me?"

"Of course, dear," came a familiar wavery voice.

Slowly, Paige turned around. The scent of lilacs filled the air and a wispy fog formed near the bed. It took shape and solidified—Millicent. This time, her chartreuse sweatshirt read, FAIRY GODMOTHERS DO IT WITH COSMIC ENERGY.

Paige walked toward her. "Tonight has been a disaster. The prince must be furious with me, and I can't blame him."

The elderly woman's wrinkles deepened, and her little shoe-button eyes closed, then winked open. "I'm delighted you invited me here." She placed her stubby fingers against her temples, and her wavery voice grew stronger. "But, dear, I don't sense an aura of anger around the castle right now. In fact, if nothing else, I think I sense peace. And love."

Millicent always claimed to read Paige's mind but no one else's. That figured. She was a figment of Paige's idiotic imagination, a product of that readable mind. But she claimed she could interpret auras. Love and peace instead of anger? She sounded like an escapee from the hippie 1960s instead of a fairy godmother.

"I want to go home," Paige sighed.

"But you just got here." Millicent sounded troubled. "I was sure this was where your destiny lay, but . . . how is your relationship with the prince developing?"

Paige's laugh was not humorous. "Relationship? It's more of a travesty. I just hope he doesn't fire me."

Millicent took Paige's hands. "Oh, my dear, I'm so sorry. What happened?"

To her dismay, Paige found her lower lip trembling. Deciding that something near the large wardrobe demanded her immediate attention, she strode over to it, biting her lip hard. In a moment she whispered, "I nearly ruined the only set of family jewels he can find."

Millicent groaned. "You didn't hurt him, did you?"

"Well, no, but . . . before that, he kissed me."

Millicent clapped her hands. "Kissed you? That's marvelous! Why on earth would you think he'd fire you?"

Paige whirled to face her. "I must have done something to encourage him, but we both immediately realized what a mistake it was. He . . . he just left me sitting there.''

''Well, the course of true love never did run smooth, did it, dear? Although why he'd resist so much . . .''

Paige snorted. ''He's a high-and-mighty snob! Besides, I'm not exactly attracting him with my gorgeous looks and scintillating personality. I thought that was where fairy godmothers came in.''

The elderly woman shook her head. ''We've discussed that before, dear. Part of the problem is that you simply haven't learned—''

''The secret of fairy tales,'' broke in Paige. ''I don't want to hear that right now.'' She sighed. ''Look, Millicent. I'm okay now. I just wanted someone to talk to.''

''So glad you called on me!''

''I should leave, Millicent. And if I can't convince Prince Niko I'll do my job without injuring him or making him pay extra compensation in the form of kisses, I'll have to leave anyway.''

''Give it a chance, Eleanora.''

''Paige. My name is Paige. Millicent, do you realize you've probably ruined my whole life by getting me this job? The one I turned down at the museum won't be waiting when I get back to the States.''

Millicent's wizened face puckered. ''I brought you here to save you from throwing your life away in the battered basements of Miller's Mine, New Mexico, Eleanora.''

''But it was the chance of a lifetime.''

Millicent started to fade. ''You already have the chance of a lifetime right here, dear. Don't throw it away.''

There was a small snapping like static electricity, a whoosh of wind and then she was gone.

Paige managed to sleep that night, dreamlessly. In the morning she felt stiff—and immediately recalled the bruising incidents of the day before. She chose optimism over realism and dressed in work clothes: jeans, her favorite black T-shirt that said SMITHSONIAN in white letters and running shoes with yellow and green neon stripes. She threw them on quickly. The more she dawdled, the more time her mind would have to rehash the events of the previous day. Besides, she had to get downstairs to face Niko. To fight for her job.

She left her room and hurried down the steps, looking about.

Paintings, furniture and even scratches in the stone wall were beginning to look familiar, thank heavens. With luck, she wouldn't lose her way again.

But she wasn't sure where to go on the castle's lower floor. Rounding a corner, she nearly ran into someone. "Oh!" she gasped, her heart pounding. It was the dirndled young woman who'd served dinner the previous evening. "Hi," Paige said. "I'm Paige Conner, and I'm lost!"

"I am Maibelle," the smiling woman said in heavily accented English. She had broad, rosy cheeks that overpowered her tiny, cupid's bow mouth, and she again wore a lacy cap. "Perhaps I can help you be found."

Maibelle led Paige to a small room dominated by a wooden table and a breakfront that held several covered dishes and a silver urn. "*Le petit dejeuner*—how you call breakfast—is served here every morning," Maibelle said.

"Will the others join me?" asked Paige.

"Everyone comes as they wish. I am up early because there is much to do. But Prince Niko is always up before me. Princess Charlotte, Prince Rudy—sometimes they rise early, sometimes late."

"I'll be early after this," Paige stated, then added, "Prince Niko has already eaten, then?"

Maibelle nodded as she bustled toward the kitchen.

Paige knew she should feel relieved that their confrontation was delayed. Instead, she regretted that she wouldn't see the prince for breakfast. Ridiculous! This way, she could eat in peace.

Surprised at her hunger, she ate more than she usually did in the morning: eggs, a heavy German sausage and two small croissants spread with jam. The coffee from the urn was delicious and rich—and the color of Niko's eyes.

Drat! She didn't want to think about him. Instead, till he fired her, she would do her job.

As she was pouring herself a second cup of coffee, Aldred entered the room. He was dressed as formally as the night before, in a charcoal suit and red tie. His hair was no more tamed than it had been when she'd first seen him.

"Good morning," she said.

"Good morning, Miss Conner. May I join you?"

She assured him that she'd be delighted with the company. She

50

would be even more delighted if she could learn something useful from the prince's longtime retainer.

For such a small man he took an enormous breakfast, twice as much as Paige had served herself. Prince Niko must keep him hopping, Paige thought, for him to maintain his slight figure.

"Last night was your first at the castle?" Aldred asked as he sat at the linen-covered table.

"Yes. My room is charming."

He nodded. "The tower room in the west wing. I'm glad Niko chose that one for you. It should give you the flavor of the castle and its ruling family." He put strawberry jam on a croissant.

"That's what I need," Paige agreed. "All the information possible about Prince Niko and his ancestors." Though she'd been hired to do a history, she couldn't help thinking, for an unfettered moment, that what she really wanted was to learn more about Niko himself.

But why? She was nothing to him—maybe not, after last night, even his employee.

Trying to keep her momentary depression from her voice, she continued, "I understand you've been the prince's servant since he was born."

Aldred's cheeks nearly obscured his blue eyes as he smiled in what appeared to be pride and fondness. He had few wrinkles; his age was disclosed more by the gray in his hair, the parenthetical grooves beside his mouth and the slackness of skin beneath his jaw. "And even before. In fact, there has been an Aldred serving the Dargentian ruling family as long as there has been a Dargentian ruling family."

Paige was impressed. "Then I should find a lot about you and your ancestors as I research this country's history."

Aldred held a deeply etched palm toward her, shaking his head so his wild hair fluttered about his face. "Heavens, no. If my ancestors did their jobs well, they were unobtrusive. You're likely to find no mention of them at all."

A thought struck her. "But what of *them?* Did they keep any old papers about the family? Journals, perhaps?" Today, everyone and his uncle, connected however tenuously to the rich, famous or royal, kept notes, aspiring to make a fortune from pitching prurient details to the press. Aldred's ancestors might have been more discreet, yet many people in the past kept diaries, a possible added resource for Niko's history—and her own historical research.

"Papers . . . I don't know." He glanced toward the ceiling pensively, then turned his bright blue-eyed gaze back on her. "I'll certainly check. As soon as I've some time when Niko can spare me, I intend to visit my own ancestral estate."

"You have an estate, too?"

The corners of Aldred's eyes drooped. "Yes, though it hasn't fared well over time. My father and I used to sneak into Dargentia now and then to check on the country for Niko's family. We would visit our own lands then, too. The house is still standing, but barely."

"Is it nearby?" An excursion might be interesting—especially if it led to more historical information.

"Not far from D'Argent City. But in the meantime there is one interesting tidbit you might be able to use—"

"Tidbit? Eating again, Aldred?" Niko stood in the doorway. Paige looked up at him. Today he wore an outfit that looked more American: a soft plaid shirt with short sleeves and khaki trousers. The common clothing did nothing to minimize his rare good looks.

She met his eyes, then immediately glanced away, inclining her head so her hair flowed about the edges of her glasses. She swallowed. Was he about to fire her? At least he probably wouldn't do it in front of Aldred.

Or would that matter? She supposed powerful people considered their servants part of the wallpaper.

"Ready to get to work, Niko?" Aldred asked. He half stood.

The loyal retainer's reaction to his master's entrance irritated Paige. Surely Niko could wait long enough to let Aldred eat.

"How about some coffee, Niko," she said, "while Aldred finishes his meal?" If he was going to fire her anyway, what was one more demerit added to her list?

To her surprise, Niko docilely poured himself a cup of the hot brew that was as rich in color as his eyes. He sat at the table between Aldred and Paige.

"I was just about to tell Miss Conner about my little contribution to the legend of the crown jewels," Aldred said to the prince.

He was? He'd said nothing of the sort to Paige.

"We were discussing contributions my family made to the Dargentian annals," he continued.

"I hardly think a riddle qualifies as much of a contribution," Niko retorted, running the back of his hand along the base of his beard in apparent irritation.

That was enough to make Paige eager to hear what Aldred had to say. "As I do research," she said, "I might find references to the missing jewels. If so, I should be armed with all the information possible to help me track them down for you."

"You've more to worry about than mythical riches, Ms. Conner," Niko retorted. His head was raised imperiously.

"But those 'mythical riches' might just help you save your country, from what I gathered last night." She was feeling brave enough this morning to bait him. What difference did it make?

He snorted. "To satisfy Rudy's legend?"

"If nothing else," Paige said, meeting his glare with one of her own, "then to satisfy Edouard's loan."

After one heart-stopping moment his stare softened, and Paige thought she glimpsed a hint of admiration in his eyes. Her imagination was on overtime again, she told herself.

"You may be too perceptive for your own good, Paige Conner," he said softly. He turned toward Aldred. "Go on. Tell her your riddle."

Aldred's narrow face lit in a smile as he faced Paige. She felt that he tacitly thanked her. In fact, without his having said a word, she felt she'd found an ally.

"You need to understand, Miss Conner—"

"Please call me Paige," she interrupted Aldred.

"—Paige, that I was made by my father to memorize what I'm about to tell you when I was a small child. We went over it again and again as I grew older. My father said he'd been taught it by his father, and his father had learned it from *his* father, and so forth. But I don't know whether it means anything at all."

Intrigued, Paige asked, "What is it?"

"My father told me that it originated with the Aldred at the time the crown jewels first went missing. That was during the reign when Dargentia lost its freedom, the time of Nicholas the First. It's purported to be a clue to the location of the crown jewels."

"Enough introduction," growled Niko, standing to get himself a coffee refill. "Tell her the riddle." He grabbed Paige's cup from the table and filled it with coffee, too.

She murmured her thanks as Aldred, his eyes seemingly fastened on a point on the distant wall, began intoning,

"Our king is fleeing. He will not risk carrying Les Fabuleux. They will be needed most sorely when the throne is restored to ensure its longevity.

"Oh, how sad is the day that the rightful rulers of Dargentia, King Nicholas, Queen Anna, Prince Stephan and Prince Wenzel, can no longer gaze upon the precious and powerful Fabuleux."

Wenzel! Paige's breath caught in her throat. Was this related to her own mystery?

She forced herself to continue listening to Aldred's words.

"But their names and spirits shall remain with their kingdom.

"Have all our protective spirits fled, too? How else could the throne have fallen?

"And thus shall the crown jewels be found."

Aldred stopped speaking. Paige stared at him. "Is that all?"

He nodded.

"But what does it mean?"

"Not a thing," Niko said. "From the time I was a child, probably even earlier, my whole family tried to dissect it. It's incapable of comprehension because it means absolutely nothing."

"Not true!" Aldred protested. "I know it has a meaning."

Niko turned a look on Aldred that Paige interpreted as vaguely sympathetic. "Why? Because your father made you learn it, and his father before him?"

Aldred's stance remained stalwart. He opened his mouth as though to say something, then closed it again. Paige had the distinct impression that the loyal Aldred was disloyally keeping something from his employer.

Well, she'd help her new ally. "No matter what, the riddle is fascinating," she said diplomatically. "Let's see. . . . There really was a King Nicholas, wasn't there? You showed me his statue, Niko.''

Niko, still standing with his coffee cup in hand, nodded curtly. ''My illustrious namesake who lost the kingdom.''

''Then were there really a Queen Anna, Prince Stephan and Prince Wardell?'' She purposely stumbled over the name that was so important to her.

''Wenzel,'' corrected Aldred. ''So say the legends, and you should be able to confirm that they were the last ruling family of Dargentia before Niko.''

''Would you write it all down for me, Aldred?'' Paige asked. ''Just in case I find something in my research that suggests an interpretation.''

He agreed.

''Now I'll get to work.'' She shot a glance at Niko. He didn't protest.

She took a last sip of her coffee, then left the room. She stood outside the breakfast room, orienting herself. She'd be darned if she'd ask Niko for directions to the library after that fiasco last night.

Down the hall, she recognized a hunting scene on the wall. The nearest door had to be to the room where they'd eaten the previous night. From there, she reconstructed the route to the library.

There were windows along one side of the room. Dim light straggled in, for the day was overcast. Lovely weather for swans and geese, Paige thought, grimacing at her recollection of her set-to with the birds the night before. That reminded her of the attack at the airport—and Millicent.

She scowled. No matter how she'd gotten this position, she was going to do a good job with it.

And if Millicent thought she'd done Paige a favor by putting her in the proximity of a handsome prince . . . , well, that interfering fairy fraud-mother would have to think again.

Although . . . last night, in the moonlight by the moat, Paige had had a sense, for a fleeting moment, that Niko might actually see her as a person, too.

Well, that hadn't lasted. And he certainly thought of her only as his employee today. At least he hadn't fired her—yet. Rubbing her lips as though to erase the memory of Niko's kiss, she sighed and flicked the switch near the door. The room was bathed in bright artificial light.

Paige strode in and stopped abruptly. The computer was set up at the end of the room, on the large table.

Had Niko already decided not to fire her? She felt inordinately relieved. Maybe he really wouldn't hold last night's kiss—and her knee—against her.

She hurried to the table and pulled out a chair along the antique Oriental rug. She sat and looked around. Boy, were there a lot of boxes! Her palms grew sticky, and she rubbed the bridge of her nose beneath her glasses. Maybe she'd taken on more than she could handle. Especially since the prince wanted enough information for an impressive brochure in just two weeks.

But each of the cartons was full of *history!*

She smiled in glee. This was her passion. All that untouched material. Who knew what wonderful mysteries would unfold?

Besides, the answer to her own small historical mystery might be right here. She already had heard of one Wenzel. Too soon to tell if he was the right one. But just maybe . . .

Then there were Les Fabuleux. What if she could solve Aldred's riddle, locate some obscure reference and find the country's missing riches?

She could satisfy the legend that the crown jewels had to be found before the prince married, so the country would survive. She could also satisfy the prince's need for wealth to save the country.

*She* could save the country. And then, maybe Niko would be so grateful, he'd . . .

What? Pay attention to her? Hardly. He'd simply pay off the nobody with glasses whom he'd imported as his historian, then wed his gorgeous princess.

Back to earth, Conner, she ordered herself.

# *Chapter Five*

Paige knelt on the floor beside one dilapidated box piled on another. She lifted the flaps on the top carton, coughing at the dust cloud she raised.

The box was filled with brittle, yellowed papers. Carefully, she lifted some out. They contained household accounts—very old ones. What fun she'd have going through them!

She wouldn't admit it to Millicent, but this beat the miserable archives of Miller's Mine, New Mexico, any day.

The next box contained books. The third, too. She held her breath as she unleashed each carton's musty smells. She scolded herself for attacking them so haphazardly. Well, she'd don her scholar's hat once she got some of the excitement out of her system.

She pried open the flaps of the fourth box and lifted the top page, a hand-printed sheet with a list of guests at a mid-seventeenth-century party in Paris. "Oh, my!" she exclaimed. "So many Wenzels!"

She heard a soft, sweet voice in her head say, "I knew you'd be pleased, dear!"

Paige groaned. Gritting her teeth and scrunching her eyes beneath her glasses, she concentrated on thrusting her imagination aside. She didn't need any interference with her work, not even something—or someone—who wasn't really there.

Fortunately, Millicent forbore from materializing. Paige had a job to do—and it wasn't baby-sitting her blasted imaginary guardian.

Now she had a further clue to the mystery most dear to her. But which Wenzel, if any, was the one for whom she searched?

She studied the fragile guest list. The time frame was perfect. Her Wenzel would have been about twenty-three years old.

"Hi." A soft voice from the doorway startled Paige. She looked up to see Niko's cousin Rudy. He wore a short-sleeved white shirt buttoned to the neck, and dark blue, creased trousers. He regarded her with his body turned partially away, as though he were ready to run if she didn't want him there.

She wasn't pleased by the interruption, but she said nothing to hurt Rudy's feelings. She, of all people, knew what it was like to feel awkward and scorned.

"Come in, Rudy," she said, punctuating her words with an exaggerated invitation with her hand.

He sidled in a few steps, then stopped, looking about. "Spinning wheel," he said.

"What?" Paige felt her nose wrinkle in her confusion, lifting her glasses.

"You need a spinning wheel, like in *Rumplestiltskin,* to spin the raw materials in all these boxes into gold.

Paige laughed. "Maybe that would help."

He still hadn't quite met her eyes, and the way his head was turned gave her a sidelong view of his sail-like nose. "I'm sorry," he said. "Am I disturbing you?"

"Maybe you can help."

A big smile lifted the corners of his mouth, revealing a set of large, almost even teeth. "That's what I hoped. I know a lot about legends, Dargentia's especially."

Paige didn't want to disappoint him, but what she needed was information on real-live history. That was what Niko had hired her for. Still, she said, "They seem fascinating, all wrapped up in crown jewels and who the prince is to marry."

Rudy frowned. "Niko's making a mistake."

"You mean the ball?" Paige didn't want to dwell on her own opinion; the idea of Niko's wooing a princess had sharp edges that seemed to slice at her. Even though it was none of her business.

Rudy moved closer, still looking as though he thought she'd pounce on him if he got too near. "Not necessarily. It might attract tourists. But he shouldn't say he wants to marry a princess. He shouldn't consider marrying at all until the crown jewels are found."

That idea held a certain allure for Paige. "Here, sit down," she said, designating a chair near hers at the table. His nervousness made her own stomach flutter in sympathy. "Where did the legends come from?"

Rudy's Adam's apple bobbed as he sought a response. His pale eyes gazed over her shoulder. "Where do any legends come from? They're simply passed along over time."

"Then why do they matter?"

"People believe in them, even if they seem skeptical. And legends can come true. Do you know, one actually predicted Niko's freeing the country?"

"Really?" That got Paige's attention. She leaned forward, her elbows on the edge of the table. "What did it say?"

He laced his fingers and studied them as if they were his crystal ball, though their boniness made them look like bent twigs to Paige. "I can't remember it perfectly, even in French, but it was something like, 'A plucky prince with a tongue more silver than his forebears' will wield a sword with power beyond the French king's swiftest rapier, and the Dargentian crimson, silver and purple will fly once more.' "

Paige stifled a giggle. "There isn't a French king now, and the president doesn't exactly swing a rapier."

Rudy's mouth melted in a hurt frown. "It's allegorical."

"I know. But, Rudy, what you quoted could fit any prince who happened to restore the throne." Though Paige did enjoy the image of Niko out-talking and out-rapiering an evil despot.

Rudy sighed, sitting back in his chair. "I suppose. But the people are so excited. They believe they were intended to wait for Niko's return all along."

As Paige leaned back, she caught sight of the boxes gaping temptingly. She had history to research, but she didn't want to just kick Rudy out.

He noticed her look. "I'm keeping you from your work," he mumbled, his chin down.

"I appreciated the break," Paige lied.

"Look," he said more forcefully, "you should ask Dargentians about their legends. They're part of our history—the really important part. Niko needs to understand how much his people believe in them. True or not, they govern our lives."

Paige pondered Rudy's vehement words. "Then you think his people's feelings should be more important to Niko than whether he accepts the legends himself?"

"Exactly!" Rudy stood in excitement, and his eyes very nearly met Paige's.

# Linda O. Johnston

What he said made sense. Any leader needed his subjects to believe in him. And, for that to happen, he needed to believe in *them.*

"Talk to them, Paige," Rudy continued. "You'll see that the people have faith in the legends. Then you can let Niko know."

Paige suddenly grasped Rudy's intent in telling her this; he wanted her to convince Niko. There was a major flaw, though, in his reasoning. "But Rudy, Niko won't listen to me. I'm just his employee." And not a very noteworthy one at that. Paige thought for a moment. "The legend you described at dinner last night— Niko must find Les Fabuleux first, marry a commoner second. What do the people think will happen if he ignores all that?"

"Yes, indeed, Rudy," said a deep voice from the doorway. "What happens if I ignore the legend?" Niko strode in. Though he still wore his American outfit, his bearing was as regal as though he were, indeed, the stuff of legends. He was followed by his aunt Charlotte.

For just a moment Paige tilted her head so her hair swayed forward. She certainly didn't want the prince to see the goofy smile that suddenly lighted her face. She didn't dare act pleased just to see him.

She quickly got her expression under control. Serene. Suave.

Rudy mumbled something so low that Paige couldn't hear. "What was that?" she asked gently.

"They say the kingdom will fall again," he repeated.

"Now, Rudy!" Charlotte's voice chided in her thick-as-mousse accent as she stopped behind her son's chair. She wore a dress and lipstick nearly the shade of her artificially orange hair.

Standing close to Paige's side, Niko held up his hand. "He's right, Charlotte. That's exactly what the legends do say. To some extent they're correct. If I don't find the crown jewels, I'll need a miracle to hold on to the throne."

"Because you need money?" Paige ventured.

"Because Dargentia needs money," he contradicted, looking down at her. His dark eyes held a bleakness that sent a sympathetic pang cascading through her.

"Then we have to find the jewels," she said with determination. "Tell me about them."

They all looked at Rudy. "Go ahead," Niko said. "You're our resident expert on legends."

Rudy seemed to be hammered down into his chair by the attention trained on him. Paige could see the effort it took him to start to speak, but once he began enthusiasm carried him ahead. "Les Fabuleux are reputed to be incredible! Amethysts, rubies and diamonds, the colors of the country, all set in gold. There's a scepter, of course, plus crowns for both the king and queen. And adornments, such as collars and bracelets and rings. Simply . . .*fabuleux!*" He paused. "They *must* be found by the king who'll keep the country free." He said the last defiantly, very nearly looking Niko straight in the eye. Then his eyes found his fingers again.

"Fine, Rudy," Niko said impatiently, placing one booted foot on a chair and leaning on his leg with his arm. "You've heard Aldred's little clue that has been chanted through the centuries by his ancestors, haven't you?"

Rudy nodded jerkily.

"All the family has," murmured Charlotte.

"So tell me how to interpret it. I'd be glad to find the jewels to keep my kingdom, but how?"

"I'm sure to find something in my research," Paige said encouragingly, then wished she'd bitten her tongue. She shouldn't offer something she might not be able to deliver. How did she know what those dusty old boxes might divulge?

"You do that," Niko said. "In the meantime, I'll keep on looking for the jewels—while I plan the ball."

"That is good, Niko," Charlotte said. "I'll help as you witch—"

" 'Wish,' Mother," corrected Rudy.

Without missing a beat, Charlotte continued, "But to marry a princess—" She looked at her son, who once more seemed to shrivel in his seat.

"You can't" Rudy pleaded in a strangled voice.

"I'll do whatever it takes to save this kingdom!" shouted Niko. "And if that involves a political alliance with a kingdom that would share some of its wealth with this miserable beggar of a country, then so be it, legends be damned! There is no such thing as a supernatural solution to problems. There's no such thing as the supernatural at all!"

Paige suddenly detected a strong scent of lilacs. "No!" she cried.

61

# Linda O. Johnston

"I'm glad you agree, Paige," said the prince.

"Agree?" The lilac smell grew heavier. What was Millicent up to? She'd never interfered in Paige's life except when they were alone. "No, he wasn't serious; were you, Niko?" Paige spoke more to the air than to him.

He replied through gritted teeth, "I meant exactly what I said, and I thought you were supporting—"

Paige interrupted. "Surely a prince must keep an open mind."

"About what? That some legend is going to save my kingdom? It didn't for more than three hundred years."

"Time had to pass, Niko," said Rudy, looking as though he expected to be struck for contradicting someone. "That was part of the legend." He tilted his head back. His odd-shaped nose seemed to sniff the air.

Oh, no! Paige thought. She wasn't the only one scenting lilacs. "Anyway," she said, searching for a way to diffuse the situation—whatever it was—"it doesn't matter what you accept, Niko, so long as you honor your subjects' beliefs."

"Give credence to their superstitions? Never! In fact, if I do exactly as I wish and the kingdom doesn't fall, perhaps they'll come out of the Dark Ages and into the twentieth century. Legends are for fools, and so is anything else purportedly supernatural."

As the smell of lilacs cloyed about her, Paige swiveled in her chair. Surely there was no way her personal figment could contradict Niko. Her imagination couldn't play tricks that anyone else could experience. Just in case, she whispered, "No, Millicent. He doesn't mean anything."

"*But he needs to learn, dear,*" came the dreaded reply inside her head.

Suddenly Paige noticed a column of smoke in the box farthest from her. It was white, writhing as it rose.

Rudy spotted it, too. "Fire!" he cried.

"No!" Paige said. "It's . . . it's . . ." But she didn't know what it was either. And she couldn't swear that it wouldn't hurt the box—or them. *Millicent,* she cried out in her mind, *stop! Please!*

*Just watch, dear,* came the silent reply.

Niko, not unexpectedly, wasn't standing still long enough to watch the apparent fire spread. "I'll get water!" he said, running toward the door.

"Wait!" Paige cried. She cringed as the white smoky column grew, reaching the bottom row of wooden library shelves on the near wall.

And then it turned into a mass of moths. Their white wings sparkled like sun-drenched dew despite the spare library light. Half turned toward the hearth of the huge fireplace at the stone wall across from Paige's seat, the rest wheeled in the other direction. A window was open; they all soon migrated toward it, then flew outside.

Niko, now by the door, stared in astonishment. His amazed expression was mirrored on the faces of Rudy and Charlotte.

Paige tried to seem surprised as well. She *was* surprised. But she also felt embarrassed. Guilty. As though she had caused the fuss.

Indirectly she had.

She knew the mind was a powerful thing, but was her imagination really capable of such chicanery?

To cover her confusion, she ran toward the errant box. Reaching inside, she pulled out sheafs of yellowing papers—all intact. "Everything's fine," she said in relief.

Niko was suddenly standing beside her. "Everything's not fine," he contradicted. "What was that all about?"

"What?" asked Paige, striving for innocence in her tone.

"The smoke. Those odd moths." He towered above her, and his large, stiff body seemed threatening.

Trembling slightly, Paige maintained her guileless guise as she looked up, and up, and up till she could see his glowering face. "Oh, that. I don't know. Maybe they'd been breeding for centuries in that box."

"Has that happened with any other box?" he asked.

"Well . . . no," Paige admitted. "But I haven't yet opened them all."

Still at the table, Rudy chimed in softly, "You were denying the existence of the supernatural, Niko. Maybe the castle is haunted, and a ghost was making its presence known."

Paige was relieved that Niko's dagger-filled look was no longer trained on her. Rudy cowered beneath it.

"By turning into a boxful of butterflies?" Niko didn't sound believing. "Besides," he said to Rudy, "you've lived in the castle

63

a few months longer than I. Have you ever seen a sign of a supposed ghost?''

''No,'' Rudy admitted in a rasp.

Niko turned to Charlotte, who stood behind her son. ''Have you?''

She shook her head with such fervor that her artificially orange curls bobbed. Her rodentlike front teeth chewed on her lower lip.

''Then enough of this nonsense. I don't know what it was all about.'' He turned his fearsome frown on Paige, and it was her turn to cringe where she still knelt on the floor. He suspected her. He'd send her away now.

Unwanted tears crowded behind her eyelids, and she concentrated on keeping them there.

''Now,'' he continued, ''we'd better let Paige get back to work. I have a ball to prepare for, and she has a brochure to write— and maybe some boxes to clean, if there are any more of those damned moths.''

Paige felt herself sag in relief. She wasn't fired!

But just wait till she got her fingers on that fairy firebrand Millicent!

# *Chapter Six*

When the door had shut behind the others Paige sat in her ornate wooden chair. She hissed, "Millicent!"

No reply.

Who would ever believe in a chicken fairy godmother?

Who would ever believe in a fairy godmother at all? Especially one who played miserable pranks.

With a sigh, Paige looked about. The library's crowded wooden shelves were untouched by flame or moths. The computer confronted her, and she was surrounded by boxes—smoke-free, thank heavens.

She certainly had work to do.

She booted up the computer. It chirped a few notes to signify that it was on, as the small printer beside it hummed. Fortunately, the machine was loaded with a word processing program she knew well.

She stood and lifted the heavy box that had been the subject of all the hullabaloo. She recalled Niko's furious stare as the box had cast up its butterflies.

Well, no matter what he'd thought, it hadn't been her fault . . . exactly. She hadn't intentionally loosed Millicent on him.

She hadn't intentionally loosed Millicent on herself, either—but she seemed to be stuck with her.

Millicent appeared to Paige to be tromping on her own toes. If she'd set things in motion for the brave and handsome Niko to fall in love with plain Paige Conner—fat chance!—he surely wouldn't if he believed her responsible for inexplicable goings-on in his castle.

Just as well. Paige knew it would take a bigger miracle than Millicent could create to make Prince Niko think of her as more than an inept employee. And besides, she had no intention of catching any man—prince or not—by magic.

She opened the fragile cardboard flaps of the box. There just

# Linda O. Johnston

might have been a supernatural reason Millicent had focused on it. Could it contain the secret of where to find Les Fabuleux?

Now that would make Niko notice her.

"Stupid!" she called herself aloud, shaking her head. How could she find the crown jewels in the short time she was likely to be in this job, when dozens of monarchs' minions had failed for centuries?

And even if she found them, she would still be ordinary, bespectacled Paige Conner, genius of the gauche.

She began gently to pull items from the box, listing on the screen the ancient books it contained and making notes on her preferred order in which to tackle them. She was in the middle of doing the same with another box when Maibelle came in to announce lunch.

"No more moths, mademoiselle?" the maid asked in a timid voice, touching her fluffy white cap nervously.

News apparently spread like wildfire here at the castle. "No problems at all," Paige replied, forcing a smile.

"*Bon.* That is good." Maibelle seemed to relax. "Prince Niko waits to dine with you."

Paige was too embarrassed to deal with Niko right then. Too nervous. Too—hopeless. Besides, she was on a roll. "May I just have a tray here?"

"Certainly, mademoiselle." But the maid chewed at her bottom lip as though troubled.

"Oh, and please apologize to the prince for me, but I'm all wrapped up in the research he asked me to do."

The maid's face lightened again, and she left. As soon as she was gone, Paige slumped in her seat, depressed by her own decision. She stared half unseeing at the huge stone fireplace across the room. Maybe she could have diffused Niko's irritation. Maybe she could have made him see that whatever had happened with the box, she was an innocent—almost—bystander as well.

Well, no use crying over spilt opportunities. Sitting straight enough at the computer to be ergonomically correct, Paige delved into her work.

By the end of the afternoon she had made a preliminary pass-through of most of the boxes of books. More than a dozen held papers, and their contents weren't so easily categorized. The paper itself was fascinating, a veritable timeline of how materials had

66

changed over centuries. Some of the older sheets, of higher quality fibers, seemed of more substance and longevity than more recent pages.

But she'd a lot to look through. One day had nearly passed; she'd only thirteen more before the brochure was due. And no suggestion yet that her own quest might find fulfillment.

She took time out for dinner—but only after Niko raised his imperious bearded chin at her from the library doorway. "Do what you wish for breakfast and lunch," he said, "but I want you to join us for dinner."

Paige agreed. She hadn't a choice.

She wouldn't have chosen otherwise anyway.

First, she returned to her room to shower. Her hands were filthy, covered with the grime of centuries. At least she was learning the way to familiar rooms without hesitation. And her soreness from the occurrence at the airport and the goose attack had nearly gone, so she could move quickly.

She peered inside as she arrived. No Millicent. Good—for now. She needed to scold the irritating imp, but she hadn't time at the moment. She put on a tailored yellow shirt and beige skirt.

That night, Charlotte and Rudy joined them in the same small dining room. Aldred was there, too. Obviously, he wasn't a run-of-the-mill servant. He again wore a dark suit, this time with a conservative paisley tie.

Niko had remained somewhat informal, in a striped shirt and dark trousers. Again the others sat as he took his seat at the head of the table. Paige tried to gauge his mood.

"How did your work go this afternoon?" he asked, passing a basket of bread.

Sensing the softly spoken question was a test as well as an expression of interest, she took a deep breath, then told him of her computer cataloging. She concluded, "I think I've made good progress."

He nodded. She couldn't tell whether he liked or hated her answers and decided to take that as a good sign; if he'd hated them, he'd surely have let her know.

Again the meal was delicious. "My compliments to the chef," Paige told Maibelle, who once again served them.

The dirndled maid grinned widely and curtsied. "*Merci*, mademoiselle." Then she hurried from the room.

"*She's* the chef?" Paige was surprised.

"She was educated at Cordon Bleu school in Paris." Niko sipped claret from a delicate stemmed glass.

"Niko's father set up a scholarship fund for deserving Dargentian youths," Aldred explained. His wild salt-and-pepper hair formed a cotton-candy halo about his head.

Out of the corner of her eye, Paige saw Rudy move and turned toward him. His white shirt was again buttoned all the way to the collar, and he faced away from her so she was treated to a side view of his sail-like nose. Staring at the fragile wineglass in his bony fingers, he said softly, in his slight French accent, "Seven League Boots."

"Pardon?" said Paige.

"Like the fellow in the story of 'Seven League Boots,' the reach of the exiled Dargentian monarchs extended far. They all did what they could from abroad to help their people. You might consider putting that in your brochure, too."

"I will," Paige said, then asked Rudy, "Where did you live till Dargentia was freed?"

His mother, daintily patting her protruding mouth with a linen napkin, answered for him. "*Ici.* In town, I mean. You see, my husband Wenzel was Niko's ankle—"

" 'Uncle,' Mother," said Rudy.

As usual, Charlotte kept speaking. "He was Niko's *grandpere*'s second son. Only the one who would inherit stayed away. Other family members were sneaked back to serve as—" She hesitated.

"Regents, Mother," supplied Rudy.

She nodded. "Rudy grew up here."

"Was that scary?" Paige asked. She knew that the Wenzel Charlotte had mentioned could not be the right one, but she'd held her breath for an instant anyway on hearing the name. "I mean, did the French government know who you were?"

"Loyalty," Rudy commented. "Dargentians wouldn't tell." His pale eyes were fastened on his food. "If the French were aware, they said nothing so long as Dargentians stayed quiet."

"That was still brave," Paige said, wanting to stroke poor, bashful Rudy's ego. And then she hazarded a glance at Niko. Would he think that she considered his staying away a sign of cowardice? That was the last opinion she'd have of the brave man who'd saved her from the forklift. Even though she knew her life hadn't really been in danger.

Or had it?

Fortunately, Niko did not seem affronted. Instead, he took a forkful of his beef Wellington.

I'm being absurd, Paige told herself. He was merely her employer. She didn't have to wonder about his reaction to her every word.

After dinner Paige changed back to work clothes and returned to the library. She was absorbed in a box of papers when a soft cough made her jump up and whirl around, her heart thudding.

It was the prince. "Sorry, Paige. I didn't mean to startle you."

"That's all right." There was no one she'd rather be startled by.

She looked up to meet his dark eyes, then immediately bent her head to let her hair fall beside her glasses as she collected her thoughts. She'd talk business, of course. Turning back to the boxes on the table, she said, "There's a lot here. I don't have a feel yet for how to get the sexy information you want as quickly as you need it."

"Sexy?"

Heat suffused her face. She wished she didn't embarrass so easily. "Appealing. Likely to attract tourists."

"I knew what you meant, but you blush so irresistibly, I had to tease you."

She pretended to arrange some of the papers piled beside the computer. Flirting must come as naturally to this gorgeous man as eating or sleeping, but it unnerved her. She preferred it, though, to his seriousness the night before; that had led to that unforgettable but unfortunate kiss. Now she had to change the subject. Without looking at him, she said, "As far as I can tell from the little I've read, your family has been the ruling house for as long as Dargentia has existed. That's unusual."

"Very," he agreed. "Since we had no complete history, as a child my father had me recite the names of all the Dargentian kings from the eleventh century through Nicholas the First in the mid-seventeenth century. He'd learned them as a child, too."

Excited, she spun to face him. "Really? Do you still remember them?"

One broad hand stroked his beard, and his expression grew

pensive. "I think so, but you'll have to try to verify that I'm correct." He pulled out one of the carved chairs beside her and threw one leg over it so he sat straddling it backwards. She settled herself again at the computer. Then, staring over her shoulder toward an empty bookshelf, he began to rattle off a list of names.

"Slower," she said, laughing. She had opened a new file on the computer and was trying to enter them all.

There were a lot of Friedrichs and Stephans, Wenzels and Henris, showing the combined influences of Germany and France. Paige paid particular attention to the Wenzels of the seventeenth century, though she remained unsure whether any were the one she needed to learn more about for her personal research. When he was finished Paige said, "I don't suppose you memorized the queens' names."

"Mere women? Of course not."

Paige felt her chest expand in outrage till she heard him laugh.

"Teasing you is fun, Paige Conner, since you're so serious. No, though the omission is appalling, my education didn't include the names of the rulers' honored consorts. Now, I'll leave you to your work, unless there's something else I can do to help."

"There is one thing." All day Paige had mulled over what might speed up her work and had had an idea. "If I can tap into computer data banks around the world, there may be information I can retrieve quickly to short circuit the research. It'll cost a lot, though, for the long-distance calls."

"Do it," Niko said.

"I'll call my brother in Washington to have him send some software, okay?"

"Of course." He stood and looked down at her, and her heart began to somersault in her chest. Surely he wasn't going to kiss her again. But he bent, slowly. She closed her eyes, lifting her chin—only to feel his lips graze her forehead. She opened her eyes quickly, mortified that she'd misunderstood him.

"Should you have any other requests tonight, I'll be closeted in my rooms with Aldred. We've a lot to discuss about the ball, so I expect I'll be awake for quite a while. You can reach me from any telephone at extension one. Don't work too late."

Paige had no intention of working too late. But when she finally catalogued her last computer entry of the night she wasn't certain what time it was.

Her eyes were bleary, but the rest of her still felt energized. She didn't want to go upstairs to bed yet. She needed to psych herself up to scold Millicent first; surely her self-styled fairy godmother would be waiting for her to rehash Paige's first full day at the castle.

Unless Paige's sanity had won out over her imagination, of course, and had sent Millicent back to fantasyland.

In any event, her bedroom didn't yet call to her. And then she realized what *was* calling—the sweet, serene scene by the moat that Niko had shown her last night.

Not that she wanted to go there with him again. Not after that sensational but strictly charitable kiss he'd shared with her. But he'd said he'd be up late working with Aldred. Surely she'd be alone if she went out now.

First she wended her way to the kitchen, where she found some bread. Then she went outside into the unseasonably warm, moist spring night, where the crickets serenaded her as she walked to the gate through the bulwark wall.

She started to push it open—then stopped. In the dim light cast by the sconces on the outer wall, she saw a shadowy figure sitting on the bench where she'd been with Niko the night before.

That couldn't be Niko, she thought. He was busy inside. Besides, whoever sat there did not have the straight back and regal posture of the poised, self-confident prince.

Who could it be? Paige watched for a moment.

The figure was bent forward from the waist. He seemed to have shoulders as broad as Niko's, but they were hunched forward. He did not look as though he posed a threat to the castle, but Paige believed she owed it to her employer to identify him.

She inched ahead, trying to be silent. She wished the geese were honking at the man for handouts; they would have hidden any sound she made. But though a few milled about on the bank of the moat, they seemed oblivious to the man, as though he'd sat there long enough for them to consider him part of the scenery.

In a minute she'd gone far enough to recognize him: Niko.

But not a Niko she'd seen before. His elbows were on his knees, and he'd dropped his head into his hands. There was a deep sorrow in his demeanor.

Embarrassed, Paige turned to leave. The prince was entitled to solitude in the refuge he'd been kind enough to share with her

71

last night. She would leave him alone.

Unfortunately, though, the geese spotted her. A couple waddled up the path, terrible squawks emanating from their orange beaks.

The prince turned, and Paige froze.

"I—I'm sorry," she said, loud enough to be heard over the honking. "I didn't expect you to be out here."

He stood. He was dressed once more in the peasant outfit that hugged his broad, brawny body. "Come here, Paige," he commanded.

She obeyed, holding out a handful of bread. "I thought I'd feed the geese before I went to bed."

"They'll like that."

He sat again, and she joined him on the bench. Together they fed the geese as they had the night before. His usual arrogance returned to starch his posture. Once more, the lovely black swans stayed far out in the water, condescending to snatch a piece of bread now and then.

As neither of them spoke, Paige's mind kept returning to the way she'd seen the prince a few minutes earlier. So forlorn. So apparently in need of a friend.

She wasn't the most impulsive of people, but she suddenly found herself blurting, "Niko, is something wrong?"

"Wrong?" His voice sounded affronted, yet there was a note of appeal in it that made her continue.

"I know it's not my business, but you looked . . . well, *unhappy* when I came out here."

"You're right," he said in a deceptively soft tone that shouted of his royal heritage. "It is none of your business."

Ducking her head forward to let her hair act as a buffer between them, Paige squirmed as mortification rolled through her. Then she rose in a rush. "Here." She handed him the last of her bread. "Good night, Niko."

He grabbed her arm as she started to leave, his strength making her gasp and turn. "I'm sorry, Paige," he said, truly sounding so. "I appreciate your asking about me."

In the dim light from the outer-wall sconces shining over her shoulders, she found herself staring into the depths of those potent dark eyes—and blinked quickly at the pain she thought she saw there. Impulsively, she grabbed the hand that still held her arm. "Niko, if there's anything I can do to help . . ."

She stopped. How stupid she must sound. She, ordinary Paige Conner, offering to solve a prince's problems.

But he was also a man. And a sad one.

She tried to pull free of his hand, but instead he gripped her tighter. "Stay here with me, Paige, for just a little while."

What else could she do? She sat.

The geese seemed to sense there would be no more handouts that night; they waddled back to the water and glided out among the swans. Without their squawking, the loudest noises of the night were the frogs, garrumphing over the gurgling of the water and the whispering of the slight wind.

Paige ached to soothe the silent man whose fingers remained laced with hers. Despite the humid heat of the evening air, she was not discomfited by the extra warmth of his body close beside hers, only by her own inadequacy. She stared off toward the lapping water, and from the corners of her eyes she saw that Niko did the same.

After a minute his hand tensed. "I have to do what's best for my people," he said, "even if they don't understand. I was speaking with Aldred before about some decisions I made. Now, I have to deal with their consequences."

He spoke in riddles, yet she sensed he wanted to explain. "What decisions?" she prompted.

His voice was almost too low to hear. "I mortgaged my country's soul."

"How—"

"Edouard." The single word was imbued with an agony that Paige did not understand. "I was so sure I couldn't lose. I'd have my entire country behind me. But rebuilding a crushed culture takes time. And time is something I no longer have."

"Niko—?" He'd paused, and she tried to fill the silence with something that would help. But without comprehension what could she say?

He rose, drawing her up with him. They walked slowly toward the bank of the moat. He picked up a stone and skimmed it across the water. Paige heard the *plop-plop-plop* as the stone skipped three times.

Abruptly, he turned toward her. His face was shadowed and craggy in the dim light, and it held no expression. "I borrowed money from Edouard to build the hotels. A lot of money. The

73

due date for the first payment is in six weeks.''

Paige knew the question she was supposed to ask. She also guessed the answer. "Can you pay it?"

"The bargain called either for a lot of cash or evidence that the hotels would be successful. That meant having them ninety percent filled by the day the first payment was due and remaining full for at least a month.''

Now Paige understood. "You haven't the money, so despite what the legend says, you have to hold the ball to find a princess to marry. A fairy-tale situation like that will bring in a lot of tourists right away, and the promise of a royal romance will keep them coming.''

"I told you before that you were perceptive.'' His grin looked genuine, but the lift of his mouth didn't erase the misery in his eyes.

"But if you found Les Fabuleux, wouldn't you sell them to make the payment?''

Any hint of a smile disappeared. "If they're even real . . . but yes. I'd have to sell them. And then I'd go down in history as the prince who tossed away the country's most priceless, legendary assets.''

Paige heard his pain. "But what will Edouard do if you simply can't make that first payment, Niko? If he takes over the hotels, he'll just have to find a way to make them run at a profit himself. Would that really be so bad?''

Niko's laugh was bitter. "Bad? Try almighty awful. He'll take my people's dreams for a bright Dargentian future, crush them into oblivion and toss them out like so much trash.''

"What do you mean?''

"First thing he'll do is import experienced hotel help from other countries so Dargentians won't get the work.''

Paige kept her impatience in check. The answer seemed obvious. "But you're the prince. Can't you prevent that by enacting immigration laws?''

"I could now, but not if I renege on my first payment to Edouard.''

Maybe even a sovereign's solutions weren't so simple. "But why?''

"I promised that if I couldn't pay him, I'd name him prime

minister. He'd be able to dictate the country's fiscal and other policies.''

Paige was shocked. Niko had pledged power. No doubt Edouard would seize it gladly. "And he won't just rely on tourists.''

"Dear Edouard wants to make this a mecca for the money interests of the world, with low taxes, numbered bank accounts and whatever else will turn Dargentia into the worst that Switzerland and the Cayman Islands have to offer.'' Niko's hands flexed into fists as he turned back toward the water. "And if a few less savory interests are enticed here, too . . . well, all the better. He won't let immigration laws keep them out. They've the bulk of the money, after all. And judging by Edouard's standard of living, I suspect he's already pocketing investments by insidious outsiders just itching to be the first to launder money in Dargentia.''

"But he's a banker, isn't he? Is his standard of living above—''

"He's got caviar and champagne habits in a milk-and-mutton economy,'' retorted the prince. "And his bank's lending policies don't exactly encourage local small business ingenuity. He'd make a fine Dargentian prime minister—for everyone but Dargentians.''

"I see.'' Paige paused, then blurted out, "Then there's a lot riding on the ball.''

He pivoted to face her. "An awesome lot. Even my title, since a Dargentian prince can only be crowned king if he is wed.''

"Then,'' she said, looking encouragingly into those deep, dark, distressed eyes, "it'll have to be an awesome ball.''

He laughed humorlessly.

"And,'' Paige continued, "we'll have to lure a lot of tourists here.'' She turned away for a moment, watching a beautiful black swan glide across the moat. A sudden inspiration had struck her. "Niko, I think . . . if you'll give me a little latitude, I believe my brochure can bring people for longer than a month.''

As she faced him once more, his expression was more than skeptical. "How?''

"Rudy gave me part of the idea, though I wasn't sure how to use it. I've been worried about the time it will take me to sort history into coherent pieces for your ball brochure. But Rudy said

Dargentia is filled with legends, and not just the ones about the jewels and the prince's obligation to marry a commoner.''

She had to look away from him again on that one. She didn't want him to think she was nominating herself to fill that role.

"But lots of others, too," she continued. "People everywhere love legends and fairy tales, and your country can give them both if they come here to visit. And there's something else people love.''

"What's that?''

"Contests. We can let the tourists help you pick your princess!''

# Chapter Seven

"Ridiculous!" Niko was astonished. How could this strange young woman think he'd agree to a group of total strangers choosing his bride?

So far, she'd acted appropriately respectful of him and his position. In fact, at times she'd seemed charmingly shy, unsure of how to act around royalty.

Or was that just part of her game? Was this just a new twist on an American's attempt to land a prince? He could just see her arranging for oceans of her friends to show up at the ball and vote for her to become his wife. A commoner to boot, to fulfill the legend.

Though he somehow doubted that quiet Paige Conner had enough friends to rig the ball and fill the hotels for a month.

Still, there was something about her that might have made him feel her capturing him was almost a pleasant idea. If, of course, she had been born a princess who could bring money to the country's coffers and tourists to its land.

She'd wanted to help him, to ease the burdens of leadership from his back.

Well, she had certainly come up with an absurd idea. Having tourists pick his bride, indeed!

But the louder he said no, the more Paige doggedly dug in her heels. "Think about it, Niko," she said. "It would bring in tourists. Maybe there's some variation you could live with."

"Never!" He felt so angry, he could have tossed her into the moat. Instead, he paced along its edge, barely avoiding sliding in himself. Lingering geese squawked and scrambled to get out of his way. He should have gone back into the castle—but something in the back of his brain taunted him that she just might be right.

She didn't seem intimidated by his anger. Beyond where he walked, she tucked her skirt under her and sat on the grassy bank

77

# Linda O. Johnston

of the moat, her legs to one side. Reaching forward, she dangled her fingers in the water.

Her coolness made him all the more outraged. "How would you feel," he said, "if someone suggested that you be married off at the whim of somebody else?"

The look she tossed up to him was astonished—and anguished. He had the distinct impression that this was not the first time the suggestion had been made to her.

But who would try to marry Paige Conner off against her will?

She stood slowly, and her words were uneven. "You're absolutely correct, Niko. I had no right even to suggest it."

Perversely, he now did not want to abandon the idea. She trudged up the path toward the bulwark wall, and he hurriedly caught up with her near the crumbling swan statue. He swung an arm about her shoulder, causing her to turn and look at him with those amazing amber eyes beneath her ugly glasses. He smiled at her. "Let's," he said, "consider the variations."

On their way toward the castle they brainstormed together. He concentrated on her words so he wouldn't think of the curvaceous, charming body pressed tightly against his as he kept his arm about her. Their steps automatically coordinated so their hips swayed in unison; they fit well together. He inhaled her fresh aroma of baby powder. Unavoidably, he recalled lying on top of her on the airport tarmac and how she had felt beneath him.

But that was irrelevant. He himself came up with a related contest idea. It was astoundingly simple yet wonderfully alluring. Crowds were sure to come. "We'll use your brochure to speak of Dargentia's abundance of legends, including the missing crown jewels. People love mysteries. Then we'll lure them here to help me pick my bride by a drawing."

"What?"

She stopped walking on the shrub-surrounded path, and he laughed at her surprise. "It's simple. Each attendee at the ball and visitor to Dargentia for a month after will have one vote, though I'll choose the winning candidate myself. But all those who vote for the princess I actually choose to wed will have their entries placed in a drawing. The winner whose name is selected at random will return here for the nuptials, all expenses paid, and be part of the wedding party."

"Then you pick the princess you want," Paige said, "but

78

everyone who agrees with you has a chance of being rewarded for their good taste. Like a lottery. I love it!'' Her excitement glimmered in her eyes as they reflected light from an upper castle window.

Somewhere inside him, the word *love* hovered for a moment. What would it feel like, someday, to have her use it in regard to him? What would it feel like if, someday, he used it in regard to her?

Nonsense! With his drawing idea, he'd foiled any notion she might have had to capture him at his own ball. And the contest would surely draw tourists to Dargentia.

They entered the castle through the kitchen door. He was amused at Paige's hesitation when they reached the dimly lighted hallway.

"That way,'' he said, pointing to their right.

"I know.'' She sounded miffed. Then, more softly, "Good night, Niko.''

"Thank you, Paige,'' he said, "for trying to help me.''

Paige practically ran down the hall. Her emotions battered about inside her as though they were spun by the agitator of a washing machine.

Niko had battled doing something against his will, like having his bride selected for him. She knew how horrible that could feel.

But what if he knew the whole ball idea was the result of Millicent's manipulation, of supernatural skullduggery?

She could be wrong, of course. Paige prayed that the ball was a coincidental contrivance of Niko's own mind.

But balls were certainly the traditional tool of fairy godmothers.

Niko had made it clear in the library earlier that day what he thought of things that oughtn't be real.

Maybe she should try to make him forget the ball before he realized he might have been been set up.

She reached her bedroom door. Ah, at last—another distressing thought to occupy her mind. Millicent.

But after the moth cavalcade of that morning Millicent was still hiding. Paige thought about shouting for her; she wanted to blow off steam by giving the prank-playing pixie a good scolding.

Silly, to try to scold someone who wasn't even there. She gave up on the idea.

She only wished she could give up so easily on thinking about Niko.

She sat on the edge of the tester bed. In the mirror above the bureau across the room, she saw the reflection of a woman in glasses, with straight, dark hair. Plain. Ordinary. A nobody.

But one in whóm a prince had confided! And not just any prince, but Niko. The reflection smiled at her, for she felt, at least for this moment, special.

That night, out by the moat, he hadn't tried to kiss her. She was glad.

Wasn't she?

He'd laid his problems on her, then argued against her proposed solutions. Her brother had done the same hundreds of times. Better to think of Niko fraternally than to imagine any other kind of interest—

Her brother! Oh, my, she'd nearly forgotten that she needed to call Joe. She checked her Timex watch for the time. Fortunately, Washington, D.C., was six hours behind. It would be evening there. She might be able to get hold of him.

As Niko had said, the Dargentian phone system was modern, though the castle's internal system was confusing. She'd never placed an international call before; most of her communications while negotiating for this job had been with American diplomats in the States, followed by a confirming letter from the prince. Despite a couple of false starts she finally got through—only to reach Joe's answering machine. She left a message, asking him to call her back as soon as possible. It served him right for not being home that the next call would be on his dime.

As she got into her carved tester bed, she looked up at the ceiling of the curved tower room. Which myth did it depict, with its sorrowful wood nymph longingly watching a handsome youth? Greek history had not been her focus. She swallowed and looked away. She could suddenly imagine how that ignored nymph felt.

She slept well that night, only to be roused early the next morning by a ringing telephone. "Hello?" She tried to sound as perky as possible despite her abrupt awakening.

"Paige? It's me."

Joe! She sat up, cupping the phone in her hands as though it were a direct contact with her brother. "Hi. Aren't you up rather late?" She could picture him in his Washington condo, tall and thin and looking a whole lot like their handsome dad. Fortunately, his personality was a world apart; he was a sweetheart of a brother.

"All-night diplomatic session. I figured I'd better call early to be sure to reach you. How's everything going? Did you get to Dargentia all right? What's your job like? The country?"

Paige laughed. "Hold on! Let's see: I got to Dargentia without a hitch. The country's beautiful, everything's going well and the job's why I called." She explained her need for a modem and certain software to allow her to tap into a European university's network to give her access to the Internet. "Prince Niko wants me to have enough preliminary information to put together a zinger of a promotional brochure for a ball he's holding in a few weeks. I'll mostly focus on the country's legends, but I want access to all sources of information as soon as possible."

"A prince hosting a ball. Sounds familiar. Am I speaking to Cinderella?"

Paige laughed. "The prince has met me already and hasn't started chasing me with a glass slipper. I'm simply an employee."

"Too bad."

"Not bad at all," Paige said. "I get to live in the castle, if only for a little while." She hesitated. "Have you heard from Mother and Dad?"

"Of course. They're still talking about your new job."

"I can imagine what they're saying."

"Now, Paige—"

She ignored the familiar ache. It was bad enough that she'd never learned to scintillate, but to have two such driven, scintillating parents . . . Her father was a top advertising executive, her mother a TV newscaster. Both were beautiful. Both had done all they could, as she was growing up, to beautify both her and her personality: expensive clothes, modeling school, acting classes, contact lenses. But none of it ever took.

Joe and she talked for a few more minutes, and he promised to send the things she needed as soon as possible. "Thanks, Joe."

"Take care, Cinderella."

She laughed despite herself. When he hung up she was still holding the phone to her ear, reluctant to break the connection. Dear Joe; she missed him.

When she started smelling lilacs she slammed down the re-

# Linda O. Johnston

ceiver. "Okay, Millicent, where are you?"

A sparkling column began to shimmer near the window. In a moment Millicent materialized.

She stood with her hands folded before her, looking absolutely angelic despite the cerise sweatshirt that depicted a grinning, flitting fairy complete with wings and magic wand. The shirt read, WHO YA' GONNA CALL? OGRE BUSTERS! Her sad eyes lit on Paige, and her usual smile stretched wider. "Hello, dear," she said.

Much of Paige's outrage of the day before had faded. That angered her all over again. She knew Millicent had avoided her so assiduously in the hope that she'd decide to forget her fairy godmother's troublesome frolic.

"I didn't forget, Millicent," Paige warned.

"Never thought you would, dear. Wasn't my smoke simply lovely? And the way it transmogrified into butterflies . . . why, I simply had to go home and show my friends. Although," she said wistfully, "when I tried it there the smoke fizzled and turned into slimy caterpillars. And my friend Glenda's terrified of crawly things. She didn't stop screaming for—well, never mind. But I think you must be a positive influence on me, Eleanora."

Paige sighed. Just as she'd been a sucker for the prince's melancholy the previous night, she now felt sorry for Millicent. "Your trick was wonderful."

"Do you really think so?" She began waving her small, wizened hands until tendrils of smoke trailed from her fingertips.

Paige watched in fascination—for only a moment. "But Millicent, you still shouldn't have worked your magic yesterday. I wasn't alone."

"That was the point, Eleanora. You even told the prince it was important for him to have an open mind. If he doesn't, you won't get to be princess."

"I don't want to be princess, Millicent. All I want is—"

But Millicent was already fading away, the smoke from her fingertips following her. Her wavery voice reverberated off the walls. "You need to keep an open mind, too, dear."

An open mind, Paige thought as she dressed in jeans and T-shirt for the day's research. How open could it get? She kept seeing fairy godmothers, for heaven's sake!

As quickly as she could, she hurried downstairs.

"Good morning," Paige called as she entered the breakfast room. The aroma of cinnamon and bacon filled the air.

That morning, Niko was there. So were Suzanne Pelletiere and Aldred. And Edouard Campion—though Paige wondered why Niko let the nasty man hang around so much when he was the source of so much of the prince's pain.

Though they lived somewhere in the castle, Charlotte and Rudy hadn't joined the breakfast party.

Edouard, Aldred and Niko stood. Niko wore the same kind of outfit in which she'd first seen him: a loose off-white shirt that displayed a thatch of furred, muscled chest, snug pants and boots. He looked devastatingly handsome, but she wondered how she'd ever mistaken someone with his air of authority for a chauffeur.

Catching his eye, Paige considered how to act with him that day. Unless he said something to the contrary, she wouldn't hint of his shared confidences of the previous night. She simply smiled at him and ducked her head.

Aldred looked as casual as she had ever seen him, a dark blue sweater vest pulled down over his white shirt. "Good morning, Miss Conner," he greeted.

Silver-fox Edouard was impeccable in a charcoal business suit, and Suzanne wore a green sheath that covered all the appropriate parts yet still managed to seem on the wrong side of risque. Or maybe Paige found the dress all the greener as she looked at it through jealous eyes. The woman, slender, sloe-eyed and sizzling, was drop-dead gorgeous.

Paige's only consolation was that Suzanne must be ready to chew raw ticket stock; the travel agent would soon lose Niko to a royal, and as yet undiscovered, bride. Slim comfort. The idea did nothing for Paige's mood, either.

"I trust you slept well last night, Paige," Niko said. She had; better than her first night in the castle. She was about to assure him she had when he said, "I certainly did." There was such gratitude and warmth in the look he turned on her that she felt the heat of it turn her skin pink.

Not wanting to see Suzanne's expression, Paige turned and took a plate from the breakfront. She wondered how Suzanne would feel if she knew Niko was about to raffle himself off at the ball—sort of. With a grin, she filled her plate with an omelet and a delicious-looking sugared sweet roll.

Edouard had resumed his seat and ate with apparent gusto. Niko and Aldred had remained standing. Niko held out the tall antique chair for Paige, making her smile at the floor despite herself. She'd simply have to get used to this courtesy.

Taking his seat beside her, Niko said, "I'm heading to town around eleven today. You'll need to come."

So much for the basking she'd done in his earlier pleasure. Paige felt her toes curl as she dug in her heels. "I'm sorry, Niko. I want to sort all those boxes first, so I can't afford the time."

She caught Aldred's shocked glance from the corner of her eye. Apparently, he was not used to anyone denying his favorite dictator anything.

Niko's sensuous lips tautened, drawing his tawny mustache and beard closer together. "You can't afford not to."

Talking to people about Dargentia's legends had become critical to her plans, but he could have asked her opinion. Still, she'd save arguing for something that mattered.

After conversing for a while Niko took a last sip of coffee. "Paige, I'll wait for you by the front entry at eleven."

He said his farewells and left the room, followed quickly by Aldred and Suzanne. "Oh, Niko, there's something I forgot to tell you," called Suzanne.

Paige was left alone with Edouard. The guy was still impeccable. He hadn't even loosened his tie to eat breakfast. She wanted to fling something nasty at him—words or breakfast debris, it wouldn't have mattered. Instead, she bit back her vindictive thoughts and asked, "I don't suppose you've some deep insight into the history of Dargentia to share, do you?"

He snorted, slanting his usual sly gaze at her beneath silvery brows. "Dargentia's history? It's the future that matters. And I mean to have a lot to say about that."

As Paige well knew, he meant it. But he'd fall flat on that smooth, pompous face if she had anything to say about it. She quickly finished her coffee and hurried to the library.

Paige dug eagerly into her first box of the day but couldn't get fully absorbed because of the anticipated interruption. At ten thirty she dashed to her room to wash and change into a skirt, peach blouse and low-heeled pumps. Looking into the bathroom mirror, she ran a comb through her straight, dark hair. Her bangs touched the tops of her glasses, and she wished she'd gotten a haircut before leaving home.

The prince, still in his alluring peasant outfit, was waiting outside the front door promptly at eleven. This time he drove a small Fiat. He came around the car and opened the door for her, looking her up and down with approval. "No jeans?"

"I'll change back later, when I can get back to work."

"My dear Paige, all work and no play will make you a dull girl." His dark eyes sparkled with amusement; gone was his earlier autocratic air, and she tried to respond lightly.

She didn't succeed. "I'm dull already. And hard work will allow me to meet your deadline."

"Fishing for a compliment? All right. You, lovely Paige, could never be dull."

She said nothing. He was simply being kind.

The day was sunnier than the one before, and light glinted on the flowing Argent. A coal barge made its way downriver.

"What about a water tour of the area to attract tourists?" asked Paige. "Maybe a dinner cruise, with local entertainment?"

"Great idea!" Paige warmed at the prince's praise. "I'll ask Suzanne to look into it right away."

They parked near the central square, with its statue of Nicholas I, and began to walk. A Dargentian flag fluttered from a flagpole nearby. Paige hurried to keep up with Niko's rakish stride. Immediately, a swarm of people surrounded them, slowing their progress. The women in town seemed to favor flowered skirts and lacy blouses, the men shirts in bright, solid colors. Again, Paige was unable to catch more than a few of the quickly spoken French words in the more gutteral Dargentian dialect—but chief among them were *bal* and *danse*. The word was out about the prince's ball.

Though most people seemed quite deferential to their monarch, there was an air of concern evident in the shaking of heads and quick, worried glances shared among the townspeople.

A couple of men in overalls edged through the crowd. They got Niko's attention; Paige gathered they were working on the reconstruction of the town's only department store and needed Niko's guidance on the air-conditioning system.

"I need to go with them," he told Paige. "Care to come?"

Of course she did. She'd noticed the building when they'd

# Linda O. Johnston

driven through town—quite old, with stone steps and pillars, and full of history. It was only a few blocks away, so they walked.

Standing outside in the warm spring air, Paige wondered what the building's gargoyles, with their staring, grotesque faces, could have told her about the history of D'Argent City if they could talk. She didn't have any particular interest in the air conditioning, so when they went inside she asked to speak to the store's manager.

His name was Monsieur Pologne, and he looked like Santa Claus without the beard—short, round and red-faced, with a wisp of white hair behind his ears. His shirt with straining buttons was bright green, and he wore a loosely knotted necktie. "Non, mademoiselle," he answered her question. "I am desolate that I know nothing about the history of *Le Grand Magasin*"—this the accurate but prosaic name of the shop, meaning "the big store"— "before I began working here, and I have only been here for about *trente*—thirty—years. Oh, *mais ma mere*—my mother— perhaps mademoiselle would care to visit her one day to learn what she knows of the history of Dargentia?"

Monsieur Pologne was probably in his sixties, and Paige figured his mother would have to be twenty years or so older. "I'd like that very much. Do either of you know much about the country's legends?"

His moon face shone with an eager light. "Ah, oui, mademoiselle. There are few who know more about such matters than my *maman!*"

Inviting Paige for tea at the store's ornate first-floor restaurant, Monsieur Pologne paraded in several of his staff, who also were up in years. One still had a grandmother alive. "Oh, yes, mademoiselle," said the thin woman, whose dark crepe dress was nearly as crinkled as her face. "*Ma grandmere* is quite lucid and able to talk so that you think she will never stop. And the legends she tells us of Dargentia—oh, my, there were even knights and dragons to go with our wonderful castle."

"That's fantastic!" Paige made arrangements to meet with everyone who appeared able to give her insight into Dargentia's history, whether real or mythic. She was still annoyed by Niko's heavy-handed ordering of her out of the boxes and into the town, but he'd been right. She had a promotional brochure to prepare— one grounded in local legends—and how better to do that quickly than to get an oral history from Dargentia's citizens?

How enjoyable this project was becoming!

And how sensitive, too. Somehow she had to do all she could to help the prince win his tourists and his bride, to ensure him the continuation of his throne.

While she was at it, she'd even look out for the missing jewels.

Monsieur Pologne brought Paige a delightful herbal tea, full of cinnamon and cloves and other sweet and tart flavors she couldn't identify, in a fine porcelain pot. As the manager's parade of employees wound down, she lifted the warm pot, admiring its pink painted roses. She poured more tea into the matching cup, careful not to spill any on the starched white tablecloth.

She kept her eye on the arched doorway in the irregular, cream-colored walls of the restaurant. The room began to fill with diners, and Paige felt guilty for taking up a table without eating. She'd just requested a menu when Niko arrived. "Oh, here you are," he said.

"How's the air conditioning?" she asked as he sat.

"Infernally obstinate, like the proverbial woman." There was a gleam in his dark eyes, and he seemed to work to keep his beguiling lips from smiling. He was baiting her again. Despite her initial irritation, she felt pleased; she preferred this mood to his regal aloofness.

At Niko's recommendation, they each ordered oxtail soup and a plate of popular local cheeses and bread.

He chatted about the reconstruction. "Everyone's working together. There's such a spirit of camaraderie; it's wonderful. They really don't need to consult me on details like air conditioning, but I like when they keep me involved."

The camaraderie between Paige and Niko increased, too, or so she thought. She gave him a rundown on the people she'd met and the legends she hoped to collect from them.

But the question that had been on her mind since breakfast finally blurted itself out. "Niko, why do you include Edouard at the castle as though you like him?"

His expression shuttered just as their soup was served. He looked down at the thick, deep red concoction and began to eat.

"I'm sorry. It's not my business." Paige took a spoonful of her soup. It was robust and tasty.

"No. After all I told you last night, you should know every-

87

thing.'' He paused, his voice low. He looked around as though making sure no one could hear, his longish hair catching on the neck of his peasant shirt. Though other diners looked at him frequently and smiled, the noise level in the old room was high enough to hide their conversation. ''Edouard himself was part of his deal. You see, he was raised here and became quite a successful French businessman. He was against freeing Dargentia and was quite vocal about it.''

Paige shouldn't have felt so shocked about the behavior of a man she already believed to be amoral. ''But he's a member of your family, isn't he?''

His laugh was bitter. ''By marriage. And he was influential. I had to promise he could spend time at the castle, giving people the impression he already had my trust, until I showed whether or not I could meet my obligations.''

''I see.'' Paige paused, then blurted out, ''Then you've got to tell everyone the truth once you've paid him off! Even if you can't find the jewels, you'll fill the hotels. Dargentia will become the best darned tourist attraction since Walt Disney World.''

Niko looked at her again. The brilliant smile that crinkled his eyes and arched the lips she loved to watch made her feel as though someone had increased the wattage of the dining room's antique electric lights. ''Not EuroDisney, though, I hope.''

Paige knew the European venture had not had the success of its siblings. ''Perish the thought!''

They gazed at one another for an endless moment. A tingling began in Paige's toes. Heavens, even this man's grins were supercharged with sensuality! Good thing he wasn't touching her, especially the way he had a few nights ago.

''Niko, darling, I'm glad I found you.'' The voice coming from over Paige's shoulder was jarringly familiar.

Jolted back to reality, Paige tugged her gaze away from Niko, who stood. ''Fancy meeting you here,'' he said to Suzanne. His expression had turned bland, and Paige couldn't tell whether he was pleased or annoyed to see the slim, sexy travel agent.

''I hope I'm not interrupting anything,'' she purred as he held out a chair for her. She sat down, tossing her head so her blond hair caressed Niko's hand. She still wore the green sheath, and its skirt rode high on her thighs. ''I had a few matters to discuss with you, Niko dear.'' She drew a sheaf of papers from a leather briefcase—sharkskin, Paige assumed—and placed them on the table before the prince as their meal arrived.

Niko thanked the waitress for serving them, then picked up the papers. "What's all this?" he asked Suzanne.

"I've been doing my homework. Rather, Dargentia's homework. Since you hope that tourists will book rooms in your hotels, you'll need suitable places for overnight stays for royalty the evening of your ball—" She couldn't quite hide the distaste in her voice at those last words, and Paige found herself stifling a smile. "So I've been asking around. All these people with appropriately stately homes are willing to help their prince, nearly everyone I've asked so far—"

"Wonderful!"

"—even though the consensus of the more affluent and influential is to side with the common people. You should pay more attention to our legends and forget the idea of this ill-conceived ball."

"And you should forget your objections." Niko's voice rang with a forcefulness that made Suzanne squirm.

She quickly smiled, not slackening her pace. "I've come up with other ideas to amuse our royal visitors. A tour of the castle, of course. A genteel croquet tournament, perhaps. Tennis, too."

"Paige suggested cruises on the Argent. I think that's a great idea for both royalty and regular tourists."

"Of course." Suzanne regarded Paige as though a cockroach had managed to speak.

Paige couldn't let that pass. She racked her brain for another brilliant suggestion. "How about a culinary contest? Ask Dargentia's citizens to cook and sell the best local dishes the country has to offer, and let the visitors vote." Another audience participation contest, she thought, glancing at Niko.

He got the idea and laughed. "How marvelous!"

"But Niko—" Suzanne sounded upset, and Paige looked at her. Her lovely face was contorted into a mask of anger. Was she simply upset she hadn't thought of it? Or did she hate the idea?

Or did she hate Paige?

That shouldn't matter, but Paige didn't like the idea of making enemies, even of people she didn't like herself. "I'll bet Suzanne's full of other kinds of tourist-attracting ideas," she said with an encouraging smile at her lovely nemesis.

# Linda O. Johnston

Far from appeasing Suzanne, the comment made her glare all the more fiercely. Quickly, Paige found something of great importance to study in the center of her cheese plate.

Suzanne turned to the prince. "Niko, dear, with all these wonderful ideas for attracting tourists, surely you don't need something as trite and childish as a ball."

"Trite, childish and necessary," he contradicted. "It will kick off our tourist program. And if I meet a suitable princess to court in the process . . . well, all the better. It's not as though I've a little black book full of them."

"I understand, Niko. A childhood in the United States"— she spat the words as though they were poisonous and cast an accusatory glance at Paige, obviously blaming her for the ills of the whole country—"wouldn't exactly let you meet the right people. But you're home now. And the legend says you must marry a commoner."

"Even so, I need to do this. For Dargentia."

Paige understood. The whole world would be aware of Niko's ball. Romantics would swoon to see the handsome prince woo, and then wed, a royal princess. Then they'd spend good money to come here, hoping to glimpse the happy couple.

And if Niko left behind a trail of broken hearts . . . well, hers wouldn't be among them. She wouldn't let it. And she had no sympathy for Suzanne.

In her mind, Paige watched Niko dancing with a lovely princess, gazing down at her with those dark, smoldering eyes, speaking words of love with the lips Paige found so perfect, so sensual . . . damn! She swigged her tea as though its herbs contained something intoxicating. Then she poured herself another cup from the porcelain pot.

Niko soon decided it was time to return to the castle. Fortunately, Suzanne had business in town.

As they walked to Niko's car, Paige spotted Charlotte and Rudy across the street in a crowd of workers. The group, pointing and talking animatedly, surrounded scaffolding that scaled a two-story stone building. Both of Niko's relatives wore hard hats, and even the reticent Rudy appeared to be right at home.

Niko lifted his hand in greeting as Rudy nodded shyly toward them. "His father worked here in construction," Niko explained with a smile. "Displaced royalty has to earn a living. Uncle Wenzel was quite good at it. He taught Rudy a lot. Now the towns-people ask his advice.''

They stopped for a short while at Niko's new hotels. One was modern and sleek, with a white stucco and red tile facade; the second was more old-world European, of stone and half-timbering and charm. Both were huge. Both were luxurious. And, Paige hoped, both would appeal to tourists. Lots of them.

Edouard stood in the nearly complete lobby of the second hotel. The impeccable silver fox stood with several hard-hatted construction workers beside a scaffolded wall in the throes of being painted a regal white. The workmen were laughing uproariously. Edouard simply smiled his sly smile. The scene smelled to Paige of more than the overbearing odor of wet paint. ''What's he doing here?'' Paige asked, feeling irritated on Niko's behalf.

''Keeping an eye on his investment, no doubt,'' the prince replied dryly.

Their ride back to the castle was pleasant. Paige made it a point to ask questions about Dargentia, its charming capital, the shimmering Argent, the upcoming ball. No way would she act like Suzanne and appear as though the ball bothered her.

But the more she got to know Niko, the more attracted to him she felt. The only future in that was to be hurt. There were many things she wanted here, all involving history—and none involving heartbreak. She'd keep herself in line.

When they reached the last switchback before the bridge over the moat Niko asked, ''Shall I give you your tour of the castle this afternoon?''

Paige hesitated, tempted. But she mustered her resolve to take care of herself. ''Maybe later.'' When he pulled up to the castle entry she burst from the car with a quick, ''Thanks,'' then ran up to her room to change.

First there was something she had to know. She made sure her door was locked, then turned around. ''Millicent!''

# Chapter Eight

In a moment she smelled lilacs. A hazy pillar suddenly shimmered before the wall near the carved tester bed. It took shape—Millicent.

"You called me, Eleanora, dear?"

Eleanora again. Paige bit the inside of her lip to keep from yelling at the gold-haired old woman with the gray roots, sympathetic eyes and annoying smile. She had, after all, called *her*— this time. There was a question she had to ask.

"Millicent, did you make up the Dargentian legend about the prince having to marry a commoner?"

"I didn't have to. Wonderful, isn't it? It fits perfectly with the prince falling in love with you."

Paige hooted. "Right. Well, you've gone to a lot of trouble for nothing, Millicent. I suspect you planted the idea of a ball in Niko's brain, but he's fixed your fairy finagling. He's only interested in finding a princess, one whose presence will bring in tourists and whose family will bring in money. No chance of either coming from me."

For the first time Millicent looked worried. Her tiny brow caved into more crinkles than Paige had ever seen there, and she raised one finger to her puckered lips. "Well, dear, I suppose I could try to turn you into a princess."

Paige decided to humor her. "Only a beautiful one, of course. Permanently. And one who scintillates."

Those shiny, down-turned eyes grew sad. "Eleanora, dear, that's not in the rules. The secret of fairy tales . . . if only you'd recognize it. It just requires concentration."

"I know better than to concentrate on fairy tales, Millicent. I did that when I was a junior in high school, and all it got me was the most miserable time I could imagine."

Millicent sank onto the bed, shaking her head. "I remember only too well."

# The Glass Slipper

Paige looked down at the small seated figure. The mattress didn't sag. Of course not. There was no such thing as a fairy godmother. It wouldn't matter, then, if she took out her frustration on someone who wasn't there.

She couldn't explain that frustration, though—how she was attracted to Niko, and how she actually, deep down inside, wished with all her heart that fairy tales could come true. Millicent would think her fairy godmothering had resulted in something right for a change. Maybe she already did, if she could read Paige's excited aura or her inanely imaginative mind. In self-defense, Paige resurrected a gripe for which she'd blamed Millicent forever. She sat on the bed next to the elderly being who wasn't there. "I remember, too. I was so shy that I hadn't a prom date till my brother arranged one with Robert Cox, the coolest guy in school."

"Smart, too," Millicent murmured.

Mr. Everything, Paige recalled. His girlfriend had come down with the measles.

"Wasn't that serendipitous?"

"Stop reading my mind, Millicent," Paige grumped. She paused. "I've always thought it was magic."

Millicent looked shocked. "But I explained then, dear—"

"Never mind." Paige rose and paced the room. "It was disastrous." They had double-dated with her best friend, Leah. What was her date's name? The new guy in school who earned spending money by selling fish bait?

"He was such a nice young man."

"Millicent!" Paige tried to shift her thoughts to something else, but now that her painful memories were stirred they poured forward like a mud slide—ugly, relentless and very sticky.

She'd been unable to decide whether Leah's date smelled more like fertilizer or dead worms. She knew Robert would never ask her out again once his girlfriend got better, but she just hoped for a nice evening.

For some reason she'd never been able to explain to herself, she'd triggered it all by sitting on her bed, her head in her hands, and begging for a fairy godmother.

To her shock, Millicent had appeared.

Now Millicent rose, standing beside Paige in a flurry of pixie dust. "I appreciated the opportunity, dear. We fairy godmothers have the most delightful retirement facilities, now that hardly anyone believes in us. Pools, fountains, gardens, and all the pastry we can eat. But it's so much nicer to feel wanted. When you called for one of us, I felt fortunate to have been chosen.'' She hugged Paige. It was as though a soft baby sheet enveloped her.

Paige's eyes misted at the love radiating from this creature. She pulled away, reminding herself that she was angry. ''I wasn't so fortunate,'' she snapped. ''Sure, you helped me dress: lovely gown, hair up, even helped me wear those dratted contact lenses my parents had bought. My eyes didn't water all evening. That part was perfect!''

Then her date picked her up, and the disaster began. Robert *had* looked impressed, but when he talked she didn't know how to respond. She wanted to scintillate, but the only scintillating one was Leah. Paige learned more about digging worms from Leah's date than she'd ever wanted to know.

She turned on the older woman. ''Darn it, Millicent, why couldn't you have packaged scintillation into that beautiful gown? All I wanted was one wonderful evening.''

''But you simply didn't understand—''

''The secret of fairy tales. I still don't, but I'm a glutton for punishment.'' She had called on Millicent in desperation occasionally since then, but she'd never gotten exactly what she'd wished for—though her appearance had certainly been improved for an evening or two. ''And now—well, why did you set me up with this job? Even if you succeeded somehow in getting Niko to notice me—a highly unlikely prospect—he'd never marry me. He's after a royal bride.''

''I know.'' Millicent looked so sad that Paige considered comforting her. How absurd; *she* was the fairy godmother. She was supposed to take care of Paige.

''Sorry, Millicent. You can't help it that your magic's flawed. Anyway, I'd better get back to work.''

Millicent began to fade. ''My magic is as it should be, Eleanora, dear. Things can still work out.''

''In your dreams, Millicent.''

With a crackle and the scent of lilacs, the old woman was gone, and Paige was left alone with her stupid dreams.

She quickly changed back into a T-shirt and jeans and hurried to the library. That afternoon she made notes on the computer. She had lots of ideas, plus plans to talk more with the people she'd met that day. She jotted down the local folk tales she'd heard, printed and saved them to a disk, then turned back to the first box of papers.

When Niko came in to take her on the tour she declined: too many documents; too little time. And too much futile attraction toward Niko.

Especially as he stalked regally into the room, still in his peasant outfit with the loose shirt that emphasized the breadth of his shoulders, the tight pants that stressed the narrowness of his hips. Holding her breath and lassoing her libido, Paige managed nevertheless to refuse. She swallowed as he glared down at her. His sensual lips formed a stiff line. If there was hurt in his dark eyes, she didn't want to see it. But she considered—just for a moment—changing her mind.

She probably would have, had he evinced even a shred of the vulnerability he'd shown the previous night. But he didn't. "Dinner will be in two hours. I want you to join me." He was in one of his imperious moods again.

She was his employee, not his subject. And she didn't take orders well. "*I* want to continue with my work." She glanced at him looming above her. "Look, Niko, you were right about the trip to town today. I loved meeting people, and everyone was helpful." Except Edouard, she thought. "But you hired me for a job with a difficult deadline. I need to catch up."

His deep voice could have frozen the moat. "I'll send Maibelle with a tray." He stalked out, leaving Paige empty inside. Maybe she should spend a few minutes more with him. She'd love a tour of the castle. . . . No! She was being ridiculous.

She worked till late, finishing one box and delving into a second. Thank heavens for the legends, especially those she'd yet to learn. She doubted she would have been able to put an honest-to-goodness history of Dargentia together in less than two weeks. Relying on folk tales would be fun, though it wasn't her forte. She was a historian. She thrived on verifiable facts, not colorful fiction.

Paige grew tired. She knew she'd concentrate better if she started fresh the next morning.

Rather than going straight to bed, she wended her way to the kitchen. There, she rounded up some bread.

She wanted to unwind someplace peaceful. Someplace solitary.

Not her bedroom, where Millicent might appear at any moment. She wanted to be by the moat.

Maybe she also wanted to be by Niko.

He might be there again. He might go there every night.

Well, she wasn't intending to intrude on him again. If he was there, she'd simply ask if he minded her presence. He wasn't shy about telling her what to do. If he wanted her to leave, she would.

And she'd retreat on her own if she felt at all uneasy about his presence. But he hadn't even hinted at wanting to kiss her again last night. She was safe.

Why didn't that make her feel good?

A few slices of Italian bread in her hands, she stepped outside the kitchen door and proceeded along the path. The air was cooler that night than it had been the previous evening. But she didn't want warmth; she wanted serenity. Still, her T-shirt hardly lent any protection. She reached the gate through the bulwark wall and peered through.

No one sat on the bench. The only visible movement was from the moat, where the water shimmered in the slight breeze.

Paige sighed—in relief, she told herself. She was alone.

Sitting on the cold hardness of the stone bench before the swan statue, she shivered. She could go back inside where it was warm . . . but not yet.

The light from the castle walls was dim. A sliver of a moon cast a pale, shimmering light on the water. Paige wondered for a moment if she'd come too late, if the geese and swans had gone to bed. "I'm here," she called. "With treats."

She heard a splash and some honking to her right. As though they'd understood, the mother goose appeared with her goslings and two males following behind. Paige laughed. "Here," she said, and began to toss them pieces of bread, careful not to rush them or get her fingers—or shins—too close.

Suddenly she heard footsteps. She stiffened. No need for her heart to pound so outrageously fast. Maybe she'd hoped, down deep, to see Niko, but he couldn't be the only one who knew this perfectly peaceful hideaway. Perhaps it was Aldred, or Charlotte or Rudy. Maybe even the opprobrious Edouard.

But it wasn't. She wasn't sure how she knew—maybe from the steadiness of the stride. But she was certain. It was Niko.

96

Sure enough, when she turned he stood in the shadows by the open gate.

Niko had been watching Paige for only a minute before she turned. In that time he'd heard her call the geese, listened to her melodic laughter as they squawked and swam, watched her smooth motions as she threw bread into the water.

Her dark hair skimmed her slender shoulders. She was a study of graceful, shifting shadows in the dim light that turned everything to shades of gray and black, softening her work clothes and ugly glasses.

He hadn't come out here every night before Paige Conner had arrived. Now it seemed like the most natural thing in the world to feed the water fowl. She expected it of him.

He hadn't planned to pour out his troubles to her the previous evening, but she'd been so easy to talk to. She seemed to care about his pain—and more. She'd offered a solution that just might work, with some modification.

Now he joined her on the bench. "Hi," he said softly.

"Hi." Her voice was a whisper, but somehow it conveyed pleasure piqued with uncertainty. Was she disturbed by his presence? He certainly was disturbed by hers.

"I brought you more bread." He showed her the paper napkin in his right hand. It was wrapped around several small dinner rolls.

"How did you know I'd be here?"

He smiled. "Wishful thinking."

She looked quickly away. "I don't see the swans tonight."

"They'll come." He held out the extra bread. Their fingers brushed as she took it, and that tiny contact stirred him. He inched closer on the bench. The seat was hard and cold, but her nearness warmed him. He stopped when their arms touched.

She stiffened but didn't move away, though she should have. Wasn't she singed by the burning inside him that made him want so much more than that tiny touch?

He wanted to douse the conflagration. But to do that he'd have to stoke it further first. He pivoted and took the bread from her hands, placing it on the bench.

"But you were right," she protested. "The swans are coming."

"They'll wait." The coolness of the air intensified as a breeze buffeted them. He saw the tautening of her nipples strain her T-shirt. Or could their budding be a reaction to his warm hands, now rubbing her arms? Her gaze followed his. With a tiny cry of embarrassment, she tried to pull away.

He didn't let her go. Instead, he drew her close, holding her awkwardly on the stone bench as she remained rigid. But the clumsiness disappeared when he used his fingers to caress her cool cheek beneath her glasses. He touched the edge of her mouth. She relaxed against him as her lips opened, and he bent and brushed them lightly with his own.

His hands stroked her slender back. They moved downward until they grasped her buttocks, and he used their feminine fullness to pull her closer still.

He was behaving badly. He was a prince, but the days of droit du seigneur were long past. He could offer this woman nothing but a job that would soon end.

Yet he was the one who felt commanded by the presence of Paige Conner—and his desire for her. It was almost magical, if he believed in magic. Which he didn't. But he did believe in his desire. . . .

"Paige," he whispered against her mouth.

Her lips moved as they responded. "Niko, I—"

He silenced her by deepening the kiss. He moistened her with his tongue, explored the inside of her mouth as though he were one of his remote ancestors discovering a new kingdom.

Touching his beard with her fingertips, she sighed. The sound stimulated him to greater exploration. He moved his hand upward and around, to grasp gently one firm, full breast. His thumb brushed across the already alert nipple, causing it to form an even tighter nub.

His mouth tore from hers and trailed heated kisses down her cheek, along her arched neck, over the soft fabric of her shirt.

She pulled away. Her breathing ragged, she looked at him. Her amber eyes, framed by the black rims of her glasses, were the only color in the grayness of the dim light. "I'm sorry, Niko. You don't . . . I can't . . ." She pulled away, then stood and ran toward the open gate.

## The Glass Slipper

Fleeing mindlessly along the dimly lighted path, Paige ignored the cold spring breeze that made her shiver.

Or was it losing Niko's heated touch that turned her to ice?

She hadn't wanted to run. She'd wanted desperately to stay with Niko. To share those incredible kisses. To feel his hands on her, to let the softness of his beard tickle her chin, to savor the scorching of his mouth.

But self-preservation had prevailed.

How could he tease her with such abandon, make her feel desirable, when she knew it wasn't so?

To him it was a game.

To her it was impassioned, incredible reality.

She tugged open the first wooden door of the castle, barely hearing its creak as it closed.

Her ears strained in the eerie silence of the empty kitchen. She half hoped to hear Niko. To have him grab her from behind, whirl her into his arms, kiss her till she couldn't remember why she shouldn't be near him.

She heard nothing.

She should have felt relieved. Instead, she was disappointed. Angry. Why had he kissed her again?

She hurried through the kitchen and down the red runner along the first stone hallway.

Alone in her room, she locked the door. If only she could lock her feelings outside, too.

Sitting on the bed, she closed her eyes, trying to keep her anger alive. Instead, she relived every moment from her noticing Niko by the gate to her flight. She spent most of her time recalling his hard, heated body, his hands, his lips. . . .

Damn him! And damn herself, too. And Millicent. And even her brother Joe. Here she was, in the middle of a modern-day fairy tale that could never come true.

She hated fairy tales.

In reality, a plain, ordinary heroine who fell in love with the handsome prince would remain plain, ordinary . . . and unloved.

# Chapter Nine

Rising early the next morning, Paige planned to have a little talk with Prince Nicholas of Dargentia. Recalling her body's treacherous response to him the night before, she dressed in a baggy cotton shirt over a nondescript dark skirt.

She found him alone in the breakfast room, where the aromas of bacon and coffee filled the air. He rose at her entrance, regal and handsome in his customary peasant clothes. To avoid his eyes, she looked straight ahead, only to feel uncomfortable anyway as she found herself staring at his broad chest. Burnished gold hair peeked from his open shirt. After stammering, "Good morning," she hesitated, then said stiffly, "About last evening . . ."

"Yes?"

Her words flowed out in a rush. "I realize that the spot out by the moat is a special place to you. I apologize for disturbing you there the last couple of nights, and I won't do it again."

"Think nothing of it," said the prince. His expression looked so icy that she imagined he was glad of the dusky beard to warm his face. "It doesn't matter to me whether you're there or not. I don't visit the spot every night anyway, and you may continue to do so—for the rest of your employment."

In those few words he put her in her place. Last night's kiss meant no more to him than the first. She was just a temporary hireling.

That was fine with her. She'd gotten her emotions in line after a nearly sleepless night. What she felt for Prince Niko was a silly infatuation, one any American woman would feel, faced with a charming European prince. She'd keep it to herself. Her professionalism was at stake.

But it still hurt to be reminded of reality—that a man as exciting as Niko found the kisses of a nobody like her no more memorable than a discarded paper towel.

She got her food and joined him at the table. Shrugging aside her pain, she made conversation by tossing out a job-related request. "I'd like to use a car, if you don't mind. I've arranged to visit people I met yesterday to learn some of Dargentia's legends."

"Of course." His earlier aloofness eased as an approving smile displayed perfect teeth beneath his eminently appealing lips. "You're not wasting any time."

Her heart leapfrogged into her throat. She couldn't help but smile back, but she quickly wiped it away. Be professional, she admonished herself. Stay distant, cool.

When they'd finished eating he showed her to the stables, a huge stone building at the far end of the castle's driveway within the bulwark walls. Though there were a few horses in immaculately kept stalls, much of the stables had been converted into a garage. The odor inside was a not unpleasant combination of horse, gasoline, car polish and disinfectant.

They passed a large black stallion moving skittishly in his stall. Paige pictured Niko astride the powerful steed as it bounded through fields, the prince's dusky blond hair waving behind him, his seat perfect, his broad shoulders thrust back as he easily handled the reins. His thighs tightly compressed, controlling the untamed horse as its hoofbeats pounded a wild rhythm . . .

It was a good thing that the prince drove a car. And that Paige was practiced in keeping her imagination under control.

She quickly passed the stalls to stand beside the cars. "Here," Niko said. He gave her the keys to the small Fiat and showed her the buttons for the automatic garage door.

"I don't suppose you have time for your tour of the castle." His voice was a flat statement.

"I'm looking forward to it, but not today." She didn't dare to share an hour or two of his company alone. Despite all her careful self-control, he still drove her to foolish fantasies. "I need to get to work."

But as she turned away, she stifled a sigh. Maybe she'd be better off just taking the tour, getting her curiosity out of her system.

Or, she feared, stimulating her interest in the prince all the more.

* * *

# Linda O. Johnston

Before leaving for town, Paige needed to return to her room for her purse and notepad.

As she reached for the doorknob, she heard noises inside. She sighed, her shoulders slumped, then straightened, preparing to deal with Millicent.

She was surprised to see Aldred instead. Niko's majordomo wore a long apron over his trousers and white shirt. He held a feather duster in one hand, and his salt-and-pepper hair was even more wildly askew than usual. He must have brought the step stool on which he stood, for the slight man was stretching the duster far along the top of the carved bedstead.

She didn't want to startle him while he leaned so precariously. Instead, she watched him for a moment. He was limber for his age, and he hummed what sounded like an off-key march.

Paige looked around uneasily. Fortunately, there was no sign of Millicent, not even the slightest scent of lilacs. Good. The last thing Paige needed was for anyone else to suspect she'd arrived at the castle with an imaginary companion in tow—if they didn't already suspect her of playing juvenile pranks after the smoke-and-butterfly incident.

In a moment Aldred straightened, placing one hand on his hip as he surveyed his work. Apparently pleased, he backed down the steps, then turned and saw Paige.

He gasped, his hand rising so swiftly that a feather from the duster fluttered to the floor. "Oh, Paige," he said. "I didn't hear you come in. I hope you don't mind my being here, but I'm helping out the very busy Maibelle."

"I don't mind." She knew she didn't sound very convincing, so she continued, "Sorry I startled you. Look, I hate to see either Maibelle or you go to any trouble on my account. Why don't I just see to my own room while I'm here? And please, call me Paige."

His bright blue eyes widened between his aged, pouched lids as though he was scandalized. "Oh, no, Paige. Guests of the prince of Dargentia don't clean their own rooms."

"I'm not a guest, Aldred," she reminded him. "I'm an employee."

He lifted his chin obstinately in a gesture that reminded Paige of his employer. The loose skin beneath his jaw lost a little of its slackness. "But while you are here, you are also a guest."

Paige recalled her feeling, on meeting Aldred, that he could be an ally. She certainly didn't want to alienate him over his kindness. She smiled. "Thanks, Aldred," she said. "You'll spoil me."

"Such a lovely young lady deserves to be spoiled," he said gallantly.

Nonsense! Paige figured he'd taken blarney lessons from his charming boss.

With a shake of her head, she began to gather what she needed for the day's venture to D'Argent City.

"You are going into town?" Aldred asked.

Paige nodded. "I'm gathering legends."

His small mouth broadened into a grin accentuated by the parenthetical grooves beside it. "Good! Then you must see some of our most noteworthy raconteurs—other than young Rudy. He is perhaps our country's expert. But you should also hear stories from the others; then he will help you assemble them." He gave her a few names, which she wrote down. One or two were familiar; the rest were new to her.

"Thanks," she said. As she hoisted the strap of her purse over her shoulder, she thought she smelled lilacs. "Oh, no," she commanded in a whisper. "Don't you dare!"

"I'm sorry, Paige," Aldred said, confusion on his aging face. He'd been in the middle of moving the step stool to the other side of the bed. "You don't wish me to dust the rest of the headboard?"

Paige thought quickly, then spoke as though she hadn't quite finished her statement. "Don't you dare do anything to hurt yourself, Aldred. I saw how you were leaning when I came into the room."

She no longer smelled lilacs, thank heavens. Maybe she'd been mistaken. Or maybe, for once, Millicent was minding what Paige said.

Aldred smiled broadly. "I will be careful, Paige."

Paige left the castle without another glimpse of Prince Nicholas of Dargentia. She drove the little Fiat herself. It was the first time she'd gone down the switchback on her own, her first trip to town without Niko's company.

She was better off this way. Much better, since her mind still

103

played pitiful games of reliving those meaningless kisses.

She intended to take up Monsieur Pologne's offer to meet with his mother. She stopped first at the Grand Magasin. Its rotund restauranteur, again clad in a shirt of emerald green, ushered her to a stone cottage several streets away.

Madame Pologne was a delightful, pink-haired octogenarian with a small, immaculate home. She insisted that Paige take the seat of honor—a delicately carved sofa with velvet upholstery and spindly legs. Wearing what appeared to be the traditional Dargentian white lacy blouse and flowery skirt, she served fruit-filled pastry she'd made herself. Her voice was high-pitched but strong as, in French, she spun the most glorious tales—all true, she insisted. "My family, you see, has been Dargentian as long as our dear Prince Niko's."

While Paige made notes, madame told the tale of the first king of Dargentia, Wenzel I, who rallied the local citizens to fight off invading Normans.

Then there was King Michel, who, during feudal times, watched his subjects succumbing to the Black Death. He rode his steed many days until he found the Valley of Darkness, where he defeated *L'Ange du Mort*—the Angel of Death. When he returned to Dargentia the rest of his subjects were recovering.

And their current prince, too, was a legendary hero. Just as the story had foretold, he had single-handedly—except for the wise counsel of his mentor, Lord Aldred—freed Dargentia from its recent oppressors.

"He is so brave, so wonderful" tiny Madame Pologne gushed, pouring Paige more tea, her fragile hand surprisingly steady.

Paige couldn't argue with the brave part. As to wonderful . . . well, he certainly had his good points. His looks. His body. Even his alluring personality, if she excused his arrogance. But there was nothing particularly wonderful about his taunting her with trivial kisses out by the moat.

Those kisses, though . . . *they* were wonderful.

"But our prince is so misguided, Maman," said the madame's Santa Clauslike son, who sat across the room on a chair too small for him.

"Ah, yes," sighed madame. "The ball. It should be so exciting, but . . ."

Feeling as though she were sticking a dagger beneath her own skin and twisting it, Paige asked, "Aren't all Dargentians glad that Prince Niko is looking for a bride?" She sipped her tea; her mouth was suddenly dry.

"Mais, oui!" Monsieur Pologne answered. The red-faced man stood to pace the small parlor. "Our Prince Niko's idea to make this poor country a rich tourist haven was ingenious. He has brought back our freedom, and now he wishes to assure our survival. Yet he goes about it so wrong—"

His mother interrupted, waving her small hand as though erasing an ugly thought. "A royal princess. That is what he wishes. But he must instead find a commoner."

Paige winced. She still saw the smoky fingers of Millicent in this treasured legend. But surely the inept fairy godmother couldn't have engraved the tale into so many minds. No; more likely, as she'd said, she'd known it existed before uprooting Paige and planting her in this impossibly fairy-talelike kingdom.

"I've heard the Dargentian legend," Paige said. "It's a fascinating story, but—"

The petite madame drew herself up with dignity. "Our legends, mademoiselle, are what sustained Dargentians for centuries, until our homeland was freed. And they were correct, for they predicted the return of our prince. But now, he, too, must learn their importance, or Dargentia will face ruin anew."

Paige pondered for a moment. "I'm sure Prince Niko could find a suitable commoner bride if that's what he decides." The lovely, snide face of Suzanne sneaked into Paige's mind. She thought about sticking out her tongue at the image, then turned her internal grimace into a smile at her host and hostess. "The harder part of the legend to fulfill will be finding Les Fabuleux. Do you really think they exist?"

Did they ever! Madame and Monsieur Pologne spoke together, spinning stories of the jewels' magnificence. No false fable at all were Les Fabuleux.

And did the stories say where the jewels could be found?

Monsieur Pologne offered a butchered version of Aldred's recitation, but neither had more to suggest.

"Perhaps, mademoiselle, you will learn more as you search for Dargentia's history." Madame Pologne sounded so hopeful that Paige nearly wished she'd stayed away from the subject. No one should count on her for anything—certainly not to save the country.

She thought of Niko again, so suited to the role of prince. Surely he would do what was right for his people.

Paige eventually asked about the Wenzels of the royal family in the era of her greatest interest. The Polognes didn't know, though, who'd married Leticia Adamson of Williamsburg in the late seventeenth century.

Nor did anyone here know the secret Paige hugged to herself about Leticia and Wenzel, and the controversial connection to Paige's dreams that made her care.

When the mother and son had spun all the tales they remembered monsieur took Paige to the thatch-roofed cottage next door. "My neighbors, *les* Le Blancs—they will tell you such stories. . . ."

Before waddling back to his own home he introduced Paige in French to two dark-haired brothers. One was a thin, middle-aged man with thick glasses; the other, also lanky, would have looked years younger if he'd shaved off his unkempt gray mustache. Both wore shirts of bright blue, though the first brother's looked as if it was the veteran of many a washing day battle.

The Le Blancs, too, invited her in to tea. Their home was far from the tidy habitat of the Polognes, though their frayed furnishings were also antique. The place smelled of old cigars and undiscarded ashes, and here and there Paige noticed burn marks on the edges of wooden end tables.

Andre, the one whose long upper lip was devoid of hair, had a new story to offer Paige. His voice was as thin as he. "One of our princes long ago, mademoiselle—he was a brave hunter. But one day he went into the woods and found a great bear with a thorn in his paw." The story was a fairy tale familiar to Paige. The bear was in such pain that the prince took pity on him, removed the thorn and spared his life. Years later, the bear repaid him by saving the prince.

"Oh, yes, mademoiselle," he concluded, "this story is true. It was related to me by my grand-aunt, whose own second cousin thrice removed learned of it from the descendant of that very prince's valet."

Perhaps that valet also knew where to find the missing jewels,

Paige thought as she dutifully jotted a few notes. That story was equally fabuleux.

Jean, the other brother, first told the tale foretelling the return of Dargentian sovereignty. He finished with the story that most Dargentians now had etched into their minds. Then he leaned toward her, his blue-veined hands set into tight, threatening fists. "Mademoiselle, this ball of our prince's is a wonderful idea—so long as he chooses a commoner for his bride."

He shook one fist, as though to punctuate his vehemence. His look was stern, even forbidding, despite the ludicrousness of his bushy, mouse-colored mustache. Paige almost shuddered.

"Yes, mademoiselle," echoed Andre, equally assertive. His gray eyes glowed with fervor. "His people will tolerate no less."

Certainly that spoke for the Le Blancs. Were other Dargentians as unswerving?

Uneasy, Paige swiftly changed the subject. But no news here, either, about Paige's favorite Wenzel.

The Le Blancs finished reciting all the tales they recalled. With a final admonition for Paige to tell the prince that he must listen to the legends, they took her to the half-timbered house across the street. There, they introduced her to a plump, friendly widow named Madame de Font. Wearing a frilly pinafore over a flowered dress, the ruddy madame served Paige a delicious bread delicately flavored with basil and rosemary—and more tea. Paige collapsed into the offered chair. She hadn't realized how the Le Blancs had disconcerted her till her nerves were permitted to relax.

Madame de Font told Paige a Robin Hood story of a brave band of men who fought the French after Nicholas I had fled, making sure the distraught Dargentians had enough to eat. "They say, mademoiselle, that their leader, the Eagle, was the exiled king's own brother."

"What happened to him?" Paige asked.

"After he did all he could to settle the people and find them food, they say he flew away."

Paige didn't laugh. It would have been rude.

Of course Madame de Font put in her two francs' worth of worry about the future of the kingdom. "It is so wonderful to be free, mademoiselle. But our freedom could just fly away, too, if our dear Prince Niko fails to follow our legends."

Paige asked her, too, about the Wenzel who'd gone to America.

She shook her head till her round cheeks quivered. "I regret, mademoiselle, that I do not know."

When she'd exhausted her repertoire of recounted tales, Madame de Font took Paige through the riotous, verdant herb garden in her backyard, filled with fantastic fragrances. The gate in her fence led to another neighbor's yard—the Martins, a youthful couple who also invited Paige inside.

Clearly more modern than the others Paige had met, the Martins had discovered the comfort of T-shirts and blue jeans. Their living room looked like any back home—nicely furnished, an antique here and there, but not filled with the Dargentian charm she'd been exposed to all day. They seated her before a coffee table, then sat close together on the nondescript stuffed sofa across from her.

In moments they made it clear that, despite being around Paige's age, they, like other Dargentians, worried about the future of their country, thanks to the tales from its past. Unlike the rest, they spoke to her in English.

Annette Martin, dark hair in short, bobbing curls, looked at Paige with earnest gray eyes. "I'm a schoolteacher, mademoiselle. I lived in Paris for a year. I am, how you Americans might say, cosmopolitan. But I am also Dargentian. I grew up with legends. I believe in their significance to our people. The prince must pay attention."

"I find the legends fascinating," Paige said.

Her husband Marcel had been trained in hotel management in London. He was short and intense. He held Annette's hand on her knee, and Paige could gauge his emotions by the whiteness of his knuckles and the flinches of his wife. "But you believe Dargentians are a bit crazy for the importance they attach to them, do you not?"

Paige shifted uncomfortably. "I wouldn't exactly say—"

"The legends may be foolish, but they cannot be discounted." Marcel's knuckles paled. "Our prince fulfilled one himself by his return, and I cannot tell you how pleased our people are." Color returned.

"That will be a wonderful anecdote to put in the historical material I'm gathering," Paige agreed.

"But that cannot be all. Next Niko must find Les Fabuleux. Only then can he marry—a commoner. His people expect no less.'' His hand grew white, and Annette's pretty face scrunched in pain.

From the Martins, Paige learned another tale or two, taught to them as bedtime stories as they grew up under French rule in Dargentia. The Robin Hood story of *L'Aigle,* the Eagle, was the favorite of both.

Again Paige reached a dead end when she asked about her Wenzel.

As Paige stood to leave, Annette crossed the room and touched her shoulder. ''Mademoiselle, you are the employee of our prince. You must make him listen to the legends.''

Paige hazarded a glance at Annette's glowering husband. ''But—I am *just* an employee.'' She felt depressed, deflated. The people here lived the history she'd studied with such relish back home. They'd opened their homes to her. They'd shared their dearest treasures—their legends.

She owed them something.

She owed a lot to Niko, too, for bringing her here. Could she help him learn to live peaceably with his people's legends? The only way was to find Les Fabuleux. Before he had to repay Edouard. Before he picked a bride. Before the ball.

Impulsively, she asked, ''Do your tales give you any clues as to where Les Fabuleux can be found?''

''Have you spoken with Monsieur Pelerin?'' Michel asked.

''Who is he?''

''Why, the town jeweler, mademoiselle. His family has been in the business for centuries.''

According to the Martins, the jewelry shop was on the second block south of Le Grand Magasin. They were short blocks; D'Argent City, although the capital of a new country, was still a tiny town. Its ancient beginnings still shone in old-world charm, delighting Paige as she imbibed its historic atmosphere.

The one-story buildings here had no scaffolding obscuring them. The shops were small, with wide windows dominating weathered stone facades, just as they must have centuries earlier.

Paige passed a butcher shop. Through the window she saw a man in a blood-spattered apron use a wicked cleaver to carve steaks from a large hunk of meat. No modern electric slicers here. But, as at the castle, the quaintness of the old place must have been tempered by modern necessities such as refrigeration; the air didn't slap her with the odor of rotting flesh as she walked by.

No smog here, either. There was, however, a tiny traffic jam on the narrow two-lane street as a pickup truck tried to pass a parked compact Ford. Paige imagined the width of the street more suited to horses and carriages of days long past.

Her steps scuffled in her flat shoes over the cobblestones. Meeting the eyes of a few other strollers, she nodded and returned their friendly *"Bonjours."* All wore the usual Dargentian dress of blouse and skirt for women, bright shirt and subdued trousers for men.

A small bank stood in the center of the block. Paige peered in the large front window.

Edouard Campion stood behind the counter, his dapper dark suit emphasizing the bright blue shirts of the people with whom he spoke—Jean and Andre Le Blanc, the men who'd so discomfitted Paige when they'd insisted on Niko's listening to Dargentian legends.

What business did they have with Edouard?

Their own business, Paige admonished herself. The bank was, after all, open to the public.

Edouard spotted her. He turned quite deliberately to look at her. His silver hair was, as always, immaculately in place—and his sly, secretive smile made her shudder. Paige walked quickly on.

The Pelerin Bijouterie was near the end of the short block. Paige peered into the eye-level window, where wristwatches and clocks were displayed along with a few plain wedding bands. No *bijoux* were exhibited as representative of the *bijouterie*. But Paige suspected that the people of D'Argent City, despite its being the capital of the country, hadn't much money to spare for diamonds instead of dish soap—not till Niko enhanced the economy.

Paige pushed open the shop door. A cowbell clanged. She flinched as the loud sound reverberated in the small room, then smiled at the cluttered appeal of what she saw there.

The room ticked with a large assemblage of cuckoo clocks along one wall. A disarrayed workstand behind a sales counter indicated that the shopkeeper must repair clocks, too.

A tall, narrow display case near the work area held an assortment of rings and bracelets. Paige approached and peered in. A light inside the case set off the sparkling stones. They looked mostly like diamonds to Paige—small ones. Nothing extraordinarily expensive. Not, certainly, Les Fabuleux.

"*Bonjour,* mademoiselle," boomed a voice whose owner Paige did not see at first. "Can I help you?" it asked in French.

From an open door beyond the work area emerged a bear of a man who ducked his head to avoid banging it on the doorframe. He was wide enough that he filled the doorway horizontally, too. He wore a bright red shirt, and his gray trousers strained about his bulging middle, held up by gaily embroidered suspenders.

Paige wouldn't have thought someone so large could work well with tiny jewels or delicate clock mechanisms.

She introduced herself. "I'm here as an employee of Prince Niko," she explained. "He's hired me to gather the history of Dargentia."

The man's fleshy face fit his ample body. His large lips curved down as Paige spoke, and his bushy black eyebrows, shaped like dueling diagonal accent marks over French vowels, emphasized his frown.

"Are you Monsieur Pelerin?" she asked. She hated the way her voice halted and wavered, but the unfriendly-looking man didn't do much for her nerves.

He nodded, rippling the folds of skin that obscured the place his jaw should be.

"Annette and Marcel Martin sent me. My first assignment for the prince is to prepare a promotional brochure for the ball he plans to hold." Monsieur Pelerin's scowl deepened—here was yet another opponent of Niko's plans, Paige thought. She hurried on. "I'm going to focus on the legends of Dargentia, including the one about how the prince should find Les Fabuleux—the crown jewels—before he marries. I'm looking for any information Dargentians have about that legend, and the Martins thought you would be a good source. They said your ancestors were the town jewelers, and—"

"It's about time!" boomed the angry voice of the jeweler. "Yes, I have information about Les Fabuleux. I've been waiting to tell it. But you tell our prince not to send his servants to collect what he, and he alone, needs to know."

111

# Chapter Ten

Niko sat in the garden before the castle. It was cooler there than in his office, a more pleasant atmosphere for going over the depressing figures of the Dargentian tax rolls.

He wasn't concentrating well. Perhaps the hardness of the white metal chair made him uncomfortable.

Or maybe it was his thoughts of Paige Conner.

He wondered how she was doing on her expedition into town, learning what she could about his country's legends.

Why was it that his mind turned to her so often? And why had he kissed her again last night, out by the moat?

More to the point, why had it bothered him so much that she'd stormed away?

As though he'd called her, he saw her drive the little Fiat onto the castle grounds. She stopped as near to him as she could get on the pavement.

She hurried from the car, running gracefully in her ugly dark skirt and sensible flat shoes. Her face was flushed, and behind her glasses there was a gleam in her unusual amber eyes.

She stopped near him, out of breath, seeming so excited she could hardly speak. "The jeweler has information about Les Fabuleux," she managed. "Only for you."

His heart thumped. But he knew better than to jump to conclusions. "He probably wants to sell me replacements."

She scowled. "Don't be so cynical. You have to come."

He'd never taken orders well, and certainly not from a subordinate. "I don't think so."

She reached out with both hands, then drew them back. He sensed her urge to throttle him. Despite how fragile those hands looked, she was used to lifting big boxes and books with them. And there'd been that ready knee when Aldred's arrival had startled her . . .

He decided to listen.

She told him then of her day's discoveries. His people expected him to live up to the legends. "No matter who you marry," she said, "at least give them this, if it's at all possible. Find Les Fabuleux for them first."

Disgust washed through him. He'd heard enough about imaginary jewels to fill the moat with mud. "They're fabled," he snorted.

"They're real."

There was a stubborn tilt to her chin that intrigued Niko. "How do you know?" he asked obstinately. "Do you believe in the legends? In the supernatural?"

She turned her amber eyes on him. He could have made a frozen daiquiri with their ice. "What I believe doesn't matter, Niko. If I'm right, you'll have enough money to save your kingdom from Edouard if you decide to sell the jewels. And, more important, you'll save your right to rule in the eyes of your people."

A few hours later Niko slammed the Fiat into reverse, trying to shoehorn it into a tiny parking spot. The engine growled, and so did he.

What the heck was he doing?

Sure, he wanted to find the Fabuleux. If they still existed—which he doubted. Maybe they never had.

He saw Paige swallow without saying a word. Her eyes were wide beneath her black-rimmed glasses. Obviously she thought he'd smash into the cars in front and behind of the space he was trying to enter. A space just in front of the Pelerin Bijouterie.

Well, it was his right, wasn't it? He was the prince.

He was also a damned good driver. He wouldn't hit anyone's precious car. But he was a bit more careful as he maneuvered his own.

He'd deliberately taken his time deciding whether to come. Despite Paige's insistent nagging. For hours.

Les Fabuleux? Unlikely.

If so, why had Pelerin waited till Paige asked about the jewels to reveal that he had a clue? Why hadn't he come to Niko, who'd been home for three months now? Why not tell his cousin Rudy, who'd lived in Dargentia all these years?

Still, the Pelerin family had been the country's jewelers since

113

heaven knew when. Probably as long as Niko's ancestors had been royal and Aldred's had been their servants. Traditions survived a long time in Dargentia.

Paige was right, damn her stubborn historian's heart. He'd had to come.

"We're here," he grumbled, stopping the car engine. Paige looked relieved.

"Are you sure you want me to go with you?" Though the words were appropriate, her eager expression begged him to say yes. "Monsieur Pelerin said that you alone needed to know what he has to say."

Despite his annoyance with her, he found her excitement contagious. The inveterate, intrepid historian, hunting down clues to the past.

His past. His jewels. His triumph.

But one he would want to share. And why not with eager, persistent Paige Conner?

"Come on." He reached for the handle to the car door. "Let's learn what Pelerin has to say."

He went around to Paige's door to open it, and she waited for him. The first time she had done it, she'd seemed astounded at his ordinary courtesy. She still looked shyly toward the ground, as though he did something special for her.

He didn't, though it gave him a kick to know she thought so. She didn't expect impeccable manners, the way most women seemed to from a prince. And now, after all that nagging, she was shy with him once more. He shook his head. This woman was an enigma.

He looked toward the jewelry shop. What did Pelerin know? Probably nothing worth the trip down the hill.

Still, how wonderful it would be if he found the jewels before the ball. That would appease his subjects; part of their legend would be fulfilled. Then he could marry as he intended—for his subjects' benefit, whether they realized it or not. They'd never be allowed to know that he'd sell the jewels to keep the vulture Edouard from swooping in, to keep Niko's rule alive.

But it would feel as though he'd sold his own right hand.

He pushed open the shop door, his arm extended to allow Paige to enter before him. Her quick smile again gracing the floor, she complied.

# The Glass Slipper

The cowbell sounded, but the place was empty. "Pelerin!" called Niko.

The large form of the jeweler appeared immediately in the doorway to the rear of the shop. "Your Highness," said the bulky man in French, inclining his fleshy face. But his head shot up again as his small eyes, beneath thick, dark brows, lit on Paige. "I'm sorry, Your Highness, I must see you alone."

"Miss Conner is discreet." Niko spoke with certainty, allowing no contradiction. "She's my historian, and if what you have to say reflects on this country's past, she needs to know about it." He paused. Had he asserted his authority too strongly? He was the prince, but he was also a virtual stranger to this country. His subjects were already restless because of his reluctance to bow to their silly superstitions. If he lorded it over them too much, French rule might start sounding good to them.

But Pelerin looked abashed, his gaze falling. "Whatever you say, Sire. If you would follow me . . . you, too, please, Miss Conner." The last was said in English, and his tone was respectful, even toward Paige.

She looked at Niko, gratitude glowing with the excitement on her face. "Thank you," she murmured.

"You're welcome," he said stonily, not wanting to reveal how good that glow made him feel. Motioning Paige to join him, he turned to follow Pelerin.

What could it be, Paige wondered—this clue Monsieur Pelerin had for Niko.

By all rights, she shouldn't be here, accompanying the two men—one huge, stout and ursine, the other broad-shouldered, slim-hipped and altogether too appealing. Both with jewels on their mind.

Pelerin led them into his back room. It appeared to be his home, for it contained a sofa and a television, a kitchenette, with a cot pushed against the wall. Unlike in his store, here there was no clutter. Not even any clocks that Paige could see. It smelled slightly of some evening's fish dinner.

"Please sit there," he said, pointing toward the couch. Pelerin's favorite spot on the overstuffed seat was easily visible, for there was a deep, wide indentation. Paige primly took a seat on the other side, then wondered if she'd made a faux pas. Maybe the

115

prince would rather have had the good end.

He appeared indifferent as he settled himself in the crater. Both watched as Pelerin used a back door to leave the room.

"Do you suppose his family has been guarding Les Fabuleux all these years and he's gone to get them?" Paige whispered, not wanting Pelerin to hear.

"More likely, he'll just give us a recitation of old Aldred's mysterious clue."

But Paige's imagination was wandering. "If he does have them, how will you announce it to your people? Will you walk down to the town square and show them their legend is coming true? They'd be so excited that—"

Niko's laugh stopped her. Abashed, she turned toward him. His dark eyes twinkled despite the poor light in the room, and his perfect teeth showed behind his smile. "Let's wait to see what Pelerin has before we count the jewels, shall we?"

Paige dipped her head immediately till her hair flowed about her face, hiding the flush she felt creeping from her neck upward. She'd done it again. How gauche could she get?

She was relieved when, a moment later, Pelerin returned. She glanced at him. He looked the same as before: large, in red shirt and suspenders, unfriendly. His arms were held behind his back.

He stopped before the prince. "Your Highness, this is for you."

He drew his arms forward, extending one hand.

It was a surprisingly slender hand for so large a man. The fingers were long, almost beautifully formed. Paige wondered that she hadn't noticed them before. They explained how someone as bear sized as Pelerin could work with the intricacies of small jewels and clock mechanisms.

In the center of his hand was a small wooden box. The mahogany veneer gleamed, as though it had been recently polished.

Niko reached for it, but before he could touch it, Pelerin dramatically drew it back. He opened the box with his other hand.

Inside was a signet ring. It was made of silver, the swirling metal brilliant and baroque. Pelerin must have polished it, too, for it sparkled. The combined smells of the sweetness of jewelry polish plus the mustiness of tarnished metal assailed Paige's nostrils. The metal odor must have lingered in the box, for the ring looked spotless.

Set in the ring was a trio of large stones. The one in the center was the biggest, a square diamond that Paige guessed to be more than two carats. Its smaller companions, on either side, were also square: a ruby on the left and an amethyst on the right. Above them all was an arch of small purple stones; amethysts, too, Paige supposed.

It was lovely. It was probably invaluable. But surely, Paige thought, this was not all of Les Fabuleux.

Niko voiced the same thought to Pelerin. "Rudy has described the legendary Fabuleux jewels to me," he said. "I don't recall this ring among them."

"No," Pelerin agreed. "This is not what my father and his father described to me, either. But they explained that this ring has been passed to each new Pelerin for centuries. It is held in trust for our ruler, to be given to the first prince of Dargentia to regain the throne. That is you, Your Highness. I am honored to be the one to restore it to you."

"Thank you." Niko accepted the box. He pulled the ring from it and placed it on his broad right hand. It seemed to fit, and despite its large size did not look out of place. "I will treasure it always. But if it was not among Les Fabuleux—does that mean that the crown jewels are, indeed, only a fable?"

Pelerin's skilled, smooth hands flew up as though fending off a demon. His head shook vehemently from side to side till the wave action in his jowls alarmed Paige. Was he having a seizure? "No, Your Highness. I did not make myself clear. This ring is a clue. If you can decipher it, it will lead you to Les Fabuleux."

Paige stared at the jewels as they sparkled in the sunlight shimmering through the windshield. Niko's strong hand lay restively on the dashboard of the Fiat, the only place in downtown D'Argent City where they could be alone to ponder the riddle of the ring. His forefinger tapped an uneven rhythm.

Niko had driven around to the back of the shops, into an alley free of traffic, where no greetings of his subjects disturbed them, no prying eyes stared, with them, at the ring.

A breeze blew through the open car windows, keeping them from suffocating. Back here, by the trash bins, Paige sniffed the foul odor of rotting meat from the butcher's refuse. Still, understanding Niko's need for the three of them to be alone—Niko, her and the ring—she didn't complain.

"Does the way the stones are set mean anything to you?" she asked. With her fingertip, she reached out toward the jewels, careful not to touch Niko, at the same time—though she would have loved to still the annoying beat of his finger. The stones were smooth and so warm from the sun and Niko's body heat that she could imagine they had a soul of their own. Especially the way they vibrated as Niko continued to tap-tap-tap.

"That's the way our colors are striped on our flag: crimson, silver and purple." Niko voice was a barely contained explosion. Paige couldn't read whether his hopes were raised or dashed by this odd turn of events. A ring. It hinted that Les Fabuleux were real. Were recoverable.

Or was the whole thing just a tantalizing farce?

Paige couldn't believe that. She *wouldn't* believe it. Niko had been restored to his throne. He needed Les Fabuleux to retain it—whether for their monetary or legendary value or both. They existed. And Niko and she would find them.

Gritting her teeth against his ceaseless tapping, she thought for a moment. "Any idea what the curved row of amethysts could mean?"

Niko shook his head so vehemently that his tawny mane of hair tossed about his shoulders. "If I had, I wouldn't be hanging around here."

Paige had no doubt that Niko wasn't used to sitting and waiting for answers; he made his own.

"Well, then," she said, "we'll work with what we have. Let's think about the order of the stones. You said it's the same as on the Dargentian flag. Any flags from centuries back, when the jewels disappeared, would probably have rotted by now. Could there be any ancient flagpoles that still exist?"

Niko's irritating tapping stopped. He pivoted in his seat to look at her. His heart-stopping lips arched in a broad grin. "Paige Conner, you're a genius!" Without warning, he leaned forward on the small car seat. His hands cupped her face, and he planted a quick, decisive kiss on her mouth.

She missed a breath or five, waiting for him to let go, to leap from the car toward the clue he thought her musing had triggered—but he didn't. His hands remained at the sides of her face, and he held her firmly.

This time his kiss was anything but quick. She tasted the sweet moistness of his lips on her mouth. There was an aching tenderness in the way he teased out her response. His tongue darted boldly after hers, then retreated in seductive shyness, inviting hers to follow.

She should have pulled away. She didn't. She couldn't. Not if her life depended on it. No matter what the consequences, she wanted to experience this kiss.

Her arms circled him, pulling him closer. That was all the encouragement he needed, and he let go of her face. One hand splayed hard against her back, pressing her to him awkwardly over the console. His heart beat a contrapuntal rhythm to hers as her chest met his, softness against solidity in the cramped quarters of the car. His other hand burrowed into her hair, keeping her close, ensuring that her mouth could not escape from his.

As though she wanted it to.

His tongue dipped again inside her mouth, where it found hers waiting once more to play. And oh, what luscious, lascivious play it was! She murmured something against him, though not even she knew what it was.

His hand on her back began to rove—downward at first, tantalizing her as he touched the top of her buttocks. She arched toward him despite her uncomfortable position in the small space, wanting to rub her body along his, wanting—

Here? In the car? In full sight of any of the prince's fascinated subjects who came to dump their garbage?

He must have had the same thought, for suddenly it was over. Both of them pulled back into their seats.

Paige tried to catch her breath. She stole a look at him—and found him smiling at her. If she'd been clutching a lightbulb, she knew it would have glowed; she felt illuminated by the brilliance of that smile.

"I believe," he said, "that treasure hunts are rather stimulating."

"Very," she agreed solemnly, feeling her own lips twitch. She wanted to grin right back.

"Well, we'll have to be careful of that since, my dear Ms. Conner, I think we have a clue or two to track down."

* * *

# Linda O. Johnston

He took her hand as he led her through the short, narrow streets of D'Argent City. He didn't stop to talk to the people who greeted him, but his greetings sounded most cordial to Paige. She hoped his subjects thought so, too.

They stopped at a small domed building. It was made of mottled white marble, and a wide phalanx of steps marched up to its door. A Dargentian flag waved from the roof, right in front of the dome.

"This," said Niko, "is the Dargentia provincial capitol building. It was constructed by the French right after they kicked my ancestors out of the country. They didn't want to use the castle for governmental matters, not while the wounds of lost sovereignty were fresh in Dargentians' minds. What an irony it would be if Les Fabuleux were hidden here."

"Do you think—"

"I don't think anything," he replied, moving forward. "But the flagstaff is the right age."

Their footfalls scuffled on the well-worn steps. Inside, the building was ponderously formal, with marble block walls, columns and floors in a great gallery that occupied the entire first floor. The domed rotunda rose in the center. The building was cool and smelled faintly of mildew. There were few people about, and those who were there hurried by as though on business of their own, smiling and nodding at their sovereign.

"The D'Argent City Council will continue to meet here." Niko's voice pealed hollowly in the vast room. "The mayor's office is here, too. I'll handle the affairs of state on a national level at the castle."

He led her to a stairway at the back of the gallery. Up they went to the second story, where bureaucratic offices circled the perimeter of the building. Paige heard the murmur of voices behind closed doors. A balcony at the center looked down on the gallery and up at the dome.

There was another set of stairs, and they reached a locked door. Niko had the key, and he opened it. It led to the roof, where a railing ran around the edges.

Still holding Paige's hand, Niko pulled her outside. "Come on," he said.

The breeze up here blew stronger than on the ground, wafting Paige's skirt about her knees. She heard the flapping of the flag

120

almost at the same time she spotted the pole that held it. It stood across from where they'd come out on the roof, beyond the dome. They hurried toward it.

The flagpole, though not particularly tall, extended high enough over the roofline to be seen below. It held the proudly waving Dargentian flag—in crimson, silver and purple. It was rooted in a pyramid-shaped stone base nearly as tall as Paige herself. The stones looked ancient and worn from the unforgiving weather of centuries—but the cement between them had clearly been replaced in the recent past.

"Will you have to take the whole thing apart?" she asked worriedly. That could take time, and Prince Niko wasn't the kind to wait for anything.

"Let's see."

He stooped on the roof, and Paige couldn't help noticing how his tight trousers pulled taut against his firm buttocks. She made her wayward eyes focus on his strong hands instead—and particularly the one on which he'd put the glittering signet ring.

After a lot of searching he finally found a spot where he was able to tug some of the surface stones. He groped along the exposed area, then replaced the rocks. He spent some more time examining the pedestal and pulling at worn stones and knocking gingerly on exposed cement with his bare knuckles. Then he stopped and stood, eyeing the thing critically.

"What's wrong?" Paige asked.

"Nothing, except that the whole base was rebuilt, I'd guess sometime within the last twenty years. The stones are just a facade now. Behind them, the base seems to be solid cement."

"Are you sure?"

He looked up at the flagpole, then back at its base. "I can't be positive, but to hold up a post like that, the thing is unlikely to be hollow."

"Could the jewels have been hidden there and removed when the base was replaced?"

"Maybe, but I doubt that a find like that would have been kept quiet for long. In any event, I'm convinced of one thing."

"What's that?" asked Paige.

"We won't find Les Fabuleux here."

# *Chapter Eleven*

"So where are they, Miss Credulous Conner?" Niko slammed the car into gear.

"Where's your next old flagpole?" she replied, tartness flavoring her voice. He shouldn't take their failure out on her.

He stopped the car and glared. His face was set into its customary arrogance. She considered reaching over to pluck a strand from that golden head, just to get him to react.

But he relaxed first. "There's an antique flagpole at the castle we can look at," he said. "I'm the one who raises and lowers the flag, and I have to admit I've never taken its pedestal apart to see what's inside."

As they drove off, Paige asked hesitantly, "Are there any other flagpoles that might be old enough?"

He slammed on the brakes. "There's one more place to look before we leave town."

He found another parking spot—a larger one, this time. Then he led Paige into the park, toward the statue of King Nicholas I. Not far from him, a Dargentian flag on a tall pole fluttered in the breeze.

A thought struck Paige. The statue certainly didn't look new. "How long has he been here?" she asked Niko.

"Ages. Since Nicholas was chased out of the country."

"But why did the French allow the building of a monument, after deposing him?"

Niko snorted. "They built it as a punishment. My dear namesake wasn't exactly beloved by the people. He squandered his subjects' hard-earned taxes on himself, then had no money to pay the soldiers who fought to keep Dargentia free."

"Oh." She'd need to put a healthy spin on this country's history to attract tourists, but the guy who'd lost the throne, Nicholas I, had been made of less than the noble stuff of legends.

Niko laughed, obviously sensing her dilemma. "Keep to the

truth about him, Paige. That will be more fascinating than to tell the world how wonderful all Dargentians are."

She had to agree. "Why is the statue still there?"

"As a reminder."

"To the townspeople, about how easily a kingdom can be lost?"

"To me, of the same thing."

Paige had no response to that.

The stone pedestal was more flimsy than the one at the capital. Paige helped Niko pull aged stones away with little effort. Soon they had an audience. "Safety issue," Niko explained to the gathering townsfolk. "We're checking on its sturdiness. I'd hate to have it fall and injure someone."

Several friendly workmen joined them. Using tools to chip away the unreinforced mortar, they removed the pedestal stone by stone, then eased the flagpole to the ground. A middle-aged woman with tears in her eyes was entrusted with the care of the Dargentian flag till its pole was reconstructed.

The pedestal was empty.

"Could anything be hidden in the statue's base?" whispered Paige.

"Not when the French built it," Niko replied. "Besides, how would the ring provide a clue to old Nicholas?"

Paige had no suggestions.

They returned to the car. Niko, extending his arm over the seat, looked at Paige. "Thank you," he said simply, touching her shoulder.

His fingers sent a thrill racing through her. "For what?" She leaned forward so her hair covered her face; that was easier than meeting his eyes.

"For being there today. For making me come to find out what Pelerin wanted. For helping me look for the jewels. For looking out for this country—and me—whether I wanted you to or not."

"You're welcome," she whispered.

He turned away, starting the car, and they headed back toward the castle.

Paige groped for something to say. The moment called for something suave. Something cool. Scintillation.

She could think of nothing. The silence lengthened, making her feel utterly wretched.

He was such a sweet man, she thought, for an arrogant prince. His gratitude had seemed sincere.

She liked him. And, given an ounce of encouragement, she could fall in love with him.

Where had that thought come from? She looked around. Niko, blessedly, was unaware of her thoughts, which were more fantasy than Les Fabuleux and even Millicent. His driving was still straight and steady.

Well, she'd given herself not an ounce of encouragement. Not even a milligram. There was no future in it. He'd want someone— a princess—who scintillated. And even if he discovered he wanted a commoner, it would not be her. It couldn't be her. She refused to allow Millicent's magic to buy her a prince. If she ever found someone to love her, it had to be for herself.

A highly unlikely scenario.

The sound of the tires washboarding on the bridge over the moat startled her; she hadn't expected to reach the castle so quickly.

This lovely day was drawing to an end. And she'd said nothing at all, the whole way back, to Niko.

But as he parked in front of the huge wooden door, he said, "I'm sure Maibelle will have dinner ready soon, and I don't want to keep her waiting. Afterward we'll go check the flag pedestal on the ramparts, though I doubt we'll find anything there. Then I'll take you on your castle tour. Okay?"

A refusal was on her lips. She'd be dooming herself to stay in his presence for an extended period. No big deal to him. They'd continue on their treasure hunt, then take a look around.

Soon he'd accompany complete strangers on tours of his castle to bolster Dargentia's economy. He'd consider her no different. And she? She'd fight her attraction to this exciting, enchanting man every step of the way.

At least there would be other people at dinner; there always were. And after . . . well, she could beg off. She should beg off, right now. But instead she found herself saying, "Sounds great!"

"Millicent!" Paige hissed, hurrying into her room. She only had a few minutes to shower and dress for dinner.

She was about to do something stupid. But it would only be

for one night, she promised herself. And after that ride up from D'Argent City, she needed—

A glimmer of dust began swirling near the tester bed. It turned into a column, and the aroma of lilacs filled the air.

"You called, dear?" asked a wavery voice. Her body didn't materialize until a few more seconds later.

Millicent's sweatshirt this time was neon orange. BE CAREFUL WHAT YOU WISH FOR, it read, displaying a glittering stack of gold coins. From the center of the pile poked the head of a trapped, distraught demon.

"Yes, I did call," Paige stated, her voice strong and sure. "Millicent, this is it: prove yourself. Just for tonight, for no particular occasion, I want you to make me scintillate."

"But, Eleanora, dear—"

Paige rushed to her. She took one warm, wizened hand in her own, squeezing it tight. It felt real.

For once she hoped the being to which it belonged *was* real.

"Don't give me that line about secrets of fairy tales. Millicent, if you're real, you have to do it."

The elderly woman's eyes grew even more sad. For once she forgot to smile. Paige's resolve began to slip. She sighed. "Okay. It's all right. You don't exist anyway. I don't know why I even asked." She pulled away and sank onto the bed. "I wish you hadn't brought me here. I never wanted to catch a prince's attention. I never even dreamed of such a thing."

"Except when you were a child, dear." Millicent sat beside her on the bed without making a dent. "You believed in fairy tales then, and you should now. You see—"

"All I believe in, Millicent," Paige said in a defeated voice, "is that I should write Niko's brochure, so I don't leave him in the lurch, then go home. I can't find the missing jewels for him, unless—" She looked at Millicent hopefully.

But the aged elf shook her head. "That's not part of my magic, dear."

"Then I just don't belong here."

Millicent stood. "That's not true. You do belong. You'll find it out soon enough."

Paige shrugged. She looked down at the Persian rug and sighed.

"Look at me, Eleanora," demanded Millicent.

Slowly, Paige raised her head.

# Linda O. Johnston

"Okay," Millicent said.

"Okay what?"

"You made a wish for this evening, and it will come true."

Paige stood immediately. She felt her jaw drop. "You mean I'll scintillate?"

"Was that what you asked for?"

Paige nodded, unwilling to believe what she was hearing.

"Then I will use my magic to help you."

Paige grabbed Millicent by the hands and began to dance around the room. It felt like dancing with a feather bed, only lighter. "Really? Do you mean it?"

Millicent pulled away. "Now, let's get down to particulars. Do you want me to change your appearance?"

"Oh, no. No, he'd notice. And I'll wear some of the clothes I've brought. All I want different is to scintillate."

"You understand that the normal rules apply?"

"Like . . . ?"

"Fairy-tale rules." Millicent sounded faintly annoyed. "You know, the usual. Every spell lasts only till midnight."

"Oh." Paige stopped for a moment. She looked at the small Timex watch she wore. Seven-thirty. Four and a half hours of scintillation. "That should be plenty of time for dinner, the flagpole and the tour. Yes. Oh, yes, thank you, Millicent. You won't regret this."

"I only hope you won't, dear." Millicent waved her arms about in the air as though playing helicopter. A whoosh of something like sequined talcum filled the air. Paige coughed and closed her eyes.

When she opened them again Millicent was gone.

They were alone at dinner. Niko hadn't planned it that way, but Charlotte and Rudy were attending the dedication of a building Rudy had helped to reconstruct in downtown D'Argent City, and Aldred was off on an errand.

They sat at one end of the large dining table, he at the head and Paige at his right. A large candelabrum, filled with flickering tapers, gave the room its only illumination.

"How are you enjoying the asparagus and leek soup?" he asked, feeling like the host of a lovely woman instead of this historian's employer.

126

"It's wonderful," she replied, taking a dainty sip. She was wearing a silky yellow blouse, and the contrast with her straight, dark hair, drifting about her shoulders, was almost startling. Her amber eyes, reflecting the faint candle luminescence, seemed to shoot tendrils of magical light at him, enticing him to look nowhere else. She glanced away first, though he had a sense that the next tiny spoonful of soup she ladled with deliberation was not intended to reach her mouth. She glanced at the watch on her wrist, then raised her eyes to meet his. "I think, Your Highness, that I'll have to ask you to send me to Cordon Bleu school as your father did Maibelle."

He was amused at her formal words, uttered with just a touch of teasing. "And why is that, Mademoiselle Conner?"

"Well, this country is so taken by its legends that this food brings to mind an age-old saying."

"What saying is that?"

" 'The way to a man's heart is through his stomach.' " She stuttered a little on the last and hazarded a look at him that seemed almost panicky after her earlier flirtatious gaze. But then she recovered her composure. "There are men at home who would be quite smitten by Maibelle's food, and I intend to smite them as well, when I return. I realize, though, that the way to the heart of the prince of Dargentia is much more complicated."

He played along. "And what is this circuitous route you envision?"

"It will take a princess quite unique, I'm certain. One who has family background and money. One clever enough to capture your attention at your ball. One who . . . scintillates."

He thought about that. What would he want in an ideal woman? If he didn't have his country to think of, he wouldn't worry about titles and substance. But clever? Yes. He couldn't see himself with someone witless, no matter how wealthy.

And, yes, a woman who scintillated would be just fine.

Someone as clever and scintillating, perhaps, as Paige Conner.

He'd never thought of the word *scintillating* in relation to her before. Most of the time she seemed more starchy and shy. But tonight . . . she did, indeed, scintillate.

"Yes," he said. "One who sparkles, who can keep me amused. Who can surprise me." He stared deeply into those enticing golden brown eyes, trying to get her to blink. But all she did was send him a small, suggestive smile. Somewhere deep inside he shivered deliciously.

The absurdity of the situation struck him. As the next king of Dargentia, he would, in a few weeks, have his pick of the unmarried daughters of the world's royalty. But he found himself ridiculously attracted to a plain American historian. Not just tonight, but today as well, when she'd prodded him until he had joined her treasure hunt.

And yesterday at the moat, when he'd kissed her and she'd run away. And the night before, when she'd let him pour out his heart to her about all his hopes and fears for Dargentia. Even when, startled, she'd tried to knee him where it hurt.

Ordinary Paige Conner was a wealth of contrasts. She surprised him.

Ordinary? She wasn't ordinary. Her amber eyes, so expressive, were magnified by her silly librarian glasses. Her dark hair was beautiful, her skin smooth and soft, her lips full and enticing—despite the sharp words that so often came from them. Maybe because of them. She was a challenge.

She had responded with exuberance and passion every time he'd kissed her. And so had he. His groin pulsed now, with just the reminder. Maybe they should do something about that.

"So you like surprises, Your Highness?" she asked. "But I'll bet your parents couldn't surprise you for your birthday or Christmas when you were a child. I'll bet you always knew just where to look to find what they'd hidden."

He discovered he was blushing quite uncharacteristically. How would she know that? "Too bad I can't find all my ancestors' favorite hiding places so easily."

He'd enjoy taking this beguiling, bewildering creature to bed. He couldn't marry her, of course; not with the future of his country at stake. He had to ensure its economic improvement. Tourists loved royalty or, at least, fame. Prince Rainier of Monaco, though he hadn't married a princess, had chosen Grace Kelly, an American movie star, whom many had wanted to see. Niko, too, would marry suitably.

But perhaps he could take a lover. Other monarchs did.

Yes, and look where it had gotten them. Britain, for example, and the scandals of Prince Charles and Princess Diana.

Besides, he didn't know how Paige felt about *him*. Was she only interested in his title?

Suddenly angry, he asked, "Do you honestly think you can singlehandedly save Dargentia by finding Les Fabuleux, Ms. Conner?"

About to take a bite of the cucumber salad Maibelle had just served, Paige dropped her fork into her plate with a clatter. She stared at him, but only for an instant. As she looked down again in that irritating way she had, her dark hair flowed in front of her face, partially obscuring those unattractive glasses. He'd hurt her feelings. Well, what did it matter? He glared at her.

She looked up then. There was a mysterious smile on her lips that lit up her face like starlight. "Yes, Your High and Mightiness. I might even continue to let you help look for them, if you're nice. And thanks to me, your kingdom just might be saved."

"What's in it for you?" he shot back.

"Satisfaction," she said. The tip of her tongue shot out to lick her lips, and she ate another morsel of salad without moving her eyes from his.

Maibelle came in with their main course then, a tasty chicken casserole. Paige again glanced at her wristwatch. Was he boring her? She certainly intrigued him. Niko decided not to continue their conversation in the uncomfortable yet fascinating manner in which it had begun.

"Tell me about the rest of the legends you've learned," he said.

It was working! Paige was astounded at how easily scintillation came to her. More than scintillation—out-and-out flirtation.

She hadn't actually believed Millicent would give in after all this time and weave this sort of spell for her. But she'd come through.

*Thank you,* she thought in boundless gratitude. She glanced at her watch. Eight-fifteen. Plenty of time left.

By the way Niko responded to her, she could tell that he enjoyed her scintillation, too. With lighthearted glee she responded to his request to tell him about his country's legends. She noticed the ring on one of his long, strong fingers, the source of perhaps the most intriguing legend of all—if it ever revealed its secret.

"The legend that sounds most exciting to me is the story of

L'Aigle, a Robin Hood clone. Usually that kind of legend is grounded in fact, and I can't wait to see if my research reveals who he really was.''

Niko rested his bearded chin on one hand, his elbow on the table, and leaned toward her. ''Tell me more.'' His eyes said his attention was fully on her.

The old Paige would have blushed and looked away, but not this new and scintillating model. She put her own embellishments into the tales she retold. More than once Niko laughed out loud. Never did his attention stray from her. She felt as though heaven had fallen down to meet her.

All too soon dinner was over. ''Let's go to the ramparts to see if we can look into the castle's flag pedestal,'' Niko said.

Paige checked the time: 8:45. ''Sure,'' she said.

There were no lights up on the castle's roof, but Niko brought a bright lantern. Tucking her skirt about her legs, Paige knelt beside him. The pedestal that anchored the eagerly whipping flag looked even newer than the one at the capitol, not even disguised by a facade of old stones. If it had existed in the days of Nicholas I, it had clearly been rebuilt since then. And if it had once held Les Fabuleux, it probably didn't any longer.

Niko did not seem particularly upset about it. ''I knew it was a long shot. I'll have to think about another way to decipher this.'' He held out the ring, and it caught the lantern light, the facets of the jewels radiating spikes of red, white and purple. ''Now, how about your tour of the castle?''

Not a good idea, Paige told herself. But she was too involved in scintillating to be sensible. Still, was there time? She looked at her watch. It was nine o'clock. They had almost three hours. She was fine.

They went all the way downstairs to start with the ground floor. It was vast, and the scent of cleaning materials hardly masked its ubiquitous mustiness. Paige had noticed many hallway entrances and closed doors in the paths she'd already taken, but she'd had little opportunity to explore. What Niko showed her was as dramatic as she'd expected—an impressive habitat for an impressive prince. ''Not bad,'' she remarked when he'd turned on the lights in an opulently decorated salon. ''Maybe I'll bring some work in here someday. Soaking up atmosphere is bound to help this little ol' historian's success.''

There was the obligatory Great Hall, complete with a balcony with carved wooden railings. Its granite block floor was a smooth sea of gray. "We've no separate ballroom," Niko said, "so this is where the ball will be held."

Paige made no comment to this. Though she thought of scintillating things to say—oh, how wonderful this night was!—the idea of the ball could make her lose her shine.

But not for long.

He showed her to a room housing a collection of hunting memorabilia. The trophies, including the heads of wild boar and deer, peered sightlessly from positions along the walls. Paige, who'd rescued many an injured bird in her youth, shuddered. "Not a pretty sight," she said.

Niko's arm wrapped around her shoulders. "I've given away the guns. And I'll give these away, too, if I can find someone to take them."

There had to be something to dislike in this man. Paige needed to find it and dwell on it. Otherwise she was heading for horrible heartache.

Without her having to ask, he showed her to the portrait gallery. It was in a large room off the first landing of the grand stairway. One by one, he introduced her to his ancestors, including his father and mother. They looked like kind people, not stuffy monarchs, and Paige had a gut feel she would have liked them. She wondered what had happened to them, and asked.

"Car accident," Niko said curtly.

She wondered how old he'd been. At least someone had been there for him; he'd had Aldred assigned to him at birth. She'd always heard fondness in Niko's voice when he spoke of his servant, and having met Aldred, she found it justified.

She changed the subject. "Why are there so many portraits here? I'd have thought after dear Nicholas the First was kicked out on his behind, there'd have been no need to have them painted."

"Tradition. Each generation hoped to be the one restored to the throne, so while in exile everyone had a portrait made. Many of the paintings were in storage in the United States. I had them all shipped home."

When they left the portrait gallery Paige made note of landmarks. She wanted to be able to return to study Niko's ancestors.

# Linda O. Johnston

The idea of learning more about these people, who together had resulted in the man beside her, made her smile.

Ridiculous, of course. She needed to know about Niko's heritage for her work, and to learn about Wenzel, nothing else.

She looked at her wrist. They'd spent nearly an hour in the portrait gallery. She'd have to be careful.

The rest of the tour became a blur of stone-walled, antique-filled rooms. There were parlors, pantries and sitting rooms, an area once used for boot removal, another for weapon storage and even a gallery with a row of medieval armor.

"Were all of these actually used here?" Paige asked, studying a standing suit of armor, complete with a lance clutched in the metal glove.

"Probably, though some could have been brought while the castle was in one of its museum incarnations."

"Was it being used as a museum when you returned?"

"Partially. Dargentia was being treated as a separate province within France, and its governor lived here, too."

"It must have been hard for you to see it that way." Not a particularly scintillating thing to say, but she felt sympathy for the man beside her: losing his parents in some unmentionable accident, seeing how his country had been treated in his absence.

His smile was grim. "Not as hard as my exile."

Niko took her hand at the bottom of a staircase. They began to climb. She tried hard not to think about the contact—even as every nerve in her body seemed to center itself in her warm and tingling fingertips.

She needed to get him talking again. What could she ask that was scintillating? She tried, "Did you ever visit Dargentia before you returned as its prince?"

"Several times. My father came as often as he could to see his country and visit his brother, Charlotte's husband, who kept an eye on the place. He brought me along to see my birthright. I'll always remember the first time I reached that spot in the road where the castle first becomes visible."

"That sight alone should bring thousands of tourists." Paige's enthusiasm was genuine.

Just as they reached the top of the stairs, she tripped. Tears came to her eyes. Not that she was hurt—but even scintillation wasn't enough. Her usual gaucheness overpowered magic.

"Are you all right?" asked Niko.

Maybe she could turn this around into something she'd want to remember. "Sure," she whispered—and looked up into his eyes as though she were lying.

Paige suddenly found herself swept into his arms and up the remaining steps.

She glowed inside. She wished the staircase were endless and Niko would never put her down.

Stupid. This wasn't a fairy tale. She wasn't a gorgeous princess to be swept off her feet. Beneath the temporary scintillation, she was still a nobody.

She swallowed her sigh at the top of the stairs as he set her gently on her feet. "Can you walk?" His tone was solicitous, and she found herself looking into eyes as enticing as molten chocolate.

She couldn't draw her gaze away. Her mouth went dry. "Of course, Your Very Royal Highness."

"No doubt." The amusement in his tone was overlaid with huskiness. She swallowed, still locked in the exquisite dungeon of his gaze. His lips parted, and she found herself wanting to trace their outline, beneath his masculine beard, with her fingertips. There was a sensuality in the way he stared, his eyes filled with a longing that her soul mirrored.

Was he going to kiss her? She couldn't stand that. Not again. Not without wanting much more.

Suddenly she was afraid Millicent was right. She shouldn't have wished to scintillate. She'd bitten off much more than she could chew.

She cleared her throat. "So," she said. "How many bedrooms are on this floor?"

She could have chomped on her tongue. The last thing she wanted, with that unrestrained desire in the prince's gaze, was to remind him of bedrooms.

Then what was she doing on this floor with him? Other than the portrait gallery and the balcony to the Great Hall, there probably weren't many other chambers besides bedrooms on the castle's upper levels.

But the question had broken the spell. "I've never counted," Niko said. "You can do that for our history."

He took her to the gallery overlooking the vast Great Hall.

# Linda O. Johnston

"This is where the tourists will be during the ball," he said. "We'll have to come up for a peek, too. I can't tell you how many times in my youth I imagined a grand party in the castle. I can't think of a more perfect place to view all the activity."

*She* might come up here to watch out of curiosity, for she most certainly wouldn't attend the ball, even though everyone in Dargentia would be invited. And *he* might come up here, too, with one of his stunning and eligible princesses. But there would be no *we* about it. She'd no intention of making the ordeal harder on herself than necessary. And on the big day Prince Nicholas of Dargentia would have no idea whether one of his employees was there or not.

He took her hand again, leading her from the gallery, up one hall and down the next till she lost track of the number of bedrooms. All were spacious but musty, with paneled walls, rug-covered stone floors and muraled ceilings, and filled with precious antique furniture that needed a good polish. Niko noticed that, too. "Starting next week, a battery of townsfolk has been hired to come in and spruce up the rooms. They'll all be occupied, of course, for the ball."

"Of course." Paige had no doubt of it. The world was full of princesses who couldn't wait to dance with Niko.

As they visited one room after the next, she began to wonder if there was some kind of electric current of desire that resulted from the hands of two incompatible people touching one another—positive stimulating negative, some perverse attraction. She found herself making an enormous effort to avoid looking at all those large, carved antique beds.

Still, she felt unable to withdraw her hand from his. The current clamped her as strongly as an electromagnet.

He pointed out the hall that led to Charlotte and Rudy's rooms. "I leave them to their privacy," he said, "but maybe they'll give you a tour of their wing."

Paige should have considered that, among all those anonymous rooms, would be the prince's suite. It was down a wide hall lined with some of the oldest paintings. They stepped into his sitting room first, a spacious, airy chamber containing his office. His large teak desk was piled with neat stacks of papers. There were nearly as many boxes on the magnificent hand-woven tapestry rug as in the library. "I'm still getting settled," he explained.

# The Glass Slipper

The room gave the impression of impatience combined with organization. Paige supposed that was a reflection of the prince's inner thoughts. "I can't imagine all there is to do to launch a newly freed kingdom," she said. "I'll do all I can to help, of course. . . ." She stopped herself. She was his employee. After tonight she wouldn't scintillate. It was foolish to pretend she was a friend offering assistance. And to suggest that she, a nobody, could help set up his new country—how presumptuous!

He'd been pulling her gently toward a door at the end of the room. Opening it, he stopped and looked down at her. "Thank you, Paige." His voice was softer than the down on the goslings in the moat, smoother than the silken curtains at the windows. "I appreciate your offer, but you're already helping more than I can tell you."

She was afraid to meet his eyes, afraid of what she might see. Still, her gaze was drawn up, as though he'd issued an unspoken command. As she'd feared—as she'd hoped—a fire smoldered in his dark eyes. Or was it a whirlpool, a swirling eddy of desire? It seemed to tow her closer.

His arms drew her tightly to his hard chest. She fleetingly remembered the feel of him atop her at the airport. A shudder of desire leapt through her. She tried unsuccessfully to pull away.

Only then did she realize that they had reached his bedroom. She peered around him. It was larger than the sitting room. The furniture was heavy, dark wood, carved and masculine. There were a sturdy chest of drawers and matching dresser; a huge German shrunk instead of a closet . . . and the bed. With elaborately carved headboard, posts and canopy, it dominated the room, jutting onto the tapestry rug covering the floor.

"Well, well. Very nice indeed." Paige's voice was thick, muffled by the way he held her.

"*You're* very nice, Paige Conner," said Prince Niko. "In fact, you're—" He didn't finish, and she looked up, wondering what he'd been about to say.

She wasn't skilled at reading people's expressions. The tightening of Niko's brow, the twisting of those sensuous lips, the slow, pained opening and closing of his eyes . . . they all confused her. If she'd had to guess, she'd have thought she glimpsed an odd combination of anger and indecision, arrogance and warmth, all wrapped up in deep, overwhelming desire.

# Linda O. Johnston

"Paige, I won't—"

Amazed at her own temerity, Paige placed her finger on his lips. They were as smooth and moist as she'd imagined. And sensuous. They kissed her fingertips, then opened slightly to allow his tongue to touch her.

Paige shivered. She closed her eyes, yanking her hand away as though she'd been scorched.

But she wasn't free yet. Those incredibly sexy lips of Niko's captured hers. As at the airport, she felt the vibration, this time against her mouth, when he groaned softly. Then he swept her into his arms.

# *Chapter Twelve*

Paige felt as though she was floating on a feathery cloud as Niko laid her gently on the duvet covering his bed. She opened her eyes enough to notice the heavy carving on the canopy's underside: honeycomb cells imbedded with swirls and flowers. She was enveloped by Niko's aroma of autumn leaves and citrus. She closed her eyes as though drugged.

The hard mattress dipped beneath her, and she was surrounded by Niko.

Gently, he removed her glasses. She considered protesting, but he was so close. So very close. And she could see all she needed in the faint blurriness beyond the delicate curtain of her eyelashes.

She sought something scintillating to say. Then she realized she didn't have to talk at all. Not now. Her scintillation would show in the way she reacted. Gracefully. With finesse.

How wonderful scintillation was! It had brought her here, with Niko.

But should she be here? She couldn't think.

His mouth found hers again, first softly, then full of sweet insistence. His tongue gently forced her lips apart, then plunged inside, teasing hers till it joined in the play that shot ripples of desire clear to her toes. The soft bristles of his beard brushed her chin.

Her time was limited. She had to watch out for midnight. She had to remember . . . what time was it?

One of Niko's hands stroked her back while pressing her closer. The other squeezed between them to take firm possession of her breast.

She felt rapturous. She felt confused. Niko was her employer. And what would happen when her scintillation disappeared? Would she say something, do something in her normally gauche way? Oh, that could not happen. Not when she had to remain—

His kiss grew more heated. His lips demanded an answering

137

fieriness from hers. His tongue suggested a primal rhythm, and despite her misgivings she moaned against him. She felt his free hand rove her back till it grasped her buttocks, pulling her tightly to him.

She had to remain sensible.

She could not stay still, though. She let her own hands explore beneath his shirt, outside his trousers, around to the front, where she encountered a thick, pulsing bulge. She drew in her breath as he pressed forward against her eager hand.

But wasn't there something she had to remember? Oh, yes. "Niko," she gasped against his unyielding mouth. "What time is it?"

"What?" His hands began to unbutton her blouse.

"Wait," she insisted. "Please. I need to know the time."

Niko grew still. She wanted to know the time.

He wanted to know where his brains had gone.

Rolling over to look at the clock on the bedside table, he felt foolish. He had let his hormones overrule his common sense. He'd been making love to Paige Conner. If she hadn't asked the time, he wouldn't have stopped.

How the heck could she turn herself off so quickly and completely to worry about the time?

"It's eleven fifty-eight," he grumbled.

The woman beside him gasped. "Oh, my. I . . . I'm sorry. I have to go."

"Catching a train?" He hated the sound of his own sarcasm. But why was she leaving him now?

She leapt from the bed. Her fingers flew to her blouse, rebuttoning herself. She opened her kiss-bruised mouth, as though she had something to say.

But nothing she could utter now would make a difference. She seemed to know that. She straightened her skirt, then ran to the door, pulling it open forcefully. Turning back toward him one more time, she said, "Niko, I—" She stopped. She shook her head slowly, as though in sorrow.

And then she was gone.

He picked up the pillow on which her head had lain and slammed it back onto the bed with a loud *whump*. Damn Paige Conner. To him, their lovemaking had been nothing short of astonishing. He wouldn't have believed his mousy little employee had it in her. Cleverness, yes; she'd dreamed up that silly contest that was sure to attract tourists. A bully, of course; she'd gotten him, unwillingly, to visit Pelerin's that day. He knew from their kisses at the moat that her knowledge of the human body wasn't just historical. But such sensuousness . . .

Obviously she not only had it in her; she'd found him lacking. That didn't sit well with his ego.

No matter. He was saved from himself, from having to fight off this woman's claims of seduction. Her typical American claims that after sex came marriage.

Or was this part of her plan? Get him so excited that he'd do anything to get her into bed—even wed her?

Well, that wouldn't happen.

He wouldn't let it.

He started to get out of bed, though he felt deflated. His body seemed stiff, uncomfortable, uncooperative. He hiked up his trousers at the waist, pulled down the tails of his peasant shirt. Maybe he should remove his clothes instead. What he really needed was a cold shower.

He had his shirt over his face when he heard a sound in the room. Quickly, he dragged the material over his head and off.

Paige was back. She stood by the door, her head bent forward, her straight, dark hair hiding her expression. Was she laughing at him?

"I'm sorry," she rasped, her face flaming. She didn't meet his eyes, but seemed to stare at his bare chest.

Was she coming back to tease him further?

Or maybe she'd realized what she'd run out on.

He certainly was tantalized by what he'd missed. Should he give her another chance?

"Well, Paige?" His voice was cool. Still, he found himself walking toward her.

She was apparently back in her mouse mode, for she did nothing, said nothing. Not until he was close to her. His chest nearly touched the tips of those bewitching breasts. He smelled her scent of baby powder. He heard her deep, ragged breathing.

His arm reached out. He grasped her shoulder, then ran his hand up her neck, to nest in her hair.

The look she turned on him was tortured. Then she pulled

away, running across the room. She nearly tripped on the bed, then hurried to its far side. To the table, where she reached out.

She sped past him, once more on her way to the door.

"I forgot my glasses," she moaned, and left.

Paige ran through the dimly lighted halls, only getting lost twice before finding the entry hall. Once again she met Aldred coming in. As usual, he was dressed formally, in suit and tie. This time he wasn't sneaking.

The last thing she wanted was to speak with him. Or anyone.

But he saw her before she got away. "Good evening, Paige."

She considered asking him what was good about it. By his concerned expression, she was sure he could see something was wrong. But he was much too polite to ask. Instead, he ran a hand through his wild hair and asked, "May I see you to your room?"

"I can find it just fine," she murmured—and proceeded to head down the wrong hall. She knew it as soon as she'd taken three steps.

A firm grip fastened on her elbow. "Please allow me."

She walked slowly with Aldred. His quiet presence was somehow comforting.

They soon reached the stairs to her tower room. He insisted on coming up with her.

At the door, he said cryptically, "There are opportunities, you know, in the most terrible of impediments."

Little did he know that she'd just gotten done playing a game of boudoir circus with his boss, and that the prince would think he'd been treated like the clown.

But Paige was, after all, the one who'd fallen flat on her face.

"May I see you safely inside?" Aldred tried to edge past her as she opened the door to her room.

Smelling the scent of lilacs, Paige quickly headed him off, planting herself in the opening. "Thank you. No, I'll be all right now. I appreciate your accompanying me here."

She hurried inside, smiling wanly. Aldred seemed to hesitate, as though he wanted something else. Finally he turned his small frame and sauntered toward the stairs.

Paige locked the door behind her, then leaned against it. Suddenly she lost the control she'd been hanging on to so carefully. Sobs wracked her body.

# The Glass Slipper

Scintillation, hah! She'd blundered something fierce.

Through her stuffed nose, she still smelled the scent of lilacs. "Go away," she whispered. All she needed was Millicent's "I told you so."

Millicent's form appeared in a sparkling haze in the center of the Persian rug. She sidled past Paige, unlocked the door, then looked out. "I thought I heard voices."

"The prince's majordomo accompanied me here," Paige said with little interest. She pulled Millicent inside, then shut the door again. "The last thing I need is for someone to know you're here. Especially when I don't even want you here. Please leave me alone."

But Millicent turned toward her, stirring a swirl of pixie dust. "You did it!" she exclaimed, clapping her hands. "I told you the prince would be attracted to you, and now you've engaged in the most delectable lovemaking with him. Oh, Eleanora, how wonderful!"

Aghast, Paige gasped. "Were you watching?"

"Of course not. At least not for very long." She followed Paige across the room. Her neon blue sweatshirt said, DO IT WITH MAGIC!

"Well, you stopped too soon. We were together. It was nearly midnight, and . . . and . . ."

"And you ran out on him?" Millicent sounded horrified.

"You were the one who imposed the stupid rules."

Millicent shook her small head till her gold cap of hair bobbed. "I didn't impose them, dear. I only reminded you about them. And this scintillation thing—"

"I couldn't have gone through with it anyway," Paige stormed. "I don't want the prince attracted to me because of your magic. I don't want him attracted to me at all."

Two tiny tears appeared in the corners of Millicent's sad eyes. As they rolled down her face, they caught the light and swirled prisms of color sparkling through the room. "I'm sorry, Eleanora dear. I wish you understood. It wasn't my magic that attracted the prince to you." She began to fade, and a crackle filled the air.

"No, of course not," Paige shot back sarcastically. "It was my own scintillating personality."

"You must, Eleanora," whispered a voice from the walls, "learn the secret of fairy tales."

Paige didn't sleep well that night. She sat in a chair for hours. Bed reminded her too much of Niko.

She didn't dare look at the clock as the night crept by. Time reminded her too much of Niko.

What did he think of her now? What would he do to her in the morning? Firing her was probably not an excruciating enough punishment. If this were the old days, he'd probably have her drawn and quartered. Boiled in oil. Fed to the geese.

One shouldn't fool with a prince's sensual nature.

She hadn't meant to tease him. She, too, was the victim of her own bad judgment.

That very wonderful day had led up to it. She'd heard the legends, experienced his people's earnestness, learned a clue to the whereabouts of the Fabuleux jewels.

Then they'd been together so wonderfully long, searching for the meaning of the ring. Running their ideas up empty flagpoles till they fell flat.

Was it any wonder she'd wanted the evening to end with scintillation?

To have to stop in the middle of such incredible lovemaking, though—

Well, enough of that. She had a job to do . . . if she still had it.

She finally sneaked a peek at her wristwatch. Six fifteen. Maybe she could get some work done before Maibelle set out breakfast.

She donned her favorite work outfit to bolster her mood—her Smithsonian T-shirt, blue jeans and neon walking shoes.

She'd be fortified for any punishment Niko decided to mete out.

Paige didn't see Niko that day, not even so he could snub her. At least he didn't stomp in to fire her.

She worked in the library in the morning, then took the Fiat to town in the afternoon to visit more townsfolk and listen to their stories. She was getting quite a repertoire of legends; soon she'd be able to write the promotional brochure without feeling she mightn't have ferreted out the country's most magnetic folk tales.

In the evening, after she dined with Charlotte and Rudy, worry rumbled through her mind. Would Niko avoid her for the rest of her stay in Dargentia? Perhaps that was best. But she deserved an opportunity to apologize, even though she couldn't exactly explain.

She decided to go out to the moat. Niko might be there. She'd just express her regrets, then exit.

Express them how? Sorry I teased you, Your Highness.

Sorry I stopped in the middle of the most wonderful lovemaking I could imagine, but at any moment I was going to change back into the ugly, ordinary creature you see before you. Sorry I invoked magic so you'd see me as someone special.

Paige sighed. Maybe she should keep her unscintillating mouth closed. But she still wished for the peacefulness of the moat.

She headed first for the kitchen to get bread.

"Paige!" She turned. Aldred hurried toward her. "Niko tells me you like to feed my large feathered friends at night. May I join you?"

"Yes. Please." No matter what the prince's opinion of her now, it was kind of him to have thought of this. She craved company, and Aldred's was ideal. Other than Niko's . . . stop that! she ordered herself. He undoubtedly despised her.

After they'd found some stale bread Aldred and she headed outside. The spring evening was hot and humid. Clouds blanketed the sky, racing to see which could next cover the moon.

When Aldred and she reached the moat he chose her favorite bench. In the dim light from the electric torches on the outer wall, he pointed to the aging swan statue. "There have been swans here as long as there's been a castle. Our legends compare them to the ravens at the Tower of London; if the swans leave, the country will fall."

The geese swam eagerly toward them, squawking to be fed. From the distant shadows the black swans, too, began their disdainful approach. The disturbed water lapped at the moat's grassy banks.

"Did the swans leave Dargentia back in the time of Nicholas the First?" Paige asked, tossing out a piece of bread toward a lagging gosling. The floral aroma near the moat was strong in the cool evening air.

"That's the legend. You should hear that one, too, in your research. But sometime afterward they returned—a good omen, we hope, for Niko's reign. Did you know swans mate for life?"

She didn't want to talk about happily ever after, even for swans, so she changed the subject. First, she asked what Aldred knew about the Wenzels of the seventeenth century.

Was it her imagination, or did his shoulders stiffen as he sat on the bench beside her? If so, his tension lasted only for an instant before he again stretched out to cast bread to the birds. His voice sounded normal as he replied, "Not a lot, I'm afraid. Why? Have you come across some interesting history about one of Niko's ancient relations?"

He'd turned the tables. She wasn't sure how to urge him to speak without sharing her own secret reason for being there. Despite the camaraderie she felt with the kind older man, she sensed he was hiding something.

As was she.

She tried yet another new topic. "How long were you away from Dargentia?"

"This trip, only a few months. But really, generations. My family has served Niko's since before the exile. We were able to sneak here to visit the country and remaining relations now and then, but I'd consider this my real return to Dargentia."

"How wonderful! Can you tell me more for my research?"

Aldred confirmed much of-what Paige had gleaned from the townsfolk. Each oldest son of the heir to the throne had been raised outside the country, groomed to resume power. "That's where I came in." Aldred's family had been schooled to teach the young princes royal etiquette and statesmanship. "Meantime, the youngest son or another male relation was always sent secretly back to be raised in Dargentia, to keep an eye on the country and its politics. The citizens kept their secret, for that gave them hope of eventual freedom. Et voilà, it finally happened!"

Aldred threw bread toward the lingering swans. With only a little prodding he launched into the tale of how Niko won Dargentia's freedom. "He used the statesmanship I'd taught him. But I can't claim much credit. He's got his own special talent for seeing inside people, promising them what they want but getting, instead, what he wants."

Paige worried she'd seen that side of him.

Aldred's face turned grave. "But now the country is faltering. It will fall again if we fail to improve the economy. Encouraging tourism was Niko's idea. The ball was mine."

Paige took a slow, deep breath, allowing her pain at the reminder of the ball to dissipate. "What a good suggestion," she said, "to have Niko invite the world's royalty to pick out a bride."

Aldred shot a shrewd look at her. "I thought so at first. But maybe there were other ways to attract tourists fast. Ones that wouldn't antagonize the prince's subjects."

"Or Niko." Paige sighed. "Did he . . . I mean, is he very angry with me?" She rushed forward so he wouldn't ask why. "We had a bit of a disagreement last night, and I was hoping he wouldn't fire me."

"No," Aldred said. "He didn't mention wanting to fire you. But I can usually tell when there's something bothering him. I think," he continued shrewdly, "that you bother him."

Paige stood and threw her last bit of bread toward the swans, unsure how to respond. She changed the subject. "Did he show you the ring?"

"What ring?" The small, formal man regarded her with interest.

Paige swallowed. "I hope I'm not talking out of turn, but I thought he always confided in you. Look, don't tell him I mentioned it, but we found a clue to Les Fabuleux. Or at least that's what we were told."

She explained her visit to Monsieur Pelerin, their return visit and the treasure hunts at the flagpoles.

"I think," said Aldred, "that I want to see this ring."

When they reentered the castle Aldred again saw her to her room. Once more, he seemed inclined to walk her inside, but she gently sent him on his way. Was this sweet older man developing a crush on her? Unlikely, but just in case she'd stay friendly but firm.

She had no visit from Millicent that night. The next day she saw no one but Maibelle at breakfast, which was fine with her. She catalogued the contents of some boxes in the morning, then headed for town.

The afternoon was rainy, Paige's first less-than-perfect weather

# Linda O. Johnston

in the fairy-tale kingdom of Dargentia. The Fiat crept cautiously down the switchbacks as Paige worried about skidding over the steep sides. Sheets of water swept over the car, but she didn't dare lose a day of research.

The dismal gray of the sky and the stormswept surface of the swift Argent mirrored Paige's turbulent mood. Why had she messed with Millicent's magic?

She couldn't think about that. Or about Niko and his unleashed sensuality that had made her sensibility flee. His angry gaze as she'd come back for her glasses . . .

Instead, she concentrated on the job she had to do—and finding her own elusive Wenzel.

She might as well have stayed in the coziness of the castle. The moods of the townsfolk of Dargentia whom she'd come to see had reflected the irritability of the weather. She visited several people she'd met at Le Grand Magasin's tea room but hardly gathered a single new story before heading back up the mountain.

She parked in the stables and sat for a moment in the car, thinking. The day was partially wasted, a problem she could ill afford. She'd barely a week left to complete the promotional brochure for the prince's ball—the ball where he'd find a bride to bless with those incredibly inflammatory caresses. Someone who could be with him every day, every night, with no deadline to slay her scintillation.

Someone Niko would love.

With a slam on the steering wheel and a shake of her head, Paige thrust herself out of the car.

She dashed from the stable-garage into the castle but still got soaked. In the entry she ran into Rudy. "Frog Prince," he said in his soft, shy voice.

"Pardon?" Paige was used to his comments that seemed to be non sequiturs, but she still seldom understood them at first.

"This weather," he rasped. "It's fit only for a prince who's a frog, too." She laughed with him. Then he asked, "How is your research going?"

"Not badly—before today."

"Can I do anything to help?" The poor guy sounded eager, but he never met her gaze.

"Sure," she said. "Come to the library with me."

The day wasn't wasted after all. Rudy helped her place each

146

tale she'd learned into order. He'd studied most himself and had a sense of their origins, whether based on true-life historical figures or myths cadged from other cultures.

Paige was most interested in the people who'd really lived, whose stories had become bigger than life. They were the ones on whom she'd concentrate in her promotional brochure. What tourist could resist coming to the country where L'Aigle had once flown? Where missing crown jewels could hold the key to a newly restored prince's survival?

Where visitors were invited to participate in a contest to help the prince choose his royal bride, no matter how opposed his subjects might be.

And no matter how much it might make one insignificant employee ache inside.

During the next few days Paige saw nothing of the prince. That suited her just fine—didn't it?

She saw little of Aldred, as well. She wondered now and then whether he'd gotten Niko to show him the signet ring, whether his knowledge of Dargentia and its past gave him, in its jeweled surface, a clue to finding Les Fabuleux.

She remained busy with her research, still cataloguing the contents of boxes, visiting Dargentians despite the continued gloomy weather and working on the brochure, often with Rudy's useful input.

Now and then Charlotte or Aldred would stop in, too. Never Niko. But that was dandy with Paige. She didn't know what to say to him anyway. Especially not now, after she'd teased him with scintillation.

She wished, though, that he'd discussed further with her what the ring might mean. Time was growing short. How was she to help him find Les Fabuleux before the ball? Surely Aldred would have let her know if they'd been located.

She found oblique ways to quiz everyone—Niko's relatives and subjects—on all they might know about square jewels in the country's colors. No one told her anything helpful.

She got into the habit of asking Maibelle for meal trays. Apparently the prince had given the order that this was acceptable, for her presence was never commanded, even at dinner.

# Linda O. Johnston

Not until several days had passed since the fiasco in Niko's bedroom.

She was engrossed in drafting the brochure when a deep voice cut into her concentration. "It's dinnertime, Paige," stated the prince.

She stiffened. Her breathing stopped, then started again.

What should she say? How should she treat him?

Biting her lip, she kept her eyes glued to the monitor, her fingers shaking on the keyboard. The clicking, less rhythmic now, did not cease. "Thanks, but I can't stop now."

His footsteps resounded on the wooden floor between the Oriental rugs. "You've avoided me long enough. Join us tonight. You can come back after we've eaten."

Who had avoided whom? Paige ducked her head abruptly, closing her eyes, stilling her fingers. Her train of thought was already derailed. She looked up. Niko towered above her, his large hands on narrow hips hugged by his tight peasant trousers. She noticed that he did not wear the signet ring. As always, his masculinity, enhanced by his aroma of autumn leaves and citrus, enticed her. But ignoring her delight at seeing him again, she focused on her irritation at his heavy-handed arrogance. That was the only route to self-preservation. "Certainly, Your Highness." She stood and bobbed into an absurd little curtsey, holding out the edges of her T-shirt in the absence of a skirt.

Those deep, dark eyes narrowed as he raised his bearded chin autocratically. "You're quick to use my title."

She felt herself redden from the base of her skull to the top of her head. Several nights earlier she'd used his title and variations of it scintillatingly to tease him. Now she used it sarcastically, in annoyance.

"I'm impressed by your being a prince, of course."

He scowled, and when he finally spoke his tone was glacial. "I'm delighted to hear that. So delighted that now I'll give you the choice: Come to dinner or don't."

He didn't care, of course, whether she was there or not—except as evidence that he'd exerted control over her. "Thank you," she said, keeping her voice calm as a wave of sorrow suddenly swamped her. "I'll stay here. Would you mind asking Maibelle to bring me a tray later?"

"Yes, I'd mind." He stalked from the room.

Paige looked back at the screen, unable to focus through her tears. She dashed them away as she re-read what she'd last typed. With enormous effort, she returned to her work.

Later, when her eyes blurred again from exhaustion, she realized she was hungry. True to his word, Niko hadn't asked Maibelle to bring her a tray. No matter; she'd scrounge some leftovers in the kitchen, then head out to the moat to eat with the geese and swans.

When she reached the kitchen door she found it locked. Her stomach growled in protest. She went out the main door and around the castle, but the outside door to the kitchen, too, was locked.

Darn that prehistoric, power-mad prince! He was punishing her for her failure to subject herself to his will, like one of his subjects.

Or maybe this was his retribution for what had happened a few nights back.

Maybe she merited a wrist slap. Still, she'd half a mind to stalk upstairs and yell at him.

She decided not to give him the satisfaction. Instead, she fled to her room.

But she was hungry. How could she go to sleep on an empty stomach? "Millicent!" she cried.

# Chapter Thirteen

A column of shimmering stardust spun near one pole of the tester bed. The scent of lilacs swelled. "Hello, Eleanora," said a sweet, wavery voice.

As soon as the elderly imp took shape, Paige stepped forward and held her cool, papery hands. Millicent's neon green sweatshirt read, ENCHANTMENT? ENCORE!

"Millicent, I'm going to ask you a very big favor."

The kindness in the small, shoe-button eyes was nevertheless suspicious. "What's that, dear?"

"I'm hungry. Can you feed me?"

The wrinkled brow furrowed. "That's not exactly a matter within my mandate as fairy godmother, but—"

"A hex on your mandate!" Paige released Millicent's hands and stood on her toes to intimidate the fragile-looking creature the way Niko liked to loom over her. "I've dared to disobey the high-and-mighty prince you've picked for me, and he's sending me to bed without my supper. And all because . . . because I dared to dabble in your magic. All I want now is to do my job and go home. Your fairy tale is full of—"

"Enough!" Millicent scowled and swept away from Paige, putting out her arms. Purple lightning crackled from her fingertips, and she was suddenly surrounded by a sizzling cloak of sunbeams.

For an instant Paige cringed. She was so used to snapping at Millicent with no dire consequences that she hadn't thought twice about it now. But she'd never seen Millicent truly miffed before. She must have pushed her too far.

"If you want food, I'll give you food!"

The crackling increased in intensity. The air about Paige grew heavy. A thick, moist fog formed about her and began to swirl like warmed butter being folded into batter. It thickened to the consistency of melted marshmallows. "Millicent," Paige whispered. She inhaled deeply, unable to catch her breath. "I'm sorry. I—"

Suddenly a bright light blinded Paige, but just for an instant. When she opened her eyes she found herself sitting on the floor in a sea of cookies, stretching to chest height. Sugar, chocolate chip, peanut butter and macaroons—all her favorites.

Extending her arm till she created an avalanche, Paige picked up a chocolate chip cookie and brought it to her mouth. She took a bite. "Mmmmm. Delicious. But not exactly health food."

"Best I could do on the spur of the moment." Millicent stood in the middle of the mountain of cookies, her grin stretching from one corner of her small, smooth face to the other. She tasted one, too. "What do you think of my magic now?"

Paige savored the taste of the cookie and took another, sugar this time. "It's sweet. Could you always have done this?"

"I don't know. It stretched the limits of my duties, that's for sure. But I guess it goes along with fairy tales."

"Don't suppose you'd tell me the secret, would you?"

"Sorry, dear, it's against—"

There was a knock at the door. Millicent hushed as Paige stared with horror in the direction of the sound. Who was it? What would anyone think if they found her here with a living figment of her imagination, surrounded by a sea of cookies?

"Sshh!" she whispered in a panic. "Who's there?" she called aloud.

The deep voice she dreaded answered, "It's Niko, Paige. Please open up."

"Just a minute." She picked her way through the mountain of sweets to the door. She opened it just a crack.

Niko stood there, a tray of food in his hands. "Were you practicing another scene? I thought I heard voices."

"Scene?" Paige was puzzled until she recalled the last time Niko had nearly caught her with Millicent. Her excuse then had been a play rehearsal, with herself cast in key roles. She thought fast. "Oh, yes. Peter Pan this time. I was Wendy and Captain Hook."

"I see." The incredulous inclination of his brow contradicted his words; he didn't see at all. "Paige, I'm sorry. When I told Maibelle she wasn't to feed you I meant she wasn't to bring you a tray. But she must have believed I intended that you not eat at all. I thought you might be at the moat and was going to check on you. When I stopped at the kitchen its door was locked.'' He thrust the tray toward her. ''If you'll let me in, I'll put this down and you can eat.''

Paige swallowed. ''Thanks,'' she said, falsely cheerful. ''I appreciate this. Just give it to me, and I'll—''

''It's heavy. I'll bring it in.''

She recognized the imperiousness in his tone. What could she do?

Panicked, she turned to implore Millicent to do something—and discovered that the room looked normal. No fairy godmother; no ocean of cookies. ''Thanks,'' she said, begging her knees not to buckle in relief.

He strode in with that regal gait she knew so well and placed the tray on the dressing table. He turned to her, earnestness dipping his strong brow. His broad, callused palms turned up in a gesture of apology. ''Paige, I'm sorry. I never meant . . .'' His voice tapered off.

She turned to follow his gaze over her shoulder. At the end of the dressing table were two glasses of milk and a plate with two chocolate chip cookies.

She shrugged and attempted to smile. ''I brought them with me from town earlier,'' she improvised. ''Like some?''

''Sure. Thanks.''

They stood there, she eating the sandwich he'd provided, he nibbling cookies. Paige enjoyed watching the way Niko's jaw worked beneath his beard as he chewed. She found herself gazing deep into his dark eyes. They never quite lost their puzzlement, and that made her smile secretively. She rather liked the idea of his recognizing her resourcefulness, even if he didn't know its source. She didn't depend on him for anything, not even food.

It was better that way. So what if she was attracted to this imperious hunk? He might be kind enough to keep her fed, but he did no less for his subjects. She might have a fairy godmother, but she was hardly a scintillating siren who would attract a prince.

That thought made her sigh for the umpteenth time as she lay in bed that night, long after Niko had left.

Paige was eating breakfast the next morning when Niko strode into the small room, immediately dominating it with his regal presence. She supposed she should, by now, be used to seeing him in all his broad-chested splendor in his becoming peasant garb, but as usual her heart leapt into a tiny tap dance.

She was proud of how poised her "Good morning" sounded.

He wasted no time on niceties. "There's an answer to this, Paige." He thrust his hand toward her.

The signet ring once again dominated his strong fingers, its stones glittering despite the meager light of the breakfast room. Did he now know what it meant? "Tell me," she urged.

Before he replied, Aldred hurried into the room, straightening his light-blue necktie. "Oh, I see you and Miss Conner are already discussing our pilgrimage."

"*Your* pilgrimage," Niko said. "I'm just tagging along for amusement."

Paige didn't see the joke. "What do you mean?"

While Aldred poured coffee, Niko joined Paige at the table. "After our uninspired barking up flagpoles the other day I figured this ring was just a valuable relic. I hid it away, but I understand you mentioned it to Aldred."

Paige let her head droop forward. So she *had* spoken out of turn. "I'm sorry. I know you share some confidences with him and assumed—"

"Don't let him bully you, Paige," Aldred said, lifting her coffee cup to refill it. "You were right to let me know. But it took me till yesterday to convince this stubborn young buck to show it to me."

"Did it mean something to you?" Paige looked eagerly toward Aldred.

"Perhaps," said the majordomo, taking a seat. "As I recall, there's a certain arch at my own ancestral manor where colored rocks were embedded in the stonework to resemble the Dargentian flag. And above them are an arc of purplish stones. The effect resembles the appearance of the ring."

"Then that might be where Les Fabuleux were hidden!" Paige clasped her hands tightly together.

"We will never know until we look," Aldred said. "I haven't visited my estate for several years. The trip will be a pilgrimage for me."

"And a pleasant ride through the Dargentian countryside for

me." Niko sipped his coffee. "I have few expectations that those dratted jewels are there."

"But Monsieur Pelerin said the ring was a clue!" Paige couldn't contain her excitement. "Les Fabuleux have to be there."

"They don't have to be anywhere." Niko's tone was stern. "But we'll rule out that possibility this afternoon."

"May I come, too?" Paige rushed ahead before Niko could respond. "It would make a wonderful anecdote for the promotional brochure to add a section describing how the newly restored prince restored the jewels of legend to his kingdom."

"That's the stuff to attract tourists," Aldred agreed. "I vote to take Paige."

Niko placed his cup on the table. "I suppose I second it."

Paige was doubly relieved: first that Niko hadn't said no, and second that they wouldn't be alone. Aldred would be a buffer between them.

Drat that interfering old son of a gun, Niko thought as he aimed the Fiat over the drawbridge that afternoon. Paige sat quietly in the bucket seat next to him, thumbs twiddling uneasily in her lap. Her head was bent forward in a mannerism he now knew well; her lovely dark hair spilled over her face. She seemed not only to wish to veil her expression from him, but her entire curvaceous body.

Thank heavens she hadn't succeeded in the latter. Even if he was still as angry with her as a cat cast into the Argent, he enjoyed looking at her.

But Aldred was not in the back seat. He was supposed to be. That had been the plan.

The majordomo's moaning had begun just after breakfast. "Ohhhh, my stomach," he'd said. He had clasped his offending middle and leaned forward from the waist, crumpling his inevitable suit coat and letting his tie flow forward in an uncharacteristic, less-than-impeccable manner. They had been alone in Niko's office. No way would such a performance have taken place in front of Maibelle; the poor chef would have been horrified to think something she'd cooked had made the man so ill.

The only thing sick about Aldred, Niko was sure, was his conniving mind. He'd wanted Niko and Paige to go off together; nothing subtle about him.

The man had apparently taken the legends too seriously, and the most available commoner to entice Niko was Paige.

But he was unenticeable. Especially by the difficult, discomfiting Paige Conner.

His thoughts turned to the last time they'd gone on a treasure hunt, and how much he'd enjoyed her company.

How much he'd enjoyed having her in his bed that night—until she'd run away. Damn her! He was hardly a man to appreciate teasing. And her teasing had left him hard indeed.

Making sure that the car was safely in the center of a switchback, he glanced at her. As he'd advised, she wore work clothes; he'd no idea what the condition of the Aldred estate might be. He, too, wore blue jeans and a T-shirt. She seemed to favor that Smithsonian shirt and those neon-striped running shoes. Staring out of the car window, she presented him with the back of her head. He wouldn't be surprised if her thoughts were also on that night—and how he'd made a fool of him.

She hadn't seemed eager to go off alone with him. When he had met her by the car without Aldred she had offered to wait till the older man felt better.

"I suspect," Niko had told her in a voice he kept so dry it nearly spouted sand, "that my poor servant will not feel better until you and I have gone on our expedition."

She had shot him a look both curious and cautious, but she'd gotten into the car.

They had a drive of more than an hour into the countryside to reach the old Aldred estate. It was a long way to go in utter, uneasy silence, the way the ride began.

When they reached the bottom of the mountain he stopped the car. "Paige?"

She turned to him quickly, her full, moist lips parted as though eager to respond to whatever he asked. But her lovely amber eyes darted to the side beneath her glasses, unwilling to meet his gaze.

Reaching over to take her small hand, he was surprised to feel it trembling. "Truce!" he asserted. "Looking for buried treasure is stimulating, and we both got carried away a few days back. But we learned our lesson. No apologies, but now we'll just stick to business. Okay?"

# Linda O. Johnston

Her body seemed to relax visibly. Her hand turned in his and grasped it, giving it a firm shake. "Okay." Her smile made his heart—and other body parts—leap.

Concerned that he took his own orders no better than Aldred did, he turned on the car's air conditioning to cool himself down.

Paige should have felt better after the bargain she'd struck with Niko. They would just have a companionable day searching for Les Fabuleux. She'd behave professionally. No need for scintillation or magic; she'd just be herself.

But oh, how she wished she could hold an intelligent conversation with the prince.

Intelligent? That was it! She'd try something she knew well. "Would you like to hear what I've learned about Dargentian history?" she asked.

"Only if it's my country's *real* history. I've had my fill of those damned legends."

"But, Niko, to your subjects they *are* Dargentia's history."

He glanced at her, and those marvelous lips arched into a sardonic grin that lifted the sides of his magnificent beard. Paige's heart wobbled inside till she willed it to settle down. Silly to go all mushy over a meaningless smile.

"Maybe you spent too much time in the United States," she continued, her bravery bolstered by his smile, despite its wryness. "People there have learned not to have much imagination."

Like her, she thought. She'd stopped believing in fairy tales long ago. Now if only she'd stop believing in Millicent.

"Then you support my people's ridiculous beliefs?" His tone was mild, but she sensed tension as taut as a compressed spring.

"Who's to say they're ridiculous? One story actually predicted your return."

"But—"

She interrupted. "If you go blithely on with your plans without your people marching behind you, they'll veer off in their own direction."

He was silent. Had she gone too far? But she'd just restated truths he'd heard before.

She glanced at him. There was a pensiveness in the way he studied the road.

"I planned for years how to protect my kingdom once I had it

156

back," he finally said. "I never considered that myths might be my downfall. Many Dargentians are superstitious, uneducated. They're like children. They need to be cared for."

"Kids love to disobey overprotective parents." Besides, his subjects didn't seem like children to her. Charmingly credulous, yes. Naive—no. "They love you, Niko." She kept her voice soft and pleading. "Just listen hard enough so they'll let you lead."

He made no reply. The Fiat turned onto a narrow, twisting road that followed the curves of the Argent. The gloomy weather of the previous days had been transfigured into a glorious bout of sunshine. As Niko steered, the light streaming through the window settled on the stones in the signet ring he wore. Rainbows flashing red, white and purple shot through he car.

Below, the river meandered slowly, a shimmering, silvery ribbon tied between rich green banks.

They passed great rolling acres of grape arbors. "Wine?" asked Paige, eager to find a less intense topic.

Niko, too, seemed inclined to ease the atmosphere. "Wine not?" he quipped. They laughed together. "Yes," he said. "While we were part of France, this wasn't the premier area, but wineries have existed here for many years. That's another industry I hope to cultivate."

"Grapes need cultivation," Paige agreed. They smiled at one another.

Once they'd tacitly agreed to keep away from controversy, Paige found it easier to talk. "Most of the materials I've been cataloguing are fascinating," she said.

"Like what?"

"Grocery lists, wine lists, party guest lists. Even laundry lists." She glanced at him. His lips puckered as though she fed him cod liver oil. "I suppose fascination is in the eyes of the beholder," she admitted.

"Now, if there were budgets and balance sheets, maybe even a paper or two on royal public relations, that's where I could get excited."

Paige wrinkled her face. They laughed again. The day's sunshine seemed suddenly to multiply.

She began a description of the history she'd collated, careful to keep away from anything seemingly fabled. A lot was based on his ancestors and the way they'd lived.

# Linda O. Johnston

"Niko," she finished impulsively, "what was it like? I mean, when you were younger. You grew up knowing you were important. You had a history behind you. You were destined for greatness."

His expressive, tawny brows knit into a stern scowl. "I always had a sense of what I wanted to accomplish," he admitted. "My country was part of me, even though I couldn't come home. I visited but hated it. I was spirited in and out, as though my coming was shameful. But worse was realizing my father was just as driven as I, yet he didn't succeed in freeing our homeland."

"The world was different then," Paige said, half wishing she hadn't brought up the subject. It caused him pain.

Niko nodded. "My grandfather fought for the Allies during World War II, then tried for Dargentia's freedom when the war ended. But the Allies were too territorial. Then, during the Cold War, my father didn't think it wise to break from France and leave Dargentia vulnerable."

"They had to wait for you!" Paige spoke teasingly, but she meant it.

The look he turned on her seemed tender, and she had to force herself not to look down at her lap. Still, she felt the usual redness creeping up her neck. She liked this man. His vulnerability touched her. Given half a chance, she could even love—

No. None of that. There wasn't half a chance. There wasn't any chance at all, no matter what Millicent schemed.

But maybe they could be friends.

Ordinary Paige Conner, the friend of a wonderful prince? And a wonderful man . . . She could live with that. She hoped.

Paige enjoyed the scenery for the rest of the ride. With the prince's permission, she clicked off the air conditioning. She rolled down the car window, enjoying the fresh, though warm, air. This part of Dargentia was beautiful, mountainous country that meandered about the banks of the Argent. Past the grape arbors were forests and, beyond them, farmlands. Niko, too, seemed mesmerized by the changing landscape. "I've only been this way a couple of times." His voice was hushed. "It's beautiful."

Paige heard his unspoken words: It was his home.

They eventually turned down a wide drive off the main highway. "We're here," he said.

158

## The Glass Slipper

They were where? All she could see was a rutted road over-grown with willow roots from below and hanging branches from above. The Fiat bumped along so fiercely that she felt her insides churn like a blender turned on high.

Finally they stopped. Before them was a large house—a mansion, really, of a gray stone similar to Niko's castle. But there the resemblance ended. The place was a three-story box, with no interesting angles. Many windows gaped open, glass free and grim. Bushes grew around the place in wild profusion, adding to the atmosphere of abandonment.

"Poor Aldred," whispered Paige.

Niko didn't disagree. They continued along the overgrown drive, the car still bumping and bucking. From what Paige could see the side of the house was no better than the front. As it turned out, the box was instead a U; the place had matching wings on both sides. Along the perimeter, at least, most of the windows appeared paned and intact.

Then they reached the rear. "Oh," Paige breathed. Even Niko sat still.

Speaking of fairy tales, the place looked as forbidding as something any diabolical witch could have conjured up. An enormous wall of the same dark stone as the house rose between the edges of the U. Parts of the parapet had crumbled at the top, but most seemed grimly intact. The wall was hardly visible through the profusion of trees, bushes and other flora whose height rivaled the barrier beyond. In the center of the wall stood a huge iron gate.

"Shall we take a closer look?" Niko asked. His voice suggested that his enthusiasm had ebbed.

But Paige was game. They'd come this far. She leapt from the car without waiting, this time, for the prince to open the door. She studied the leafy obstructions, then picked her way through bushes and over undergrowth. Fortunately, no brambles waylaid her, but she spared time for a quick prayer that the plants hid no snakes.

The close air among the bushes smelled green as her progress broke off branches. Twigs caught at her arms, bare beneath the short sleeves of her T-shirt, cracking off as they scratched at her. In her eagerness to search for Les Fabuleux, she hardly noticed.

A chorus of songbirds serenaded her as she plowed ahead, rustling leaves in her wake. Reaching the gate, she held its rough, oxidizing bars, warm in the summer sun, and peered in like a child at a closed toy store. Weeds along the fence obscured whatever waited beyond. She tried pulling the gate open, but it wouldn't budge; its padlock was as corroded as the rest. Turning, she called, ''Niko''—only to find him close behind her.

''Aldred gave me a key,'' he said, reaching into an athletic bag he'd taken from the trunk of the car. From an inside pocket he withdrew a large old-fashioned skeleton key. He edged past her to put the key into the lock. He turned it. Nothing happened.

''Drat,'' he muttered, then tried again. This time Paige heard a metallic protest, and the lock sprang open.

''Great!'' She clapped her hands.

Niko unhooked the open lock, then pulled at the rust-reddened metal of the gate. It, too, protested, but after he worked with it for some moments, the muscles and sinews in his taunt arms straining, it squealed open like the door of a haunted house.

Paige preceded Niko inside. She found herself in a courtyard, also littered with profuse plantlife, though not as overgrown as outside. A fountain complete with fauns and cavorting nymphs stood off to one side, and Paige dashed to examine it, disturbing a large, black crow. Its loud caw as it took off startled Paige, and she jumped back.

The fountain's marble had weathered well over the years and, despite a couple of nymphs lying down on the job of emptying jugs into the fountain, it was in good condition. A pool of brackish water puddled inside the base, more than would have remained after the recent rains. Combined with the smell of mildew in the air and the moss blanket along one side, the amount of water suggested to Paige that the fountain might be fed by an underground spring.

She heard a footfall behind her and turned. ''It must have been lovely once,'' she said.

He nodded. ''It looks salvageable, but Aldred has his work cut out for him.''

Beyond the fountain Paige saw that a crumbling cobbled path bisected the courtyard. Weeds sprang up among the stones, but it was still passable. ''This way?'' she asked.

Niko nodded. ''Aldred said he recalled a couple of arches that could resemble this.'' He held out his hand and eyed the ring.

"There's one outside and several in the house."

Niko led the way. Paige smelled the pungence of the weeds he disturbed on the uneven path, and her throat closed in an allergic reaction. The first arch they reached was at an opening into a granite wall that spanned the entrance to the house. The arch hadn't survived the years, though; half of its rounded stonework still perched precariously, but much had tumbled onto the walkway. Paige couldn't tell if there was anything about it resembling the jewels in the signet ring; any likeness was long gone.

Niko examined it, running his hands along the rough, crumbling wall. He picked at the stone. Pieces fell out into his fingers. "I doubt this was it," he finally pronounced.

They maneuvered around the arch and up the path until they were confronted with a wooden door. It hadn't fared well over the years; parts had rotted away. Without unlocking it, Niko poked his hand inside a hole and pulled. The door opened easily.

"Want to wait out here?" he asked, peering inside. "It doesn't look pleasant."

"Not on your life!" Paige wasn't about to be left out of the treasure hunt when she'd come this far. Although . . . "What do you see in there?" she asked tentatively.

The smile he turned on her was wicked. "Cobwebs," he said. "I hope you're not afraid of spiders. It'll be hard to see them in the dark. At least I expect them to be smaller than the rats."

Paige suppressed a shudder, refusing to rise to the bait. "No problem. I'll just follow you."

He laughed but preceded her inside.

The place had the dry, stifling smell of dust accumulated over the ages. Paige had to force herself to breathe. Niko hadn't lied about the cobwebs; they were everywhere. A layer of dirt carpeted the floor, and Paige suspected that he'd been right about the rats, too.

But this was no time to chicken out. Rats would be more scared of her than she of them . . . she hoped. And she was a lot bigger than any spiders. They wouldn't bother her—but she still put one hand on her head so she'd know right away if attacked from above.

They had entered into some kind of large gathering hall—she looked about in the dim light from the half-broken windows. She couldn't see far into the grayness.

## Linda O. Johnston

"Here." Niko reached into the bag he carried and pulled out two large flashlights. "One good thing about growing up in the United States was how easy it was to join the Boy Scouts. I'm always prepared."

Paige just bet he was. But she gladly took the proffered light. She turned it on, shining it about, only to have its beam captured in the pervasive, unreflective sheets of cobwebs.

Maybe coming here hadn't been such a good idea.

But Niko grabbed her hand, holding it tightly so they both clutched the straps of his bag. "Come on!" He used his free hand to forge a path through the cobwebs. "I think I see something."

He led her through the grimy, hanging gunk toward a doorway leading from the large room. The blackness beyond seemed singularly uninviting. Maybe, Paige considered, he should explore by himself. She could guard the door for wandering marauders, giant gila monsters and the like.

"Here," he said. "This could be it!" Letting go of her, he pulled his own flashlight from the bag and trained its beam overhead. The doorway was tall and broad—and framed overhead by a thick stone archway.

Paige could make out a pattern in the focused light. Instead of the black stonework that made up the rest of the arch, colored stones had been used. They were square—in red, pale gray and purple. And above them was a rounded row of smaller purple stones.

"Hey!" Paige cried. She grabbed for Niko's hand and held it upward, training her light on the ring. There was no doubt; it was the same pattern.

Letting go of him, she looked all around. "Where could Les Fabuleux be hidden?" she whispered.

"Someplace not very obvious," Niko replied. "Otherwise the Aldred who hid them would not have kept them on the ground floor, so accessible to outsiders."

He ran his hands along the stonework on one side of the archway. The rocks here, not having been exposed to the elements, weren't so prone to crumbling.

Swallowing her distaste for touching anything covered with cobwebs, Paige, too, began feeling the wall. It was rough, cool, wallpapered with sticky webs—and solid.

She wasn't sure how long she stood there, gingerly examining

162

the wall. She lost track of the time. Niko must have, too.

She went up one side of the stoneworks, then stood in the archway itself, exploring the doorway.

And then she felt it—a narrow recess. Only someone caressing the cobblestones could have noticed it. But Paige did. She stuck two fingers inside and felt a smooth metallic protrusion. "Niko—there's something here!"

He joined her immediately, his hands grasping her shoulders. "What is it?"

"I'm not sure—" She strained to maneuver the small lever. It didn't budge. She wiggled a third finger inside—all she could fit into the opening. Managing to move her fingers to the top of the lever, she concentrated on pushing it down. That did it! There was an irritating, scratching sound, as though one rock rubbed against another.

"There!" Niko pointed to a large stone several feet above the spot where Paige's hand rested. It had moved out a few inches. He pulled it easily from the wall, then reached into the hole it left. "There's something here!"

In a moment he had extracted a long metal box. It was large enough to hold a crown, maybe two. A little short for the renowned scepter—but maybe just the jeweled head had been hidden away.

Paige waited till Niko placed the box on the ground, then stooped beside him. She placed her hand on his arm, wanting to have even a distant contact with the box as he opened it.

Its rusty metal hasp objected to the rough treatment, but Niko was obviously too eager to let a small barrier stand in his way. He ripped it open, and it groaned.

Paige shone her flashlight beam inside—and then she groaned, too.

Niko reached inside and pulled out the only thing the box contained: a gold chain. On it was a single quarter-sized charm, in the shape of a swan.

"So much for your fabled Fabuleux," Niko said.

# Chapter Fourteen

Paige refused to leave. "This can't be it," she insisted. Swallowing her distaste for the decrepit state of the mansion, she grabbed Niko's hand and dragged him from room to room. Through dark, hot hallways they followed their flashlight beams, sweeping sheets of cottony cobwebs out of their way. Paige could hardly breathe as the disturbed dust clogged the air. They entered rooms where furniture, smelling of birds' nests and rodent-droppings, sagged and rotted. They climbed stone stairways covered in carpets so threadbare that they consisted of matted patches of threads. Only their footsteps sounded in the stillness of the huge, empty house.

They discovered several more archways, but none was decorated with the design on Niko's ring.

"Give it up, Paige," he finally said as they peered into the last bedroom on the second floor.

"I never give up."

"I know." His tone was so tender that Paige looked at him, startled. He regarded her with those marvelous deep, dark eyes. They sparkled with something that, if she hadn't known better, she'd have identified as admiration.

She swallowed, her gaze as trapped as if she'd been a panicky deer pinned by headlights on a dark country road. Biting her lower lip, she cleared her throat, then coughed into her hand. "Dust," she explained, though it had been strictly a measure of salvation. It gave her an excuse to look away.

"Ready to leave?" His voice was gentle.

She nodded slowly, furious at the feeling of defeat. "This can't be all." She pulled the swan pendant from where it dangled atop her T-shirt. Niko took her free hand and led her, flashlight in hand, toward the stairway that would take them back downstairs.

"It's all that's left," Niko contradicted her.

"I won't believe it."

"You've no reason to believe otherwise."

"The legends," Paige persisted. "Your people believe Les Fableux existed. Still exist. And you have to believe in your people."

Niko said nothing more until they'd returned to the rear courtyard. Then he took Paige by the elbow and swung her around so he could look her in the eye once more. "Legends are simply that," he said sternly. "Stories. Lies that people want to believe in so badly that they do. Just like all other kinds of superstitions—unbelievable and unreal."

Flinching, Paige looked over his shoulder. The last time Niko had expressed incredulity at the incredible, Millicent had retaliated. She couldn't have followed them all the way here, could she? But she'd followed Paige to Dargentia. Would they be bothered with a blizzard of butterflies here?

Fortunately, nothing happened. Still, Paige didn't relax her shoulders until she settled herself in the seat of the Fiat. Niko shut the car door behind her. She felt gritty and covered with cobwebs, almost ashamed to ride in even the most mundane of Niko's cars. But he didn't hesitate before climbing in himself, and his jeans and T-shirt were as filthy as hers.

She watched him as he turned the key in the ignition and put the car into gear. He sat tall and erect in his seat, staring straight ahead. His broad shoulders stretched his shirt, and his muscles bunched as he turned the steering wheel and guided the car around the side of the house whose crumbling walls seemed to mirror their crumbling hopes.

"Are you very disappointed?" she asked softly.

"Those damned jewels would have gone a long way toward saving this country," he said to the windshield. He headed the car back down the rutted road.

Paige wilted. *She* was disappointed, sure—but more, she felt dismal and defeated, as though she'd let Niko down. Maybe she had. Maybe she should never have encouraged him in this wild goose chase. He had enough tame geese to worry about back at the castle.

She thought again of Aldred's riddle, then of the signet ring from the jeweler Pelegrin. They'd been passed along through the centuries as clues to Les Fabuleux. They had to mean something.

If only she could figure out what.

"Don't look so depressed, Paige," Niko commanded from beside her.

"I'm not," she contradicted, lifting her chin. If he could be brave, she could do no less.

"The day's not wasted," he said. "We still have the picnic lunch Maibelle prepared for us. Are you hungry?"

Surprisingly, she was. But she wasn't so sure she could eat, feeling as grungy as she did.

"Can we wash our hands somewhere?" she asked.

"We are pretty raunchy," he agreed, leaning over to brush something from her cheek. She closed her eyes. Funny, how that trivial little touch made her whole body tingle. "I have an idea. Aldred told me about this little spot . . ."

Instead of driving toward the narrow main road, he headed up the mountain on an even skinnier one. Paige prayed they wouldn't meet any other vehicles coming down; though there were plenty of trees on both sides of the road to break their fall, some seemed to cling pretty precariously to the side of the cliff.

She thought of asking Niko to go back, but why bother? There was no place to turn around, and she wouldn't suggest he back the car down such a wild and winding drive.

Besides, he was concentrating on his driving.

"Let's see," he said eventually. "Aldred hasn't been here himself for years, but his directions seemed pretty explicit. If he was correct, we should come to a turnoff right about . . . now!"

And there it was—a paved road through a thick stand of tall pines. "Are you sure we should . . ." Paige stopped talking when she heard the quiver in her voice.

"If what Aldred described is here, this will be worth the ride."

The pavement quickly ended, and they bumped along a needle-carpeted path for a few more minutes. The path widened and finally ended in a grassy glade. On one side the mountain climbed straight up, across from which appeared to be the jagged edge of a cliff.

"Come on," Niko said.

This time Paige waited for him to open the car door. The place didn't look particularly inviting. In fact, now that there was a place to turn around, maybe she should hint . . .

But Niko didn't give her time to object. He took her hand and

166

led her slowly toward the edge of the cliff. "The view here is supposed to be—"

"It's gorgeous!" Paige gasped, interrupting him. Far, far below was a vista that took her breath away: tiny farmhouses, checkered fields and, slithering between it all, the ubiquitous Argent.

There was a haziness in the valley, giving the scene a sense of unreality. But the sun smiled down on them from above, its reflection glinting through the mist off the Argent, way below.

She made herself stand back from the edge, though she wanted to see all she could from this roost that seemed as high as an airplane's route. This was an aspect of Dargentia that she hadn't imagined, a distant, storybook quality: Once upon a time there was a magical kingdom whose kind and friendly people built beautiful farms, and through it all flowed a magnificent river tying one end of the country to the other.

She had a sudden sense of yearning. If only she could belong here. If only she dared to dream she might someday achieve happily ever after. . . .

She glanced at Niko. He was watching her, not the view. Quickly she turned away. She might be more credulous than he about things that couldn't be explained, but she wasn't crazy. Fairy tales didn't come true. Not for her.

She took a cautious step closer to the cliff edge. The sound of a breeze hummed in her ear as the slight wind, cooler than when they'd started up the mountain, blew her hair into her face. There was another sound, too, that she couldn't identify. It was more of a low roar.

"Let me show you something else," Niko said. "If I'm not hearing things, I think the other thing Aldred told me about this spot might be true."

Paige let him take her elbow and lead her to the more solid safety of the ground near the towering mountain wall. No plant life grew along it, and the rock formation, in red and gray strata of irregular widths, spoke of great upheaval in this area in prehistoric times.

Niko headed toward the farthest part of the clearing, where evergreen trees grew in as much profusion as along the road. As they walked, the roar grew louder. "There," he said, stopping short.

"Oh!" was Paige's awed response. She stood silently beside

# Linda O. Johnston

Niko, absorbing nature's spectacular show.

A sparkling sheet of water cascaded down the mountainside. The graceful stream dove into a rocky pool beside the spot where they stood. Shielding her eyes from the shimmering sun, Paige looked up, trying to see the source, but it was too high up. Though portions of the mountain above stuck out in sharp, knifelike crags, the artistic power of the water had rounded the rocks of the pool, creating a masterwork of stacked and sorted boulders.

She took a few steps closer, till she could have stepped right into the pool. Niko stayed at her side.

Near the base of the roaring falls, the water was the foamy froth of whipped egg whites. Closer to where they stood, though, the water sighed its way to rest. It grew so clear that the brown, smooth stones of its bottom were easily visible. Even from the distance, though, Paige felt the cool mist from the falls tickle her face.

"Now then," Niko said. "You asked for a place to wash your hands. That's one request this prince can grant."

Paige laughed. "That's sort of like supplying someone with a towel factory when she asks for a washcloth."

"Oh, but I never do things in a small way." His smile was so smug that Paige couldn't quite let him get away with it.

"Is that so?"

He nodded.

"Well, neither do I."

Before she could warn herself how unwise she was being, she knocked her hips sideways into the side of his leg. The earth around the pool was wet and muddy—and just slippery enough. The prince's strong, bare arms flailed for a moment as he lost his balance—and went sliding into the water.

"Good day for a swim," Paige remarked as Niko righted himself.

"Not bad." Water cascaded from his broad body. His T-shirt had hugged his muscular torso before; now it stuck like a second skin. Paige could hardly tear her eyes away.

She watched him even more carefully for a sign of righteous royal fury. Oh, why had she done such a silly thing? What would happen to her job now?

"It's an even better day for a shower, though," Niko continued conversationally. Did she dare believe his smile was genuine?

Before she had time to react, he'd bounded from the water and grabbed her arms with unyielding hands. He pulled until she, too, lost her balance. In a moment she was on top of him in the middle of the mountain pool, soaked, startled and unable to see through her wet glasses.

"Hey!" she tried crying, but only succeeded in swallowing a mouthful of the fresh, pure water.

He didn't stop there. Twisting so he was at her side, he grabbed her with one strong arm and began swimming, his free arm stroking at his far side. Paige tried to resist, but her attempts to get her footing were foiled by Niko's smooth, sure kicks through the water.

In a moment they reached the base of the falls. "Shower time," Niko called, then gave Paige a soft shove.

Holding her breath, she sat down in the middle of the seething froth. Water stronger than any shower she'd ever taken poured over her head. She gasped, shaking her head till her wet hair slapped her own cheeks.

She felt surprised. Shocked. Then she was as angry as a wet hen. Why had His Royal Highness undermined her already diminished dignity?

And then, as she sat there, water still falling fast upon her head, she began to laugh. She sputtered as water poured into her mouth. She'd deserved it, but she wasn't about to give in just yet.

Quickly, she removed her glasses and looked around. Though her vision was highly blurred, there seemed to be an area behind the falls . . . She slithered on her backside along the smooth rocks at the bottom. As she cleared the base of the falls, she took a deep breath of the damp air that smelled like wet rocks. Waving her glasses to shake off what water she could, she put them back on. She couldn't see Niko through the pouring water. That meant he couldn't see her, either.

With luck, he'd think she had drowned.

She'd give him a few minutes to worry, then leap out and shout "Surprise!" Give his heart a few extra palpitations.

She sat in the deep shadows of the rocks behind the cascading water. The cool, clean moistness felt good after their day of dirty digging at Aldred's ancestral home.

If she sat here long enough, she'd be totally cleansed.

If she sat here long enough, she'd be totally nuts! What was she thinking of? What if Niko really thought she'd drowned? He'd run off and leave her stranded here, in the middle of nowhere, while he looked for help. "Hey," she called out, standing so quickly that she slipped back down onto her butt. Her bottom smarting, she rose again. "Hey, Niko!" But her words were lost in the tumult of the falls.

Panicking, she fought her way back toward the falling curtain of water—and as she stepped into the pelting shower, she ran into a thick, solid wall. Niko.

His firm hands grasped her tightly. "Paige! Paige, are you all right?"

She tried to answer, but the falls drowned her words. He lifted her easily into his arms and hugged her to him till they were clear of the falling water.

Then, not putting her down, he looked at her. His eyes were even darker than usual, shadowed by his worried frown. "I was afraid—"

He didn't finish his thought, for as he'd spoken, his mouth had moved closer to hers until he cut off his own words with his kiss.

There was a savagery in it, as though he wished to command her to live, to breathe. His lips were cool and moist, yet tempered by his body heat. She threw her arms about his neck, the better to meet his determined mouth. She wasn't concerned about falling into the pool again; Niko's arms were strong and sure about her.

His tongue plunged into her mouth as though conducting a search-and-rescue of its own. It found hers, and she met its inquisitive thrusts as though assuring him she was alive—*very* alive—and well.

She felt his soft, soaking beard against her chin. The kiss gentled, his tongue lifted, and she sighed. Was it over?

No. She wasn't ready to stop. She used her hands at the back of his head, twisted her fingers in the wetness of his hair, to bring him closer. She moved her head in a slow, sensual circle so she could taste him from other angles. Softly, she touched his lips with her tongue.

He responded with even more ardor than his previous kiss. Paige lost track of where she was, of who she was, as she was engulfed by the hypnotic power of Niko's mouth capturing hers.

Too soon, though, it ended. Niko pulled his head away. Still holding her in his arms, he started striding toward the far end of the water. He didn't release her. She didn't want him to. She was too limp, drowned not by the water but by the liquid fire flowing through her veins from his kisses.

She hung on, her arms still around his neck, her head resting on his chest. The coolness of his wet T-shirt rasped against her cheek.

She was alive to all sensation, one of his arms wrapped about her shoulders, the other beneath her knees. The breeze whispered against her soaked body. Niko's muscles flexed tautly against her as he walked.

A stirring inside her signaled her sensual awareness of the man in whose arms she lay.

Lifting her head, she studied him through the veil of her still-wet glasses, not really wanting to reach the shore. There was determination in his expression, a royal imperative in the lift of his chin. He said nothing. She said nothing.

Would he finally fire her this time for her impetuousness? But his admission of defeat had goaded her into her little jokes: pushing him into the water, hiding beneath the falls.

And those kisses had been worth everything.

Niko didn't break his stride as he walked from the water and over the muddy bank. He didn't stop till he reached the overgrown grass waving along the shore. Then he gently set Paige down. His arms remained about her back, as though to hold her steady as she sat on the thick cushion of green.

Afraid to move, she nevertheless hazarded a glance into his dark, unfathomable eyes. They bored into hers. What was he thinking? Was he angry?

Unsure of herself, she tried to duck her head but felt his fingers beneath her chin. "Is it time for our picnic?" she managed, staring at his chest.

"Are you hungry?" The question rumbled deep in his throat, and Paige, still not looking at his face, had a sudden, sure sense that he wasn't talking about food.

Was she hungry? Here she was, alone with the most gorgeous, most wonderful man she had ever known. They were both soaking wet. His T-shirt was plastered to him, hugging every hard, firm muscle. She was afraid to look down to see how much her own wet clothing revealed.

Was she hungry? "Oh, yes," she whispered.

# Linda O. Johnston

He gently pulled her down on the grass, then stretched out beside her. She hazarded an upward glance. His heated gaze pinned her like a trapped butterfly. She held her breath as his hand reached toward her. His long, strong fingers stroked her side over her clinging shirt, then continued onward. As he reached the base of her breast, she gasped and closed her eyes.

Her mind swirled in an eddy of sensation, though a sudden, unwelcome though intruded. What if . . . ?

Surely not. Surely whatever Niko's reason for kissing her, for touching her, it couldn't be magic.

But just in case, she let her mind call, *Millicent!*

Nothing. No reply. Not even any lilacs.

Thank heavens.

And then she thought no more as Niko's exploration expanded to the use of both hands. Paige, used to being a participant in her life and not merely passive, conducted an expedition with her own fingers, touching the wetness of his T-shirt, stroking the protrusion of his collarbone, feeling with her palms the rounded hardness of his pectoral muscles. As his hands moved downward, hers did the same.

His wet jeans both stimulated and frustrated her. They clung to him, hinting at all beneath. He seemed to feel the same frustration, for he tugged irritably at the buckle of her belt.

She turned to allow him easier access to her clothing. He took off her glasses and laid them gently behind her. Then he pulled her sopping shirt over her head. Her bra followed. Her skin was still damp, and she felt her nipples blossom even before he brushed them with his fingers, then with his lips.

His hands again dipped lower, and she drew him close, but only for a moment. The scraping of his shirt on her naked breasts irritated her. She reached for the offending expanse of material. Her trembling hindered her, but not for long. Soon his chest was as bare as hers. Thick whorls of golden hair covered his well-defined muscles, tapering to a narrow line above the waist of his pants. Her breathing quick and irregular, Paige let her finger follow the line till his belt stopped her.

With a growl deep in his throat, Niko again captured her mouth with his. She sensed the last of their clothing disappear. His hands were all over her, his touch tender yet inflammatory. She explored him, too: the angles of his shoulders, the planes of his back, his

172

tight buttocks. He reached between them, urging her to open to him. Her voice made small, unfamiliar sounds and her body writhed of its own volition. Wanting to create in him a similar sweet suffering, she followed the tantalizing line of the hair on his abdomen. Her hand grasped him, hardness and heat, and she wasn't certain whether the gasp she heard was his or hers or both combined.

He shifted until he was on top of her. His strength and weight felt familiar; they'd been in a similar position at the airport, and once again in his bedroom, the night she had temporarily scintillated. But the stirring she'd felt then was a mere hint of the pleasurable sensuality rocking her now. She was melted by his heat, weakened by his hardness.

And then he began to enter her. He seemed inclined to gentleness, but she felt alive, feral, needy. She urged him onward, gasping at the sudden burst of pain.

He hesitated.

"Please," she whispered. "Don't stop."

The rhythm of her hips further entreated him to continue. She was scaling an unknown, rapturous precipice, and to stop would be more torture than she could bear. He met and surpassed the cadence she set, and when she soared over the edge his soft cry and sudden stillness told her that he flew beside her.

She didn't move. She wanted to savor the moment: his weight and warmth atop her, the slowing movement of his chest as he caught his breath, their combined moistness, his aroma of autumn leaves and citrus mingled with muskiness.

As her own breathing became regular, she was struck by a sudden nervousness. She had made love with the prince of Dargentia, her employer. What should she do now? What could she say?

She didn't regret what had happened. It had been everything she could have imagined that such a royal experience would be. She would remember it as a miraculous interlude in a rather ordinary existence.

But what now?

Rolling over beside Paige, Niko was angry. He had let his common sense be overruled by the overwhelming combination of

# Linda O. Johnston

his relief that Paige hadn't drowned and his hormones. What was he to do now?

Paige Conner was a bewitching creature, full of contrasts. Who would have thought such boundless sensuality could be found beneath her sensible clothes? Her bookishness, her straight and ordinary hairdo, her glasses—they were camouflage, hiding from the world a tigress.

He didn't regret the experience. He'd enjoyed every moment.

But he'd have fought harder for control had he known she was a virgin.

Would she assume now that he owed her something? Was this part of a plot to get him to marry her?

She was an American, after all. But he'd met good Americans as well as bad. And despite the mistrust he carried like a shield, there'd been nothing about Paige Conner to suggest she was a schemer.

Instead, she was a banner-waver, carrying to him the voice of his own people. Shoving legends at him, for heaven's sake. Looking for legendary jewels.

Though he'd have to fight his instincts, he would give her the benefit of the doubt.

When he turned again her back was toward him. She'd half covered herself with her wet clothes.

Was she ashamed? A pang of guilt shot through him. He leaned over, watching her. Her lovely amber eyes were wide, blinking rapidly as they looked everywhere but at him.

He put his arm around her as she remained cocooned beneath the meager cover. "You should have told me," he said softly.

She jumped. "What?"

"This was your first time, Paige. You should have told me. How old are you?"

"Twenty-nine. Does it matter?"

She sounded defensive, and he laughed. "No, but you're a rarity."

"I've done some experimenting," she said huffily. "Out of curiosity. But the situation never seemed right."

"And this was?" Niko kept his voice soft.

"This was," she whispered. Then she cleared her throat, rolling over to face him, again clutching her T-shirt to her. She looked at him steadfastly, despite the unfocused look in her eyes

174

that said she needed her glasses. "My curiosity got the better of me this time. I—I'm glad it did. But I don't want this in the way of our professional relationship." Her small, determined chin lifted, as though challenging him to contradict her. "I'll do my job as we agreed. And I want to keep looking for Les Fabuleux. But we can just forget about this . . . if you want."

Did she mean it? He searched her beautiful sunshine-bright eyes and found nothing there to contradict her words. A feeling of tenderness flooded him. He touched her cheek with his forefinger. "I *don't* want, Paige."

She closed her eyes as though in relief, then opened them again, smiling. She swept her gaze down his body. He remembered that, though she was partly covered, he was still naked. He wondered how nearsighted she really was. The idea of her stare made him throb. He considered this development but decided enough of a good thing was enough—at least for now.

She turned her back as she slipped into her underclothes. As he dressed, he watched her lithe, graceful movements. He almost reconsidered his decision to let her go. But they had to get back to the castle. He'd have time to get to know her better there. To teach her more—although she seemed to have the knack naturally. He grinned.

When she was dressed she ran her fingers through her hair. "My glasses?"

He found them for her where they'd gotten buried in the thick grass and slipped the sidepieces over her ears. Pushing them gently up the bridge of her nose, he bent down and kissed her.

"Time to go back," he said softly.

She nodded. Then, as though on impulse, she threw her arms about his neck and drew his head down till his lips were again ignited by hers. Her tongue plunged into his mouth, and he groaned as his body responded to this renewed sensual stimulation.

But as he pulled her damp T-shirt from where she'd tucked it into her jeans, she danced away from him.

Her captivating dark gold eyes sparkling beneath her glasses, she laughed. "Time to go back," she repeated.

# Chapter Fifteen

Niko had a miserable time keeping his mind on his driving. Not that he had much choice on the way back down Aldred's twisting, tree-shrouded mountain road. But he had a problem with his hands. They itched. He wanted more than anything to lift them from the steering wheel, reach over and run them through the soft, moist satin of Paige's still-damp hair. To touch the creamy texture of her cheek.

He glanced at her. Often. Not once did she dip her head to hide her expression behind the veil of her beautiful black hair. Her unique amber eyes sparkled gold in the leaf-mottled sunlight, never wavering from his face.

Maybe he should give in to his subjects' demands. Marrying a commoner might not be so bad—not if that commoner was Paige Conner.

He darted yet another look at her. She smiled shyly, curving those sweet lips that were still puffy from his kisses.

"We forgot about lunch," she said suddenly.

"So we did." His surprise lasted only a moment. The satisfaction of another, more avid appetite had completely obliterated his urge for food. "Do you mind?"

She shook her head, then raised her fingers to curl around that puny swan pendant they'd found instead of Les Fabuleux. "We can't give up, you know."

Of course she wouldn't let him give up. Her tenacity was one of the things he found most endearing about her.

"If you have any other suggestions, tell me."

"I want to study your signet ring and hear Aldred repeat his clue at the same time. Maybe one of us will have a thought."

He had a lot of thoughts, all of them about Paige Conner. How had someone so sweet and shy blossomed into such a sensual vixen?

He wasn't sure, but he wanted to test it again. And again.

Maybe he could announce at the ball that he'd found his commoner, and . . .

The car hit a rut and bounced jarringly.

"Oh!" Paige gasped beside him, reaching for the dashboard.

Niko fought to keep control, quickly steering the vehicle back on track. But the sharp motion had shaken him.

Control. He needed better control of his thoughts. What had he been thinking of? No matter how many skyrockets he'd seen, how singularly enthralling the experience had felt, he'd merely made love with this woman.

Merely? Hah! The act had been phenomenal. It had been a sensory smorgasbord, touching him from the top of his head to the tip of his toes—and some other tips in between. It had made him feel, for a few minutes, more powerful than had the liberation of his kingdom.

But was he forgetting so easily years of anguish at the hands of women scheming to ensnare a prince? Maybe he was wrong about Paige Conner. Maybe she had simple goals—sex, then scandal, unless he offered marriage and a crown.

Despite the shade blanketing the car from the hanging boughs and the dampness of his clothing, he felt, suddenly, very warm. He closed the open window beside him and turned on the air conditioning.

"Why did you come to Dargentia?" he asked abruptly, his voice so sharp it could have stabbed her. When he glanced at her she did, in fact, look wounded. Once more, her head dipped forward.

"You hired me, Niko. As a historian. And I'm a damned good one." Her hurt voice was soft as a feather, yet it pounded at him as though she'd kicked him with a steel-toed boot.

"I heard you turned down the job of curator of a museum to come here. Why would you do that for a job you knew was temporary?"

He saw, with his peripheral vision, that she was studying him. Obviously she hoped to see why his mood had changed so swiftly. He couldn't explain it. He didn't know himself—except that he'd been hurt before by wily Americans wielding sex like a weapon. He wouldn't let it happen again.

"It was a small museum in a small town," Paige said. Then,

more loudly, "Maybe I should have gone there instead. It was a wonderful opportunity."

"And this wasn't?" Perversely, he felt wounded.

"Nothing could have been more wonderful than coming here." He could hardly hear her voice. He glanced toward her. There were tiny tears in the corners of her eyes beneath those big, black-rimmed glasses.

He reached toward her, squeezing her hand atop her knee. "Paige, I'm sorry. But I need the truth. Was this job the only reason you came here?" It had to be, of course. This woman couldn't be the kind of schemer he'd run into before. She was too open. Too straightforward. Too . . . lovable.

"No, it wasn't." Her whisper struck him as though she'd cracked a whip.

He withdrew his hand, saying nothing for a long moment, absorbing the pain. For a moment he'd been willing to believe the best of her. "Why, then?" he demanded, curving his fingers around the steering wheel till they ached.

She sighed. "I should have told you the truth right away. Maybe you could even have helped me. I was looking for the right Wenzel."

The car had reached the end of the narrow drive to the main road. He stopped it, staring at her. "What do you mean?"

He'd expected a confession of maneuvering and manipulating for a title. Her quiet statement made no sense.

She found a spot outside the Fiat on which to focus. As far as Niko could tell, all she saw was the peeling bark of a willow's trunk. "I wrote my Master's thesis just over a year ago. It was a scholarly treatise on one of Williamsburg, Virginia's, oldest families, the Adamsons. I researched more than their genealogy; I interwove the way the political and sociological climates of their times influenced each family member through the centuries to the present."

Niko enjoyed the lilt of enthusiasm in her voice—even if she was avoiding the subject. Maybe because she was. "Something like what I hope you'll do for Dargentia," he prompted. He sat back; his fingers tingled as the stress on them eased.

She nodded. "That's one thing I hope to achieve here. A lot of people found my Williamsburg analysis worthwhile, and they're paying to use it. It's now the basis for history courses in several universities, and it gives me a small side income.'' She turned to Niko, a question written in the dip of her dark eyebrows. ''I suspected that was one of the reasons I was chosen for this job.''

He nodded. ''I let Aldred narrow down the list. His favorite of the final candidates was a person who'd written a fine text on an obscure historical subject. I agreed on his selection.''

A smile tipped the corners of Paige's mouth. She steepled her hands in front of her, and her face glowed with pride.

''Tell me more about it,'' he encouraged, though he had no idea how this might relate to her reason for coming to Dargentia.

''It was great fun,'' she said. ''A lot of work, too, but it gave me the chance to delve into all sorts of reference materials.'' A bore to him, but the excitement in her eyes said she'd found it anything but. ''I followed leads about the Adamsons till I felt I'd shaken hands and shared tears with everyone connected with the family—almost. But there was a dead end, and . . . Niko, there's something you should know.''

She sounded serious. Here it came, her real reason for accepting this job. Niko turned off the engine. He couldn't quite sit back against the seat; his back felt as stiff as if it were supported by a buttress. He crossed his arms, ready to listen.

Paige bit her lower lip. She'd determined to keep this secret because she was sure he would misunderstand. But now he had to know.

She considered what to say. ''My family is distantly related to the Adamsons, Niko.'' She hazarded a glance at him.

''So?'' he asked, staring straight ahead.

Paige cleared her throat nervously. ''One of the earliest Adamsons I learned about was my ancestor Leticia. She was an only child, the belle of seventeenth-century Williamsburg—until her parents died, leaving her destitute. The debts her family left scared off every suitable suitor. Out of desperation, she married an older man, and the few records of the time that mention her after that said she was treated terribly.''

''How sad.'' He sounded singularly unsympathetic.

That irritated Paige. ''Imagine what it was like then for a woman. She needed a man to support her, and poor, beautiful Leticia got stuck with a crotchety old codger. He kept her holed

# Linda O. Johnston

up in their house, didn't let her friends visit and, I suspect from hints I read in others' journals, he even beat her. He—"

Niko cut in. "Get to the point, Paige." His voice had assumed a suspicious tone, as though he waited for her to bombard him with a bombshell.

Even after their special time together, he still expected the worst from her. Pain raced through her, churning the soft approach she'd intended into anger. "Okay," she shot back. "The old man died. Leticia got married again, to a man named John Wenzel. A footnote I found indicated that this Wenzel was a member of the Dargentian ruling family. I came here hoping to find out the truth: was Leticia's Wenzel a member of the deposed Dargentian monarchy?"

She winced at his expression: rage that would have done a rabid dog proud. Though perhaps there was a touch of hurt in him as well. . . .

She felt miserable suddenly. Letting him goad her into a show of temper had done neither of them any good. "It's not what you think, Niko," she said quietly. "Actually—"

"What *I* think doesn't matter here." His voice emerged through gritted teeth. "I suppose *you* think that, if you find proof that this Wenzel was my ancestor, you'll have a claim through your Leticia to the Dargentian throne." He flexed his fingers, as though he had the urge to throttle her.

"Niko, no!" Paige felt tears well in her eyes. She'd handled this all wrong. "That's why I didn't tell you; I was afraid that was what you'd assume. But if you'd let me explain without interrupting—"

"Okay, I won't interrupt again," he interrupted. "Tell me exactly why I should believe you're not after my kingdom."

Paige's jaw ached as she clenched her teeth. Her unhappiness about their argument was waging war with her simmering indignation at Niko's arrogant attitude. Still, she'd nothing to gain by holding back the truth. Her voice sounded tight, even to her. "I can prove to you, Niko, that I didn't come to make a claim on your throne. The only thing good that Leticia's first husband did for her was to give her a sweet little baby girl. I brought with me some papers that show my distant relationship to that baby. I have no blood ties at all to Wenzel, no way I could make a claim on your kingdom even if I wanted to. Surely someone who wanted

180

to exploit a connection wouldn't bring along evidence that the claim had no merit.''

"Then you didn't come here planning to become a princess?'' Paige had heard skepticism in voices before, but none so clear and cutting as in Niko's.

She knew that her entire relationship with him—as employer-employee, as potential friends . . . and as lovers—hung in the balance. He'd made it clear what he thought of women who pursued him for a title; he'd have no greater affection for someone claiming ancestry to gain elevation. "No, Niko,'' she said firmly. "Becoming Dargentia's princess was the last thing on my mind when I took this job.''

"I'm supposed to believe, then, that your ulterior motive for coming here was to research this one little historical footnote?''

"Yes,'' she said. It was, after all, the truth. She had wanted to believe that Leticia had enjoyed a happy ending when she'd lost her weasel of a husband and found Wenzel. And, oh, what a fantastic finish if she'd actually married royalty.

Someone with whom Paige was connected, however remotely, had had a fairy tale come true.

It was the closest she'd ever come.

"I'm a historian, Niko,'' she went on, knowing he needed further explanation. "And I'm especially interested in genealogy.'' She kept her voice soft and pleading as she watched him. "I go berserk over loose ends from the past: family trees where limbs, even twigs, disappear without a trace; birth records without evidence of death; even death records where there's no hint there was a birth.''

She held her breath for a moment. If she could interpret body language, she thought Niko was finally beginning to believe her. Just a little, though; the easing of his stiff shoulders was barely perceptible.

"Then there was Leticia Adamson,'' she continued cajolingly. "She seemed to call out from the past and urge me to learn all about her. She'd had everything, then lost it all when she was orphaned. The idea of her finding happiness—well, I wanted to make sure it happened. Her Wenzel rated a mention in an obscure scholarly work of the time, the kind of dry treatise that never hints of mystery. But this one did.''

# Linda O. Johnston

"And that was it? You were simply intrigued by this historical trivia?"

She nodded.

"Like grocery lists, wine lists, party guests and laundry?" His tone was nearly conversational now, and the anger had fled from his face.

Nodding, Paige said, "I'm sorry, Niko. I should have told you right off about Leticia and Wenzel, that they were my special reason for taking this job."

"Yes," he said, "you should have. Historians!" He shook his head, as though he were discussing an incomprehensible alien culture.

She closed her eyes in relief as he reached over and pulled her to him along the cramped seat of the Fiat. He pressed her head beneath his chin and kissed her hair. She sighed and ran her fingertips up the hardness of his chest.

"I forgive you," he said in his most regal voice. "But don't keep secrets from me again."

There was, Paige thought, just one little bitty secret left that she hadn't spilled her heart about.

Millicent.

But what was there to say about a being whose existence was highly suspect? No; there was no sense putting her sanity at issue.

With respect to her Wenzel quest, her confession hadn't been so horrible. In fact, she felt a whole lot better. Niko hadn't fired her, kicked her out of the country . . . or repudiated the rapture they'd shared by the waterfall.

While they drove from their mountain aerie, her damp clothes still sticking to her body, Niko spoke of the Wenzel he'd heard most about while growing up. "As I told you when I gave you the list of all the Dargentian rulers, the first king of this country was named Wenzel. But he was much earlier than the era you're interested in. Legend has it that he won this country's freedom from Germany in a duel back sometime before the Middle Ages."

"Then you do believe in legends?" Paige teased.

"I believe in real people about whom legends are created," he contradicted. "Aldred tried to convince me of more as I was growing up, though."

Paige thought of a regal, realistic child with golden brown hair

182

and dark, penetrating eyes, and smiled. "He wanted you to believe in legends?"

Niko nodded. "He said that a king-in-the-making had a duty to accept everything that made his subjects tick. All of Dargentia's legends, he said, had a basis in truth, and many were interrelated. But when I asked what about them was real, he told me I'd have to grow up to learn that."

"And now that you're an adult?"

"Their truth still eludes me."

Paige laughed. "I don't suppose anything will turn you into a believer."

He momentarily moved his eloquent eyes from the road to rest them on her, and she felt a lethargy as warm and sweet as microwaved molasses flow through her bloodstream. "People believe in legends for all sorts of reasons. Perhaps I can be convinced to follow my country's, even if I don't buy all the disasters that are supposed to befall us if I don't."

Paige quivered inside. Was that a suggestion that he might marry a commoner after all? And could that very lucky commoner be her?

Oh, yes, she prayed. For she had to acknowledge it to herself: She'd fallen in love with Prince Nicholas of Dargentia.

She'd known it before that day, before their magnificent lovemaking by the waterfall. But their passion had sparked the knowledge to such proportions that it felt like a forest fire igniting her insides, threatening to burst into bright and shining flames that only he could control by his touch, his kiss.

Not that she'd tell him that. Not unless he confessed feelings for her first.

And then only if she were certain that whatever he felt for her wasn't the result of Millicent's interference.

At least Paige hadn't sensed the presence of her personal meddler today. Her lovemaking with Niko had been magical, but it had been the magic of two people attracted to one another—there was nothing supernatural about it.

She hoped.

She struggled to make a reply to his statement that wouldn't seem self-serving. "Your subjects would be very pleased if you listened to the legends," she finally said. "They'd never have to know that you don't really believe."

# Linda O. Johnston

"You're kind to worry about my subjects." Niko lifted his hand from the steering wheel and gently caressed her cheek with his knuckles. She closed her eyes, revelling in the soft and tender touch.

"Your subjects are kind people," she said simply.

"Oh, look!" Niko exclaimed, just as Paige's ears were assaulted by a commotion outside the car.

Her eyes popped open. Crossing the road in front of them was a line of sheep, earnestly herded by a frantically barking dog with high, flopping ears. A man with a tall, rounded staff ran through the field beside the highway, shouting something Paige could not quite hear. The last of the line of animals were a couple of large mother sheep accompanied by tiny, frolicking lambs. Niko turned off the car air conditioning and rolled down the window, and fresh country scents filled the Fiat.

The shepherd approached the driver's side of the car. He was a small man whose outdoor living had tanned his skin to the dark, crumpled leather from which his pale eyes peered. "I am sorry, Your Highness," he said in French, recognizing the prince. The poor man appeared as though he was about to grovel abjectly in apology.

"You've given me a delightful experience, my friend," Niko said. "It's not every day that I come to such a wonderful obstruction in my travels."

The man's hidelike face lightened, and his broad smile revealed two missing teeth. He bobbed his head reverently, then dashed forward to shoo the last of the lambs from the road.

Paige laughed in pleasure. She settled back into her seat, knowing the grin on her face rivaled the shepherd's in depth. But hers, at least, wouldn't show any gaps between her teeth.

"You were wonderful with him, Niko," she said softly. He shared her smile, and she felt so happy she had to look away. Otherwise she'd say something stupid. Instead, she found a topic she'd wanted to continue anyway. "Tell me more about some Wenzels."

They shared stories on the rest of the drive. Niko told her of the only other Wenzels he'd heard about. "Most of what I know I told you from my memorized list. The last Wenzel who was king was Wenzel the Fourth. We've talked about number one. Number two was his son, and to my knowledge the most memorable thing he did was to follow in his father's footsteps and keep Dargentia free.''

"A remarkable feat," Paige said.

The prince nodded. "Especially in those hostile times." He paused, stroking a finger along his furrowed brow. "I can't remember anything about numbers three and four, except that they didn't directly follow the first two."

"Were there any Wenzels who weren't king?" Was she really having this conversation? wondered Paige. She was speaking about her favorite topic with the most wonderful man she'd ever met. Who needed magic? Who needed scintillation? Who needed Millicent?

Somehow she, plain Paige Conner, was living her dream.

"Sure," Niko replied. "Wenzel is a common family name. My father was Lucien, and his brother, who was married to Aunt Charlotte, was named Wenzel. I think there's been a Wenzel in every generation. Nicholas the First had a son named Wenzel."

That one was the Wenzel from Aldred's clue to Les Fabuleux, where the fleeing king, queen and two princes had been mentioned. Paige hadn't learned any more about this Wenzel yet, but he was from the right time period. He could be the John Wenzel of Williamsburg, but she needed to confirm it.

They ran into little traffic on the way back to the castle. As afternoon turned to early evening, the air outside cooled. Niko had left the air conditioning off. A breeze blew into the car from the open windows, lifting Paige's hair and drifting it over her glasses and into her face.

So what if she was ugly and wore glasses? Maybe, just maybe, it didn't matter. Niko had noticed her nonetheless. And now he chatted with her about Dargentian history, the farms they passed, the places he'd seen, as though they were old friends. Leaning back against the creaky leather seat of the Fiat, Paige savored every moment.

The Argent shimmered beside them, and Paige wished that it would continue to meander; the road followed the river, and she was in no hurry to return to the castle, to let this marvelous day draw to an end.

But soon the hillside houses of D'Argent City came into view. They passed the two hotels and crossed the bridge toward the castle.

"Do you have any plans for this evening?" Niko asked, turning the car up the first switchback.

"Some writing," she said. "I've begun the brochure, but I want to finish a draft."

"Fine," he agreed. "We'll have dinner in a couple of hours, you can work for a while after that, and then we'll meet at the moat. Is that all right with you?"

He was asking, not commanding. She'd have been delighted in any event, but his treating her as an equal touched her. "Just fine," she said—one of the world's greatest understatements.

But there would be a major disruption to their plans, Paige learned a few minutes later. Niko parked the car in the stables and came around to open the door for her. He took her hand and she slid her legs around to scoot out.

It was then that she saw them.

Aldred stood by the stable door, absolutely beaming, darn him. Two people were with him.

Though they were backlighted, outlined by the dwindling sun in the stable doorway, Paige immediately recognized their silhouettes. She stiffened.

One of them was a tall, thin man whose hair waved boyishly. His shoulders were encased in a nattily cut sports jacket; his trousers hung just so.

Beside him was a woman whose shadow revealed a perfectly chignoned coif. Her suit was Chanel, her legs were long, her shoes high-heeled and elegant. Her scent, an Armani original, managed to overlay the usual stable smells like a soft admonishment.

Paige immediately looked down at her own dirty T-shirt and clinging, still-damp jeans. She swallowed. *This* was a woman who had attracted, even for a moment, a prince?

With a sigh, she started forward, her arms outstretched as eagerly as if she reached for a bottle of skunk oil. "Mother? Dad? What are you doing here?"

# *Chapter Sixteen*

"What a charming bedroom," said Alexandra Conner.

Paige always thought of her mother as Alexandra. Like her own real first name, Eleanora, Alexandra sounded to her like someone cultured, glamorous . . . scintillating. And that certainly described Paige's eloquent, head-spinningly attractive, TV-newscaster mother.

But it wasn't a whit like Paige.

Paige hadn't wanted to bring her mother to her room, but Alexandra had insisted. "I have to see where my baby girl lives in a real castle."

Paige felt like sticking her thumb in her mouth and gurgling, "Goo."

She shouldn't have been worried about bringing her mother here. Millicent had been buzzing in and out of her life for years, and she'd never popped up and made her presence known to Paige's family.

Paige still glanced about the bedroom. No scent of lilacs, thank heavens. No shimmering column of pixie dust. It simply remained the wonderful tower room with curved walls and tester bed that she'd begun inhabiting a short time before. She'd added a couple of personal touches—history books from the library to read in bed, a few pads of paper and fountain pens. It felt like home to Paige. She thought it was lovely. She felt warm and cozy here.

But what did this room look like to Alexandra?

"So my baby girl sleeps here. How . . . delightful." Model-perfect in poise, Alexandra glided over the Persian rug toward the bed, one foot sliding smoothly before the other. Her skirt was slim and short enough to reveal her perfect legs. She wore her hair, as black as Paige's, in her favorite style—a tight, muss-free chignon. The way it swept back from her face emphasized her wonderful bone structure and gracefully hollow cheeks. Her makeup was, as always, perfect.

187

# Linda O. Johnston

She examined the carved roses and leaves lavishly decorating the headboard, then touched her finger to the polished wood. Thank heavens for Aldred, thought Paige. Her mother didn't wear white gloves, but Paige would have been mortified if Alexandra had wiped a dab of dust from the headboard.

Her mother looked up. "That mural is quite . . . interesting. Do you know who it's supposed to portray?"

"N-no," Paige stammered. "I mean, it's a scene from Greek mythology, but—"

"Well, love, you're the historian."

Since she'd chosen to become a historian against her parents' wishes for their bookish daughter—"With brains like yours, love, you surely should become a doctor. Or, if you must, a lawyer"—Paige realized she should have known exactly what the historical scene showed. She dipped her head in shame.

"The tour you gave us of the castle was quite charming." Alexandra slid agilely to a new subject, obviously unaware of Paige's mortification.

It had been nothing at all like the tour Niko had given her: quick and quiet. Paige hadn't at all done justice to the many rooms and their magificent contents. But it had been a time in which she'd felt able to converse with her parents on a neutral topic.

Of course, no tour could compare with Niko's. Remembering it reminded Paige of the night she'd wished so hard to Millicent—the night she'd had to flee from Niko before midnight's arrival erased her fleeting taste of scintillation.

Oh, what she wouldn't give for a smidgeon of scintillation now. She just had to show Alexandra how well she was managing.

Smoothing the quilted coverlet, Alexandra gracefully turned and dipped her legs until her derriere perched on the bed, then daintily crossed her ankles. She smiled at Paige, looking at her daughter as though she expected her to utter a profound comment or two.

Paige racked her brain for something. Anything. Nothing came to mind.

"It was kind of your Prince Niko to invite us to dine tonight." Alexandra broke the silence.

"He's not *my* Prince Niko. He's my boss." Still, after that miraculous afternoon in the mountains Paige could feel a red vine of embarrassment reaching tendrils up her face. "And, yes, it was very nice of him."

"You plan to dress for dinner, of course," her mother said.

Paige looked down at herself. Her jeans had dried, but her Smithsonian T-shirt still wore dabs of mud from the shore of the pond.

She wanted in the worst way to say that this was how they always dressed for dinner. But she couldn't stay like this—not with her mother in one of her very pretty, very proper, very expensive tailored suits.

"Sure," she said.

"I'll wait right here while you change."

With a sigh, Paige reached into the closet and withdrew one of her beige blouses and her flowing black skirt. Not exactly designer style, but at least they were an improvement over work clothes.

"Surely you've brought something nicer than those." Alexandra's words were a statement. "That shapeless black skirt simply brings out the darkness of the frames of your glasses. Have you tried wearing your contact lenses recently?"

Paige quickly put the skirt and blouse back on hangers and withdrew her blue dress.

"That will have to do," Alexandra said.

Paige felt a surge of relief. Other than her ugly navy suit, this was the dressiest thing she had.


Niko sat in a burgundy leather chair in the trophy room. Why they'd wound up here, surrounded by former castle residents' elks and eland, minks and monkeys staring from the walls, he wasn't sure. He didn't know whether the lumpy chair or the limpid eyes of the animals bothered him more.

But Paige Conner's father Frank seemed right at home.

He was a tall man, thin, with few age crinkles marring his beaming narrow face. His hair was a deeper, sleeker brown than usual in a man his age. Niko wondered ungenerously if it sprouted that way from the man's own follicles or whether nature had been foiled by a bottle.

"To bring tourists to fill those hotels," Frank was saying, "you need promotion. Everywhere. The whole world." His slim fingers circled through the air in illustration. "Of the right kind, of course. Some of that sexy subliminal stuff always works well; that's how I've grown some of my biggest accounts.''

Apparently, Niko thought with only a bit of amusement, he was being pitched to become another of Frank's promotional clients.

"I'd be delighted to prepare a presentation for you," said Frank.

"I'll consider it seriously," Niko said. He already had considered it and was seriously thinking of tossing this smooth salesman out on his subliminal behind.

But the man was Paige Conner's father. After the wonderful afternoon Niko had just shared with her—marred only by that unfortunate but momentary misunderstanding—that counted a lot.

He could see how Paige's determination had developed; these two people would have nurtured it. But with these parents, how had she become so sweet and shy? Living with people like this could train anyone for the Outspoken Olympics.

Well, however she had managed to turn out the way she had, he was glad. Her only secret seemed to be a desire to find an obscure ancestor of his because of curiosity about her own forebear, not a plan to become a princess. Despite his initial, instinctive mistrust, she'd turned out to be guilt-free and guileless. He now believed that no soul of a scheming siren had taken up residence in her very lovely body.

From what Niko had gathered Paige's parents weren't planning on staying long. For her sake he would play the charming host—for a while, at least.

But he looked forward to the next time he could get Paige alone.

If only, Paige thought, Niko and she could be alone together this evening. How, with such a crowd, could she savor the memory of their mountaintop idyll that afternoon?

But he'd been kind enough to invite her parents to dine. He'd been even kinder to turn the event into a dinner party. She felt overwhelmed—and dismayed—by such kindness.

Now he sat at the head of the long wooden table in the granite-walled room where suppers were generally served. Dim lights glowed from the crossed-torch sconces along the walls. Flickering light from small, slender candles placed in several candelabra danced on the faces of the few guests who seemed too many.

Paige, happily, sat beside Niko. He looked wonderful in the loose white peasant shirt that revealed his strong neck and a glimpse of his chest.

He looked even better in nothing at all. But Paige didn't dare think about that. Not here. Not now.

To her right sat her parents. Along the other side of the table were Charlotte, Rudy, Suzanne . . . and, despite the fact that his presence galled her and should have been vetoed by Niko, Edouard.

"Tell me who you are and what you do," Alexandra was saying to Edouard in her most cajoling interviewer's tone. Paige had heard it thousands of times on TV. She'd never known anyone not to respond.

"I'm a very distant relation of Niko's," said Edouard in a silky smooth voice that suggested he enjoyed Alexandra's attention. He wore a dark suit tonight, and his tie was striped in Dargentian crimson, silver and purple. "And what I do is collect things."

Paige took a sip of a full-flavored consommé, concocted by an attentive, hovering Maibelle, that hinted of a dash of wine. What, she wondered, did Edouard mean?

Her mother wasn't shy about asking. "You must do better than that, Edouard," enticed Alexandra. "Tell us exactly what you collect." She'd freshened up before dinner, changing into a sweet little confection, as she called it, for dining at a castle—a glittering blue sequined dress that shimmered as she moved. So much for Paige's muted blue shirtwaist; it seemed to fade into the woodwork. Alexandra's hair had been rearranged so that a perfectly coiled dark curl hung down on either side of her fine-boned face.

"Little things." Edouard waved his perfectly manicured hand in the air, apparently enjoying his own obfuscation.

"Tom Thumb," blurted Rudy, blushing into his soup. "A little money, a little power, a few small people."

What a brave thing for such a bashful man to say, Paige thought, wishing he were not so far away across the table. She wanted to pat him on his bony back. As everyone looked at him, he grew ripe-tomato red above his buttoned white shirt. He tipped his head till his angelfish nose nearly touched his spoon.

"Rudy," his mother admonished mildly. But Charlotte seemed to have trouble maneuvering her upper lip over her protruding teeth as she fought a smile. Her bright orange hair stuck out in sausage curls that evening, but the gaudy yellow of her paisley print dress went quite well with the color.

Suzanne laughed aloud. Niko's beautiful blond kissing cousin had worn a black sheath that dipped way down in the front. Paige wondered how any man in the room could concentrate on his consommé. Perhaps none did.

"Touché, Rudy," Suzanne said. She turned to Edouard, who was on her right. "Any other small things he missed?"

"Hotels," Edouard said, turning his sly smile on Niko.

Why did the prince let that terrible man get away with such snideness? Paige wondered. But she knew the answer. Niko had no choice.

She found herself fingering the swan pendant they'd unearthed at Aldred's earlier that day. Why couldn't it have been the whole cache of Les Fabuleux? That would have shown Edouard.

It might even have impressed her parents.

"No," said Rudy. "Not hotels. The ball will fill them up fast."

"They can empty just as quickly," Edouard growled. Paige recalled that the terms for deferral of Niko's first loan payment required that the hotels stay filled for at least a month.

"But they won't." Suzanne's voice was as smooth as the delicious pâté Maibelle had prepared as an appetizer. "We've plenty of ideas to keep packing people in."

Paige's appetite ebbed in response to Edouard's poisonous scowl.

Niko ended the uneasy silence. "What I want to know is what brings our guests, the Conners, to our country. Beside visiting their lovely daughter, of course."

Paige could hardly miss the astonished look that passed between her parents. She quickly passed her empty bowl to the tuxedoed Aldred, who had donned the invisible hat of extra servant that night. The long parentheses at the sides of his mouth bowed out as he grinned encouragement at her.

She knew her answering expression fell short of a smile. She was surprised, though, at how hurt she felt. Why couldn't her parents accept a compliment for their plain daughter—even if merely kind, and not true?

Her father turned toward Niko first. "You guessed it, Niko.

We were dying to see how our Paige was doing here, in her first little job outside her country.''

Little job? Paige opened her mouth, but her mother beat her to taking the floor.

''We've brought a few things, you see. Paige called her brother Joe and asked for some computer gadgetry. I don't know exactly what it is, but we'd been thinking of taking a European tour anyway. Hand-carrying these things to Paige gave us the excuse we needed.''

Oh, Joe, Paige groaned inside. Why had he even mentioned her call to their parents? But she couldn't blame him, not really. Alexandra Conner was known for luring secrets from stones. Her husband Frank talked with such a highly polished tongue that other people's confidences sometimes slid right out.

A garlicky odor of tomato, fish and spice filled the otherwise candle-scented air about the table. Aldred wheeled a covered cart through the door, then began with a flourish to dish onto plates a mouth-watering concoction of pasta in a seafood sauce. Ever-dirndled Maibelle dealt the dishes swiftly onto the table.

''Maibelle is a Cordon Bleu chef,'' Paige revealed proudly to her parents.

''Really?'' asked her father. He turned with new interest to the softly blushing Maibelle. ''Have you ever thought of marketing your recipes? Maybe even your pasta sauce?''

''Oh, non, monsieur,'' Maibelle said, her hands putting on the brakes in the air. She continued in heavily accented English. ''I am so happy to be the servant of our wonderful returned prince. This is all I ever wanted.''

Paige's father looked undaunted, and Paige wanted to crawl beneath the long slats of the dark wood table. Would he really try to lure the prince's chef away with the promise of promotion? She wanted to take the delicious pasta sauce and push it into her father's handsome face.

She wouldn't, of course. Not even she would do something that gauche. Especially to her parents. They meant well. They always had.

''It was so wonderful of you to hire our Paige,'' said Alexandra, seated at Paige's right. ''I mean, we always knew she was a wonderful historian''— She uttered the word as though it defined some exotic enigma—''but for someone of your stature to recognize it—we couldn't be more proud.''

Paige couldn't have been more mortified at the comment. Still, she said nothing. Again, her parents meant well.

Despite being multiple place-settings down the table from the prince, Alexandra leaned forward and addressed Niko directly. ''Has she ever told you that her dream has always been to become a princess and live at a castle?''

Paige heard a clatter and glanced at Niko. His silver knife and fork were strewn on his plate, as though he'd thrown them there. A few spatters of tomato sauce littered the table and clung to his wineglass. Fortunately, his white peasant shirt was unstained. Had he dropped the pieces accidentally? Or had he actually tossed them?

She dared to meet his eyes. Their former darkness was nothing compared to the angry black stare he shot at her.

She shivered, even as her heart shriveled inside. He was furious. She couldn't blame him.

Her earlier humiliation was a tiny trickle contrasted with the great wave of shame that flowed over her with the force of the mountaintop waterfall. She had to explain. ''Mother,'' she said, ''that's every little girl's dream at age ten. Fairy tales seem real then.''

''But you didn't stop dreaming, love,'' continued Alexandra. ''You chattered about fairy tales long into high school. There was even some silly talk about fairy godmothers around the time you went to your junior prom.''

Paige remembered how, in her horror at what had happened that evening she'd spent with the fish-bait king of Hamilton High, she'd attempted to tell her parents why things had gone so wrong. She'd gotten no further than her first sentence before their laughter had poked pinholes into her tale, bursting it into ridiculousness all about her.

She'd quickly shut up, never mentioning it again—especially since she couldn't quite believe in Millicent herself.

''That was just a story, Mother,'' she said. ''I never meant—''

''Oh, but you were so cute,'' her father said. ''Speaking of fairy godmothers and Cinderellas and how some day you'd show us all.''

''Become a princess,'' Alexandra added.

Paige wanted to run weeping from the room. She clutched her napkin in her lap so hard, she felt her short, work-worn fingernails dig into her palms. How could she save herself from this horrible humiliation?

Niko would think her even more of a liar than he had before.

Across the table, Rudy lifted his eyes just long enough to show his sympathy. Charlotte chewed at her protruding lower lip, also, it appeared, feeling bad for Paige.

Not so Suzanne. There was a feline smile on her model-perfect face. Oh, how she seemed to relish this kick in Paige's commoner behind.

Edouard, too, doubtless derived great pleasure at seeing even someone as unimportant as Paige Conner squirm at the hint that she dreamed to aim that commoner behind throne-high. Only he dared to do such a thing.

She didn't quite hazard a look at the prince. Not again. She let her head dip forward, wishing she could disappear into the haven of her dark hair. She considered removing her glasses. Everything else would blur for her. Maybe her pain would, too.

*A joke,* came the words into her mind. Millicent!

She was the last thing Paige needed to contend with now. *Go away,* she prayed inside her head.

*But, dear, maybe you need just a touch of humor—*

*I have to be touched myself to be having this conversation with you here and now,* Paige retorted without a sound.

But she considered Millicent's unsolicited advice. Maybe she *could* treat the situation as though her teenage follies had been a festive jest on her parents. "Oh, Mother, Dad," she laughed, waving her hand in the air as though tossing the thought into insignificance. "I'd no idea I was so successful. I was teasing you back then, didn't you know?"

Her father trained his eyes on her. She'd always aspired to sharing his eyes; their glowing amber made hers seem washed out in comparison. He shook his handsome head as he regarded her with kind bewilderment.

"I only wish," he said, "that that were true. My little girl never learned how to tease."

"We took her quite seriously, in fact," Alexandra said earnestly. "Not that we knew any princes—before, I mean." She batted her eyelashes almost flirtatiously at Niko, and Paige was

195

amazed that her mother seemed unaware of his furious frown. "A friend of ours knew a British consul," she continued, "who was a peer of the Realm. He had a son about Paige's age, and we thought we had things worked out. You see, the young man was eager to date an American woman of good family. He even seemed to have marriage on his mind."

Paige wondered if the heat from her face would flame the food on her plate. She'd been twenty years old. Her parents had pushed her to marry little Lord Luffington, he of the skinny body, acned face and loud mouth, who had had a bad case of itchy fingers that he'd scratched by touching her in the most inauspicious places and at the most embarrassing of times. But never in front of her parents or his.

He'd had a sense of propriety.

He was the reason Paige had quickly backed off her original idea of a contest to choose Niko a bride. The last thing she'd wanted was to be coerced to wed so nasty a nobleman. No way would she foist such misery on her most irksome enemy, let alone a man she cared for.

"You see, Mother," she said as brightly as she could, "I mustn't have been that eager for a fairy tale to come true. I managed to avoid marrying Lord Luffington."

"Clearly you were waiting for someone better to come along, love," said Alexandra with a sugar-sweet smile and a sidelong glance at Niko.

Paige had never been so glad to see her parents' backs. Aldred had kindly offered to drive them down to D'Argent City. In the limousine, of course.

They hadn't refused. They'd convinced the manager of the more modern-looking of the two new hotels to let them stay in a finished room in the nearly completed establishment.

She'd promised to visit them there the next day, before they departed for the French Riviera. Or Monaco. They hadn't quite decided which.

In their wake, Paige felt she'd been drowned.

Now, Niko had seen her charming, sophisticated, scintillating parents. They'd inadvertently underscored just how gauche their glasses-wearing daughter was.

What had possessèd Niko to make love with her before? It had to have been Millicent after all.

Paige would have to confront her fanciful friend about it. But not until later.

For now, she had to see if she could salvage her job.

Edouard had driven Suzanne down the hill as soon as dinner had ended. Charlotte and Rudy had retreated to their quarters at the castle. As Paige had seen her parents off with Aldred, she'd noticed, from the corner of her eyes, that Niko had emerged through the outer kitchen door and was striding toward the moat.

Was he waiting for her there? Or did he just want to be alone, away from the disastrous dinner?

She had to find out.

Hoping he'd brought enough bread for her to feed the geese and swans, she hurried down the dimly lighted path behind the castle and through the gate in the stone wall. The night was cooler than those previous. Or maybe it was her own overcharged emotions that made her shiver.

He wasn't where she expected. Niko hadn't sat on their favorite stone bench.

Instead, she had to search the shadows with her squinting eyes. In a few moments she saw him, leaning on the crumbling swan statue.

She took a few tentative steps toward him. "May I join you?"

"You were joined with me plenty earlier today."

Paige felt shocked at the crudeness of his reply. "Niko, I just wanted to explain—"

He strode from the shadows till the light from a sconce shone full on his face, and she stopped her speech. There was anger in the crease between his golden brows. Unyielding flatness whitened the sensuous lips she loved to watch and had learned to taste. His beard seemed elevated, his body stiff. And she didn't dare stand in front of the flames shooting from his black, fiery eyes.

She glanced around for the geese, but even they knew enough to stay away. If only she had a gosling to hug; she needed comfort desperately.

She could understand his irritation, but why was he so rigid, so remote? So enraged?

"I think your parents did a fine job of explaining. And aren't you lucky? Here you are, with your childhood dreams within your grasp. A castle, a prince—and one with a legend haunting him to boot. He needs a commoner to marry. And you, wonder of wonders, just happen to be a commoner. Who needs a distant ancestral connection when you can plot in the present? Oh, but of course you said the last thing on your mind when you came here was to become a princess.''

"Niko, please. You don't understand—''

"I understand everything I need to.'' His laugh sounded anything but merry. "And here I thought *I* was the one seducing *you*. A poor, pitiful bookworm who hid behind her glasses, who'd never even had sex before. Or was that an act, too? If so, you're good, Cinderella. You're really good.''

Paige didn't realize she had lifted her arm. But she became aware of it suddenly as she cast her hand quickly forward.

Abruptly, she stopped it, just inches away from its intended target. She stared at it in horror, as though it belonged to someone else. Someone she didn't know at all.

She had nearly slapped Prince Nicholas of Dargentia.

She blinked at Niko as tears blurred his frozen features. She opened her mouth to apologize, but nothing came out.

Quickly, she turned and ran back toward the castle.

# Chapter Seventeen

Paige sat on the edge of the only chair in her room. She wondered vaguely if its spindly carved legs would collapse under her. She couldn't stop shuddering.

She had nearly slapped the prince.

How had such a magnificent day ended so monstrously?

"Eleanora!" The sound seemed to surround her.

With a defeated sigh, Paige dropped her head. Millicent; the crowning touch to a catastrophic time. She hadn't found the crown jewels. Then she'd made an enemy of Niko, the man whose very handsome head wore this country's crown. The man who'd made love to her so superlatively on the mountaintop.

The man she was beginning to love.

The lilac scent laced the air, nearly choking Paige. She stood and headed for the window, turning her back on her bedroom. She didn't want to see Millicent materialize.

She didn't want to see Millicent at all.

She stared out at the courtyard. Its dim electric light was enhanced by the brilliance of a full moon. The gray-green, shadow-shrouded yard was empty, thank heavens. If she glimpsed Niko now, she would probably start to cry.

From somewhere high in the sky, a tiny moonbeam flashed, hesitated, then shot by her right side. Paige gasped, stepping away from it, but it was already gone.

One more pelted on her left. Then another. In moments she was surrounded by a river of sparkling spots. They glowed from an inner light, as though filled with fire. Still, the stream flowing over her felt cool and smelled as fresh and invigorating as this afternoon's mountain clearing.

She turned to follow the path of the current. Her bedroom glowed from the glimmering pellets that swirled in a miniature Milky Way. They coalesced into a column near the post of the tester bed.

# Linda O. Johnston

Millicent.

As her petite fairy downfall took shape, Paige shook her head in resignation. "That was quite a show," she muttered as Millicent corporealized and scurried toward her. In moments she was enveloped in a surprisingly strong hug, considering its perpetrator had been nothing but formless flecks seconds before. "Was that a new trick or just something I hadn't seen before?"

"Oh, it wasn't a trick, dear. It was just a manifestation."

"Of what? Lunacy, come straight from the moon?"

"Energy. I'm so excited I can barely keep my particles together." Stepping back, tiny Millicent looked Paige up and down. Her shiny, shoe-button eyes studied Paige, as though seeing right through her. Her hot pink sweatshirt read, EXCELSIOR! "Oh, my dear," she continued, her wrinkled little hands rubbing together in glee, "I was there with you at Aldred's estate—and after. For a while." Again she stepped forward and enveloped Paige in a bear hug. Her head hardly came to Paige's chest, and Paige looked down on her close-cut cap of gold-gray hair. "You'll never know how tempted fairy godmothers can be to become voyeurs—"

Paige tried to pull away, but those small arms had an amazingly strong grip. "Millicent, how could you—"

"—but of course that's not in our mandate," the fairy godmother finished. "I have to know, though. How was it?"

Paige managed, with effort, to extricate herself and step back.

Millicent was grinning so broadly that the corners of her mouth appeared to reach for the edges of her droopy eyelids. Paige wanted to wipe that smile away. And quickly.

"How would you imagine it was?" she asked sweetly.

"Fabulous, of course. A private pool on a mountaintop. Alone with the most marvelous of monarchs. He saves you from drowning—or so he thinks. He carries you to a clearing, gently puts you down; then . . . of course, that's when I left. But wasn't it wonderful?"

"Sure. Sex was even better than I ever imagined it. We even talked about my mysterious Wenzel on the way back here."

"Eleanora, how can you sound so blasé?"

Paige walked toward the dresser and looked in the mirror. Her eyes appeared a dirty, dismal yellow, shadowed by circles. There was moisture in them, which she forced to stay there without falling. "My parents are here, did you know? But of course you did. Fairy godmothers are omniscient, aren't they?"

"Not really, dear. I can read your mind, of course, when I concentrate. And then I can think myself from one place to another, a delightful way to travel. But omniscient—"

Paige hadn't intended to invite a dissertation. She interrupted to return to her point. "We had such a pleasant dinner, my beautiful parents, the gorgeous prince and his guests, and there was me, looking ludicrous as usual." She swept her hands over her plain blue dress.

"Eleanora, you simply must stop being so hard on yourself."

Paige whirled around to face the fairy godmother who wasn't really there. But, oh, how she needed someone to be there for her now. A lump crept up her chest, lodging in her throat so she could hardly speak. "Then I'll be hard on you instead. How could you do this to me?"

"Eleanora, if you tell me what happened, maybe I could—"

"You've done enough, Millicent. You brought me here to taste heaven, then let me be kicked like a kid's football, straight to he—"

"Eleanora! Stop this now and explain." Millicent's hands were suddenly on her hips, and she wore a sterner expression on her usually sweet face than Paige had ever seen. There was sympathy in her droopy eyes now. And certainly no syrupy smile.

With a sigh, Paige sat again in the spindly-legged chair. She related as quickly as she could the way her day had begun, progressed, soared to spectacular heights, then belly-flopped—but good. "And then," she ended, "I came close to slapping him."

Millicent gasped. Her small hand flew to her mouth. "Oh, dear, how could you?"

"It was easy. He was standing right beside me as he skewered me with his sarcasm. I simply pulled back my hand, then shot it forward fast. Too bad my brain worked faster than my fingers." She wiggled them in embellishment. "Now I'll never know how it feels to deck a prince."

"Speaking of sarcasm, Eleanora." Millicent's voice was curt and chastising. "Well, we'll simply have to work around that. Though it might be difficult. Strategy—that's what we need." The abbreviated entity sank down onto the bed. As usual, she

201

made no dent in it. She wasn't there. And Paige wished she'd just leave.

Strategy, no. What she really needed was solitude, peace, a return to her own, ordinary, fairy-godmotherless life, maybe even the dusty cellars of Miller's Mine, New Mexico.

But first there was something she had to know. "Millicent, you said you were with me up in the mountains. Did you ply any magic to make Niko feel attracted to me?"

Millicent shook her head sadly. Her short, straight hair vibrated atop her scalp. "If you'd just realize the secret of fairy tales, you wouldn't ask such a thing."

"I don't know your darned secret. I've never figured it out, and I probably never will. But there's one thing I am certain of." Paige rose from the delicate chair so quickly that it toppled behind her with a clatter. She picked it up deliberately and set it back on its spindly legs. Then, she faced Millicent. "I'm through."

"But Eleanora, you need a little patience. The prince may take a bit of finessing, but he'll—"

"You don't get it. I'm through with fairy tales. Well and truly. My parents showed me, this evening, that even when you pulled that awful prank when I was in high school, I didn't really stop believing in fairy tales. How could I? I kept calling for you."

"I appreciate that, dear. But don't throw it all away; not now, when we're finally so close to realizing—"

"I'm done realizing. This is it. No more fairy tales, Millicent. No more magic. No more pixie dust and pretty clothes. No more believing I've a tiny shot at scintillating. I'm finished."

Millicent leapt from the bed so quickly that Paige saw in her the remnants of a younger being, full of life—or some force. "Please, Paige, you can't give up."

Paige, and not Eleanora? Good! Millicent was finally taking her seriously.

Paige suddenly realized she could see through her so-called fairy godmother. Not that she'd transfigured herself into her shimmering column of pixie dust; she'd simply turned transparent. Even her bright pink sweatshirt wasn't completely there.

Millicent looked down at herself. "Oh, Paige," she whispered. "You have to believe—"

But Paige slowly shook her head.

"How about some butterflies in your boudoir?" Millicent

asked brightly. She waved her small, clear hands. Immediately, a sliver of smoke rose from a lace-draped wastebasket near the carved wooden dresser. It reminded Paige of the trick Millicent had pulled in the library in front of Niko, Charlotte and Rudy. Only the smoke was thin. And it fizzled before forming into a column of moths.

Paige strode to it and looked down. In the center of the wastebasket was a single, skinny caterpillar. It arched its middle into the air, then took a few steps with several pairs of front legs, straightened—and disappeared in a puff of sweet-smelling vapor.

"I didn't really see that," said Paige. She closed her eyes. When she opened them again Millicent was moving her fingers in the air again.

"I'll show you," insisted the being who'd never been. "Cookies." She closed her little shoe-button eyes tight, then opened them again.

Paige found her own hand hanging palm up in the air. A single chocolate chip materialized in the middle. She popped it into her mouth. "I don't taste that."

"Then let's see what we can do about that dress you don't like." But Millicent's voice was faint, as though she'd wandered to the end of a long tunnel. Paige could see the bed right through her. Her hands meandered in a circle, as though in slow motion. She pointed at Paige.

Nothing happened.

Guilt niggled at the edges of Paige's mind, but she shrugged it off. How could she regret turning her back on a creature she'd always considered the creation of her own overimaginative mind?

Her attitude was harder to maintain now that others had witnessed Millicent's manifestations. But Paige had had enough of fairy tales.

"Oh, Eleanora." The sound was a soft breeze that rustled the hair around Paige's ear.

Without her usual crackle, with no scent of lilacs, Millicent faded away.

"Well, of course she has to leave." Niko stomped about his office late the next morning, slamming papers onto his desk. What a mistake it had been to bring Paige Conner to this suite a week earlier—when she'd run away right in the middle of their lovemaking, leaving him a foolish, befuddled wreck.

No wonder he'd been so eager to get her alone up on that seductive mountaintop.

His suite had seemed filled with her quiet presence ever since. Quiet? Hah! He'd never met a woman more full of life, more brimming with passion. Her fresh, baby-powder scent still seemed to hang in the air.

"Of course." Aldred sat on Niko's leather desk chair. His demeanor, calm as usual, sparked the prince's anger even further. "But I don't entirely understand the problem."

"*She's* the problem. She's supposed to research Dargentia's history, put all the juicy material in the literature to entice tourists. But *she's* the one doing the enticing." He made a fist, and the signet ring he'd worn since yesterday pressed painfully into his fingers.

Aldred rose, leaning his slight body over the desk. Niko knew the bland expression on his wrinkled face only too well. He'd seen it often ever since he was a baby. It meant Niko was about to be taught a lesson. "Oh, dear." Aldred ran a hand through his uneven shock of white hair. "If I'm getting the drift here, you mean she seduced you."

Niko didn't need a lesson. He knew how foolish he'd been. He brushed past Aldred, still pacing recklessly. "Yes." He paused. To be fair, he'd been as eager as she. Maybe more so. He sighed. "There was a sense of inevitability about it," he admitted. "The first time I met the woman she set my blood boiling." Niko didn't usually discuss his sex life with anyone, but Aldred had shared many other secrets. His counsel, even when least wanted, always helped Niko find the proper course.

Aldred smiled sagely. "That incident at the airport?"

Niko nodded. "I knew my interest was just stirred up by the adrenaline of the moment—"

"Not to mention your lying on top of her."

Niko glared. "Never mind. She's just another American impressed by a title. Her parents made that clear, even if she didn't. But it's all right; I've gotten her out of my system. She needs to go, the sooner the better."

"Of course. I'll find our list of other historians immediately so we can keep the process moving."

Niko abruptly stopped his wild pacing. They'd discussed the

list after Aldred narrowed the field to the top candidates. They'd concluded that most notable historians charged accordingly and wouldn't necessarily do a better job than the young lady with the sterling reputation for detailed research and quality writing. There weren't many other skilled—and reasonably priced—historians who'd already attained her stature.

With a sigh, he sat on the corner of his desk, tapping the toe of his laced boot on the floor as he pondered. Then, in resignation, he stamped his foot resoundingly against the wooden desk. "Don't bother. No sense punishing Dargentia for my folly. I'll stay away from her. I can't let anything interfere with my plans to save Dargentia's economy, not even my own raging hormones."

He wasn't prepared, then, for the tap on the door. It was Paige Conner. She wore a beige blouse and a dark skirt, not her usual working attire. In her hands she carried a thin sheaf of papers.

Niko decided that his suddenly increased heartbeat was a function of his fury; it had nothing to do with happiness at seeing her. The warmth he felt inside was simply his overstimulated sex drive after the time they'd spent together the day before. He had absolutely no feelings for the woman.

"I've finished the copy for the brochure, Your Highness. Here it is." She handed it to him—careful, he noticed, not to touch his hand.

He had an urge to grab her, to pull her close—at the same time as he wanted to order her out of his sight.

"Early, isn't it?" He was glad that his voice had come out in an emotionless monotone.

She did not meet his eyes but continued to look at the pages he now held. "It's due in a couple of days. I've been working on it as I've completed my preliminary research, and I believe it works well." She flushed, as though flaying herself for the compliment. "I'll be leaving with my parents today," she continued. Her amber eyes blinked dully as she raised them for just an instant to look into his. "I'll take the time without pay, of course. And I'll be back to finish Dargentia's history." He had a sense she'd more to say—but instead she pivoted quickly and hurried out the door.

He'd just got through telling Aldred all the reasons she should leave, and now she was going, at least temporarily.

But would she really return?

He had convinced himself that she had to stay for the good of the country, but he would surely be better off himself to be rid of her.

Why, then, did he feel as dismal as if his country had disappeared from beneath him?

# *Chapter Eighteen*

One afternoon, ten days later, Niko sat at his desk shuffling RSVPs for the ball. There weren't enough for a deck . . . not yet. He'd only sent out invitations a week earlier, and the replies were already pouring in—positively. Nearly every noble family in the west was sending representatives—mostly female. He was, after all, quite a commodity on the royal marriage market.

He'd quickly gotten over the fleeting fancy of marrying a commoner, no matter how highly his subjects regarded their absurd legends.

But someone also born to nobility would understand the burdens he bore. His responsibilities to his people.

He'd not be troubled with hidden motives; there'd be none in a marriage of convenience.

There'd be no passion, either. But he'd had a taste of that when Paige Conner was here, and where had it gotten him? A mind full of memories that needled him as though he'd grabbed a cactus and left his flesh full of spines, that's what. Memories of the moments he'd shared with Paige.

He had to stop thinking about her. Now.

He turned back to the RSVPs, as determined to concentrate on them as if they held the secrets of the ages. He hardly looked up when Aldred walked in.

"She's back," he told Niko, straightening his slight shoulders beneath his gray suitcoat.

"Who?" Niko felt an absurdly excited smile niggle the edges of his lips, and he quickly stanched it with a scowl.

"Don't pretend to be obtuse . . . sire." The majordomo sat in his favorite high-backed chair facing Niko's desk.

"Then don't be sarcastic, Aldred." Of course he knew whom his servant meant. "I presume," he continued coldly, "that you're speaking of your prodigal Ms. Paige."

"Well, yes," his majordomo admitted, his aging face wrinkling

207

as he frowned. "Though she's not exactly mine. *Yours* would be more like it."

"Don't be ridiculous," Niko snapped. But then he had to ask, "Where is she?"

"In her tower room, unpacking. She promised to get back to work on your history this afternoon."

Five minutes later, after Aldred had left, Niko found himself climbing the stairs to the tower. He had business to discuss with the errant Ms. Conner, he told himself. That was the only reason he was there.

He hesitated outside her door—but only for an instant. He was the prince, and this was his castle. If she didn't want to see him . . . tough!

He rapped sharply on the hard, polished wood of the door, feeling the strength of his knock punish his knuckles.

"Come in," called the sweet voice he remembered.

He turned the cool metal knob and pushed open the door.

A faint scent of baby powder hung in the air, filling Niko's senses so he wanted to inhale over and over. It reminded him of mountain air and flowing water—and a warm, willing and wonderful woman who'd—

He halted those thoughts abruptly, as though he'd crashed into a castle wall. He stared angrily about.

Paige stood by the carved wardrobe hanging some clothes. Seeing him, she stopped, holding a plain blue dress against her body like a shield. "Hello, Niko." Her voice was tentative, her expression wary, her amber eyes wide as a frightened doe's.

Well, she should be worried. Maybe he should just make her pack again, send her on her way.

But no, damn it! She'd been hired for a purpose that was only partly filled. He needed a history of his country. She was a historian, and a good one at that; he'd loved the brochure she'd written, even though she'd stressed those stupid legends.

And her idea about the contest had been inspired. Since the publicity had first gone out reservations had begun pouring in to the two new Dargentian hotels.

He needed her creativity. He needed her drive.

He stared at the soft, moist lips he'd kissed so completely more than a week earlier, now parted slightly and trembling. He needed . . . her.

No. His interest in her was purely professional. He'd just keep her around for a few more months, until she'd finished. Then he'd never have to see her again.

"You're back," he said brusquely.

She looked down at herself beneath the dress she still held. "It appears that way." She turned and hung the garment in the wardrobe. As she faced him again, he noticed that she wore the swan pendant. The small gold charm rested beneath the collar of her tailored white shirt. It didn't quite dangle down long enough on its chain to reach the valley between her breasts. Still, he wouldn't have minded resting there—

"Did you enjoy yourself?" He kept his voice gruff. The last thing he wanted was for her to think her enjoyment meant a whit to him.

"It was . . . fine. After Cannes we went to Paris. Someday I'd like to go back, by myself. My parents—" She stopped, tilting her head so her glance at him was sidelong. She seemed to think better of discussing her parents with him. "Anyway, I'm ready to get back to work." There was a quizzical note in her tone, as though she'd asked him if he still wanted her.

Of course he still wanted her . . . to work. "Fine," he said, rubbing the back of his hand over his beard. Then he blurted out, "You did a great job with the brochure. The artwork has been added, it's been printed and now it's being sent all over the world."

She smiled so brilliantly beneath those glasses of hers that he thought the sun had begun streaming through the tower window. But it was storming outside that day, as dark as the bleakness that still slithered inside him at her betrayal.

She immediately ducked her head the way she did, hiding her pride beneath a spray of her beautiful red-tinged black hair. Why did that motion make him feel so mushy inside, yet so miserable at the same time?

He shrugged the feeling off. "Just keep me informed about the progress of your history."

"Certainly, Your Highness," she said. Her voice didn't sound sarcastic. But he had a sense that she'd reduced him to the size of the small swan that hung in such a sweet, strategic place.

Yet, damn it all, he felt ridiculously relieved to have her back.

When Niko stalked from her bedroom with that autocratic stride Paige sank to her knees right where she stood beside the wardrobe.

She'd thought she could pull this off—come back, do her job, keep cool and professional.

Now she wasn't so sure.

Every molecule in her wretched body ached with longing. If only she could see in Niko's dear, dark eyes a shred of the sweetness and passion they'd shared. . . .

Foolish, foolish romantic, even after she'd flung the whole idea of fairy tales from her life.

That stung, too. It hurt to return to this room and know that there would be no Millicent to greet her.

She rose, returning to her unpacking. Her parents had insisted on buying her clothes. Fortunately, though they'd entered shops featuring designer originals, she'd come out with things more practical—skirts and blouses she would actually wear. Even though her parents shook their heads and sighed.

"But you must develop a sense of style, Paige, love," her mother had said. "Especially now that you're living in a castle."

She'd heard that many times in the past, too, though without the castle kicker. If she'd never developed a sense of style before, she was unlikely to now. And she wouldn't be living in a castle for long. But her mother meant well. "I'll try," Paige had said.

But the only sense of style she'd ever dreamed up for herself was the stuff conjured up for her by Millicent. She'd had to hand it to her former fairy godmother. When Paige had wanted to look good Millicent had had a way with her wardrobe.

Of course the only reason she would want to look good here had just stomped from her room. And he clearly didn't care whether she wore a boldly striped chartreuse shirt over puce polka-dotted pants.

But Millicent . . . Placing a hanger of new drip-dry skirts into the wardrobe, Paige sighed. Before she'd left for Paris, she had wondered if she'd done the right thing. Millicent's powers had melted before her eyes. Had she somehow destroyed the creature who'd shown her nothing but kindness?

Better to go back to trying to believe that Millicent had never existed. It hurt too much to think otherwise.

She looked around the tower bedroom. The tester bed looked

as it always had, its headboard with intricately carved flowers appearing freshly dusted. Aldred must have been busy. Its polished posts stretched toward the ceiling. Beside them, more than once, Millicent had materialized.

The colorful quilted bedspread was smooth. Paige recalled watching Millicent sit on it without making a dent.

The rare Persian rug on the floor had once been mounded with a mountain of cookies. The carved table beside the bed now held a plate with just two cookies and a glass of milk.

Thanks to ... "Millicent," Paige said aloud, testing. "I'm back. Are you here?"

Nothing. No lilacs, no voice in her head.

Of course not. The truth was, she'd always believed in Millicent. She knew it. But making a conscious decision to disbelieve was the way to keep her fairy godmother away. Millicent's magic was worthless. It hurt too much to hope otherwise. For Paige, fairy tales would never come true.

Paige plumped down on the bed, making a dent with her behind where Millicent hadn't. Maybe she shouldn't have come back. She'd seriously considered calling Aldred, telling him she'd decided to forgo further work in Dargentia to take the job in Miller's Mine, New Mexico.

Not that she imagined it was still available.

But she'd promised she'd compile Dargentia's history. She was far from done, and she'd met so many common folk whom she might help if she made her efforts count. Besides, she hadn't yet solved her own mystery about Williamsburg's John Wenzel.

She'd better work fast and efficiently here. That way, she'd be able to leave sooner. She'd have no time to miss the fairy godmother she'd decided to believe was imaginary.

Or the very real prince who wanted nothing to do with her.

The days melded into one another for Paige as swiftly as Dargentia's late spring wind turned the pages of the ancient books she read. When possible she brought her reading out to the moat during the day. That way, she had her fill of feeding the geese and swans without going out at night. She preferred to avoid the moatside company of Aldred, who watched her with a gleam in his eye that said he knew how she felt about Niko. And the last thing she wanted was to experience the moat's nighttime atmosphere of moonlight and shadowed peace. It reminded her of her visits there with Niko.

The prince maintained his distance now while managing to make it clear he was supervising his wayward employee.

She installed the computer software her parents had brought and did some exploration online. Even with access through the Internet to the archives of university libraries all over the world, she found amazingly little to add to the castle's collection of Dargentian historical materials.

Her other main source was the townsfolk she'd met. They often called her with bits of history they'd just recalled. Or they sent her to a friend, who'd had a grandmother whose great-aunt had written down some stuff that just might be of interest. And it usually was.

She became great friends with Annette and Marcel Martin, the young couple whose love for local legends was as strong as that of the older townspeople. Annette, who taught school, often had late afternoons free, and Paige would meet her, prepared to share her latest historical tidbits.

Nearly all the remodeling had been finished around town, and most of the scaffolds had been removed.

Both hotels were now open, and though their business was not yet booming, they served a mean afternoon tea in which Paige and Annette frequently indulged.

They usually chose Le Dargentian Royale, the more regal of the two. Not that the fare was substantially better, for both served equally memorable menus. Maibelle was not the only Dargentian whom Niko's family had bankrolled at the Cordon Bleu.

But Le Dargentian Royale offered one thing that L'Hotel Argentvue could not—Annette's husband Marcel as manager. When he could he joined them.

One day, nearly three weeks after Paige's return from France, she sat at a small table across from Annette and Marcel, toying with a loose thread in the embroidered linen tablecloth.

Annette looked tired. Even her short, dark curls drooped. "The end of the school year is approaching," she explained. "There is so much to do, and so little time to accomplish it."

Paige nodded. "That's something I can relate to."

"And your history of our small country—how does it progress?" Marcel's intense blue eyes focused on Paige. The short, burly man seemed to thrive on the business of opening and filling a brand-new hotel; he smiled frequently, but his gaze seldom stayed still. Interruptions were legion, but he seemed to welcome each new crisis to solve.

"Slowly," Paige answered him. "But I couldn't imagine having any more fun with a project." Unless, of course, her employer spent more time on it. Then again, she was much better off the less Niko poked his regal nose into her work. She changed the subject. "Last time I asked, you didn't quite have all the rooms and landscaping ready for the tourist onslaught. How's everything progressing?"

"Wonderfully well," Marcel said, with a smug grin on his broad face. For the next quarter hour the three conversed about the complexities of preparing a new hotel for its clientele.

A teenage waitress wearing a dirndl much like Maibelle's re-filled their tea, which was served in delicate china cups that went well with the rococo decor. The main dining room at Le Dargentian Royale was clearly designed with regaling royalty and charming tourists in mind. The chairs contained delicate wooden curves and ornate tapestried upholstery. Though they were undoubtedly reproductions, they resembled some of the finest furniture from the ages of one or another of the French kings named Louis. The place still smelled new, with the faint odor of paint and newly sawn wood hanging just below the scent of baking sweets.

As Paige buttered her second delicious, flaking scone, she spotted, from the corner of her eye, Edouard Campion entering the tearoom. Standing in the arched doorway, he swept the room with the kind of gaze with which a famished lion might observe a herd of sleeping eland.

Well, these hotels—and the prime ministership of the country—weren't going to be easily taken. Not if Paige had anything to say about it. She intended to help Niko, even if he didn't know about it.

Edouard let himself be shown to a seat near the table where Paige and the Martins sat. Good.

Her voice raised just enough that Edouard could not help but hear, she asked Marcel, "And how are your bookings? Are you filling all those wonderful completed rooms for the ball and afterward?"

"Oh, yes." Marcel's smile could not have been wider; it displayed uneven teeth more prominent on the bottom than the top. "Travel agents from all over the world call. They have seen your brochure, Mademoiselle Paige Conner. They are *désolé* that there are no longer reservations available for the week of the ball. But even a visit after, to such a charming kingdom, will be the crowning glory of their clients' vacations. Especially because everyone wants to participate in the contest to help the prince choose his princess."

That troubled Paige—just because she worried about misunderstandings, she assured herself. Niko's selecting a princess to marry no longer had the power to pierce her heart. Keeping her voice more modulated, she asked, "They do understand, don't they, that the contest is simply a drawing, and the entrants are those who vote for Niko's selection?"

"But of course," Annette replied. "Yet I hear our people passing the word that our prince loves his country well enough that he will consider choosing the lovely lady who gets the most votes. Even a commoner."

"But—"

"That just might be true, mademoiselle," said Marcel. "And even if it is not, the idea of pretending to choose and perhaps being selected as one of the wedding party holds great appeal. It most certainly is filling up my hotel, and even my rival's down the street."

"Besides," Annette continued, "your brochure has attracted guests for many more reasons. Travelers must see the place where such wonderful legends come from. And an opportunity to meet a storybook prince who has freed his country, but must now choose between tradition and today's values—we are told they simply cannot stop talking about it."

And neither, apparently, could Marcel and Annette. They remained steadfastly certain that Niko would make the right choice: a commoner bride, just as the legend recounted in Paige's wonderfully written brochure required.

Their praise made Paige glow with vicarious pride. She hadn't made up the legends; she'd just told about them simply, succinctly and in fairy-tale style.

She'd been good, once upon a time, at making up fairy tales.

Glancing sideways at Edouard, Paige raised her voice once

more. "Then you believe both hotels will be filled for the ball and at least a month after?"

"Absolutely," stated Marcel.

It was all Paige could do to keep her expression bland as she glimpsed the silver fox's glower and met his ugly gaze. She gave a small wave of her fingers, as though noticing him for the first time.

Though she stayed busy every day, Paige felt she'd barely skimmed the surface of Dargentia's history. Untold treasures had to be hidden within the boxes she'd barely touched—including the secret of Leticia Adamson's Wenzel.

But her progress was delightfully delayed nearly daily. Current-day Dargentians from places more distant than the capital cropped up in conversations with the Martins and others, each reputed to have more fascinating historical facts to impart to her.

She wished she could leave the country before the blasted ball. But that was just another wish that couldn't come true, not if she intended to fulfill her obligations here. And to have a final shot, perhaps, at finding Les Fabuleux in time to help Niko save Dargentia. No matter what might happen to her psyche in response, she was not one to renege on responsibilities. Plus, she enjoyed her historical sleuthing.

And if she tortured herself by being around to watch the ball and Niko's wooing of his princess—well, she'd survive.

She was proud that she'd finally learned her way around the castle. No longer did she usually head down the wrong hallway, though her improved sense of familiarity didn't keep her, sometimes, from feeling lost.

Her morning work in the library, when she wasn't at the moat, was still a quiet interlude. Though she worked quickly, she was glad for the respite from the rush of finishing the brochure.

Ever the admirable employer, the prince stopped in the library each morning to inquire about her progress. Paige's pulse always quickened, but she kept her happiness to see him tightly in check.

Others dropped into the library, too. Charlotte visited at least once a day, often with Rudy.

Occasionally, Suzanne would make her presence known. She was always quick to put Paige in her place. "Your dear little brochure is so quaint," she said one morning. "All our royal

215

guests with whom I've been chatting about accommodations mention it. A contest for the tourists to let them think they're helping to choose a princess—well, everyone just thinks that's the sweetest thing.'' But the sour expression on Suzanne's lovely face made it clear just what she thought of the idea—and Paige.

Edouard seemed never to visit the castle these days, and that was just fine with Paige.

Life was chaotic outside the haven of the library. When Paige left for lunch or an expedition to D'Argent City, she had to be careful not to trip over the ladders, buckets and sponges of the eager cleaning crews swarming the castle. Bedrooms all over the place were being refurbished for royal guests.

Afternoons, when she visited with the Martins, she began to note strangers strolling the streets, dressed not in the flowered dresses and colorful shirts denoting Dargentians but in everything from business suits to blue jeans.

The tourist influx had begun.

# Chapter Nineteen

A week before the ball, Paige immersed herself in one of the boxes containing the earliest household accounts from even before the time of Nicholas I. The steward at that time had been meticulous. Every franc to purchase flour or stable fodder was accounted for.

There were even mentions of the king's acquisitions of some spectacular-sounding jewels: a diamond and ruby tiara for the then queen; a magnificent choker set with any number of precious stones.

Paige looked down at her lonely gold swan pendant. Not exactly the same quality. No, this necklace could not have been part of Les Fabuleux. Poor Monsieur Pelerin's family had been passing a simple, though stunning, signet ring from one generation to the next for all those years, with not a clue to the lost jewels that Niko needed so badly to save his country.

The only clue she had was still Aldred's recitation. She'd had him repeat it one day as she studied Niko's ring—hand-carried to the library by the majordomo—but to no avail. No brainstorm sent a solution thundering through her mind.

Now, as she had so often over the last weeks, she went over in her head the strange words from the past. Something about Nicholas I's family having to flee while protective spirits remained. Fascinating, but what did it mean?

She hadn't a clue.

She lost herself again in the accounts for more than an hour, till a sound interrupted her. She looked up. Niko stood in the doorway, watching her. She couldn't interpret the expression on his face. If she hadn't known better, she'd have thought he looked lost, regretful.

He walked into the room, clearing his throat. "So, Paige, is everything all right?"

"Fine. Wonderful, in fact." Pushing her glasses up on the

# Linda O. Johnston

bridge of her nose, she paused, struggling for a snappy comment. She settled on, "How are your plans for the ball progressing?"

"Quite well, thanks." He sat on a carved wooden chair beside her. "Most of the responses have been returned, and almost all are affirmative. That's just our royal invitees, of course."

"I see the manager of Le Dargentian Royale and his wife frequently," Paige said. "Tourist reservations are booked there, and in the Argentvue, for weeks."

"So I've been told." He leaned toward her, so close that her fingers yearned to touch the soft bristles of his fabulous beard. She folded her hands on the crackling pages in her lap. "Our success is largely," he continued, "because of your storybook brochure and its contest."

Wishing for the millionth time that she didn't blush, Paige looked down at those suddenly enthralling papers in her lap. "Suzanne has a lot to do with it." She was careful not to let herself choke on the words. "She's known how to publicize the ball and contest." Paige still thought Niko—and Dargentia—might be best off if he heeded the legend and married a commoner. Though she didn't like Suzanne personally, practically she would be perfect.

"Yes, she's a skilled travel agent." He paused, but Paige couldn't quite look at him. His voice, when he spoke again, sounded strained. "And you, Paige . . . who will you vote for at the ball?"

She drew in her breath. She held it while her mind searched for something to say. "I'll leave that to the tourists. Employees of whoever's holding a contest can't enter anyway. That's only fair." Another inspiration struck her. "And as an employee, I'll be too busy helping Maibelle and the rest to be at the ball."

"But you're not to come as a servant." His voice sounded irrationally outraged, and she hazarded a glance at him.

Sitting stiffly, he faced her, his brows raised in incredulity. His hands clutched the arms of the chair. She could no longer bear to look at the jewel-encrusted ring while he wore it. It caused recollections that were still too raw of their marvelous mountaintop idyll.

When she said nothing he continued, "You, of all people, know the ball isn't just for royalty. Tourists will be there, picking their entries for my perfect bride. Citizens of Dargentia will be

218

there, too, and only some will act as servants. You must come—
and not as hired help, or to watch from the balcony like the
visitors, but as an invited guest.''

She couldn't explain her rationale: She didn't aspire to the agony of watching him dance with one scintillating princess after
another. Or, worse, zeroing in on the love of his life. Being on
the balcony would be as bad as being on the ballroom floor, and
she intended to avoid both. ''I'm here to do a job; that's all.''

He stood and pushed back his chair along the Oriental area rug.
He took a step toward her, one strong hand out, as though reaching for her. ''Paige, I never meant to hurt you.'' His voice was
low and uneven.

Feeling disadvantaged as she looked up from her seat, she, too,
stood, put down the papers she held and took a step away from
him. She held her head high, shoving her hands behind her
back—for they just might develop a will of their own and stretch
toward him. The aching inside was nearly unbearable. She had to
stop any sweetness between them or she'd never be able to slide
back inside her hard-won shell.

She lied with bold bluntness. ''Our little interlude near Aldred's
estate has nothing to do with this. It was a great romp; that's all.
I've just no interest in the ball.''

He flinched as she spoke. His fine lips stiffened, and his chin
raised in an imperious gesture she now knew well. ''And if I
order you to come?''

She smiled sadly. ''I've said before, I'm your employee, not
your subject. You can fire me, but otherwise you can't tell me
what to do.'' She quickly changed the subject, again lifting some
paperwork from the desk. ''Would you like me to show you the
accounts I've been working on?''

''No, thank you.'' His voice was icy. ''I have to prepare for a
D'Argent City Council meeting. We're discussing the accommodations for the ball.'' He turned and walked stiffly away. She
knew his stride, all strength and power. Usually she enjoyed just
watching him. This time, it hurt.

She turned back to her work before he reached the door.

''Paige?'' His soft voice startled her.

''Yes?''

He seemed to hesitate. ''You have all the resources you need
for your research, don't you?'' His tone was stronger, but she had

# Linda O. Johnston

a sense he'd wanted to say something else.

"Oh, yes," she said.

"You'll tell me if you need anything, won't you?"

I need *you,* she thought. She replied, "Of course."

He stood for another moment, as though there was something else he wanted to ask. Then he was gone.

Quickly, Paige turned to the box of materials she had been sorting. She wanted to lose herself in it.

But among the household accounts kept long before Nicholas I's father was on the throne, Paige kept seeing the coffee-dark eyes of Nicholas II.

The next day, Paige went through, once again, the contents of that box of early material. She'd gone through it three times so far: once in a wild, fascinated spree to see what was there, the second time to catalog its contents, and now to study it thoroughly.

The material had been absorbing, full of references to foodstuffs she'd never heard of and idiomatic expressions she didn't understand. She'd log onto the Internet one day to ask if anyone could explain them.

Life in the sixteenth century hadn't been easy.

Salaries had been paid to an army larger than the entire population of Dargentia today. Arms had been purchased. Battles fought and won.

But she knew what she'd find when she studied a later box chronologically. Despite the knowledge and strength inherited from his forefathers, King Nicholas I had not been strong enough to keep his kingdom.

Unlike his descendant, Nicholas II, Paige thought. As long as she had anything to say about it.

She laughed at herself. Who was she to say anything about how a prince could hold on to a kingdom? Especially one as headstrong and self-sufficient as Niko.

Shaking her head at her own temerity, she hefted the next box onto the table. It was the one containing the most recent materials. Standard research procedure dictated that she immerse herself next into the second oldest box, but she'd an unslaked curiosity about Niko's more immediate relations. And she meant to satisfy it.

220

For the history she was writing, of course. Her interest was strictly professional.

She was so engrossed in a stack of correspondence that she gasped and half rose when she heard a noise behind her.

Charlotte leaned over her shoulder. She stepped back, tossing up her hands apologetically. "Sorry, Paige. I didn't mean to starling you." She wore a saffron-colored dress that went well with her orange hair but left her skin sallow. She wore no lipstick, but her severe overbite still dominated her features.

"Startle me? That's okay. I was reading about you, in fact."

*"Moi?"*

"Niko's father Lucien apparently saved all the letters he received from his brother Wenzel—your husband, right?"

Charlotte nodded, setting her hair bobbing about her shoulders. "Dear Wenzel had such a sense of . . . how you say, propellor?"

Holding back a giggle, Paige grasped for a translation. "A sense of . . . pride?" Charlotte shook her head. "Progress?" Again a negative response. Words careened through Paige's head: pretentiousness; profanity; primroses; prestidigitation. With Charlotte's growing frustration, Paige felt under immense pressure. And then it dawned on her. "Oh, yes! He had a sense of propriety."

*"Oui."* Charlotte smiled and nodded, bouncing her orange curls like a fraying ball of yarn. "He wanted to make sure Lucien knew all that happened here."

"Lucien was the crown prince, wasn't he?"

"Yes. My husband was holder in trust of the crown. He was born just after *La Guerre*—World War II."

"Those had to be hard times here."

"Oh, *certainement*. Dargentia, like the rest of France, was occupied. When the war was over all hoped Dargentia would be freed, like the other allies. But that did not happen." Charlotte looked away, as though overwhelmed with emotion. "Enough of bad memories. *Maintenant,* tell me what you have been reading."

"Your husband was a wonderful correspondent. I've especially enjoyed the letters telling of your marriage and your sister Liliane's marriage to Edouard Campion." Paige hesitated, wanting to ask all sorts of questions about the marriage and Edouard's attitudes back then. She settled on something more innocuous. "That's Edouard's connection with the family, then? He's not really so distant. He's your brother-in-law.''

Charlotte nodded, then settled down into one of the carved wooden chairs across from Paige with a sorrowful sigh. ''I believe Liliane truly loved Edouard. They seemed so happy. But then my poor sister died while giving birth.''

''The child . . . ?'' Paige was hesitant to ask.

Tears welled in Charlotte's pale, wistful eyes. ''A beautiful boy, but he did not live.'' She hesitated, then continued, ''Edouard's way of grieving was not like mine; he kept it to himself. He tried to stay one of the family, though. But the knot was untried—''

Paige translated this as *untied.*

''—and neither Lucien nor Wenzel recognized it. That, perhaps, is why Edouard wishes so to obtain power, even if he must buy it. He is not the kind to forget a slight, even if not intended so.''

''I see,'' Paige said, drawing out the words. There was more to this than a rich banker wanting security for his loan, an ambitious commoner weaseling his way into power. There was ego involved here. And from what she could guess, Edouard had enough ego to fill the Argent River valleys carved between the tall Dargentian mountains, and then some.

Then there was Niko's own ego to consider. What a clashing of titans, Paige thought: the egotism of a silver fox pitted against the pride of the Dargentian lion.

Fortunately, Niko, the future king, had the upper hand in this beastly situation. And he was besting Edouard fairly, thanks to the ball, the contest, the already burgeoning invasion of tourists. But would Edouard accept the inevitable?

''I'm not sure how far Edouard might go to protect his interests,'' Paige mused aloud.

''How far? Oh, he travels all over the world in his business.'' Charlotte spoke with all seriousness.

''No,'' Paige said. ''I meant to ask whether you think he's ruthless.''

''Ruth-less? Ah, *non.* My *pauvre* sister's name was Liliane.''

Paige decided to carry the quickly deteriorating conversation no further. Until shown the fox's tail had been clipped for good, she'd have to assume Edouard would do his darnedest to thwart Niko's intention to remain the only king of this jungle.

# The Glass Slipper

* * *

The next day Paige faced the library with relish and anticipation, as was always the case when she dug into research.

In less than an hour of work she was rewarded by a discovery that got her heart pumping in thrilled tumult. But the excitement ended much too quickly, in a heartbreaking fizzle.

She started that morning by re-examining the box with the second oldest information. It contained papers in which she'd read about the many Wenzels alive in Leticia Adamson's era. As with the first box, this time, instead of cataloguing quickly, Paige took her time reading the data carefully.

And then—there they were! Several letters from the time she sought, hidden in some brittle, folded pages. The papers she held could be correspondence to and from the right Wenzel!

This one was Nicholas I's son, the one she'd already zeroed in on as the best candidate for her quest, and he'd run off to America. Just around the right time, too.

His brother Stephan had written to him in stark prose about European politics, alliances, births and deaths. The tone of Wenzel's replies was rosier. Life in America agreed with him. Stephan was in Scotland. Wenzel was in Virginia. Both were in exile.

But as Paige read further, she found, with a sorrowful feeling of bursting balloons, that this Wenzel was not the right one. Nicholas I's son Wenzel had married a woman named Martha. They had lived in Colonial Jamestown, not Williamsburg, and Martha was not the social celebrity that Paige's Leticia was before her first marriage. In fact, she sounded dowdy.

Paige identified with her, poor woman.

And Paige's mystery still remained unsolved. Who was *her* Wenzel?

Reading on to ease her disappointment, Paige soon found that the papers in the bottom of this carton captivated her. No, shocked her—especially compared with the quaint, meticulous detail of the other materials.

She was reading them when Niko walked in.

"How are things going today, Paige?" he asked in his commanding voice. She looked up, lost in the past, almost not seeing him.

"Things . . ." She stopped, gathering her senses. "You have

223

to see this.'' She tendered the papers she held, only to hesitate. ''Maybe not.''

His golden brows slanted in a frown, and he held out his strong hands.

Swallowing, Paige relinquished her hold, then watched the play of emotions on Niko's face as he read.

These chaotic, crumbling papers described the horrors of the downfall of the Dargentian monarchy.

Paige would confirm events and dates independently. The borders of France changed frequently in the mid-1600s, and the ownership of the areas known as Alsace and Lorraine remained unsettled. The tiny country of Dargentia bordered both—till the French King Louis XIV decided Dargentia had some strategic value and stormed through it.

Letters from terrified royal family members apologized to their king for fleeing their homes. Royal proclamations of King Nicholas I must have fallen on deaf ears; the citizenry hadn't remained calm when their world shattered about them.

That had to be when the Aldred of that time hid Les Fabuleux and created his incomprehensible riddle. But Paige found no reference to them in these papers.

She watched while Niko paled as he read, holding pages in the hand that wore that memory-provoking signet ring. It, too, had been a relic of that time, passed down through generations of Pelerins. She put the papers she still held on the table, then slipped around, carefully avoiding open boxes on the floor, to pull out a carved wooden chair. With a grateful nod, Niko sat, immediately burying himself in the pages in his hand.

Eventually he looked up. His lips were set into a grim line between his tawny mustache and beard. ''Those times were . . . I can't even find words to express the horror my people—all of them—must have endured.''

Paige knew he meant more than his own royal ancestors. He felt as deeply for his subjects. And that made her feel even more deeply for him.

No. She reminded herself, as she did so often, that she was simply his employee, and not a particularly favored one at that.

''It was horrible,'' she agreed. ''But it was so long ago. You're making up for it now by bringing your country back to freedom.''

The glance he shot her with those dashing dark eyes was full of gratitude. But he just shrugged his thick shoulders beneath his American-style sport shirt. His sleeves were rolled to the elbows, revealing strong, sinewy, sexy forearms that made Paige swallow hard. "For now, at least. But who knows if I can keep it that way?" He stood and walked around the table to glance into the boxes surrounding her. "I don't suppose you've found any other references to Les Fabuleux, have you?"

She sighed. "You'd be the first to know."

"Of course."

But the question made her feel as though she were shirking her duty.

Sure, her job had been to prepare a history. She was doing that. But as a historian, surely she could locate the jewels missing from long ago, in a historic era.

If she succeeded, Niko could keep his kingdom; their wealth, and the legend surrounding them, would let him do that.

If she failed . . . who knew?

"I'll keep trying," she promised, organizing a couple of the piles on the library table. At least she could look efficient.

"I know you will." The warmth in his tone made her look up, startled. He was watching her. There was an expression on his face that she didn't want to try to interpret.

It looked . . . like the yearning she'd once thought she'd seen there.

But it had to be imaginary. Just as she'd made herself believe Millicent was.

Then why did it feel so familiar—and so good—to imagine it once again?

# Chapter Twenty

Paige didn't stay at the castle for lunch that day. She was too wrought up about the morning's discoveries: the tantalizing possibility that she'd proven who was the right Wenzel; her disappointment at finding she was wrong; the horrors of reading about the overthrow of Dargentia's early King Nicholas; her frustration at her failure to unearth clues about Les Fabuleux at the time of their disappearance.

Most unnerving of all was her visit from Niko.

She arrived in D'Argent City too early to meet Annette Martin; the classes she taught weren't over till late afternoon.

But Paige had another thought. She parked the Fiat along a side street and headed for Monsieur Pelerin's shop.

"Prince Niko sent me," she began when the big bear of a man lumbered from his work area to the glass counter. He again wore a bright red shirt and colorful suspenders. "Because of the history he hired me to research, he wanted to know if any of your ancestors left written materials about their times. I'll be asking other Dargentian citizens the same question," she quickly added.

She would, too. Though she'd been collecting spoken stories from them, she hadn't actually asked if they had any old papers she could sift through. But the idea seemed a logical one.

Most particularly, she wanted something—anything—from Pelerin. His ancestors, like Aldred's, had left behind a clue to future generations of where to find Les Fabuleux.

But the large man slowly shook his head, causing the folds of fat beneath his chin to ripple. "I am sorry, mademoiselle, but I have given to the prince the ring. That is all I have from the past."

"Did Niko tell you that it wasn't a clue, after all, to finding Les Fabuleux?"

He stuck out his lower lip belligerently, as though Paige had insulted him. "I did as my ancestors bade. And if they said it

226

was a clue, then, mademoiselle, it was a clue.''

He turned his back. She heard some clinking noises as he bus-ied himself with work on the table behind the counter.

Feeling dismissed, Paige departed.

Standing on the summer-hot sidewalk outside the jewelry shop, she sighed. What could she do now to find Les Fabuleux for Niko? Inside her head, she recited, like a mantra, what she re-called of Aldred's riddle: Nicholas I and his family fleeing; spirits in jeopardy.

As usual, it made no sense.

Passing the bank next door, she peered into the window. The place appeared busy; patrons formed long lines. She looked about for one familiar but repugnant face but failed to see Edouard.

Still too early to meet Annette, she decided to visit one place she'd meant to return to ever since Niko had shown it to her: Dargentia's capitol building. Surely if there were any archives of the country, they'd be housed there.

The heat of the early summer afternoon had grown so damp and thick that Paige considered carving it out of her way with a trowel. Fortunately, the small domed capitol was only a couple of streets away. Unfortunately, she found, as she scaled the front steps and slipped inside, that it wasn't air conditioned.

The marble-floored gallery was nearly empty, so Paige trudged upstairs, where offices hugged the periphery of the balconied sec-ond floor. The first rooms she peered into were empty, but the third was occupied by someone with the information Paige sought. A pleasant older lady with rosy, chipmunk cheeks and an odd, troutlike smile showed her to a small room with a large microfilm reader. It was lined with cabinets with small drawers. Apparently Dargentia maintained its archives in a modern fashion.

Paige spent the next hour poring through newspapers com-pacted onto microfiche. None, however, was particularly old, and most were copies of French regional newspapers that said little about Dargentia alone.

Still, Paige found a few pages worth keeping, and she paid the lady for machine copies. Then she was ready to meet Annette.

As she left the microfilm room, though, she stopped. From the balcony she could see Edouard Campion on the marble floor be-low, beneath the circular rotunda. He wasn't alone. In fact, there were quite a few people with him, including Monsieur Pelerin, the Le Blanc brothers and others Paige had met while doing her research.

The acoustics in the old building weren't the best, and Paige heard an echoing sibilance as Edouard spoke. She couldn't quite make out what he said, but she didn't particularly like the way those with him grumbled and nodded at almost every word.

She decided to enhance her eavesdropping by going downstairs, but by the time she arrived the crowd had moved on. Perhaps Edouard worried that it was easy for people to hear what he said.

Or perhaps Paige was the only paranoid one around here. Maybe Edouard was giving a simple lecture to some of his banking clients.

She learned a little later, though, that her paranoia had merit. While she was having tea with Annette, Marcel came in and sat with them. His normally round face looked asymmetric as his brows bent into stormy slashes. "I was just speaking with some of my neighbors, mademoiselle," he said in a voice so low that Paige could hardly hear him over the usual happily clinking and conversing teatime sounds. She bent toward him.

"You must warn Prince Niko," he continued. "If he selects a princess to court at the ball, the townsfolk will be upset. They believe in our legends, you see."

"Oh, Marcel," Annette said, shaking her head so her soft, dark curls bobbed about her. "I have heard this kind of talk before, but—"

"Hush," her husband interrupted. "I know it was all talk before, but today . . . We must all take it seriously, particularly the prince." He leaned closer, but only for an instant, while he whispered, "If the prince ignores the legends, there will be trouble the night of the ball." He straightened, then said loudly enough for the patrons around them to hear, "Now that's a brand-new tea you are sampling, mademoiselle. Secret blending. You tell me what you think of it."

Keeping her voice evenly modulated, Paige asked, "Does this have anything to do with Edouard's little convocation of townspeople earlier this afternoon?"

Marcel shrugged his beefy shoulders. "You did not hear that from me, mademoiselle." But he didn't deny it.

* * *

228

*The Glass Slipper*

A short while later Paige knocked on the door of Niko's suite. Maibelle had told her where to find him.

Aldred opened the door a crack, sticking his head with its untamed hair outside. "Can you wait until dinnertime, Paige? Niko is busy."

"It's important," she insisted.

The slight servant, in his usual stiff suit, stepped aside.

Hesitating only an instant, Paige entered. She wouldn't let the bittersweet memory of what she'd almost shared here with Niko—the night her ephemeral scintillation had turned her into a tease—interfere with warning him.

He sat at his desk, frowning at his computer. As Aldred and she came closer, he glanced up, not seeming particularly pleased at the interruption. "Yes?"

Paige stood by the desk, trying not to flinch at the irritated look in his dark eyes. He wore one of his peasant shirts, with laces at the neck. He hadn't bothered to tie them completely, and an expanse of chest was visible, complete with a thatch of tawny hair. Paige made it a point to look at his face. "Niko, I was just in D'Argent City. There's something strange going on there."

She went on to relate her noticing Edouard surrounded by a crowd at the capitol, followed by the warning from Marcel, whom she left anonymous. "What I was told is that some townspeople are willing to go to great lengths to make sure you listen to their legends."

"Thank you," he said when she was through. He turned back to his computer.

"Your life may be in danger at the ball." Paige felt her frustration reach inside her chest to squeeze. Surely he hadn't missed the point of her warning. She looked at Aldred pleadingly. The servant merely shrugged his shoulders.

"Not me personally, Ms. Conner." Niko's voice was irritatingly calm. "Whatever Edouard is pulling he wouldn't hurt me physically, just where it really hurts: in my country's coffers and my throne room."

Wasn't that worry enough? But Paige preferred reassurance now to I-told-you-so's when it was too late. And she was already convinced that snide, power-hungry Edouard would stop at nothing to satisfy his avid appetite—no matter in what manner someone else got hurt.

"Maybe you should talk to Edouard; make certain," she said to Niko.

"Forget that." He rose. "Edouard would tell his cohorts he has me nervous." He glowered at Paige. "The last thing I'll need, if I'm to rule this country, is to suggest I'd back down at the slightest threat to my throne."

"Or to suggest that Dargentia's future king is less than a big, brave, macho hero," Paige blurted out.

An ominous gleam glittered in Niko's narrowed eyes. He was furious and he had a right to be. She shouldn't speak that way to any man, let alone a prince. Especially one who *was* a brave and macho hero. He'd freed his country. He'd thrown himself in front of a runaway forklift to save her. She bit her lower lip. Should she apologize?

Before she could decide, his rigid shoulders relaxed. Amazingly, he smiled, those strikingly sensual lips curving up at the edges. "You're right, Paige. Dargentia's future king wants to pretend he's above the fears of ordinary men. But with you to remind me, I can't help but recall my mortality. Still, I've got to consider my country, not just my own feelings. I'll be careful about Edouard, believe me."

She didn't believe him, but what could she do? With a last pleading glance at Aldred, she left.

"What do you think?" Niko paced after Paige was gone. He barely skirted Aldred, who stood turning to and fro to watch him. He was more than a little irritated.

Aldred's cultured voice kept its characteristic calm. "Some of your subjects cared enough to warn you, Niko. I believe you should take some precautions when it comes to Edouard."

"Of course—within reason. I won't do anything obvious, though. Image is too important both to my subjects and to tourists. But that's not what I meant."

Aldred crossed Niko's path carefully. He lowered his small frame with prim slowness into an antique chair across from the desk. "What did you mean, Your Highness?"

Niko turned toward him. "I recognize that tone, Aldred, my friend. I'm in trouble when you call me 'Your Highness.' Tell me what you really think."

"About that young woman?"

Drat Aldred! He was being obtuse, and that wasn't like him. "No, blast it! She's just here on a short assignment. You don't have to think anything about her."

"But you do." Aldred's gaze, through sparkling blue eyes, was shrewd. Niko pursed his lips. During his childhood, Aldred's eyes had sometimes been more instructional than his lectures. They'd glowed when Aldred was proud of his charge, glowered when displeased. And always they seemed to see right into Niko's head.

As they did this time—not that he would admit his attraction to Paige Conner. Not to Aldred.

And certainly not to himself.

"Aldred," he said with utmost patience, "here's what I want your opinion about: Am I doing the right thing? I'm about to hold the most important social function of my life. It'll affect my future. Dargentia's future. I want to tie my kingdom to another of the world's old ruling families. That's how my ancestors kept this kingdom going, before the French interfered. The right future queen will bring tourists. Tourists mean money. Right?"

"Yes, Your Highness." Aldred inclined his head. "The ball is a fine idea, if I do say so myself."

"I hear a 'but' in your voice. Edouard's manipulations aside, you don't really buy that legend, do you, that dictates I must marry a commoner?" Niko strode to where Aldred sat and stared down. He trusted this wily old man, but things were moving fast. He couldn't afford to slow down to accommodate Aldred's serene style.

The majordomo rose. The top of his head came only to Niko's nose, but his bearing was as regal as if he were the one descended from kings. He stared steadily at the prince, his hair wild about his head, like a salt-and-pepper bird's nest. "Niko, my dear young man, a ball is a wonderful idea. I hope you find your fairy-tale princess, with whom you and Dargentia can live happily ever after. But though the reasons for following fairy tales sometimes get lost, others may arise to take their place."

"What do you mean?"

Aldred did not answer directly. "There are other kinds of fairy tales, you know," he went on.

"Aldred, you're being obtuse, and—"

The majordomo did not stop talking. "For every Sleeping Beauty story, there's a Cinderella. And then there's the Frog

231

Prince to consider. Or Beauty and the Beast.''

Niko wanted to whack his mentor for being so annoyingly whimsical. Irritably, he rubbed his beard with the back of his hand. "Let's not forget the Goose Girl," he growled. "Or the Little Mermaid. Or the one where the dancing princesses wear out their shoes at night.''

Aldred's creased brow smoothed as he smiled. "Good boy. At least your mind is expanding.''

Paige's mind spun as she hurried down the stairs toward the library. Darn Niko and his stubbornness!

She might as well not have told him about the townsfolks' unrest, fomented by his enemy Edouard. He'd ignore them and hold his stupid ball anyway, without taking Edouard seriously.

In the library she opened a new file on her computer and began making some notes of who she'd seen with Edouard that afternoon: Pelerin, the Le Blancs and the others she recognized. She didn't want to state, in writing, that she'd been warned by Marcel; if these notes got out, her friends the Martins could be in trouble.

She'd warned Niko. She'd continue looking for his damned, elusive jewels—if they even still existed.

What could she do now to save him despite himself?

Only one thought came to her mind.

Nah; it was ridiculous.

Still, she ran upstairs to her bedroom.

"Millicent," she whispered. But of course the room was empty. It had been since the day she'd made her imaginary fairy godmother disappear.

Did she believe in her now?

She didn't dare. Not when she'd finally accepted, without pain, that fairy tales didn't come true. At least not for her.

But oh, how she missed her fairy godmother.

# *Chapter Twenty-one*

The day of the ball seemed to Paige to be nearing much too quickly—more like the approach of a careening cannonball than a dance. She worried more each day.

Niko, of course, did nothing to dispel that worry. She still saw little of him, except for his usual morning meddling into her research and aloof discussions at dinner. She'd gotten good at squeezing her joy at seeing him into a wad kept confined deep inside—like blown bubble gum, always threatening to pop right in her face. Still, she made no sign to him that she felt like sighing each time he trained those dear, dark eyes on her coolly, as though their intimacy had never happened. And if she thought, now and then, that his gaze was warmer than that, she quickly chalked it up to still not quite having her imagination as controlled as she did her emotions.

Suzanne was now staying at the castle to help with ball plans and royal accommodations. To Paige's chagrin, Edouard had moved in, too, to make his mansion available to visiting aristocrats.

She was surprised, given his distaste for the ball, that the silver fox had agreed to such a noble sacrifice. Perhaps his presence here was for the best; that way, Niko could keep an eye on him—if he allowed himself to believe that Edouard actually was inciting upset Dargentians.

In the meantime, though, Edouard could keep his eyes open, too, and see just what preparations were being made for the ball. As far as Paige could tell, he'd made no move to meddle with them. And there was poetic justice in Edouard's accommodations in the castle; the room he'd been assigned was small, unsuitable for a royal visitor.

Perhaps, though, instead of putting Edouard in his place, such a slight only served to make him aspire to unattainable heights all the more.

# Linda O. Johnston

She had dropped a hint to Charlotte and Rudy about the rumors rampant in town. "Zorro! News about our dear relation's subversive activities has come to us through any number of sources," Rudy had replied, his sail-like nose averted even after his eyes actually glanced for a moment into hers. "But thank you, Paige, for telling us, too."

She'd also taken Aldred aside. The man was clearly worried about the stubborn royal ostrich who was his charge. "Niko has always been inclined to do things his own way, no matter what the consequences. That steadfast determination helped him win his country's freedom."

"It may also help him lose it again if he doesn't pay attention to the way his subjects feel," Paige retorted, realizing she preached to the very vocal choir. She'd heard how Aldred unabashedly sassed his boss when he felt Niko needed a lesson. Now poor Aldred looked mighty upset, the parenthetical grooves beside his frowning mouth deeper than she'd ever seen them.

Despite all the excitement swirling about her, Paige was determined to follow routine as much as possible. Still, on the afternoon two days before the ball she returned early from town. She had seen Annette and Marcel Martin again. The news from D'Argent City wasn't good.

She found the prince by the moat. Clad in his muscle-magnifying peasant garb, he perched on a bench looking pensively over the breeze-swept water. His thumb and forefinger stroked the edges of his beard.

Paige recalled prior visits to the moat with Niko. She touched her lips, then dropped her hands to her sides.

The prince seemed lost in thought. Was he nervous about the ball that would change his future in two nights' time? He'd be blessed—or burdened—with a bride. She sighed. There was no joy in that for her.

She wondered why he wasn't bustling about in preparation like the staff. Or maybe the staff's bustling was why he had a moment to muse.

"Niko," she said softly, to avoid startling him.

He turned toward her. His coffee-dark eyes looked unfocused at first. In a moment they found hers. "Something to show me, Paige?"

She shook her head negatively but approached anyway. The

234

wind rustled her hair, blowing wisps into her face, and she smoothed it back ineffectively. The geese paddling in the moat squawked their irritation as none of the people tossed them a crumb. They advanced upon the bank.

Niko smiled solemnly as she neared. To her surprise, he caught her hands in his. His touch was warm, but it sent shivers through her. "You don't have to do this, you know," he said.

"Do what?"

"Worry about me."

"I'm not worrying about you," she said, jutting her jaw in indignation. She tried in vain to rescue her hands as he tightened his grip. "Just everyone else. I'm here to try once more to get you to listen to reason. No one's against your dancing with all the princesses in the world at the ball. Ten times each, if you want. But with the townsfolk so upset and Edouard egging them on, if you'd only announced that you'd consider marrying a commoner, too, that would ease everything." She looked away. "A suitable commoner, of course. Suzanne, maybe. Or maybe one of the tourists will turn out to be someone special."

"My people simply don't understand. If I'd announced I might marry a commoner, would all these tourists flock here?"

"Sure, if you said your bride could be one of them. Look at the big response to the contest. Audience participation works every time. And if that participation means a prince is the prize, well—"

The coldness in his scowl could have frozen Hades. It certainly made Paige wonder if she'd better start weighing her words. "And then what?" Niko demanded. "There might be a big hoopla for the wedding, but who'd come to visit this small country for the chance to see the prince and his unknown bride? Unless you want to promise audience participation on my honeymoon, too."

Only if she were that audience, Paige thought forlornly. And he was right; who would continue to come to see a nobody bride? No one. If nothing else, that reality should keep her tiny, futile hopes from festering. Gently extracting her hands from Niko's, she turned toward the moat. The geese, grumbling softly, still waddled on the grassy bank. The swans glided by on the water, trailing small, v-shaped wakes.

"Someone royal will keep tourists coming," Niko continued.

"Plus, with such an alliance, we might get some foreign aid. I'm not proud when it comes to helping my country; I'd accept money because we gravely need it—particularly since we haven't been able to find Les Fabuleux."

That remark stabbed at Paige. She'd been the most likely person to find them, given the vast scope of her research.

But she'd failed.

She pivoted to face him, still standing beside the bench. "I wish you wouldn't be so stubborn, Niko," she managed, though her heart wasn't in the criticism. "If you only gave lip service to keeping an open mind—"

"Lip service, sweet Paige?" His voice contained a soft, sexy rasp that hadn't been there a moment before. Obviously he was trying to distract her.

And he was succeeding. He leaned forward, the sensuality of his tone complemented by his intense expression. He was going to kiss her; she knew it. And she knew she should run.

Instead, she stood still, letting her eyelids drop. For just a moment she wished she were a princess, one Niko wanted to marry.

But she was a commoner. And he had no interest in her. She opened her eyes again quickly, just as his lips began to descend on hers.

She turned away so his mouth merely grazed her cheek.

His eyes opened abruptly. He glared at her.

She sought something to say, settling on the last topic they'd been discussing. "Just think about telling your people you'll consider a commoner," she pleaded. "You can always say later that you changed your mind again."

His fists were suddenly clenched and his voice was nearly a shout. "I will not deceive my people, no matter what!"

With a small, anguished shrug, Paige ran up the path past the swan statue and toward the gate in the bulwark wall.

As she sat in the library working for the rest of the morning, a veritable menagerie of irritated thoughts roiled through her mind, punctuated by words like, *mulish* and *pig-headed.*

And kissable.

No, better stick with the animalistic thoughts she could deal with best—those that labeled Niko stubborn, not sexy.

Why not just give his people a little hope till the ball was over and his bride was picked? By then, maybe the tourist industry would be off to a rousing start and the people would be placated by money. But, no; Niko wouldn't feign, even for a little while, heeding his subjects' wishes. Not even to make them feel better.

And especially not to make *her* feel better. She wasn't even allowed to worry about him. As if his command could make that so.

She had all she could do to keep her disturbing thoughts from spewing from her fingers onto computerized catalog pages. She had more history to sort; she was finished with warning Niko.

But not finished with fretting.

She was mightily surprised when, late that afternoon, Niko came to her in the library. "You win," he growled, sounding not at all pleased.

What, Paige wondered, had she won? The pleasure of his irritable presence?

"Come with me," he ordered.

More out of curiosity than to follow his command, she obeyed. He led her out to the stables, then held the door of the Fiat open for her.

"Where are we going?" she asked.

"You'll see."

She did, indeed, see a short while later when they parked the car near the park where the statue of old Nicholas I stood. A horde of townsfolk hung about, obviously waiting for something.

For Niko.

In his becoming, beige-shirted peasant garb, he stood out from the crowd, for Dargentian men favored bright-colored shirts. He climbed onto the pedestal of his esteemed ancestor's effigy and began to orate in French.

"Thank you all for coming. I just have a few words to say because, despite rumors I've heard around here—" He stared at Paige, as though she were the one who'd begun circulating the most despicable of them. "—I care about all of you and your feelings."

A murmur circulated through the gathered townsfolk, many of whom Paige recognized from her research into folk tales and legends: Annette and Marcel Martin, of course. Also the Le Blanc brothers, Madame de Font, Pelerin and his neighbor, the butcher, both Monsieur Pologne and his sweet, elderly mother and others.

237

# Linda O. Johnston

But not Edouard.

Several people around her smiled. "He's going to tell us the ball is a fake," said a man with a ski-slope nose.

"He will marry a commoner after all," agreed his broom-handle thin female companion, whose smile lit her homely face.

Paige wondered whether her idea had been such a good one after all. Certainly he should let the people know he cared. But if he didn't do what they wanted, would his caring matter? She listened as he continued.

"I must, therefore, explain my thinking. The ball will go on, as planned. I am holding it to find a royal bride, for our country is poor. As much as I would like to oblige you all and choose a commoner for a bride, so at least part of the important legend will be fulfilled, I am trying in every way I can to put the economic condition of Dargentia back to rights. My marrying a commoner won't do that."

The crowd clearly didn't want to hear that. "It doesn't matter," someone shouted.

Another person called, "We'll manage, but not if our country falls."

And yet another cried, "Follow the legend!"

Niko raised his hands placatingly. Paige noted that he still wore the signet ring they'd found on that special day when . . . Better that she concentrate on his rhetoric than on her recollections.

"My friends," he continued, "the country is more likely to fall again because it can't survive economically than because we-'ve not heeded an ancient legend."

"He's right," called someone near Paige.

"The prince cares about us," said someone else. "We must follow him and hope for the best."

Niko spoke for a few more minutes. When he was done, and the townspeople returned up the hill, he turned to Paige. "What did you think?" His words seemed a challenge, and the lift of his chin underscored it. She wanted to reach out and wipe the haughty, teasing smile right off those sensuous lips. Maybe, if she leaned over, she could nibble it away . . . Never mind. He had done as she'd wanted. Had it had the effect she'd anticipated?

She considered her reply. "I'm sure the people who aren't rabid legend devotees were happy. They've got to be sure now that their feelings count with you."

"And those who are devotees?"

"I doubt that anything you said or did, short of finding Les Fabuleux and marrying a commoner, would make them happy."

"And you, Paige. . . ." His voice seemed to soften, sending sensual chills through her body. "What do you think?" He glanced at her as he drove, and his hand reached toward her. His warm, rough thumb stroked the sensitive skin of her cheek.

"I think," she whispered, moving her head away, "that you'd better pay attention to the stop sign ahead of us."

Paige spent the next day, the last before the ball, in the library, as usual.

She swiftly poured through old documents, duplicating earlier efforts. She hoped that she'd find, in these final hours before Niko chose his bride, some obscure reference that would help her find Les Fabuleux.

At least that would placate his people and give Dargentia economic independence.

"Paige?"

She jumped in her chair.

"I am sorry." Charlotte hovered in the library doorway, her buck teeth bulging from behind her pursed lips. "I did not mean to fry you." Frighten, Paige assumed. "May I come in?"

"Sure."

Charlotte took small steps toward the table, her lacy puce skirt swishing about her legs. She stopped near Paige. "I came to tell you that tourists are arriving in many numbers for the ball. I was up on the parrot before." Parapet? "There is such excitement in town; we have our first traffic jelly." Jam, of course. "Would you like to see?"

"Of course!"

She followed Charlotte out to the courtyard, then up stone steps in the outer castle wall to the parapet around the perimeter. She hadn't been here before. The view of the shimmering Argent River snaking through town and between mountains was breathtaking. "How lovely!" Paige said.

"The traffic jelly? It is fascinating, of course, but lovely . . . ?"

Paige laughed, focusing on the town. Cars covered the bridge and road on both sides of the river. Paige had known of the trickling of tourists over the last few days, but now guests for

# Linda O. Johnston

Niko's ball were arriving in force.

"I saw you come up here," said a feminine voice. Paige turned. Suzanne had joined them. "Four of the royal families staying at the castle will arrive on a flight later today. More are already being escorted to some of the other stately homes where they'll stay. I've boat rides and games going on for visitors who arrived yesterday and the day before, and more scheduled for early tomorrow. I wasn't for this crazy scheme, but the whole thing is certainly exciting."

Paige had to agree.

Later, when dinnertime came and Niko summoned her to join them, Paige decided this was excitement she could do without. She felt uncomfortable just walking back to her own room. The halls were crowded with strangers, and Paige hated the way her T-shirt and jeans failed to fit in with the finery of the royal guests.

She strongly considered staying in her room. Too bad she couldn't just call on Millicent for a mound of chocolate chip cookies.

Millicent. She didn't really believe in her fairy godmother after all, did she?

Of course not. Hadn't her finally believing in her disbelief chased Millicent away?

Still, the poor creature—whether a figment of her imagination or a real fairy—had meant well. All through Paige's life, she'd done nothing but tried to help.

And how had Paige rewarded her? With snipes, gibes and all-around nastiness. Not liking herself in the least, she sighed and sat on the edge of the tester bed, elbows on her knees and her head in her hands. "I'm sorry, Millicent," she said aloud.

There was no reply. Not even the smallest scent of lilacs.

Well, that capped it. If Millicent were a real fairy godmother, she'd accept Paige's apology and return. But the room remained empty, with its usual faintly musty smell.

That was okay. Paige had had more than enough of her own infantile imagination. Imagine, thinking that Niko was attracted to her, even for an afternoon. Or that the way he looked at her, touched her hand, meant anything but that he was an attentive employer.

She changed into her dressiest dress, still her dull blue shirt-waist. She almost regretted that she hadn't taken her parents up

240

on their offer to purchase fine designer garb for her in Paris. She needed all the help she could get to face the world's prettiest princesses downstairs.

When she was finished dressing she looked into the mirror. There she still was, plain Paige Conner, with her straight black hair and those darned glasses.

With a determined grimace, she grabbed a makeup kit from inside a drawer. She put on some blusher, a bit of eyeshadow, some mascara and a light shade of lipstick.

Was that any better?

Probably not.

With a despairing shake of her head, she left the room.

Sure enough, she felt frumpy at dinner.

They dined in an end of the Great Hall, where several tables had been set with fine china and crystal.

Rudy wore a tuxedo. The tightly buttoned collar and big black bow tie only seemed to emphasize the scope of his sail-like nose.

Charlotte had chosen to wear powder pink, which, as usual, clashed with her bright orange hair. Still, she seemed to sparkle as she regaled a tableful of royalty.

Niko ordered Paige to sit at his own table, near two sedately smiling royal princesses and their dignified, regal parents. One family was from Scandinavia, and its princess was a lovely, leggy blonde with a short swing dress. Her name was Gretta.

The other was Natalya, from Eastern Europe. She was dark and svelte, with a deep, sexy voice.

And of course both scintillated.

Everyone but Paige seemed caught in their spell. Niko, in a dark suit that accentuated his blond good looks, turned his attention first to one and then to the other. Now and then his eyes caught Paige's. If she didn't know better, she'd have interpreted his glances as tossing a jot of encouragement her way. She just smiled sweetly, as though she were having a wonderful time. Never mind her churning insides.

But, oh, if she only had a way to compete for Niko's attention with these charming royal misses.

Suzanne seemed to be in her glory each time Paige glanced at her. Her table held not only princesses and their parents, but their

241

brothers as well. Every male eye there was glued to her—and she clearly knew it.

Even Aldred headed a table. His characteristic reserve receded as he bantered with the nobles in his charge. Edouard had been seated with his group, and Aldred didn't seem inclined to let the sour-tempered silver fox get a word in edgewise. Not good for the guy's overinflated ego, Paige thought. But all the better to keep him from frightening off the nearest princesses.

At the end of the meal, which seemed nearly endless, Paige excused herself quickly. She saw Niko's gaze on her when she left the room, but she didn't slow down—not till she nearly slammed into a stranger who hovered outside the door.

"Excuse me," she said, stepping back.

"No problem," said the man. Paige took a moment to interpret exactly what he'd said. Used to hearing American English, though often, here, spoken with a French twist, she had to think through his words. The man's vowels sounded as though they'd been dropped into an electric blender and mixed into mush.

"I see you've met," said a deep, familiar voice behind her. Paige turned to see Niko. He closed the Great Hall's large wooden door behind him, then stood leaning with his back against the wall next to a massive painting of the icy Argent in winter. He crossed his arms and smiled.

"Not exactly," said the stranger, again speaking an unusual version of English. He was a young, beefy man with a butch haircut and a broad, pugnacious jawline. His small eyes looked Paige up and down as though cataloging every inch, not exactly making her comfortable with his presence.

"Paige," Niko said, "this is George Elkins. He's the head of the castle's temporary security force for the ball. He'll keep the people calm."

"Oh, great," she said before giving herself time to think. "You won't listen to your subjects, but you'll set the *gendarmes* on them if they express their opinions."

Niko's relaxed stance evaporated immediately. His shoulders, broad beneath his dark suitcoat, grew as stiff as the Argent's ice, and his look was no warmer. "I'm setting no one on anybody. I just want to make sure there's no trouble."

"The way to make sure there's no trouble is to show your

subjects you care about their feelings. That way they'll stop listening to Edouard.''

Paige found herself nearly toe-to-toe with the incensed prince. She was so close she felt his body heat radiating from beneath his beautifully tailored clothes. His scent of autumn leaves and citrus swirled in her head, making her slight muzziness from a glass of wine at dinner fly into full-fledged intoxication. Her head was tilted back so she could look in anger up into his face. She felt her lower jaw jut as far as his.

"I've told them I care," growled Niko. "And my subjects' feelings are not the concern of a stranger."

"Yes, they are. You've made them the concern of *that* stranger." Paige pointed to Elkins. "And *this* stranger"— she aimed her forefinger at herself—"has been here long enough to begin to care about—" She stopped herself and stepped back, dropping her head so her hair drooped about her face. "Oh, what's the use?"

"Care about what?" the prince asked, the harshness gone from his tone.

"About . . . your people. Your country." *You,* she felt her mind shout, but she let that cry reverberate only inside her own skull. Needing something to hang on to, she let her fingers grasp the folds in the skirt of her dress.

"Now, now, don't worry," Elkins said, patting Paige's shoulder with his big, beefy hand. "The prince, 'ere, 'as told me all about his people's beliefs in them legends and 'ow they're being all riled up by this Edouard bloke. I'm just 'ere to make sure things don't get out 'a hand."

Paige finally placed his accent: Cockney. Niko had hired a Cockney cop to keep the castle safe from his own subjects.

"You'll see, Paige, at the ball tomorrow." Niko's voice sounded as gentle as a caress, and she let it stroke her. "Everything will be fine." He paused. "You *will* be at the ball tomorrow."

She heard no question in his voice. He'd been lulling her, luring her off guard while he issued orders again.

The last thing she intended was to listen to an arrogant prince who hadn't gotten his priorities straight.

"Sure," she said sweetly. "And if you want to see me, just come to the kitchen. I'll be the one with the dirtiest apron."

"Paige, you will not—"

But she did not stay to let him finish. Turning her back on them, she hustled down the hallway that led to her room. It was his castle. His kingdom. She had nothing to say about how he ran it.

Just as he had nothing to say about how she would appear at the ball—if at all.

But, oh, how she worried about whether that ball tomorrow night would cement Dargentia's place in the tourist lures of the world—or fragment this tiny, needy country like a clay pigeon in a trapshoot.

That night, Paige woke often. Now and then, she thought she scented lilacs.

"Millicent?" she called more than once.

There was no reply, of course. She'd been dreaming. Millicent had gone the way of all fairy tales.

But, oh, could Paige use a little magic now.

She thought so even more the next morning, the day of the ball, when she needed all the help she could get to keep her mind on history. Nothing worked; her mind kept turning to the troubles of the present.

Finally, in the early afternoon, she gave up, hopped into the Fiat and headed for town. The schools were on holiday to celebrate the big event, but when Paige reached the Martin house not even teacher Annette was home.

She left the car at the curb of the residential lane; parking spaces seemed at a premium in the heart of D'Argent City. Walking briskly along people-packed streets, she headed for Le Dargentian Royale.

She had to pass Edouard's bank on the way. For fun—or something more Machiavellian—she stopped in. He was nowhere in sight. She spent a while there, ostensibly getting cash from the account in which her pay from the prince was stashed, but actually quizzing a teller or two about what they thought of their boss. Maybe she wasn't giving the banker enough credit. Maybe he wouldn't be such a bad prime minister after all.

But when she finally left her head was spinning. The man's veins must run with blue ink—the color of Dargentian francs.

And his heart muscle must roll like a printing press. She had heard nothing human about him.

And, yes, the people here also wished for Niko to heed their legends. His speech had been kind and heartfelt, but he was wrong. Only by obeying the legends, they thought, could the country stay free—and out of the clutches of their stingy, sinister boss, who hired and fired with no compunction, who let nothing stand in the way of his finagling another franc.

Paige headed again for the hotel, somewhat slowly. Her mind reeled and the sidewalks were crowded. It was the day of the ball. Niko would choose a princess tonight, and not a commoner.

And she hadn't even helped him by finding Les Fabuleux.

She clutched the swan pendant about her neck. If only it had been found in a cache of valuable jewels. If only the clue of the signet ring had rung true.

What did Aldred's clue to the crown jewels mean?

She'd nearly run out of time to figure it out.

Eventually she found herself at Le Dargentian Royale. The hotel's stately new lobby was thronged by a polyglot of gabbing tourists. Suitcases were piled everywhere. Bellhops had been recruited from all over the country—teens and octogenarians and everyone in between, each wearing traditional Dargentian flowered skirts and frilled blouses or bright-colored shirts, and each toting luggage and ushering tourists to elevators. How wonderful! Paige thought. Now if only things would stay that way for a month. Or ten. Or a million.

But if Edouard succeeded in rousing Dargentians to ruin the ball, the place would be as deserted as the day Paige had first seen it, before it had opened.

Surely that wouldn't happen. The whole country had turned out to welcome the tourists, if this was any indication. Who would have time to spoil the ball?

Paige spotted Annette leading a large party who insisted on carrying their own bags. She waved at Paige, signaling that she'd meet her out on the terrace.

Paige waited for her there in a spot away from the glaring summer sun. There wasn't much shade, except in the shadow of the building itself; the plantings at the hotel were too fresh and new. But in a few years, Paige believed, the small sycamores and maples, the rhododendrons and lavender and perennials planted about the garden paths, would grow to give the grounds color and shade and wonderful appeal.

She listened to the roar of the tourists inside and grinned. The noise meant success. Niko's success.

It had to continue.

Soon she was joined both by Annette and Marcel. Annette had dark circles about her pretty gray eyes, and her short, dark hair seemed to have lost its curl. Marcel's burliness seemed to have shrunken to fit his short stature. Worry clouded his expression.

"Most people love Niko and his whole idea of the ball," Annette said, leaning dejectedly against the outer hotel wall. "Especially after his speech, they believe in him, that he will do what's best for Dargentia, even if it's not the way we think things should go. But then there's this faction—"

"The fanatics," spat Marcel, throwing his arm about his wife's shoulder. As Paige had seen once before, his angry mood was reflected in the whiteness of his knuckles. "Led by Edouard. They won't see reason, even though they've been told Edouard has his own fish to net. They're tired of people in charge in this country not caring what the people think. They thought Niko was different—"

"He *is* different," interrupted his wife. "He's doing what he thinks is right."

"Tell me," Paige said, "I understand most Dargentians will be helping out at the ball. Will they act as servants, as they've been hired to do?"

Marcel nodded, his round face red. "Certainly. And most will do fine. But it will only take a few to disrupt everything. And that's what Edouard wants."

But that was not what Edouard would get. Not if Paige could help it.

Still, she thought a short while later as she headed the Fiat back to the castle, she couldn't do a dratted thing to help if she wasn't at the ball.

She hadn't lied to Niko; the only way she'd planned to be there was to stay in the kitchen and do something useful but unobtrusive. Slicing onions appealed to her; that way, if she felt like crying, she'd have a good reason.

But now she'd have no time to cry. She had a job to do. She'd keep a close eye on Niko and Edouard. She wouldn't trust George

## The Glass Slipper

Elkins, that meddling Cockney mercenary, to keep the peace. She'd do it herself.

But she couldn't do it alone. And there was only one person—or whatever—who could help her.

She parked the Fiat in the garage, managed, through gritted teeth, to utter pleasant greetings to the royal guests who meandered the halls and headed for her own tower room.

*Millicent,* she called in her mind the whole way. *Please forgive me. Or don't. But be there. I'm begging you. You know that, no matter what, I always believed in you. I'll let you dress me however you'd like. I'll even try hard to figure out the secret of fairy tales, though I'd think you'd have told me the dratted thing by now. No. Never mind. I'll do it myself. But please, Millicent, be there!*

She stopped outside her door and braced herself. Would her wish come true? Would Millicent be there?

She listened for a moment. Yes! There was a sound inside. Faint rustling, like the soft murmur of a mountain stream.

The last thing she wanted to think about in Niko's castle was mountain streams—not after the last one she'd visited with him. Taking a deep breath, she shoved open the door.

Sure enough, Millicent was there.

But she wasn't alone. She was clasped tight in Aldred's arms. And the slight, suit-wearing majordomo and the diminutive fairy godmother, in her usual bright-colored sweatshirt, were locked in a soul-searing, tongue-tangling, thrilling, torrid kiss.

# *Chapter Twenty-two*

Thinking of nothing sufficiently scathing to say, Paige blurted the first thing that came to mind. "How can you two carry on right here, in my room? We've Les Fabuleux to find and legends to fulfill. Dargentia's in danger!"

The two broke apart like kissing dolls whose magnets had lost polarity. Aldred kept his arm around Millicent, as though to protect her from Paige.

Which was a good thing, Paige thought. She wanted to throttle her imaginary—

Imaginary? Hah! She'd known all along Millicent was real, but if she'd let any doubts linger, Aldred's kiss would have convinced her.

"Hello, Eleanora, dear." Millicent's voice wasn't its familiar wavery self; it was deeper, huskier, as though she were thoroughly affected by Aldred's kiss.

"We were not 'carrying on,' Ms. Conner." Apparently Aldred returned to stiff formality when embarrassed. "We were merely—"

"Kissing," interrupted Paige's fickle fairy friend. "Now, dear, we didn't object when you kissed Niko. Or even when the two of you—"

"Enough," Paige growled. "Look, I haven't time to go into this now. Millicent, are you still—" She glanced at Aldred, unsure how much he knew.

"Your fairy godmother? Of course. I have been for ever so long."

Aldred didn't seem shocked. He simply smiled fondly at the woman—or whatever—in his arms.

"Then act like one." Paige stopped herself. Hadn't she promised to be kind to Millicent? And now that she was ready to accept the fact that Millicent was real and not just an aberration of her own pitiful imagination, she owed her a little respect. "I'm sorry,

Millicent. Let me tell you a bit about what's going on in Dargentia.''

"I've kept her filled in, Paige," Aldred said.

She'd just bet he had. "Anyway, the ball's in just a few hours. I hadn't planned on going except on KP duty, but—''

Millicent stopped her by stepping back from Aldred and clapping her small hands. "Oh, how wonderful. You actually want to attend now!"

Paige nodded slowly, as though she were agreeing to her own drawing, quartering and being served up for supper.

"Now run along, my dear Aldred," Millicent continued. "I know you have a lot to do tonight, too."

He nodded, but before he went he landed his lips once more on Millicent's. Paige turned away tactfully, yet watched surreptitiously from the corner of her eye, shaking her head in amazement.

When he was gone Millicent faced her, looking her up and down with a critical eye.

Paige felt herself redden. She was in her usual working uniform of black Smithsonian T-shirt, blue jeans and neon-striped athletic shoes. What did Millicent expect?

"I'd say, Eleanora, dear," said Millicent, with a pensive pause in her voice, "that we have a lot of work to do."

At the doorway to the Great Hall stood Niko, pride squaring his shoulders. Before him in the receiving line were Charlotte, Rudy, Suzanne—and, of course, Edouard, standing and beaming as though he loved the idea of the ball.

Niko had lied to Paige the day they'd met. He didn't have a collection of tuxedos—just this one, with its black coat and tails. A red sash was slashed across his chest. He felt its great weight, for it was covered with medals won by his ancestors in battles long ago.

He was the prince of Dargentia, soon to be king—once he'd taken a princess as bride, for only married Dargentian royalty truly assumed the throne. It was just as he'd planned. Perfect!

So why did he feel so sad and uneasy?

"Their Majesties, King Evguen, Queen Olga and Princess Stana of Leuchtenberg!"

As they arrived, Aldred loudly announced visiting royal fami-

249

# Linda O. Johnston

lies from calling cards in his pristinely gloved hands. He stood straight and regal in the bright light spilling through the doorway from the hall. His salt-and-pepper mane had been tamed to a well-styled cap on his head. With a smile, Niko recalled the grumbling from the next room as the aroma of his majordomo's hairspray wafted through the open door. The man had seemed preoccupied, but Niko had gotten no explanation from him. Oh, well. Right now he seemed just fine.

The Leuchtenberg family started down the receiving line beginning with Charlotte, and Niko's smile was formal yet welcoming. He was proud of the way the others had come through.

Charlotte was in a many-layered gown more appropriate for a woman a fraction of her age. Its pale rose shade clashed with her orange hair. Still, the combination suited her. She said something that must have amused the king of Leuchtenberg, for the pigeon-chested man preened as he moved down the line. Niko wondered what language she'd been speaking.

Rudy looked regal and sedate in his formal wear. His usual shy diffidence had been replaced with a serene dignity that became him. Blond Suzanne, in her shimmering silver gown, looked as though she attended such affairs all the time.

And then there was Edouard. Had he planned a disruption to the ball, as everyone assumed?

Well, among the royal guests on the dance floor and the throngs of tourists viewing from the gallery, George Elkins had strategically placed his security force. Each was well trained; all were on the alert. If there was a disturbance, it would be quickly and quietly taken care of. The royals and tourists need never know.

Niko glanced up to the balcony overlooking the ballroom. People decked out nearly as finely as the nobility on the dance floor leaned over and watched, gloved hands pointing at princesses as they arrived, their voices swelling, then ebbing, as each group of guests moved along. The crowd on the balcony could be distinguished more easily than the milling royalty; the illumination up there was brighter than on the dance floor, where ancient chandeliers, although electrified, were sparsely spaced.

The Leuchtenbergs finally reached Niko. He took their hands in turn, bowing slightly over the slender fingers of Princess Stana, careful not to squeeze too tightly and hurt her with his large, sparkling signet ring. She was short, with dark brows in a sur-

250

prised arch and a Christmas-ribbon halo of curls bobbing about her head. Her aqua gown sparkled with glittering sequins. "Your Highness," she murmured, curtseying daintily. Her face was expressionless, though her small brown eyes seemed to assess him.

Would this be the princess who'd capture his heart and his kingdom?

Unbidden, Paige Conner's image insinuated itself in his mind. Her amber eyes flashed angrily beneath her black-rimmed glasses the way he'd seen her last. He froze. *He* was the one who should feel riled. She had insulted his security chief—and him. And she had disobeyed him, assuring him, despite a direct order, that she would not attend the ball.

He was furious with her. And with the situation. For his countrymen's sake, he had to choose a royal bride—whether they understood that or not. But his rebellious heart kept telling him that his choice should not be for his kingdom but for love.

Well, maybe he could have both. Shelving his infatuation for Paige—for surely that was all it was—he turned his attention back to the receiving line. He smiled with determination at Princess Stana, who was still before him.

Her face brightened, as though she believed his smile was for her. "I look forward to our first dance," she said in French as she finally swept by.

For the next interminable time Niko bowed and shook hands and exchanged pleasantries till he felt like an automaton. Proud royal papas introduced an array of eligible daughters, all in designer gowns selected to secure his attention. Many dresses dipped into deep decolletages revealing more than a hint of eager bosom. Most gowns were long and covered with an astonishing conglomeration of lace, beads, and sparkling frills. The attractive ladies, duchesses, baronesses and princesses inside them seemed to blend, in Niko's mind, into fuzzy sameness. He even had trouble telling the houseguests with whom he'd eaten the prior evening, Natalya and Gretta, from the rest.

He'd be able to distinguish one from another, he told himself, after speaking with them alone. At least he hoped he would. Surely that would occur once he ended this endless receiving line and began to dance.

More than once he glanced in pleasure about the dimly lighted hall. The ever-versatile Maibelle had designed the decoration. Silver banners draped from the railing of the upper gallery, where a twenty-piece orchestra played sedate music. Aromatic floral wreaths and centerpieces in crimson, silver and purple, the colors of the Dargentian flag, shot brilliant color into the otherwise drab Great Hall. Part of the room had been partitioned off for a dining area for the supper to be served later.

Wrought-iron chandeliers spilled their softly muted light on the revelers on the lower level, the lights' far-apart spacing creating patches of shadows. People milled around tables offering champagne and punch. Black-uniformed Dargentians circulated among them with trays of hors d'oeuvres.

Royal gentlemen were present as well as ladies, in their dark and formal finery. Brothers of the bridal hopefuls, many eligible bachelors in their own rights, had also been invited, since Niko couldn't dance with all the ladies at once. As he greeted the young princes and earls, dukes and barons, they clapped his shoulder jovially. They, too, might find suitable consorts at Niko's ball.

So, Niko thought, might Edouard. That might solve everything, if some sweet foreign miss were wooed by the silver fox and he allowed himself to be swept off to her kingdom.

More likely, he would do all he could to usurp this kingdom, too. But not if Niko had anything to say about it. He and his royal bride would reign happily in the newly restored kingdom; tourists would visit in multitudes, tossing francs about like confetti; the rumors of the reality of the legends would die. It had to happen that way.

A separate supper had been set up outside, in the courtyard, for townsfolk and tourists. Some of the food being served included entries in the local culinary contest suggested by Paige. It had been a big hit, and many delicious traditional dishes had won prizes for Dargentia's proud citizens. Near the buffet table was another table that had been set up with ballots for strangers to vote for his bride.

If the sameness of those he met didn't seem to fade, maybe he'd even let majority rule.

No; he couldn't even think of letting the rest of his life be governed so cavalierly. There would be someone, in this room filled with royalty, who would capture his affection.

Finally Aldred's introductions dwindled. The receiving line diminished to an uneven trickle.

Time for the festivities to begin.

The protocol had been organized by Aldred. Niko would begin the ball by dancing with Aunt Charlotte. For the next couple of hours he'd spend exactly three minutes apiece with each young lady, scheduled consecutively based on the date of receipt of her family's acceptance to the ball rather than social standing, as was sometimes the criterion at formal affairs. That way, there could be no rubbing of royal egos the wrong way about who was considered most powerful. His dance card was full; hardly anyone had refused his invitation to the ball.

After Niko had danced with each guest on his card he'd be free to pick one to escort to a late supper at exactly nine o'clock. Later he could also choose those to dance with again. Only those still contending for his interest would be selected then.

Niko caught Charlotte's eye. "Ready for our dance, Aunt?"

She smiled with childlike excitement, revealing her protruding upper teeth. "This is so thrilling, Niko. Has anyone caught your fanny?"

"Fancy, Aunt." Holding her gloved hand at chest level, he led her through the crowd toward the area of the granite floor that had been designated for dancing. "Too soon to tell. Any indication whether Rudy's using this as his own hunting ground?"

She giggled. "Knowing my son, he will dance all the dances. You had better be careful; he is a charming young man. He may stole away the princess you choose."

"Steal, Aunt." That sounded more like maternal optimism than the Rudy Niko knew. But more power to him. If Rudy found someone special here, at least the ball would have accomplished something.

Someone special . . . He wondered what infuriating, stubborn Paige Conner was doing. She should have been right here. Had she found a niche to help out in the kitchen? Or could she have decided to join the tourists to watch the festivities?

His eyes rose to the upper gallery. The crowd was too dense for him to be sure, but he didn't see Paige. Most people up there were backlighted anyway, from the gallery's brighter illumination.

Stopping on the dance floor, he turned his attention to his aunt. "Are you ready?"

She nodded. He gave a prearranged signal to the orchestra.

# Linda O. Johnston

Immediately, the musicians ceased their soothing background music and burst into the familiar strains of the *Blue Danube Waltz*. Niko whirled his aunt onto the dance floor in the softly lighted room. After the interval dictated by protocol other dancers joined in.

In three minutes Aldred tapped Niko on the shoulder. The aging majordomo led out one of the princesses, who swept into Niko's waiting arms.

He'd no trouble making conversation for such a short period, despite the elegant throbbing of the music, the exuberant spin of the dance. "Tell me about your country," he said to his first partner, a petite, spritely young thing with an upturned nose. Her family was from Yugoslavia but had lived in exile in England for years.

Others, as the evening progressed, explained their own sad family histories. Many had not lived in their ancestral homes for decades or longer. And then there were those from England, the Netherlands, Scandinavia and elsewhere whose families had survived at home and intact and, often, had thrived.

Each one's dress seemed more frilled and elaborate than the last. Some wore heavy, exotic perfumes that made his sinuses rebel, and he stood as far from them as the waltz and the length of his arms would allow. Others' aromas reminded him of sweet, fragrant flowers. Those he held a little closer. But his senses missed the scent of baby powder.

Several young ladies stood out a bit in his mind. They were mostly the ones who spoke of his achievement in freeing Dargentia. That demonstrated a real interest in him and his small country. Of those, only a handful sparkled. Fewer yet fit into his arms as though they might come to belong there. He made a point of remembering their names, though he also gave a nod to Aldred to note them before they were replaced by the next in line.

At length his initial duties were nearly done. There were only a few more left to dance with.

Not a moment too soon, he thought. The activity had made him feel famished.

He wasn't sure, afterward, what caught his attention. He heard nothing unusual. The partner in his arms, a rather raucous young thing of Austrian descent, did not miss a step. But suddenly, he sensed something different in the Great Hall.

He looked instinctively toward the entrance, only to realize that nearly everyone in the room—and even the upper gallery—did the same. The music tapered to silence for an instant, then swelled again, as though in a triumphal march. Niko stood motionless, his firm grip on his partner's hand halting her.

A young woman stood in the doorway, tall and poised and striking, haloed by the brighter light from the hallway. Her dark hair was caught up in an elegantly sleek style beneath a shimmering diamond tiara. Her simple, flowing white dress pointed out the gaudiness of the other's gowns.

If only Niko could see her better in this dratted, dim light.

She waited while Aldred made his way through the sea of people to her, then handed him a small card. "Princess Eleanora of Monteubique," he announced to the crowd in his stentorian voice.

Where was that? No matter. Niko grabbed his dance card from his pocket.

Princess Eleanora was not on it.

Damn! He wouldn't be able to dance with her before dinner— the one princess who had, at last, seemed to stand out from the rest. Impatiently, he began leading his partner once more. He wanted this dance to be over, the last several, in fact. He was eager to meet Princess Eleanora.

For an instant a pang of guilt passed through him as a picture of Paige Conner's most soulful look flashed before his eyes. He thrust the image aside. He had to choose a princess, his feelings for Paige notwithstanding.

Whatever they were.

His eyes lit again on the stunning young woman who'd just arrived. Soon he would meet her. In the meantime he kept watch over her as one royal brother after another swept her into his arms. Surely it was the exertion of the dancing and not stabs of jealousy that took his breath away as he saw the princess gaze into the eyes of her partners and smile enchantingly.

How graceful she was, and how appealing, gliding from pale light to dusky shadow, and then back again. There was something familiar about her, too. He felt tantalized as she was waltzed to within twenty feet of him, then glided away once more.

At last there was someone at the ball he could imagine making his bride—if he went through with this folly of a plan.

But of course he had no choice.

The next minutes dragged, though Niko engaged in the same clever conversation with his remaining partners as he had with the rest.

Then, finally, Aldred was at his side.

"I don't care if it's supper time," Niko said, his eyes fixed on the white-clad princess. "I want to make sure I've danced with every princess here before we eat."

"I'm glad, Your Highness." Aldred sounded so relieved that Niko glanced at him. "I'm afraid there was a glitch somewhere, and there are three princesses here who didn't make it onto your dance card. With two, their cards showed they were to have the last two dances with you. The third is Princess Eleanora, and she wasn't scheduled at all. But, oh, what this does to protocol . . ."

"Protocol be damned!" Niko whispered. "I want to dance with Princess Eleanora next."

Aldred's salt-and-pepper brows rose in horror. "Oh, no! You must take time now for the two who should have been scheduled."

Glowering at Aldred, Niko let himself be led to one of the other waiting princesses.

The first, a light-haired miss descended from the German house of Lippe, trod on his toes. The second, a beauty from Brazil, tried to sell him an interest in a coffee plantation.

Niko kept one eye on Eleanora at all times. She certainly didn't lack for dancing partners. Once, her dark coif bent quite close to the muddy-brown hair of a youthful English aristocrat. She seemed to be enjoying herself.

He wished he could say the same thing. Maybe he'd feel better once he'd taken the effervescent Eleanora into his arms.

And maybe he wouldn't.

Again he thought guiltily of sweet, passionate Paige. Never mind. She'd understand. She had to.

If only he could convince himself.

At long last these two new dances were done. Niko looked around. Eleanora was at the far side of the dance floor from him. He noted Aldred edging through the crowd till he stood beside the young woman. The majordomo said something to her, and she smiled at Niko and began walking toward him.

From the corner of his eye Niko noted that Maibelle stood in the doorway. Aldred saw her, too, and began hurrying toward her. He was stopped for a moment by one of the kings who stood in his way.

But Niko was immediately distracted. The soft, uneven light of the dimmed Great Hall only enhanced the fact that, even from a distance, the princess gliding toward him was beautiful. Her floor-length gown showed off her feminine curves to perfection. Tantalizingly little of her creamy skin was revealed at the draped neckline. She had a perfect mouth, with full, pink lips slightly apart. Her cheekbones were high, her chin firm and determined.

If only she'd step out of the shadows so he could see her better.

Before the woman reached him, Aldred raced past her again, beating her to Niko's side. "May I speak with you, sire?" he said, tossing an apologetic look toward the princess.

With a black glare at his majordomo, Niko followed him for a few steps. "What's going on? I want to dance just this last—"

"I'm sorry, Your Highness, but we must start eating supper now. Everything was timed for nine o'clock sharp, and it's already a few minutes after. Some of our royal guests are already irritated by the breach of protocol, and our chef is worried some of the food will spoil."

"But the waltz will only be for three minutes." And he wanted to see the tantalizing Princess Eleanora close up.

"That's all right," said a sweet, melodic voice that came from behind Niko. The princess had followed them. "I'll have my dance after we eat, won't I?"

"Of course," Niko said, trying to swing around to see her. "You will be my supper companion, won't you?"

"Certainly."

But Aldred gripped Niko's elbow before he was able to turn around. "There are some other matters you must see to first, Your Highness. In the hall. Perhaps I can escort the princess to a table."

Was this it—Edouard's interruption? He glanced around the ballroom. The silver fox was chatting nonchalantly with a family from Finland.

"It's merely a personality clash," Aldred whispered. "But there'll be no supper if you don't intervene."

With a growl he barely tried to mute, Niko bowed toward the princess. "Please allow Aldred to show you to the dining area," he said through gritted teeth, then hurried toward the door.

He blinked in the brighter light in the corridor outside the Great

Hall. Maibelle stood there with Elkins, the head security guard. Their dispute only took a few minutes to arbitrate. Niko ordered Elkins and his troops out of the kitchen. He complimented Maibelle on the delicious aroma of food wafting down the hall from the kitchen and thanked her for her patience. Then he asked her to cooperate with the security chief.

Finally it was time to return to the ball. And to speak with Princess Eleanora.

She stood all alone at the entry to the area of the Great Hall partitioned from the rest for dining.

He strode toward her. It was all he could do not to run. His spirits soared at the thought that he'd found his special princess to wed.

She was watching him, this woman he might marry. A stranger. He might wind up pledging his future to a perfect stranger.

A beautiful one—but she wasn't his fun and feisty Paige.

He slowed his pace as his spirits began a new nosedive.

Reaching Eleanora's side, he said, "*Altesse,*" then repeated in English, "Your Highness," holding out his hand. She put hers into it, and he bent to kiss the soft, smooth skin on the back. Her scent reminded him of exotic travels and endless nights of passion.

He closed his eyes for just an instant, missing the aroma of baby powder.

He quickly let the princess go, fearful she'd sense the bittersweet bent of his mood. She dropped into an elegant curtsey and said in a soft, breathy voice, "Your Highness."

He looked at her as she rose. Unfortunately, this area was even darker than the ballroom portion of the Great Hall.

In the dimness her eyes seemed an unusual golden shade of green. They regarded him with supreme amusement, as though she considered the ball a joke they shared.

There was something familiar about her. In a moment he realized what it was: She reminded him of Paige.

But she couldn't be Paige. She wore no glasses. And more to the point, he had noticed a swing to her gait when she walked, an aura of self-confidence about her even as she stood still, that he'd never seen in Paige.

Wishful thinking, he told himself. His obstinate historian wouldn't show up at the ball. She'd told him so.

*His* historian? The words had a ring to them. Here, faced each moment by the difficult choice he had to make, which would affect the rest of his life, he realized that Paige Conner had captured his heart.

But, thank heavens, one princess had captured his attention.

"Princess Eleanora," he said, "would you care to dine?" As she nodded, he held out his hand, cupped at chest height. She placed hers gently on top of it, and he led her through the doorway.

In the dining area, elegantly festooned tables formed long, straight rows, and a seating chart at the entry told guests where to sit. The light was even fainter here than at the entry, for the main illumination consisted of flickering candles.

"I don't imagine I'm on the list," Princess Eleanora said, leaning over to look at it. She spoke English in a breathy voice, with the merest hint of an exotic accent that he couldn't place. Monteubiquian, he imagined. Whatever that was. "I've crashed your party," she continued.

"I've never met a more welcome intruder," he said. "Will you sit at my table, next to me?"

She touched his arm. Her words sang with a sincerity that shot a dart of delight through him. "There is no place in this world that I'd rather be."

"Not even Monteubique?"

"My home is a wonderful place," she acknowledged, "but I left it to meet you. Now I couldn't be more pleased that I did."

He smiled, then took her hand again. He showed her to a seat, then excused himself.

He sought out Aldred. "You need to do some quick checking for me," he said. "I need to know about Monteubique and its royal family. Princess Eleanora has admitted she's a gate-crasher. Why didn't we know to invite her? Could she be a fraud?"

"If she's a fraud, she's a lovely one," Aldred said with a grin. "I'll check my Burke's *Royal Families of the World*. And I'll try to discover whether Monteubique has a foreign aid program."

Returning to his seat beside the princess, Niko turned on the charm. "I apologize for leaving you, even for a short while."

Flickering candles darted tendrils of light to dance along her creamy complexion and the whiteness of her gown. Her eyes looked softly, sexily, gilt-tinged green. "Your absence only made

259

# Linda O. Johnston

me long for the moment when we would be reunited.'' Her smile
turned her words from serious to teasing.

Maybe he could come to like the frothiness of this pretty princess.

Despite missing the seriousness of his sweet historian.

Niko's family were also at the head table: Charlotte, Rudy and
Suzanne, who'd each selected supper companions. Rudy's was
blond, leggy Gretta, one of their houseguests, who wore a ruby
red strapless gown. Suzanne had chosen the brother of a princess
of Bulgarian ancestry, introduced as Prince Mihailo. He was tall,
with extraordinarly thick brown eyebrows. He appeared engrossed
in Suzanne's words as he gazed at the deep neckline of her shimmering gown. The room's dimness deterred him not at all.

And then there was Edouard. He was deep in conversation with
a member of the British royal family—one who wore an array of
diamonds sparkling in the candlelight along her decolletage.

Niko noted with a grin how gleefully most guests received the
souvenir brochure at each place. Many had seen it before, of
course, bound less extravagantly; it had been sent worldwide as
a promotion for the ball. Still, he'd have to let Paige know . . .
she should have been here to see for herself!

But then, how could he have concentrated on captivating a
princess?

Maybe he hadn't succeeded anyway. His thoughts kept flitter-
ing off to Paige.

Niko raised his wine goblet and toasted so softly that only the
princess could hear, ''To Monteubique.'' He took a sip. The wine
was a fragrant and well-aged Cabernet from his special stores.

Princess Eleanora raised her glass. ''To Dargentia and its most
kind prince, who allowed me to crash his ball.''

Niko laughed, but only for a moment. He stared as the princess
put her goblet to her lips and drank, her eyes never leaving his.
When she drew the glass away she licked her full lips with the
tip of her tongue. Their moistness sparkled in the shining candlelight. He quickly looked away, feeling disloyal to Paige.

How absurd, he told himself. Paige couldn't matter in matters
of state.

But she did.

Tormented, he appreciated the interruption as a contingent of
uniformed Dargentians marched into the dining area, serving the

first course, a delicate consommé. "Delightful," the princess proclaimed after her first dainty spoonful.

"But not half so delightful as youself," he forced himself to say, determined to direct all his attention to the princess.

She tilted a pleased look up at him, then placed her spoon on the saucer beside her soup bowl.

"Tell me about Monteubique," Niko said. "I have to admit I know nothing about it."

She shrugged her delicate shoulders beneath her flowing gown. "Few people do, I'm afraid, like poor Dargentia, until you."

His heart pounded with pride.

She continued, "Monteubique is a small island in the Mediterranean. It was independent once many years ago, but now it is a part of Italy."

He couldn't picture where it was. He glanced around. No Aldred. Niko hoped he would bring a map when he brought the information about this lovely princess and her home.

"What about Monteubique's future?" he asked. "Wouldn't you like its freedom?"

Eleanora's eyes clouded. "I am not you, Your Highness. I haven't any wonderful negotiating talents to set my country free, nor the resourcefulness to make it a successful independent nation. No, my home must stay as it is."

"What if I were to help you?" he offered impetuously. This could, after all, be the princess with whom he would form his alliance. "I could come to visit your country, maybe within the next few weeks. I could start the process. Your land and mine could be allies, and I'd help you gain and keep your independence."

A startled expression crossed Princess Eleanora's lovely face. She ducked her head forward for just a moment, then brought it back. The motion was familiar. . . .

It was Paige! Niko nearly stood in his certainty, despite the darkness of the room. He checked himself, remaining completely still.

A teenaged Dargentian served their fish course, but Niko hardly noticed. Instead he stared at the woman beside him, searching her candlelit face as she turned to thank the server.

Anger percolated through his bloodstream, starting a slow, roil-

# Linda O. Johnston

ing simmer. To think he'd even felt guilty for being interested in someone else.

But it hadn't been anyone else; it had been Paige.

The more he thought of the situation, the more ire tightened his fists.

Now that he was sure who this woman was, he had to know: What was her game?

Paige had claimed she wanted nothing to do with the ball, yet here she was. He'd invited her to come as herself, even forgoing the tourists' gallery, but she'd chosen to masquerade as royalty.

Of course he'd made the purpose of the ball clear to everyone: He was going to find a royal bride. Was Paige here under false pretenses so he'd pay attention to her? Perhaps even court and marry her? How long did she think she'd get away with such a farce?

Damn her! After their earlier misunderstanding he'd come to trust that she wasn't after a crown. But maybe there'd been no misunderstanding at all. Here he'd been, pining after her like a lovesick teenager, but she was just like every other American he had ever met. Worse. At least they had been honest in their attempts to snare a prince.

He stoked his anger purposefully to keep it searing hot. Paige had had him going, that was for sure.

With superhuman effort he kept his voice level. "You were right before. Maybe I am ignoring my other guests."

He stood and began to circulate among the tables, leaving Eleanora/Paige sitting there. He felt her eyes on him, but when he turned back he saw that she'd begun an animated conversation with the large, awkward Prince Mihailo, on her right. How could she avoid staring at the way his thick eyebrows met in the middle?

Everyone had finished their fish dish. The plates were cleared, but no other course had yet been served. Niko headed toward the kitchen to check on the food.

As he exited the Great Hall, he heard a footfall behind him. He pivoted, his nerves on edge.

Princess Eleanora had followed him. "I hope you don't mind, Your Highness," she said, "but I wanted to see more of your castle. And besides"— she lowered her head lower —"I began to miss you."

What kind of flirtatious foolishness was this? Still, Niko felt his blood pump faster. For someone who pretended to be so quiet and shy, Paige certainly played games well. She'd already attracted him, darn her, in her own personna.

If it *was* her own personna. Maybe this was the real Paige Conner.

But why would she pretend that diffidence? To catch his attention?

Then why change now?

In the kitchen he spotted Maibelle, her dirndl fresh but her white cap askew, laughing with the large, perspiring caterer. She noticed Niko. "All is well, Prince Niko," she assured him. "The next course will be served in a moment."

He thanked her and turned to go, Paige behind him. "Go back to the table and sit down," he told her, wondering if she would listen. As Paige Conner, she did not take direction well.

He went to the head of the stairs to the wine cellar. He needed to check on the supply of the evening's libations. A couple of Dargentian youths were carrying a new crate of wine up the steps. "Good." He stood out of their way as they headed for the kitchen. As he turned, he recognized a man walking down the hall as one of Elkins's men and returned his nod. The gesture meant all was well.

And right behind him was Paige.

She was following him.

Then it struck him. She might be engaged in some game to attract him, but there was more to it than that, and he knew what it was. She'd attached herself to him so he'd never be alone on the night of the ball. Paige Conner was trying to protect him!

It was laughable, in a way. What would she do if the townsfolk Edouard had incited actually caused a problem?

But warmth welled within him; he felt pleased, too. He stroked his beard as he considered how to handle her.

Why not play along? He'd still have to get to know the other young ladies so he could pick his royal bride, but he could enjoy Princess Eleanora, too.

"Let's go finish our supper." He offered his arm.

When she took it heat radiated from the place she touched clear to his toes. He heard violins—but the orchestra was between sets. Oh, Paige, he thought. Why did you have to complicate what had seemed so simple?

# Chapter Twenty-three

She'd done it!

No, to give credit where it was due, Millicent had done it. Not only had her fairy godmother reappeared right when Paige really needed her, but she'd performed just as Paige had wished.

But what the heck had that supernatural superwoman been doing, playing around with the very human Aldred?

Well, she'd worry about that later. Of course, Aldred knew several of her secrets now, but she knew an important one of his, too.

Now she, plain Paige Conner of the United States of America, sat at supper in the Great Hall of a castle in Dargentia, at the prince's ball. Her dress was elegant. Her hair was perfect, trimmed with an exquisite tiara. She wore green-tinted contact lenses without tears or squinting. Inside a tiny pocket at her side was the small swan pendant, for luck. She'd disguised her voice just a little, and she its tone sounded different even to her. Everything was perfect.

For now, at least. She'd been given the customary caution by Millicent, who'd fluttered about in the tower bedroom, examining her elegant handiwork. "Midnight, Eleanora," she'd warned. "You know the routine. Remember: You must be back here by twelve o'clock sharp. A second after, everything goes back the way it was."

Just like her scintillation the evening she'd first nearly seduced Niko. Or he'd nearly seduced her, she still wasn't sure which.

And now here she was. Before her was a magnificently appointed table, replete with fine linen, precious crystal and delicate china. At each setting was a special edition of the souvenir brochure she'd written, bound in parchment, printed in filigree, the pages laced together with thin silver cord. With a heavy sterling fork she ate a delicious squab stuffed with wild rice and truffles.

264

In the background the orchestra played a soft selection of old standards.

More important than the trimmings were the people. About her were representatives of all the royal families of the western world. She even recognized a few of the more publicized: the Grimaldis of Monaco, and several Windsors of Britain.

The gallery above was jammed with eager onlookers. Firm but friendly Dargentians had been selected for crowd control; tourists were to take turns at the balcony rails, watching the romantic drama unfold on the dance floor below. Paige wondered if any of them saw through her disguise, realizing she was no more noble than they. But she doubted it—not after Millicent's wondrous handiwork.

And at her side was Prince Nicholas of Dargentia. If she'd thought him handsome before, now he was magnificent, with his frilled white shirt and crimson, medal-clad sash emphasizing the breadth of his chest. He looked like the royalty he was, tall and straight in tie and tails. His tawny hair and beard were perfect. His coffee-dark eyes sparkled as he surveyed his domain. And her.

He thought her to be Princess Eleanora of Monteubique. Though she'd never believed Lois Lane couldn't immediately recognize that Clark Kent was Superman, the Man of Steel had never had a fairy godmother. Paige had asked that Millicent use magic to hide her identity. And the way Niko looked at her—the poor guy had no idea she was plain Paige Conner.

She smiled and looked down at her food.

"Enjoying your meal?" The gentleness in his deep baritone voice made the mundane question a caress. Still, there was a note in it that she couldn't quite figure out. Was it falsity or fascination? Whatever it was, she hadn't heard it before.

"Oh, yes." She turned her head to slant her gaze through her lashes. "But I'm enjoying the company even more."

She nearly crowed inside. Oh, had Millicent come through this time!

Not only did she look like a Princess Eleanora; for the second time in her life, Paige Conner scintillated.

Of course none of this would last. She was only here, she reminded herself, to keep an eye on Niko. To convince him, if the moment arose and his subjects insisted on his adherence to

## Linda O. Johnston

legend, that everyone's best intests would be served if he shelved his stubbornness long enough to suggest he'd keep an open mind.

Edouard was at the same table, flirting with a foreign royal. She could keep an eye on him, but perhaps he had planned his explosive plot to detonate automatically, without his overt intervention.

She would stay alert, though it was possible that Edouard had been all talk, or that the people he'd tried to incite remained convinced. Maybe nothing at all untoward would occur on this wonderful night.

Just in case, though, and just for tonight, she was a princess. Princess Eleanora of Monteubique.

She'd had a bad moment, just after the fish course. Niko had left her side abruptly. Had he found her out so quickly?

She'd followed to make sure he wasn't left alone to be confronted by any disgruntled subjects. He'd seemed glad to see her. And he'd invited her back to his table.

No, he couldn't know her game—though, ironically, that fact irritated her. She'd thought him perceptive, but he was no different from most men, swayed by pretty trappings and scintillation.

Just in case she was wrong, she devised a test for him. "This pamphlet on Dargentia's past is charming. Did you write it?"

"No, I hired it done—by a prominent scholar from the United States." His tone was bland, and he continued to eat. Was that all he had to say?

"Were you pleased with this scholar?" She shrugged prettily at his curious glance. "I might want a similar work about Monteubique."

Monteubique really existed; Millicent had assured her of that. It was a tiny Mediterranean island that had probably never been anything but Italian, but Paige's fairy godmother had professed that the potency of her magic to protect Paige's alter ego extended to adding a line here and there in history books about its fictional former ruling family.

"Yes, I suppose I'd recommend her."

*Suppose?* Nothing more glowing than that? Paige prevented herself from scowling. She knew she should shut up; more questions about herself might lead to more answers she didn't want to hear. But she pressed on. "Then this scholar is a woman?"

"Yes. An excellent researcher. Thorough."

## The Glass Slipper

What do you really think of her? Paige wanted to demand. Before she could figure out what to do with her frustration, Aldred entered the room and caught Niko's eye.

"Excuse me," the prince said. He dabbed his mouth and beard with his napkin, then stood.

Paige watched as he headed for his mentor. Darn him! His dull description of his American scholar hurt.

Well, she wouldn't let it ruin her evening. She turned toward the man on her right. "Isn't the food delightful?" she asked Prince Mihailo.

"Yes, this supper is nice." The Bulgarian's English was guttural and heavily accented. "Are you liking it?"

"Very much." Flashing Mihailo a flirtatious smile, she made it a point not to stare at the single shaggy brow hovering above his eyes.

As he returned her smile, his puffy cheeks expanded into balloons, nearly hiding his pale brown eyes. "I would like to dance with you later, okay?"

She'd planned to monopolize Niko for the evening. That way, she would always know where he was, and she'd be by his side if any trouble occurred. But she couldn't explain that to the mooselike man seated beside her. "Perhaps," she said, lowering her eyes coyly.

His smile widened, revealing a gold tooth.

Paige looked toward Niko. He and Aldred were conversing animatedly. Aldred held some papers, and both men glanced frequently toward her.

Had Aldred given her away? Even if he'd brought research material on Monteubique, nothing should refute her claims.

Unless Millicent had messed up. But surely Aldred would cover for her. Wouldn't he?

Her appetite evaporated. When Maibelle came to the head table to inquire whether everyone was enjoying the meal, she stared at Paige's half-full plate. "Is something wrong?" the maid asked, sounding troubled. At least there was no recognition written on her face.

There was nothing at all wrong with the food, just with Paige's fears. To ease the chef's concerns, Paige replied, "I'm simply too excited to eat."

# Linda O. Johnston

That was true. A huge lump formed in her stomach as Niko neared. Would he toss her out?

But he smiled and took his seat again. He didn't comment on what had called him away as he began to eat again.

She wouldn't worry about it. At least not much.

Plates were soon cleared. Paige noted that among the buspersons were the two brothers Le Blanc, the ardent legend-advocates whom she'd seen deep in conversation with Edouard. Their presence was no surprise and could, perhaps, be innocuous. Dargentians everywhere had been recruited to help at the ball and its attendant festivities. She'd keep an eye on them, too, though, along with Edouard. But with three people to watch and only two eyes of her own, she realized she might have bitten off more than she could chew.

Better—and more enjoyable—that she focus on Niko.

For now she concentrated on chewing her meal. Nothing untoward was happening at the moment. Dessert consisted of light French pastries and Italian fruit ice. The coffee was a thick, dark brew that reminded Paige of Niko's eyes.

Then supper was over.

Paige rose as Niko pulled out her chair. She turned to him, managing to stand close enough that she brushed her bosom against his chest. She looked up, her eyes wide. "How do we spend the rest of the evening, Your Highness?"

"However you'd like."

She smiled, a world of suggestion in her eyes. But all she said was, "I love to dance."

"Then so you shall."

As the prince led her back to the dance floor, the orchestra struck up another selection. Her side and hand tingled where he touched her. Then he spun her into a pulsing three-step rhythm.

His deep, dark, hypnotic eyes fastened on hers. As Paige dipped and whirled about the floor, she had an urge to run her fingertips over his sensuous, smiling mouth, to touch the soft silkiness of his beard. She laughed aloud. She felt as though Millicent's magic wand hung above her, raining down happiness. And, oh, what a wonderful evening was still ahead of her, in Niko's arms.

The first dance lasted much longer than three minutes, perhaps to make up for Niko's not having waltzed with her earlier. Still, it ended all too soon. Taking her hand, he led her to the edge of the dance floor. He released her and bowed from his waist. "Thank you, Your Highness. Now I must excuse myself."

Paige's blood froze in her veins. "But . . ." Where was Millicent's scintillation now, when she needed it? She nearly dipped her head to hide her alarm with her hair. Catching herself, she reached up to straighten her tiara instead. "Oh, but Your Highness, I'd hoped that we could dance the evening away." She dropped her hand to her side, smoothing the soft fabric of her draping white gown.

"I can imagine nothing more delightful," he said, "but, you see—" He gestured expansively toward the dancers who'd joined them, a surging sea of sparkles and black coats. "They're all my guests. I don't want to neglect anyone. I'm sure you'll get your wish and dance as much as you want. Someone as charming as you . . ." With that, he turned away. In a moment he'd taken the hand of a willowy woman in peach whose neck reminded Paige of the swans'.

She stood there, stunned. How could she keep an eye on Niko if she wasn't dancing with him all night? Wasn't that how it happened in fairy tales—the prince was so captivated by the princess that he paid cool attention to everyone else? *Millicent!* Paige's mind screamed. *What do I do now?*

*Keep scintillating, dear,* came the voice in her head.

And so she did. First she sought out the lumbering, one-browed Prince Mihailo. He was at the fringe of the dance floor, apparently attempting to make up his mind which lovely lady he'd let scorn him next. His former partner Suzanne was nearby, but she shimmered in her silver gown in the arms of a man much more elegant. Poor Mihailo's face was mournful until his light brown eyes lit on Paige.

"Princess! Are you having a most delightful evening?"

She put out her lower lip in a pretty pout. "No, I'm not, Mihailo. I'm not dancing enough."

"Would you . . . I mean, princess, may I have your next dance?"

"Why, Your Highness, I'd be delighted."

He spun her away, and she tried hard not to compare his labored dips and bobs with the graceful sweep of Prince Niko's dancing.

She watched the glitz and glitter as the other dancers swirled

# Linda O. Johnston

to the orchestra's beautiful music. The vast, airy room turned warm with all the bodies in motion. Now and then she was washed with the evanescent scent of expensive perfume.

Mihailo clearly would have been ecstatic to monopolize her for the rest of the evening. But she found it nearly impossible to maintain surveillance over Niko while nodding in rhythm for Mihailo to keep him in step.

And watching Niko was why she was here.

So she sought out a new partner. She spotted Rudy on the dance floor, dancing at arm's length from the long-legged Gretta. Thanking Mihailo, she excused herself and swept off in Niko's cousin's direction.

Happily, he stood near Niko, who'd found yet another partner. Unhappily, that partner was a gorgeous brunette. Niko's expression as he talked with her seemed rapt.

As Paige came by, though, he looked up. Their eyes met, and something unspoken passed between them. A wave of warmth surged through Paige.

Surely he felt the magnetism, too. She opened her lips, searching for something to say.

But Niko's eyes returned to the woman in his arms. And Paige's eyes stung.

She caught herself. Time to scintillate again.

Rudy noticed her over the shoulder of Gretta's strapless gown. Paige stood still, smiling flirtatiously and then glancing away. She pretended to be watching for someone, which wasn't hard, because she was. But she knew exactly where Niko was—nearby, with that beautiful brunette in his arms.

When the song ended Rudy bowed and excused himself from Gretta. He approached Paige, his eyes scanning the hard stone of the ballroom floor. "Princess Eleanora," he stammered, "may I have the next dance?"

Paige batted her eyelashes as though he might notice. "I'd be delighted."

Despite his lack of other social graces, Rudy was a surprisingly strong, smooth dancer—though not as graceful as Niko. He led her in gliding circles that weaved them among the many others whirling about the ballroom. The music was sweet, the rhythm classical, and Paige danced happily with the prince's usually diffident cousin.

Best of all, she remained near Niko and his irritatingly pretty partner.

"Dargentia is a wonderful place," she said dreamily, speaking loudly enough for him to hear over the music. "How lucky you are to live here and to have Prince Nicholas as a relative."

"Prince Charming, yes. All Dargentians are most proud of him."

"*But* . . ." Paige said. "I hear a 'but' in your voice."

"Oh, no, princess," Rudy quickly contradicted her, his eyes not quite meeting hers. "If you are the one our prince wishes to marry, you will be quite fortunate."

The idea sent a flutter of hope flying through Paige like a cluster of Millicent's magical moths, but only for a moment. She immediately remembered just who she was and why she was there. Princess Eleanora was as much a myth as Dargentia's celebrated legends, and Prince Niko was determined to select a royal bride.

Still, she decided to push Rudy a bit farther. "What about those legends I've heard so much of? The ones that say he must find the missing crown jewels and then wed a commoner."

Rudy's tact remained intact. "There are those who think the legends must be followed to the letter, princess. But all Dargentians believe Niko has the interests of his subjects at heart."

"Even if he disobeys the legends?"

"He will do the right thing, Princess Eleanora. Whatever that turns out to be."

Happy to hear of Rudy's still-steadfast loyalty, she considered confiding in him.

But that would mean she had to disclose Millicent's magic, for surely Rudy wouldn't otherwise believe the pretty, scintillating princess before him was plain Paige Conner. And secrecy was one of Millicent's many rules.

One the fairy godmother herself had broken with Aldred.

Still, Paige would stay silent, with every inch of her remaining alert. Only that way could she help Niko.

She excused herself at the end of the dance. Niko seemed in search of a new partner, and she positioned herself in his path.

He strode in her direction. Their eyes met. He stopped abruptly. He smiled—and passed her right by.

Paige felt her insides fall. She bit her lower lip, then pasted

271

back her evening's scintillating smile. She pretended not to watch as Niko bowed to the simpering young woman before him, a short, ruddy person who shouldn't have worn lavender.

Paige caught the eye of the unattached man nearest her; someone's brother, she imagined, not yet twenty. But the short-haired, lanky fellow gallantly spun her into the next dance, one she didn't know. It involved intricate slides and turns. Fortunately, her partner was proficient, and she easily followed, her gaze still following Niko.

At least here, where there were plenty of people, he should be safe.

Wouldn't he? Surely no unhappy subjects would crash the ball to crush Niko's aspirations of wedding a royal bride.

Or wasn't that exactly what they would do?

Suddenly worried, Paige glanced about. Maybe she should have befriended that Elkins person. That way, maybe she'd know which of the tuxedoed strangers sliding about the floor were security guards.

Ah, there! In the center of the dance floor was George Elkins himself, formal finery not hiding his beefy bulk. Charlotte was in his arms. What was the Cockney security chief saying to make Niko's aunt blush that way? Despite herself, Paige grinned in amusement, and her young partner beamed back.

After that dance she again captured Niko's attention. Though his smile seemed almost sad, he again chose another partner.

With a sigh, Paige sought out someone else with whom she could dance.

Edouard. He was standing alone.

Managing to maneuver toward him, she dealt coyly with the tuxedoed and traitorous silver fox, glancing away the instant his smug, sly eyes met her coquettish ones. She adjusted the shoulders of her draping white dress, knowing he watched. She was getting pretty good at this flirty stuff. Thanks, Millicent!

"Would you care to dance?" He spoke in French, his thin lips barely curling in a grin more snide than inviting. He held out his hand. His gloves were pristine white, as though he'd touched no one and nothing all night.

"*Oui, merci,* monsieur," replied Paige, trying to sound delighted. The orchestra leapt into a cha-cha, whose strong beat didn't lend itself to intimate inquisition. As it ended, though,

Paige stayed at Edouard's side while the next waltz began without them. Maybe she could learn something right from the source. "Tell me, monsieur," she said, her voice low and throaty. "I hear you are close to the prince. Isn't this ball a delightful event?"

His laugh was humorless. "It was a foolish idea. It won't save the country."

"Was that its purpose?"

"Dargentia is a cesspool of poverty," Edouard spat. "And the prince keeps dreaming of schemes to save it. But this won't do it."

Paige pretended to be shocked. "But why not? Perhaps the prince will find a rich royal bride."

You? Edouard's scornful sneer asked. "That's possible, of course," he said, "but the real reason for the ball was to launch the country as a big tourist attraction. Do you see this place becoming London or Paris or Rome?"

"It's quite charming." Paige tried to keep defensiveness from her voice; he'd no idea she cared for this country. Deciding to goad him, hoping he'd reveal his real plans, she leaned toward him conspiratorially and lied. "There are rumors he's found the missing Dargentian crown jewels. Is this so?"

Edouard was tall, and when he stiffened he seemed all the taller. "I wouldn't know, Your Highness. But if your reason for being here is to try to become the bride of a rich and powerful prince, you ought to return home."

"But isn't Prince Nicholas—"

"He certainly isn't rich, and even if you can call what he has power, I've a suspicion it'll be cut short soon. Very soon." Edouard's deep, dark laugh chilled Paige.

"Tell me more." She forced a smile, touching her tiara as she drew closer.

His brown eyes turned beady, but then he laughed once more. "No, I don't think I will. But keep your eyes open—" He seemed to choke on his own words, then regained his cool. "Consider this: If you're thinking of allying your family and country with Dargentia, you will find very quickly that it's best to look someplace other than Prince Nicholas." He reached out and stroked her upper arm with his gloved hand.

She forced herself to keep her eyes flirtatious without flinching. "I will keep that in mind," she said, her voice a purr.

273

# Linda O. Johnston

But her thoughts were careening. If she'd read correctly between Edouard's lines, he had suggested that something was indeed about to happen at the ball. Certainly he thought he was about to ascend to power. And that could happen only if Dargentia's tourist industry failed to fly.

She looked up at the crowded gallery and the well-dressed people staring down at the dance floor. She listened to the excited hum of voices from up there.

With all the tourists here, and those booked to follow, something would have to scare them off.

Tonight.

The rumors had to be true. Edouard must have incited his fellow subjects to insist, tonight, that Niko follow the legends and take a commoner for his bride.

Paige had to prevent any disturbance. Would it help to swallow her distaste and stick close to Edouard? The silver fox seemed to have taken a liking to Princess Eleanora.

But as she'd realized before, the vicious plan might have a life of its own. Perhaps no one needed to wait for a signal from Edouard.

She was better off sticking with brave, stubborn, exasperating Niko.

She looked around for him, trying not to seem obvious. "It is such a pretty sight, all those dancers," she said to Edouard. "And the interested people waving down from the gallery above."

"Haven't you heard the legends, Your Highness? If Prince Niko were wise, he'd select his bride from up on the balcony, instead of here, in the ballroom." He met her eyes with a snide smile. "Perhaps you ought to head up there and wait for him."

Did he see through her? No, surely not. He was just trying to tease the scintillating princess he thought he held in his arms. She laughed. "Oh, but then, monsieur, he would certainly not choose me. I doubt Prince Nicholas of Dargentia would wed someone who'd played a trick on him."

That was nearly the first true thing she'd said all evening. But she didn't care any more for herself. She only wanted Niko to succeed, and his country to survive.

She spotted the prince in the middle of the floor. In his arms now was a short, slim woman with barrel-curled hair, whose billowing aqua dress would have reminded Paige of something from

274

the antebellum southern United States if it hadn't been for its layer of shiny modern bugle beads.

If he was so attracted to Princess Eleanora, why did he avoid her? Surely he could spare her every couple of dances.

She didn't want to lop off her contact with Edouard, though—for she still wished to keep close tabs on him. She looked up at her companion expectantly.

"Would you like to dance?" he asked.

"Of course."

When their waltz ended Edouard appeared eager to keep Princess Eleanora's company, but Paige excused herself. "I believe I need a rest." When he began to follow her from the dance floor she smiled ever so sweetly and raised her hand. "Oh, please don't let me ruin your good time. There are many others who will be eager to dance with you. Perhaps, in a while, we can dance again."

She walked quickly away, then turned to make sure she wasn't being followed. Edouard had, fortunately, stopped to speak with a short blonde in a long black sheath.

Paige stood near the dance floor as the next waltz began. Prince Nicholas's eyes roved the crowd for his next partner, and Princess Eleanora once more captured his gaze. He smiled. She lowered her chin and licked her lips. Surely, this time he wouldn't refuse an invitation so scintillating.

He didn't. He began to approach. Paige's insides fluttered like butterfly wings.

She was just here to help him save his country, she admonished her flittery self. No need to get all excited just because that regal stride approached. So what if the smile on his sensuous lips was for her? And if the intense gaze of his coffee-rich eyes captured hers, this was still just business.

Sure it was.

He stopped before her. His chest almost touched hers, causing the points of near contact to tingle. His voice reverberated from deep in his throat. "I've been wanting to dance with you again all evening."

"And I with you," she barely whispered. Her mouth went dry. She felt dizzy with the aroma of autumn leaves and citrus.

He took her hand, then pulled her close. She gasped as his hard, warm body pressed against hers. Deep inside, she melted and moistened. His touch seemed a prelude to making love, not a mere dance.

The orchestra began a slow, evocative song, full of deep, driving emotion. It was too torrid a tune to stimulate the sweep of a waltz or any other dance Paige knew.

Niko seemed not to care. He simply held Princess Eleanora tightly against him. One hand splayed on her back, the other clutched her hand to his taut chest. She nestled her head beneath his chin. She felt the bristles of his soft beard blend with her hair.

Their feet moved to the music's sensual throb. Paige experienced an answering pulsation inside her body. She recalled her one, wonderful afternoon with him in the mountains. The memory of their moans and whispers, strokes and rhythms resounded in her mind, all embodied in the eerie, exciting rhythm of the music.

Her legs nearly folded beneath her. Niko held her upright. He pulled her closer still, making her want to collapse all over again.

She shut her eyes. She had no sense of the passage of time. She was totally enrapt. "Princess," he murmured against her hair. His arms grew tighter.

And then they loosened. Only then did Paige realize the music had stopped.

She opened her eyes. She swallowed. She tried to step back, but Niko still held her. Raising her chin, she looked at him. There was a raging fire in his dark, dark eyes. His lips were slightly parted, and Paige wanted to touch them.

From the upper balcony cheers rang out. Applause, too, though muffled by hands wearing formal gloves. Paige felt herself flush and hoped it was becoming.

Of course it would be, on this magical night on which she was beautiful. On which she scintillated.

If only the people in the gallery could actually choose Niko's bride. This was the first time they had reacted this way.

But Paige understood the rules. The winner of the tourist contest would be someone who voted for Niko's own selection.

"Thank you for this dance," he said in the deep, rich voice that sent a sensuous song skimming through her.

Then he let her go.

She felt weak, as though she'd fall right there, but he grasped her elbow and righted her.

Only then did she realize that they were alone on the dance

floor. The rest of the royals stood about, watching them, a shimmering, silent crowd compared with the avid onlookers above. Edouard glowered. In the eyes of some regal women, Paige saw envy; in others, speculation. In none was there friendliness.

No matter; she was with Niko. That was all that counted. After that dance, after their irresistible bonding, surely he understood that they belonged together—for tonight. That was all. So she could protect him.

He'd stay by her side. She knew he would.

The applause from those around the ballroom started then. It was thin at first, and then it was taken up by the crowd. A few masculine voices cheered. Paige felt herself blush again—in pleasure as much as acknowledgment. Everyone had seen it. Everyone, even the royals, had recognized the magic of Princess Eleanora of Monteubique in Prince Nicholas's arms.

If only it were real. If only she were the princess who could claim the evening's prize of the prince. If he could sweep her onto his stallion and ride off into the night. Proclaim her his bride.

But the best she could hope was that she could help him quell the unrest in his kingdom that Edouard had fomented.

The orchestra began the next number. It was a lilting tune, and Paige swayed along. She turned expectantly toward Niko—and grew suddenly still.

His eyes looked haunted. Hurt. But only for an instant. They were shuttered, and he bowed.

No! He had to stay at her side. He couldn't dismiss her again.

But he did. "Thank you, Your Highness." His voice was stiff and formal. There was an edge behind it, as though having to say it sliced something inside him. "I enjoyed this dance, but I must excuse myself again."

Paige wanted to shout, "Wait! Stop! Hold it!"

Instead, she politely offered her thanks.

She watched after him, her heart heavy with despair. Where was he going without her?

He bowed before a new partner. Desperately, Paige looked about. Mihailo was nearby, and she manufactured a smile. She had to appear calm. Gracious. Regal.

"May I again have your next dance?" Poor Mihailo. He tried hard to please a person incapable, at the moment, of pleasure.

"Of course," she said. She threw herself into the dance, lightening her steps to make up for Mihailo's lumbering.

The music went on forever. When the dance was done she looked around, then gasped.

Her eyes scanned the floor, then swept the sidelines of the room. Nothing.

Prince Niko was gone.

# Chapter Twenty-four

Paige murmured something to Mihailo, she wasn't sure what. She fled from the dance floor, then circled its periphery. Surely she was mistaken. Niko had to be here.

But he wasn't.

Well then, she had to be systematic. She scanned the room for his subjects.

She found no one. Not Edouard. Oh, no!

Not even Rudy or Charlotte, Suzanne or Aldred, or anyone else she knew before tonight. Not even Maibelle. Or that Elkins person.

If only she recognized some of his guards. For all she knew, they'd left, too.

After dinner was over she'd lost track of the Le Blanc brothers. Maybe she should have followed them instead of Niko. They were possible conspirators with Edouard, after all. And they'd certainly made it clear that they wanted Niko to follow the legends—to find Les Fabuleux, then marry a commoner.

He hadn't done the former, partly thanks to her, and now, by hosting this ball, he was demonstrating how unlikely he was to do the latter. He'd explained it all to his subjects, but that hadn't seemed to make them happy.

Were they about to demonstrate just how unhappy with him and his ideas they really were?

She had to be there to convince them otherwise.

*She* did? As though she, ordinary Paige Conner, would be more convincing than their prince.

She nearly stopped in her tracks. What was she thinking of? Why was she even here, somehow believing she could help Prince Niko in the face of an angry mob of subjects?

She glanced down disparagingly at herself—and smiled. She wasn't plain Paige Conner, not at this moment; she was the scintillating Princess Eleanora!

# Linda O. Johnston

She raised her wrist to look at the diamond-studded bracelet watch Millicent had magically created for her. It was after eleven o'clock already. Her entrance had been intended to be late, and the evening had passed so quickly. She hadn't much time left.

She swept swiftly from the room, brushing past gaily dressed people, nodding politely at their curious stares. Wasn't that what someone scintillating would do?

She looked about in the cold stone hall. The red runner in its center ran in both directions. Which way should she go?

Toward the upstairs gallery. From there she'd be able to see the entire ballroom, just in case she'd missed the prince. Or so she thought.

Tourists thronged in the narrow gallery framing the upper edge of the ballroom. She didn't count the number of times she said, "Excuse me," then smilingly squeezed her way between formally dressed men and women. Many tried to stop her, apparently recognizing her from her dancing with Niko.

"I vote for you," one matron in a low-cut black dress gushed.

"Thank you," Paige said with a pleased and scintillating smile, hiding her worry deep inside.

"Such a lovely princess," said a seventyish man in a pink tuxedo coat.

Again Paige minded her manners, managing to thank him as a poised princess might before oozing forward.

But Paige didn't see her quarry on the balcony or below.

Where was Niko? Showing off the showiest parts of the castle to the next princess on his list, perhaps. The portrait gallery was nearby. Squeezing her way back out of the gallery, she headed there. Its lights blazed brilliantly, but except for Niko's ancestors it was empty. They stared down at her accusingly from their places along the walls. "I'll help him, I promise," she whispered.

As she tried to hurry out, one particularly haughty stare halted her beside the door. She stopped before the lifesize rendering of King Nicholas I, all decked out in white uniform and shiny medals. He looked angry and uncaring in his aristocratic finery. She shivered. This was Niko's predecessor and namesake?

She didn't like the looks of him at all.

But that had nothing to do with what she needed to accomplish. As though to assuage his temper, she told him, "Niko will be fine," praying it was so. "But I wish your Aldred had been clearer with his clues. Niko'd be ever so much better off if he could find those damned crown jewels.''

*You'll find them,* came a voice in her head.

She gasped aloud. "Millicent, is that you?"

*Yes, dear. But you'd better get out to the moat,* tout de suite.

"Sure, I'll go quickly. Is Niko there?"

*Yes, and he needs you.*

Bless you and your magic, Millicent, Paige thought.

Niko needed her.

Lifting the skirt of her flowing white gown, she fled down the hall. At the base of the stairs she nearly ran into Rudy.

"What's wrong, Your Highness?" He very nearly met her eyes with his.

She answered his question with one of her own. "Do you know where Niko is? I—I promised the next dance to him."

He gave a quick shake of his head. "He's here somewhere. He called an impromptu family meeting, then called it off. . . . I'm sorry. You don't need to hear this."

But he was clearly worried. And Paige did need to hear that, but not as Princess Eleanora.

"Well, if you see him again, tell him I won't wait forever for that dance." She kept her tone frothy, but inside the bubble of hope that all was well had burst.

She sped down one hall after another. Most were empty, but, as she neared the Great Hall, milling royal guests gawked at her. Fortunately, she now knew her way about. Unfortunately, she couldn't run well in her gown. Not that she was trying to impress anyone at the moment. But her heels were high and her sweeping skirt hindered her legs.

She reached the kitchen. That was the easiest way out to the moat. Noting that there were no servants about, no Dargentians bustling around cleaning up after dinner, she shuddered. Where were they? Was there actually about to be a showdown?

As she reached for the door, she stopped. Edouard approached from the opposite direction.

If he was here, maybe everything was all right. Surely he'd want to be in the thick of the action, if there was any.

Nevertheless, her heart raced. She kept her feet still, though her toes felt like tapping. "Monsieur," she greeted him flirtatiously. "I thought you might have abandoned the ball."

# Linda O. Johnston

"You noticed my absence?" A cool, preening smile tugged at the silver fox's sly lips. He stopped stiffly beside her. "I was called away. National emergency."

"Oh, dear." Paige felt her throat constrict. Was that the reason for Niko's meeting? She kept her voice coy, her eyes flirtatious. "What emergency?"

"An attack on our prince," he said.

"What?" Paige felt tears rush to her eyes. Was she too late? "Should we call the authorities?"

Edouard laughed, a nasty, rusty sound. "I *am* the authorities, Your Highness. And the attack wasn't serious—an attack of conscience, I believe."

Then he was simply joking with her. Or was he trying to cover up for what was really happening?

Unlikely; the more visitors he frightened off from Dargentia, including Princess Eleanora of Monteubique, the happier he'd be.

He said no more about the subject. Paige believed he'd been referring to the meeting Rudy'd mentioned, and Niko's failure to follow through with whatever he'd intended to say. She felt relieved that the attack on Niko hadn't been physical—not yet. But what had been on the prince's mind?

Even if Edouard knew, he wasn't likely to tell Princess Eleanora. Paige had to get to Niko. "Perhaps we can have another dance later, monsieur," she said in her most scintillating tone. "Right now I must powder my nose."

"A lovely nose it is," he said. His gloved finger reached out and touched it. Paige prevented herself from flinching; she smiled instead and, pivoting, walked slowly down the hall.

In a moment she turned to be sure Edouard had headed the other way. Then she ducked into the empty kitchen and hurried on through.

The night was dark, the black sky barren of moon and stars. A pall of dampness hung in the air, a sign of a threatening storm.

Fortunately, the dinner for the tourists and townsfolk was over; only empty tables stood in rows to show where it had been served. The courtyard was empty.

Still, to stay in character, Paige knew she should stumble around in the dim lights from the torches on the castle walls. Princess Eleanora wouldn't know the way between the battlements to the quiet corner by the moat.

282

But she hadn't time for niceties. Niko could be in trouble.

Lifting her skirt to hustle, she sped forward.

As she hurried along the path to the bulwark gate, she stopped, listening. There were angry voices ahead, much louder than the party sounds from behind her.

Paige tried to swallow the lump swelling in her throat. Oh, Niko, she cried inside. She started forward once more, hurriedly. What could she do against a belligerent crowd? Maybe, if she was clever enough, she could still help him save his kingdom. But when had Paige Conner ever been clever enough?

Remember, she admonished herself, for this moment, for almost another hour, she wasn't plain Paige Conner. She was scintillating Princess Eleanora of Monteubique. She could work miracles.

Her stride was confident as she pushed open the gate in the bulwark wall. And then she stopped, keeping close to the wall so as not to be noticed, her heart clenched like a rubber ball in a child's fist. The scent of dampness nearly choked her—or was it the sight she saw?

Niko stood atop her favorite stone bench, looking the regal ruler in the tuxedo decorated with his country's medals of valor. His chin, in his neatly trimmed, tawny beard, was raised as confidently as she'd ever seen it.

The moat rim was dimly lit by the electric torches along the wall. But more darkness than shadow caused the bleakness on Niko's face.

He was surrounded by Dargentians. And they were angry.

Aldred stood beside Niko on the bench, trying to speak. "Listen to me," he shouted. "The legends aren't what you—"

"Who are you to speak of our legends?" yelled Jean Le Blanc. The mouse-colored mustache Paige remembered well from her conversation with the Le Blanc brothers now seemed more ominous than ludicrous.

"You lived away from here, in luxury instead of tyranny," agreed his lanky, middle-aged sibling.

"You are not to marry at all until you find Les Fabuleux." Strange, Paige thought, that Monsieur Pelerin, the bear of a man with the clue passed down through his family that had turned out worthless, would make such a point in front of this angry crowd.

# Linda O. Johnston

After all, it was partly due to him that the prince hadn't found the crown jewels.

Wasn't it?

She reached into her pocket. The small swan pendant was still there.

She noted, suddenly, that she was shivering. The warm breeze of the summer night blew against the sheen on her face caused by the humidity, chilling her. Or was it her nervousness that made her shake?

There were perhaps a hundred Dargentians present. Many were dressed in the dark uniforms they'd worn to serve Prince Niko's guests at the ball. They filled the area between the wall and the moat, surrounding Niko and Aldred. Beyond them, Paige could see the normality of this nighttime haven. White geese glided in the water and farther away, less visible in shadows behind the dimly lighted humans, were the black swans.

Swans. The symbols of Dargentia, Aldred had once told her.

Like the small swan pendant in her pocket, which she still clutched.

Like the crumbling swan statue, now surrounded by irate Dargentians.

What had Aldred's ancestor's clue to Les Fabuleux said about symbols? No, it was spirits.

She hadn't remembered the clue verbatim, though he'd written it down and she'd studied it once in a while. But now, as though the man who'd been silenced by the throng was speaking, she heard Aldred's voice inside her head, reciting the entire thing:

Our king is fleeing. He will not risk carrying Les Fabuleux. They will be needed most sorely when the throne is restored to ensure its longevity.

Oh, how sad is the day that the rightful rulers of Dargentia, King Nicholas, Queen Anna, Prince Stephan and Prince Wenzel, can no longer gaze upon the precious and powerful Fabuleux.

But their names and spirits shall remain with their kingdom.

Have all our protective spirits fled, too? How else could the throne have fallen?

And thus shall the crown jewels be found.

What could it mean?

Paige wracked her brain, trying to focus on the clue instead of the frightening sight before her. Niko's subjects were growing louder. At times their speech was so frenzied that she had to concentrate to understand their French. Fortunately, her command of the language had improved during her weeks in Dargentia.

"You're not listening to our concerns," one man shouted above the rest.

Niko raised his arms, trying to silence the crowd. "I told you before," he said. "I care more than anything about my people. And that's why—"

Another shout drowned him out. But Paige didn't hear what the angry woman said. Her mind was racing. Protective spirits. Swans.

*You're on the right track!* came an excited cry inside her mind. *Go to it, Eleanora.*

Thanks, Millicent, she thought. But she still didn't know . . .

"Please," Niko cried to his milling subjects. "I have something important to tell you."

"The only thing you can say that's important," yelled Pelerin, "is that you'll abdicate in favor of someone who cares what his people think."

"No more talk. Let's storm the castle and drive off the princesses," shouted someone Paige could not identify.

Suddenly she heard the thunking of an army of footsteps behind her. She turned toward the gate to see an army of tuxedoed thugs, led by George Elkins, heading toward her. The troops had arrived.

But what a disaster it would be for Niko if his ability to rule Dargentia and keep the peace was dependent on having his security force declare war on the people.

And how soon would the tourists arrive to find out what the commotion was about? They would surely flee the chaos soon thereafter.

Paige had to act. Now!

But how?

Her mind, almost unwillingly, returned to its previous train of thought. Protective spirits. Swans.

The names and protective spirits of the rightful rulers would remain with the kingdom. Names? King Nicholas, Queen Anna, and the princes, Stephan and Wenzel.

285

Stephan, Wenzel, Anna and Nicholas. Their first initials spelled *swan!*

Everything led to those lovely, aloof birds that adorned the moat.

She squeezed the small pendant she still held in her hand. How did swans relate to the hidden Fabuleux? What swan, besides the pendant, could have existed back then that still, today—

"*Attendez!*" Paige screamed. "Wait!" Somehow her voice carried more loudly than the angry ones around her, and the menacing footfalls approaching from behind. Suddenly all noise stopped.

All eyes were on her.

Slipping the pendant back into her pocket, she scurried from the shadows near the wall.

Immediately, her eyes sought Niko's. Although he scowled at her, there was something else on his face: fear. But not for himself—for her.

"This is not your business, Princess Eleanora," he stated. "Go back inside with the others."

"Oh, I will, Your Highness," she said in her most scintillating lilt. "But there's just one little matter I need to take care of out here first."

"Pa-princess—" Niko was so emotional, he seemed to be stuttering. Sweet, Paige thought. But she wouldn't be deterred.

She began walking forward, ignoring the obstruction of the crowd, which parted like Cecil B. DeMille's Red Sea. The skirt of her white gown swished about her legs, stopping in a single swirl as she halted before the crumbling swan statue.

So what if she wore a beautiful ball gown? So what if that gown was a pristine white? She'd only wear it for a short while anyway.

She glanced at her watch. Uh-oh. Only forty-five minutes left.

She studied the statue for a moment, examining its flaking stones and the flaws in its mortar.

She knew everyone was watching her. What if she was wrong? She wasn't; she was sure of it.

Quickly, she knelt, almost oblivious to the stain she was sure to put on her skirt. She picked at the stonework at the base; with the mortar loose, she had no trouble lifting one stone after another, though she found nothing—until she touched one at the very back. She pulled it out, reached inside—and felt the chill of metal.

"Niko!" she called in excitement.

No one stopped him as he stepped off the bench to join her. Together, they jiggled and rocked the large, rusting box, pulling until it burst from the base of the statue.

Awed whispers floated around them like feathers on the breeze. The words "Les Fabuleux" echoed everywhere.

Paige studied Niko. His dark eyes gleamed in anticipation. The corners of his mouth curved up in a nervous grin. Strong hands trembling, the symbolic signet ring on his finger, he forced open the squealing lid.

Inside were tattered remnants of ancient oilcloth.

And in them were the jewels.

An excited roar soared around them. Everyone in the crowd was cheering. "Les Fabuleux!"

The crown jewels were gorgeous! Niko and Paige pored through them, gasping and laughing. Rubies and diamonds, sapphires and amethysts, of every imaginable shape and size.

There was one golden crown for a king, another for his queen. The precious tiara and choker she'd heard of dripped with precious gems. Several huge jewels might once have been set in scepters. There were pendants, pins and loose stones in lavish abundance. Paige touched them, sifted their smooth, cold hardness through her fingers.

Gently, Niko took them from her. He turned toward his subjects, holding the large jewel-filled box aloft.

The crowd grew silent. Niko said nothing for a long moment, letting the anticipation grow. Paige felt the emotions of the people all about her. They waited for their prince to speak.

And speak he finally did. "My people, I present to you your crown jewels. Les Fabuleux."

For a long moment, all remained still. And then a shout arose. "Vive Niko! Vive Les Fabuleux!" The cry was repeated by three voices, then thirty; then the entire crowd was wishing Niko and the crown jewels to live long and prosper.

Only now did Paige allow herself to really look at the crowd. She recognized many people from her forays into town to search for legends: the Le Blanc brothers, of course, and the bearlike Pelerin. But others she'd considered much more benign had both-

287

ered to come here to try to enforce this country's legends; there was the rotund form of Monsieur Pologne and his well-padded neighbor, Madame de Font. Not Marcel and Annette Martin, though. They would have too much to do at the hotel—and, though they also set great store in this country's legends, they had too little interest in foisting them on their king by force.

Paige glanced toward the gate in the bulwark wall. Although George Elkins still stood there with his formally attired troops right behind him, they remained motionless, their advance halted by the activities by the moat.

She allowed herself to breathe deeply in relief.

Trying to remain unobtrusively behind the swan statue, she looked at the crumbling stonework and smiled. How often had she sat out here by the moat, staring at the real swans, ignoring the ancient sculpture that held the key to the puzzle that could save this kingdom?

She reached her hand toward it, stroking its cool, rough surface, feeling the dust and dirt of ages rub off on her fingers. "Thanks, friend," she whispered.

She looked at Niko. He was back standing on the bench, the box containing Les Fabuleux held firmly in his strong, steady hands. He was the ruler, and he was still in charge.

Or was he? Paige realized there was a new force afoot within the mob that already grew restless.

"That's only half the legend," shouted a gruff male voice. Paige looked up to see skinny but menacing Andre Le Blanc, arms folded before him, staring stone-faced at Niko. "This ball is still a farce. You must marry a commoner."

"Now wait a minute." Aldred, also still atop the bench, waved his hands in the air for attention. "My family has kept its counsel long enough. That legend had its origin in this country's need, but that need is long past."

"Keep quiet, old man." That was Pelerin, whose large form bore down on the bench.

"Let him speak." The Santa Claus figure of Monsieur Pologne, the manager of Le Grand Magasin, stepped to the front of the throng. "What do you mean, Aldred?"

"I've a legend of my own to tell you people," he said, his voice lower as he caught the crowd's attention. "Only it's a true story—the reason the jewel-and-marriage legend came into being.

*The Glass Slipper*

The original Aldred made it up and told his son, and the sons for centuries have passed it down. Each generation was sworn to secrecy—though at this point I don't know why it mattered, except at first.'' He paused and wiped his brow. ''Like all legends, I suppose the rationale grew less important than the tradition.''

''Get to the point, old man,'' growled a voice in the crowd—one quickly hushed by the rest.

Aldred's thin face appeared pained, as though his words hurt. ''I believe there is more at stake now than my family's honor in keeping our secret, and so I must speak.''

Paige's attention was captured, and she licked her lips in anticipation. Here, perhaps, was a true tidbit of history.

The crowd seemed willing to listen, too. It was quiet as Aldred began, a slight figure standing bravely before an uneasy horde.

''You all know the story of the way Nicholas the First was forced to flee Dargentia.''

A hundred heads nodded in the dim light. Good, Paige thought. Audience participation would keep their minds focused on the story and not their gripes.

Niko watched over them all. His dark eyes darted warily from side to side, as though he was concerned that the mob would join forces again and rush them. But all attention was trained on Aldred.

''Then, as now, my family served the rulers,'' the majordomo said. ''The Aldred of that time didn't at first flee. He had a mission. You see, the French had overrun Dargentia. There's a legend associated with that time: the story of L'Aigle, the Eagle, who swooped through the countryside, keeping the people fed.''

A murmur passed through the crowd. In Paige's research she had found the story of L'Aigle perhaps the most popular legend. Aldred had pushed a button that would keep the people interested.

Aldred puffed up his narrow chest importantly. ''I, my friends, know who L'Aigle was.''

''Me, too,'' came a small voice from the rear of the throng. Paige recognized the plump, pinafored figure of Madame de Font. If Paige recalled correctly, Madame de Font had been one of the many who'd taken particular pride in the legend of L'Aigle. ''He was Nicholas the First's brother, was he not?''

Aldred's expanded chest deflated, but only for an instant. ''So legend has said. And guess what, friends? I happen to know it's

# Linda O. Johnston

true. In fact, he was the reason for the creation of the legend you're now placing in front of our Niko as though it were law. But it was only my old ancestor Aldred, way back then, who made up a story to try to save this country."

"What do you mean?" cried the stout madame, wending her way through the crowd toward its front.

Aldred, his wild shock of salt-and-pepper hair waving in the warm summer night's breeze, gazed up at the dark night sky as though deciding how to continue. Many in the crowd let their eyes follow his, but not Niko; his attention stayed trained on his subjects. But even Paige eventually looked up; the moon was a bright three-quarters, and a myriad of stars surrounded it. Despite the dampness in the air, the sky contained few clouds.

Aldred continued, again facing his audience, "It was this way: Nicholas the First wasn't a particularly wonderful ruler. Though none of his people wanted the French to take over Dargentia, many had grown tired of him. When he fled there would have been a sense of relief in the kingdom—except for the intrusion of the French marauders. That's where L'Aigle came in."

"Nicholas's brother," repeated Madame de Font, who took a place at Aldred's feet and stood staring up at him, enrapt.

"Exactly," Aldred agreed. "He led raids all over the place, making sure the people were fed. But eventually the French caught on to him. Things got too hot, and he had to follow in his brother's footsteps. He fled Dargentia."

"Where did he go?" called a voice from the crowd. From what Paige could tell, the formerly angry mob had turned into a bunch of eager children enjoying a bedtime story.

Niko seemed to notice that, too, for he sat down on the bench and let his majordomo keep the floor.

"America," said Aldred. "Prince Wenzel ended up in the American colonies, in a small town called Williamsburg."

Paige gasped aloud. She felt Niko's eyes on her from where he sat only a few feet away. He knew of Paige's quest for her mysterious Wenzel. He stared, though, not at Paige but at Eleanora. She covered her mistake with a yawn and a sleepy smile.

But her body vibrated as though she was leaning on an idling race car. Was that *the* Wenzel? Could it be that her elusive Wenzel was the brother of Nicholas I, who'd had something to do with Dargentia's most cherished legends?

She turned her full attention back on the majordomo who'd captured the ears of the capital city with his tale.

"He married there, a commoner named, I think, Lucinda."

No, Paige thought. Leticia. Leticia Adamson was the woman who'd married the legendary L'Aigle, who'd had her fairy tale come true. But this detail, so important to Paige, would be trivial to everyone else. She said nothing, simply holding on to the statue of the swan for support.

"When things settled down the country wanted its own sovereignty back—though a new sovereign was in order. The people's thoughts turned longingly toward L'Aigle, but to many, anyone who could rout the French would have sufficed. Not my ancestor Aldred, though. Perhaps one of Nicholas's sons would have been accepted, though they were still too young. No, Aldred wanted L'Aigle to return—and he wanted his countrymen to want the same. And so he invented the legend."

"No one invents legends." The angry shout came from Jean Le Blanc, and Paige, who watched Niko nearly as closely as Aldred, noted the way the prince stiffened and began to rise. But the others in the crowd glared at Jean till he said no more. Niko stayed where he was, but his arms were crossed over his chest.

"They have to start somewhere," Aldred said mildly, wiping the back of his small hand across his moist brow. The tension was apparently getting to him, but he went gamely on. "To get the people to wait for the Prince Wenzel who'd fled to America, old Aldred circulated rumors that the only one who could permanently break the hold of the French on Dargentia had to first find the missing crown jewels. That would be easy for Wenzel; my ancestor had hidden them, and he could restore them simply enough."

"He's also the one who made up that stupid clue, wasn't he?" That was Monsieur Pologne.

"And gave my ancestor the signet ring." Pelerin's gruff voice carved through the damp air. He looked at Niko, who held his hand wearing the ring in the air. "What did the ring mean?"

"It was a clue to a hiding place on my ancestor's estate, resembling as it did an archway there. He'd hidden a swan pendant. I can only guess why now. Though he fully anticipated being right there when Wenzel returned, he put together a contingency plan, leaving clues for any royal to follow just in case he wasn't

291

# Linda O. Johnston

around any more—which turned out to be true. He must have hoped the royal who found the swan pendant would at worst recall the swans in the moat and, preferably, think of the swan statue right here.''

All eyes turned toward Paige, and she, in turn, faced the statue, again patting it as though it had feathers.

"That princess was the one who followed the clue," said Maibelle from the fringes of the crowd. Paige wondered if the versatile, still-dirndled chef and maid recognized the lowly historian.

No, that couldn't be.

"She's the one I'll bet Niko's chosen to marry." The voice in the crowd didn't exactly sound welcoming. "A princess instead of a commoner."

Paige couldn't look at Niko, though she longed to see the expression on his face.

But what did it matter? If he agreed, that only meant he'd fallen for the farce of Princess Eleanora. He had no interest in his plain historian, Paige Conner. She let her concentration rest on the rough texture of the swan statue against the heel of her hand. Better to think of how she felt on the outside of her body than inside her heart.

Aldred held up his hands to calm the restless crowd. "Wait; I'm not through with the background of the legends. My ancestor was still trying to pave the way for Wenzel the Eagle's return, remember. Wenzel had married a commoner in America. So, to the requirement that the person reascending the Dargentian throne had to find Les Fabuleux he added another twist. The one rightfully entitled to reign had to marry a commoner. It was as simple as that.''

"Did Wenzel ever try to come back?" Madame de Font had rested her bulk on the end of the bench, twisting so she could keep an eye on Aldred.

"He tried several times, but the French had assumed he would and were ready for him. Eventually he gave up and settled down in America, never to return. Aldred joined him, and eventually so did Nicholas the First's sons, who were the rightful heirs to the throne—Prince Niko is the descendant of the older one, Prince Stephan. That Aldred acted as their servant, but he kept his lines of communication open in Dargentia. So did his descendants. That was how things remained for all these centuries."

"Then what you're saying," said Pelerin, "is that the legend that our prince must marry a commoner for the kingdom to be stable was only a plot way back then to bring that Wenzel to power?"

"Exactly," Aldred said. "Niko has come back to rule on his own, all these years later. My ancestors were told to keep this quiet in case there was a need to enforce the legend again. As was I. But, my fellow Dargentians, there's no reason in the world that our Niko can't marry whomever he pleases."

Most members of the crowd turned now to stare at Niko. The prince, seated on the bench with his legs casually crossed, appeared pleased, Paige thought. Aldred had done it. He'd diffused the situation, let Niko feel comfortable continuing with his plans at the ball.

Aldred knew, of course, that Paige was no princess. But he'd paved the way for Niko to freely choose a royal bride.

She made herself smile in happiness for Niko.

But her smile froze as, practically as one, everyone turned from their prince toward her.

"Whomever he pleases," echoed a voice in the crowd as they stared at her.

Swallowing hard, Paige turned away from all the eyes on her to the only pair that mattered. Niko, too, was looking at her with his dark, intense gaze. "Whomever he pleases," he mouthed.

Niko rose. He bent to place the box with Les Fabuleux inside beneath the stone seat. Then he strode toward her.

Paige was poised to run.

# Chapter Twenty-five

Paige felt as though her legs had turned to smoke and been blown out from beneath her. Somehow, she managed to remain standing as Niko drew near.

How, she wondered, could her senses be so alert yet so numb?

There was the sound of his soft footfalls on the paved area between the bench and the statue where she stood. She heard them as though they drummed inside her head.

She watched as his large, muscular body, packaged in a perfectly alluring and sophisticated tuxedo, approached with the no-nonsense king-in-his-castle stride she knew so well.

She saw, in the dimness, light and shadows on the handsome, bearded face she had come to love. Those eyes of his entrapped hers, black in the darkness yet sparkling with something she didn't dare name.

She smelled his aroma of autumn leaves and citrus combined with the moist, floral smells near the moat. She tasted, on her lips, a yearning to place them tightly on his.

But there was more going on around her that she hardly noticed. She saw shapes moving about in a wave toward the open gate in the wall. She thought she heard whispers without focusing on what they said, except for an occasional, "Leave them alone" or "Privacy."

Hours passed before he reached her, she thought, though in real time it could only have been moments. But then, there he was. His hand took hers and swiftly drew her back to the bench he'd vacated. He helped her step up onto it, her flowing white skirt swishing about her legs.

No, she thought. What was happening here? He didn't know what, or who, she was. He was about to make a fool of himself, thanks to her—and she didn't know how to prevent it.

"Niko, wait," she whispered. "I have to tell you—"

He stopped her words with his own mouth, giving her a kiss

that robbed her of breath, willpower and even memory. What had she meant to say?

She tried to catch her breath as he broke away. "My people," he called in French, his deep voice reverberating loudly, though she thought she heard a catch in it. "I wish to introduce you to someone."

Paige saw the crowd again then, dozens of nicely dressed people, many in black uniforms, whose mob mentality had been psyched out by Aldred's ancestral confession. They were about to leave the clearing by the moat.

"Please let them go," she whispered, trying not to sound too frantic. "Niko, you don't understand—"

"Give me a little credit here, Princess." His knuckles gently rubbed her cheek in a gesture both tender and commanding.

People stood still. Faces, shadowed in the soft light, tipped up expectantly. All attention was back on Nicholas II, ruler of Dargentia.

And now the focus also encompassed the scintillating scam artist, Paige Conner. She squared her shoulders beneath her soft gown and lifted her chin. These people weren't a firing squad, she told herself, though they'd nearly fired Niko from being their prince. And what was about to happen here would certainly result in her being fired by Niko tomorrow.

But for now, she told herself, be a princess. For Niko. Then face the consequences of his rage when he had time to deal with her alone—and decide what to tell his subjects.

Her stomach, still filled with the evening's delicious dinner, began to contract like the dungeon walls in old movies, where the characters were threatened with being crushed. She stopped it midsquish by sheer determination; she had enough embarrassment to deal with.

"Now," said Niko loudly, so all could hear. His arm went about Paige. His hand gripped her shoulder, and she sensed a message in the hold. Was he keeping her there or handing her courage—or perhaps a bit of both? "I would like you all to meet the woman I intend to marry."

Sure enough, Paige began to sag, but the firmness of Niko's grip kept her standing. "Stop," she hissed from the side of her mouth. She fought for something to get his attention. "You haven't asked me to marry you."

"I'll get around to that, my love," he said softly.

Paige drew in her breath at his words.

His voice raised again, he said, "This wonderful woman is someone you saw me dancing with earlier. I'd imagine that many of those welcome tourists up in the gallery have already cast their votes for me to marry Princess Eleanora of Monteubique."

"If it weren't for the legends, I'll bet the ballot box would be stuffed by all of us, too," hollered Pelerin, amazing Paige. The crowd laughed, and Paige sensed their sweet approval—of Princess Eleanora, she reminded herself. Not of her.

"Well, thanks to Aldred, we know about the legends now," said Niko. "And I appreciate how quickly you've all accepted that what was created hundreds of years ago might not be needed today. But I have a little surprise for you. As it turns out, I'm going to be listening to the legends."

A murmur circulated through the crowd. What was Niko up to? Paige wondered.

"My friends, I would like to let you in on a little secret—one that would have been revealed soon enough anyway. There are a lot of people with courage around here. Aldred, for one, for telling you the truth." That statement was met by nods all around. "You have something to thank Princess Eleanora for—for locating Les Fabuleux." Again, there was a positive response.

Turning her with his hand, Niko looked at Paige, and the dampness of the evening seemed to sizzle away in the heat of his gaze. Then he turned back to the people who watched them. "Did anyone wonder how a stranger suddenly happened to know just where the crown jewels might be?"

An assortment of replies wafted up to the makeshift stage where Niko and Paige played their roles in this impromptu drama. "Yes." "That's right." "How did she know?"

"That's because she's done a lot of research on your behalf, my friends. In fact, some of you have already spoken with her. Allow me to present Paige Conner."

Paige thought her heart had stopped. But it made up for the pause when it started to thunk again, double time. "You knew?" She faced Niko accusingly.

He nodded and smiled.

She didn't feel much like smiling back, but she pasted a weak grin on her face and turned back to the crowd. She waved her fingers in acknowledgment of their amazed exclamations. Dozens of eyes peered at her assessingly. Could they see through Millicent's makeup and magic to the plain historian beneath? She supposed so, for several began to nod, then more. Most smiled—but what were they really thinking? "I'm sorry," she began, but Niko stopped her.

"We're sorry about the deception," he said, "but we thought Paige could be more useful to me—and the kingdom—if she was close to me rather than working or up in the tourist gallery. Now, then . . . I don't think most of you doubt that our Paige Conner, alias Princess Eleanora, is really a commoner, do you?"

No one did.

"And thanks to her we've found Les Fabuleux before I've taken a bride."

"Yes!" came excited shouts. "It's real! The legend is coming true."

Never mind that no one had to listen to the legends any longer, Paige thought. The idea had become too ingrained for them to drop at the divulging of its origins.

And now Niko had proven that he'd heard the legends. That he cared about his subjects. They would be convinced he was the right one to rule. There would be a happy ending in Dargentia.

Not for Paige Conner, though—of that she was sure. There was more to Paige's masquerade than simply appearing as a princess. Her scintillation was part of the facade. And that wasn't all. Niko needed to know the whole truth.

"Now, my friends," Niko continued, "if you would excuse us, there's a little matter I need to take care of: proposing to my bride."

A laugh rippled through the now-merry throng. "Hold out for half the kingdom, Paige," shouted a friendly voice.

Again the crowd turned to leave.

This time Niko did not call them back. Beyond the gate, the townsfolk mingled with the relaxed security guards, who turned and chatted amiably with them.

In moments, Paige and Niko were left alone.

Moments? Paige stole a look at her watch. Had all that only taken half an hour? She still had fifteen minutes to go before she'd turn back into an unscintillating historian in jeans and T-shirt. But how could she explain everything to Niko in such a short time?

He gently took her hand and helped her down from the bench. Removing his tuxedo jacket, he spread it on the stone.

"No," she protested. "You'll ruin it."

He shrugged, then tugged her down till she sat upon it in her clinging white gown. The seat was hard beneath her, and the jacket only partly protected her from chill.

He sat beside her, saying nothing at first, just looking out over the moat. In the water the geese swam toward them now that the place wasn't overpopulated by people. Still, the swans glided by.

He hadn't loosened her hand. Now he pivoted toward her until their knees touched. His thumbs stroked the soft skin of her palms. "I nearly told my relations that I was buckling under and marrying a commoner," he said.

Enjoying the sweet sensuality of the feather-light brush of his fingers, Paige asked, "That was why you called your family together?"

"Yes. Edouard joined the rest unfortunately, though, so I decided to wait. That was before you found Les Fabuleux. I figured he could gloat later, when the hotels stopped filling and I couldn't make my payments. Now that situation has changed."

"But, Niko, with the ball already in progress, there were so many lovely princesses to choose from. Rich ones. You didn't have to buckle under at all."

"Of course I did. My mind was already set on Princess Eleanora—"

"But—"

"—whom I already knew to be Paige Conner. But why the charade, Paige?"

He knew, and he wanted to marry her. She felt tears rise to her eyes—in gladness at the gift he had given her, and in sorrow that it would soon be taken away.

She tried to think of how to begin. "It's a long story. But I did what I did tonight because I was worried about you. You didn't seem to take the rumors about your subjects' intended insurrection seriously at first, and then when you did, you hired thugs. I love . . . I love your subjects, most of them. And I wanted to try to prevent something ugly."

"And instead you brought something beautiful."

"I don't know what you mean—" she began, but he stopped her by cupping her chin.

"You," he said, as soft as the breeze that carried the word away.

She froze. She melted. But she couldn't let him continue. He was attracted to her that night because of all the trappings Millicent had created. Not to mention her dratted magical scintillation.

She couldn't marry him, even if he'd been serious earlier. In mere minutes she'd be herself once more.

How could she explain—especially when he bent forward and his lips skimmed hers.

She closed her eyes, all protest obliterated by the tiny, tantalizing touch. She wanted to reach over and pull him tightly to her. Instead she remained perfectly still.

Quite suddenly, she was where she wanted to be: standing in his arms, pressed against his hard, heated body. "Paige," he murmured, and his mouth planted firmly upon hers. His lips explored for only an instant before his tongue thrust forward to find hers. She met it, moaning softly, her mouth as eager and active as his.

She was instantly lost in a surge of exquisite sensation as his hands stroked the delicate skin of her cheek and then moved on. They pioneered a path that made Paige weak with wanting: touching her eager breasts, then down to tantalize her thighs.

Shivers of sensuous pleasure shot through her, pulsing, moistening, weakening. Her fingers, too, explored smooth fabric hiding tense, taut planes; the soft silkiness of Niko's hair; the rougher texture of his beard. She wished she were again in the prince's bedroom, her masquerade ended. . . .

Masquerade. She wasn't real, and she had to tell him so. Now, before things went any further.

She broke away, bending forward in a bold attempt to catch her wavery breath. Her uneven voice erupted in a cross between a cry and a groan. "How long did you know Eleanora was me?"

One hand grasped her shoulder, attempting to pull her near again. Her body held back, though, every inch of her mind fought to resist her resistance.

"Nearly from the moment you walked into the Great Hall," he said, amusement changing his deep voice into a soft chuckle. "We've worked closely together for weeks, Paige." Giving up trying to tow her to him, he stepped forward with the same result. He whispered into her ear, "We've made love, Paige. I know

# Linda O. Johnston

your body. I've learned your mannerisms. Did you really think you could fool me?''

She gave that a moment's thought. She'd believed she could; she'd hoped she couldn't. "But without my glasses, with my hair up . . . and I scintillated, didn't I?''

"What?''

"Never mind. Niko, I didn't intend to come tonight. I didn't want to distract you from finding your princess.''

He laughed aloud. "You did a good job of it anyway.''

"But you were being stubborn," she continued as though he hadn't spoken. "I wanted to help you and your subjects, somehow create a win-win situation.''

"You've certainly done that. You won everyone's love by finding Les Fabuleux, and they'll love both of us all the more when I marry the commoner they want—you.'' He lifted her beneath her arms and whirled her about until she grew giddy. Then he set her down. She swayed, and he caught her. His coffee-colored eyes suddenly darkened as he stared at her face, as though seeking an answer written there. "You will marry me, Paige, won't you?''

She sighed and pulled away. She walked slowly toward the grassy bank of the moat. "I can't," she said, then realized she'd spoken too softly for him to hear.

But he was closer than she'd thought. He pivoted before her and stopped, blocking her path. "Why not?'' The deep voice she loved seemed wracked with pain, and she moved a step back, trying hard not to look at him.

"There are things you don't know," she said. She looked at her watch. There were ten minutes left. How could she tell him everything before her time was up?

Or maybe she didn't need to. She could stand right here and let him watch her turn back into the colorless nonentity he'd come to know and despise. If nothing else cooled his ardor, certainly that would.

But that was the coward's way. She had to explain.

Several squawking geese waddled at the edge of the bank, obviously hoping to be fed. The goslings were much larger now than when she'd first seen them. She shook her head at them all. She was even disappointing her animal friends tonight. But the worst disappointment would be hers, when she saw Niko's eyes after she told all.

"Do you remember the day I first arrived, when the forklift ran away and you saved me from its clutches? There wasn't anyone inside."

He nodded grimly. "I gave the workers the talking-to of their lives after that. They'll remember to set the brakes from now on."

"But it wasn't just—oh, listen, how about the day in the library when we thought we saw smoke? You do recall that?"

"Of course." He sounded puzzled and even a little angry, as though upset she'd changed the subject with nonsequiturs. "Turned out to be just a nest of moths in one of the old boxes."

She nodded. "It certainly looked that way. What about the cookies and milk in my room the night you sent me to bed without my supper?"

He laughed uneasily. "I still feel bad about that, but if this is to punish me—"

She whirled about to face him. "No, Niko. I . . . I'm going about this all wrong." She sighed and stared down at a clump of grass beneath them on the shadowed ground. "My parents," she said. "You remember what they told you about my childhood?"

"Yes. You liked fairy tales." There was a stiffness in his tone that made her certain she'd found the key to telling him.

"I more than liked them, Niko. I lived them." Her voice was tiny, and she cleared her throat. "It's not what you might think; you see—"

He interrupted. "I suppose you came here intending to catch a prince, as your mother said." She knew he wasn't as casual as he sounded.

"Well, no. But my fairy godmother did." There; she'd said it. Now let him think what he would.

He said nothing for so long that Paige wondered if her time was already up and he was stunned to see her transforming.

But then he laughed aloud, pulling her close to plant a hard, quick kiss on her mouth. "That's what this is about? You still pretend and make wishes as though you were a child? Oh, Paige, that's adorable!"

"It's no pretense! It's real. Ask Aldred." She drew back, though not too far. She could still feel the heat radiating from his body. Okay, she thought, spit it all out. "I'm dressed up this way thanks to Millicent."

"Who's—"

# Linda O. Johnston

"My fairy godmother. And the only reason you're attracted to me tonight is because I begged Millicent, for once, to let me scintillate. Well, for twice, really. The first time it worked was the night I went to your bedroom. But there was a deadline; there always is. In fact, mine is coming up in about—" She looked at her watch. "Oh, my gosh. Seven minutes. Niko, I'm afraid we'll have to finish this conversation tomorrow. Actually, that's a good idea, because—"

"You're babbling," he interrupted, stopping her from replying by capturing her lips with his mouth.

She couldn't babble anymore, held so tightly in his arms. She couldn't even think with his hard, huggable body so tight against hers. From her chest against his to the feel of his hips—and oh, a hardness that pressed her right in the stomach and made her whole body throb again and tense.

Well, she'd done what she could. She'd told him the truth. And if he chose to ignore it . . .

His lips were teasing hers as he whispered soft words against her skin that she couldn't hear. And then they trailed a path up her cheek till they settled on her earlobe and sent chills skittering through her body.

"Oh, Paige," he said. "My Princess Eleanora, or whoever you are. I love you."

And then his mouth was on hers yet again, silencing the response she longed to give, to return the precious gift he had just given her.

Then he pulled away. "But, Paige, if I really thought you were just like any other American vampire I'd met, who wanted me for my title, or if I believed that you could really seduce me through magic—well, let's not even talk about that. One's as true as the other."

He hadn't really heard her. It was too fantastic for him to believe: that she'd done all she did through a fairy godmother. But when he someday realized the truth—

"Now," he said, "let's get back to the evening's business. There's a ball going on inside without me, and a group of visitors waiting with anticipation. I need to announce my bride." Suddenly she was no longer in his arms. He was on his knees before her, here on the dirty, grassy bank of the moat in his tuxedo.

He was nearly surrounded by curious geese, who backed off,

honking angrily, as soon as it became apparent that there was no bread for them in the romantic scene being played before them.

Arrogant, regal Nicholas of Dargentia was kneeling before ordinary Paige Conner, begging for her hand. "Marry me, Paige."

Damn the consequences! "Oh, Niko. I love you, and of course I'll marry you, as long as you understand—"

"What a pretty scene," came a low voice from somewhere behind the prince.

Niko rose immediately, turning to face the intruder, standing alongside Paige.

She gasped. It was Edouard. The sly, insidious silver fox was holding a small but incredibly lethal-looking revolver, and he was pointing it right at her.

Niko tried to step in front of Paige, wanting to protect this strange, wonderful woman he loved.

Instead she pushed ahead of him. "Think of your subjects," she urged in a whisper. "They need you."

"Not really." Edouard sounded much too casual. He looked incongruous in his tuxedo and tails, holding a gun like an ordinary thug. "Why, tonight, for example, no one misses the two of you at all. While you've been out here, Rudy and Charlotte have been hosting the royals, and the tourists have been lapping it all up. Though they heard unusual noises coming from outside, Charlotte explained in English, in her inimitable way, that the townsfolk were throwing a surprise 'potty' to congratulate Niko on the success of the ball. Oh, and by the way, congratulations *are* in order. I hear you two found Les Fabuleux tonight. How wonderful. I'll enjoy them."

"Don't count on it," Niko found himself growling.

"Oh, I do," Edouard said. "Of course, the way the story will go is that some miserable tourist heard about the jewels and stole them right away. Strangers have no regard whatsoever for royalty. Why, they killed the prince and his bride with no compunction." He gave a great, sham sigh. "Good thing I'm around with the little promise Niko made to me in writing. Once there are no more jewels or tourists the throne will be mine. And I'll know how to keep law and order just fine."

Despite Niko's attempts to keep her back, Paige maneuvered her shoulder so she was once more in front. "I won't make you laugh by reciting that old cliché, you'll never get away with this, but you do realize, don't you, that Niko has a security force here. They'll know—''

"They think their job is done, my dear. The guards are dancing with the guests. The Dargentian mob scene for which they'd prepared has been played out, though not the way I planned it, I'm sorry to say. But never mind. I'm fine at improvising. Same result, different path. It doesn't matter.''

"It matters to me,'' Niko hissed. He grabbed Paige's shoulders to thrust her behind him once and for all, but she resisted, stopping right beside him. The fierce, determined expression on her face made him wince. She was going to try something—something that could get her killed. "Don't!'' he whispered, frantic because she seldom obeyed his orders.

"Excellent advice,'' said Edouard. The gun was pointed straight at Niko. "Stop this ridiculousness at once or I'll shoot your prince.''

Niko glanced into Paige's eyes, realizing the fear he saw there was for him. "It's okay,'' he commanded. "Paige, just get out of the way.''

He watched as she hesitated. She looked at the gun. She looked at Niko. She looked toward the moat, where those damned geese milled on the nearby bank.

And then she cried out, "Millicent, I'm hungry! Bring me food, right now. Bread. Lots of it!''

What the devil was she doing?

The air turned into a crackling chaos. A sweet, floral scent assailed his senses—lilacs? A sudden sprinkling of dust shimmered around them and swirled into a single cylinder at Paige's side. For a moment, Niko thought he saw a face in it—a beaming, beatific old lady with a cap of golden hair.

And then there was bread all about them, covering the ground. Edouard had slices at his feet, in his hair, even hanging from his pockets.

Geese waddled forward with amazing speed, honking, complaining and pecking about. Paige stooped. "Here,'' she said, shoving a mass of slices at the bewildered-looking Edouard. Now he held the gun with both hands, without lowering it. Paige nestled the bread into the crook of his elbows.

"Hey!'' he shouted as Paige walked away. He stepped menacingly forward—and was immediately surrounded by the gaggle of griping geese. They pecked at his shins, stretched up to strike at the bread in his arms. He aimed the gun first at one bird, then another, seeming too dazed to fire. With a mighty "Honk!" one big male flapped its wings and flew far enough to reach some bread in Edouard's hair with its outstretched beak. He stepped back, raising his hands to protect his face. The gander knocked the gun from his hands.

"Ow! Stop this! These creatures are hurting me!" As Edouard swatted at the offending birds, Paige knelt and picked up the gun.

Niko stared. What had happened? He hadn't a clue.

And who had that eerie, ephemeral person been?

Mustering all the wits he could persuade out of his poor, tired brain, he decided to behave as if all were normal; he had to convince himself he was still sane.

Wasn't he?

He strode toward Paige, the prince in him taking charge. He slipped the gun from her shaking fingers and trained it on the bruised and ragged figure of Edouard, who stood still with a glazed expression in his eyes. Niko gave a glance toward the geese, now happily nibbling mounds of bread along the shore. Where had all those cursed carbohydrates come from?

Shaking his head, he concentrated on reality—the gun, and the man who'd threatened to use it on the woman Niko loved. Not to mention his own royal person.

"Come on," he growled to Edouard, surprised his voice sounded so strong and controlled. "I have a security man who'll know just what to do with you."

"Of course," said Edouard, the silver fox now as meek as a lamb cutlet. His head hanging wearily, his once immaculate formal clothes now shreds of expensive cloth, he headed toward the gate through the wall.

Niko began to follow, then turned back to make sure Paige was coming, too. And to convince himself, once more, that he hadn't really seen what he'd thought he'd seen.

Fantastic fading faces indeed!

The geese, honking happily, pecked their way through the piles of bread that could not really have materialized right then and there.

Paige still stood by the bank of the moat, straight and strong, yet somehow fragile.

It was then that Niko noticed a haze around her. The night's humidity seemed concentrated in a fog that suddenly swirled about her slender body. Wispy tendrils of mist meandered toward her face, caressing the black hood of her upswept hair beneath her tiara, which seemed to shoot sparks into the air. Her long silky gown elongated into a train of wispy white.

Without thinking, Niko cried, "Paige?"

Through the fog surrounding her, she stretched out her arm and stared. For a moment Niko thought she was looking at her shimmering wristwatch. "Oh, blast those bloody rules!" Niko heard her cry, the sound reverberating and rusty as though she stood in a corrugated metal drainpipe. "Millicent!"

Before Niko could ask questions, Paige shot by him, the fog still shrouding her as she ran.

He shook his head. It had been a long, trying night, what with entertaining at the ball, calming his subversive subjects, finding Les Fabuleux, then dealing with the perfidious Edouard.

He had every right to be exhausted, to let his usually razor-sharp mind dull to muzziness.

That was the explanation for seeing imaginary faces and bread, and for this brand-new illusion as well.

Paige had only been behind his back for mere seconds before she ran off. Sure, she'd gotten her lovely white gown a little dirty digging for jewels and keeping Edouard from killing them. Her swan-black hair had begun to fall from its adorable upsweep. Maybe her eyes were tired, too, for he'd guessed she'd been wearing contact lenses; how else could their amber color have turned temporarily green?

But as she'd sped by, he'd looked at her. Hard. Surely she wasn't suddenly dressed in her grungy Smithsonian T-shirt . . . and glasses.

# Chapter Twenty-six

Early the next morning, Paige, dressed in a white blouse and dark skirt, sat inside the noisy, bustling Dargentia airline terminal. Unlike when she'd arrived, it was finished and furnished. The aromas of coffee, cooled air and snack-stand food battled the scents of newness and paint.

Surprisingly for the early hour, the place was filled with people. Some worked there: airline ticketers, porters, terminal staff. Others were travelers: new tourists arriving, royalty and more tourists departing.

Paige was leaving.

She wasn't saying good-bye to anyone, not even Annette and Marcel. She'd write and tell them . . . something.

She was calling herself every cowardly name in the books. And she had read a lot of books.

But since last night had turned into such a disaster, how could she do anything else but flee as fast as the next flight would take her?

An SAS jet to Stockholm was departing in forty minutes. She'd be on it. Surely, there would be flights from Sweden that would take her home to America.

All of her, that is, but her heart. It had betrayed her by becoming Dargentian. More specifically, it belonged to Dargentia's handsome, heroic ruler. But she'd survive, somehow, without it.

Just as she'd have to survive without her favorite athletic shoe.

Oh, she wasn't Cinderella, not by a long shot. Ol' Cindy had gracefully lost a glass slipper as she'd fled her ball at midnight.

Not clunky Paige Conner. No, she'd begun her magical transformation right in front of her prince. From gorgeous gown to dirty work clothes. From pretty princess to gawky historian in glasses. Edouard had seen her as she'd dashed through the gate where he stood, but at least now no one would listen to him. His name in this kingdom was now mud. But what had Niko thought?

Then, to top it all off, Millicent's magic hadn't even extended to tying her tennis shoes. As she'd hurried through the kitchen door, she'd lost one.

But the kitchen hadn't been empty any more, and she'd had no time to pick up the shoe. Instead, she'd had to slither between the refrigerator and a wall beside it to avoid Maibelle and the rest. When all backs were turned, she hustled out the door and sneaked to her room.

Not even Millicent had been there to comfort her when she cried her eyes out, darn her. She was probably somewhere smooching with Aldred.

That night, Paige had kept her door locked so anyone without magical powers couldn't get in.

Niko had come. He'd rattled the door at first, then pounded. "Okay, Paige," he finally said, sounding arrogant once more in his obvious outrage. "I'll get my explanations first thing in the morning."

Which was why she hitched a ride with some departing royals before the sun was up, why she sat there in the terminal, waiting for the first departing public airliner to board. The princesses and their parents were leaving on private planes.

A garbled voice crackled an announcement over the loud-speaker. Paige sighed and settled back onto the hard, molded terminal seat. She planted her feet on the tough new carpet in the royal colors of Dargentia: silver, red and purple. Then she rummaged in her carry-on for something to amuse herself—a mystery, maybe. Instead, her fingers curled around the souvenir brochure she'd written for the ball.

"Oh, you were there. Wasn't it wonderful?" A wizened matron sitting to her left clapped her hands in glee. She wore a bright blue Dargentian man's shirt tucked into a tight skirt that barely spanned her ample behind. "I don't know if the rumors are true, but did you hear they found the crown jewels last night?"

Paige nodded, saying nothing, hoping the woman would go away.

But she didn't. "Who did you vote for to become princess?"

"I'm afraid I didn't vote," Paige said. Maybe her cool tone would convey her unwillingness to converse.

No such luck. Mint hung in the air from where the woman breathed. "If you didn't vote—are you one of the princesses

308

yourself?'' She peered through myopic, pale-lashed eyes at Paige.

"I'm nobody," Paige said wearily. As a question she'd hoped to have answered crossed her mind, she perked up. This woman was a tourist. "Let me ask you something. Prince Niko was certain that the only thing that would attract tourists here regularly would be if he married a princess. What if he wed a commoner?"

The woman appeared to take great pains to ponder the question. "Well, marrying the prince would make her a princess. Then she wouldn't be a commoner any more."

Paige smiled sadly at this piece of wisdom. "That's true." Would all the world's tourists think the same and come flocking no matter who the prince married? If so, Niko's original premise had been flawed.

No matter. Not now. He had the crown jewels, and Edouard's deal would no longer hang over him. Edouard would, at a minimum, be banished. And Niko's subjects now believed he could wed whomever he wanted.

Maybe he would decide on one of the princesses at the ball. Or on a commoner. Or Suzanne.

But not Paige.

"Why not?" came a wavery voice from her right side. She thought she smelled lilacs.

"Millicent!" She looked toward the voice. Millicent walked up like any living being and sat in the molded seat. No pixie dust here in this public place, thank heavens.

"How are you, Eleanora, dear?" Millicent's bright orange sweat shirt read, FORGET KISSING FROGS. CALL YOUR FAIRY GODMOTHER TODAY.

Paige opened her mouth automatically to protest the use of her real name, especially now, when people might recognize it from the ball last night.

But what did it matter anymore?

Still, Millicent's presence, in the open, confused her. "What are you doing here?"

"Traveling, just like anyone else, dear."

"But—"

"Fairy godmothers get vacations, too."

"Ssshh!" Paige looked quickly behind her, but the matron who'd been talking to her was gone.

In fact, this area of the airport was suddenly deserted. Magic,

# Linda O. Johnston

Paige presumed. Millicent might be traveling, but not in the same style as mere mortals. If she needed privacy, she had it.

"Anyway," Millicent went on, her naturally sad eyes sparkling, "I'm overdue for a rest. You've kept me busy for years, Eleanora. You don't know how taxing it is to stay ready to act at any moment as a fairy godmother." Paige opened her mouth to comment, but Millicent waved it away. "Oh, I was delighted to do it for you, dear. But in a way it's a relief to know you won't need me anymore."

"No," Paige said sadly, "I won't. This time I'm really through with princes and wishes and fairy tales. At least I won't have to worry about scintillation any more. But Millicent, since we're not going to see each other again, couldn't you just give me one itsy-bitsy hint about the secret of fairy tales?"

Millicent laughed, causing the usually smooth parchment of her skin to crinkle at the corners of her mouth. "You know I can't, Eleanora. But you discovered the secret last night—if you only realized it."

Paige's mind somersaulted in confusion. What had she learned last night—except that Niko thought he loved her when she used magic and assumed scintillation. She didn't want him through magic—but, oh, how she wanted him.

Maybe, after all, just a touch of magic wouldn't hurt.

"Just think about it." Compassion glowed in the elderly elf's dark eyes. "You have the answers."

"Let me ask the questions first," Paige grumbled. She hesitated. "Millicent, before you stop being my fairy godmother, is there any possibility of building some honest-to-goodness scintillation into me permanently? Just a little bit. Enough to keep me from being eternally gauche."

"Certainly, dear. But you were never gauche, except in your own mind."

Paige sat up straight. Millicent was wrong, of course—but she'd agreed to cast a scintillation spell. "Should we go to the restroom or somewhere, or could you do it right here?"

Millicent's eyes lost their happy sparkle. "Oh, Eleanora, you're not thinking. Don't you want to know the secret of fairy tales?"

Of course Paige did. After all these years of hearing about it, this could be her last chance to learn, since Millicent was hanging up her magical shingle. "Help me, Millicent. At least give me some hints."

Her fairy godmother nodded, and a spray of stray sparkling dust spread about the area from her gold-flecked hair. "When did you begin scintillating last night?"

"I'm not sure." And what did that have to do with the secret of fairy tales? Still, she had to play along—especially if she wanted to scintillate forever. "I didn't notice till I got to the ball. Was it part of the magic you used while dressing me, or was it a separate spell that started later?"

Millicent used her forefinger as a zipper to close her mouth.

"Separate, I assume," Paige continued, "since there was that other night that I didn't want to change clothes, but you let me scintillate till midnight. And, oh, how embarrassing it was when I suddenly stopped."

"Did you?"

The soft question slapped Paige. "Well, sure. Didn't I?"

Millicent shrugged and gave an encouraging smile, but her elderly, puckered lips stayed shut.

"Of course I did. And I didn't scintillate again till last night."

"What about in the mountains, Eleanora?"

Paige felt herself redden. "That was different. There was the excitement of the treasure hunt, and we didn't do much talking—at least not outside the car."

"And last night? Did you talk?"

Paige nodded, feeling her straight, dark hair caress the sides of her cheeks beside her glasses. "Of course, Niko thought at first that I was Princess Eleanora. But I was in love with him. More than anything, I wanted to scintillate for him, so . . ." She stopped and stared at Millicent suspiciously. "You *did* work magic on me, didn't you?"

"Well, of course, dear. You didn't bring such a beautiful gown with you. And you know how contact lenses usually bother your eyes." Millicent's tiny, shoe-button eyes didn't meet hers. In fact, they seemed to have found some interesting spots to count in the acoustical ceiling.

"But those things were on the outside. I'm talking about the spell you cast for my . . ." Paige stopped, thinking. What if . . . ? "Wasn't there any such spell for my insides? Did I have to scintillate on my own?"

# Linda O. Johnston

Millicent leaned forward and swept Paige into a soft but substantial hug. "I knew you'd get it!"

Paige pulled away, standing swiftly to stare at the sweet-looking old creature who'd held the key to her happiness all these years—or had she? Slowly, she asked, "Then the secret of fairy tales—is it that all a fairy godmother can do is supply the trappings, but you have to supply your own scintillation?"

"Exactly!"

"And it was always within my control?"

Millicent bobbed her golden cap of hair in a nod that made Paige want to shake her till she bobbed some more. "That's it!"

Paige sank back onto the waiting-room seat, her fingertips at her cheeks as she shook her head. It was simple. "Then Cinderella scintillated on her own. So did Snow White, Beauty with her Beast, the whole sweet, fictional lot of them. Their wonderful personalities were their own; the magic was outside them. It was obvious. Why didn't I see it?"

"Because you wanted too much from magic, Paige dear."

"But the magic was in me all the time. I can't believe it. I—"

"If you think I'm going to let you fly away without saying good-bye, Ms. Conner, you're crazy!" came a wonderful, familiar baritone from behind her.

Swallowing hard, Paige looked first at Millicent, who smiled at her beatifically. Then she turned.

Niko was there, and in his hand was her dirty old neon-striped athletic shoe. "Did you lose this?" he asked.

He stood straight and tall before her, wearing his customary costume of peasant shirt and tight trousers. He looked even more magnificent than he had in formal wear at the ball. The only way he looked even better was when he wore nothing. . . .

Paige cleared her throat, wishing instead to clear her mind of such wistful thinking. "Thanks for coming to say good-bye, Niko," she said.

"I'm here for some answers," he said, "though I've learned a few already." He nodded toward Aldred, who'd stepped up behind him. The elderly majordomo, for the first time since Paige had known him, wasn't wearing a suit. Instead, he wore blue jeans and, over them, a sweatshirt that said LOVE A FAIRY GODMOTHER TODAY.

312

Paige moved her eyes from Aldred to Millicent and back again. She couldn't help blurting out, "Are you two really running off together?"

"That's right, dear. Aldred and I—well, I think it's time I had a life of my own."

"*Are* you alive?" asked Paige in amazement.

"Even better," Aldred said with a big wink that made Paige blush.

At least someone was going to have a happy ending.

"Now, Eleanora, dear, hand it over," Millicent demanded.

"What?" Paige felt completely bewildered.

"Your plane ticket. You won't be needing it, and Aldred and I have decided to hop the first jet out of here to adventure."

"But—"

Niko came closer to Paige, towering above her. His heady scent of autumn leaves and citrus made her recall a certain mountaintop haven, where they'd made love so sweetly.

He was here for answers. Did she dare divulge all?

"I'm forgetting my manners," she said. "Niko, this is Millicent. She's my—"

"Aldred introduced us already," Niko said in the deep voice she loved, "and Millicent told me a bit about you and her . . . special abilities. I have to admit I wouldn't have believed it if I hadn't seen her in action, but there it was: magic." He looked at Paige intently. "I guess you put a spell on me." His glare was accusing, and Paige felt like shriveling beneath it.

She held her ground, though. Her whole world might depend on what she said and did next. "Niko, please listen to me. I did believe in fairy tales, as my parents said. But I didn't come here to catch a prince. The magic I asked from Millicent wasn't to make you care but so I could help you."

Except maybe for a little scintillation here and there. But if that came from inside her anyhow, it didn't count.

Niko took a step toward her. He was so close, she could nearly touch him. She wanted to—but she kept her hands at her sides.

"I did a lot of thinking last night," Niko said slowly. "Maybe this prince thing isn't really for me after all. I'm thinking of abdicating, letting my people rule themselves."

Paige gasped. "Oh, Niko, no! They want you. They need you."

"If I were plain Nicholas Smith or Jones, I could ask you to

# Linda O. Johnston

marry me. And would you then?''

Moistness mounted to Paige's eyes, and she blinked to keep it right there instead of cascading down her cheeks. She'd thought that was what he had in mind last night, before Edouard brandished a gun at them. But that was when he thought she was Princess Eleanora.

No, he had known the truth by then.

But that was while she was scintillating.

On her own. Not through magic.

Still, that was last night; this was now. She was holding nothing back from him, certainly not the truth. ''Niko, it wouldn't matter to me if you had no name at all. I love you, not your name, rank or serial number. But I care about your country, your subjects. I couldn't let you do that to them.''

''You, my dear Ms. Conner, are not in a position to tell me what to do.''

Hearing the old domineering tone she knew so well, she looked up through her tears, only to find him smiling.

The public address system crackled; then a garbled voice announced Paige's flight. Whatever magic Millicent had used to clear the area had apparently ended. Passengers suddenly surrounded them, pushing into line. People in raincoats and hats, carrying books and bags and baggage, all took up their quest for the best place in the queue.

And then someone recognized Niko.

''Hey, it's the prince!''

Suddenly, they were surrounded by tourists and their comments. ''The ball was great, Your Highness.'' ''I intend to be the one to win your contest and dance at your wedding.'' ''Who are you going to marry?''

With the last question, Paige hazarded a glance at Niko. Surely he had been joking. He wouldn't toss away his throne. But had he selected his princess?

He was watching her, his bearded chin upthrust arrogantly. She couldn't read the expression in his inscrutable coffee-dark eyes.

No matter. It was over. She had a plane to catch.

Then he stepped up beside her and whispered in her ear, ''Let's see. I think we were rudely interrupted last night by Edouard.'' Seemingly oblivious of the surrounding crowd, Niko knelt on the terminal floor. ''Paige Conner, will you marry me?''

314

She couldn't hold back any longer; warm tears streamed down her cheeks as she smilingly pulled him back to his feet. "As Prince Niko or Nicholas Smith?"

"Does it matter?"

She shook her head vehemently, only to find any answer she might have made frozen. Niko's mouth captured hers. He tasted her gently, then teased her teeth with his tongue. Her arms swept about him, her fingers burrowed into his soft, nape-length hair as she centered all her consciousness on that deepening kiss. She sighed as he explored the shallow cavern of her mouth. Small, soothing sounds rumbled from within his throat. Her legs grew loose as noodles, and he swept her up into his arms, his lips not missing a beat of that deep, dampening, captivating kiss.

The flashes of tourists' cameras turned the waiting area into a frenzy of fireworks.

"Oh, Niko," she was finally able to whisper. "If you're sure—"

"I, my dear Paige, am always sure." He placed her gently back on the floor, then pulled from his finger the huge signet ring. He pushed it onto the thumb of her left hand. "This will have to do till we can get one of Les Fabuleux set into something suitable." He lifted her hand for a quick kiss, as though to seal the ring in place, then turned to the gathering crowd. "How many of you voted for me to wed Princess Eleanora of Monteubique at the ball last night?"

Nearly all the tourists raised their hands.

"Great! You're in the drawing, then. That means one of you might be our lucky winner to return for our wedding—" He was interrupted by a loud cheer that made Paige feel her cheeks go pink.

"When will it be?" someone shouted.

"Tomorrow?" Niko replied, looking at Paige.

"I think we'd better talk to your subjects—"

"Our subjects," he interrupted.

Smiling, she continued, "I recall hearing a legend about when and how a prince must marry."

Niko groaned, then laughed and picked Paige up, whirling her about as he kissed her so soundly that she wished Millicent would use her magic and make them be alone yet again.

A strange beeping sounded behind them. Paige pulled away

from Niko long enough to see a vehicle coming straight at them.

A sense of déjà vu overtook her. Hadn't the same thing happened, right here at the airport, several months before, when Millicent had engineered a near accident with a forklift to introduce her to Niko?

She focused on the barreling cart. It was one of those things used at airports to move people from one end to another when time was short or passengers needed help.

This one was captained by Aldred and navigated by Millicent.

"Hop on, Your Highnesses," Aldred commanded.

"We need to get you out of here," Millicent said. "Quickly, so we can catch a plane."

"You will be back soon, Millicent, won't you?" Paige asked as the throng of tourists parted reluctantly to let the entourage through. "I have one more wish for you."

She smiled as the fairy godmother and her majordomo exchanged worried glances. Reaching out to take Niko's hand, she leaned over to nestle close against his strong, warm shoulder. She looked up into those dark, delightful eyes she loved and said, quite scintillatingly, "I'm looking forward to a fairy-tale wedding."

**Bestselling Author Of** *A Stolen Rose*

Sensible Julia Addison doesn't believe in fairy tales. Nor does she think she'll ever stumble from the modern world into an enchanted wood. Yet now she is in a Highland forest, held captive by seven lairds and their quick-tempered chief. Hardened by years of war with rival clans, Darach MacStruan acts more like Grumpy than Prince Charming. Still, Julia is convinced that behind the dark-eyed Scotsman's gruff demeanor beats the heart of a kind and gentle lover. But in a land full of cunning clansmen, furious feuds, and poisonous potions, she can only wonder if her kiss has magic enough to waken Darach to sweet ecstasy.

_52086-9                                    $5.99 US/$7.99 CAN

# Guardian Angel

## Linda Winstead

Despite her father's wish that she marry and produce heirs for his spread, Melanie Barnett prefers shooting her suitors in the backside to looking them in the face. Then a masked gunman rescues her from an attempted kidnapping, and Mel has to give him the reward he requests: a single kiss.

Everybody in Paradise, Texas, believes that Gabriel Maxwell is a greenhorn dandy who has no business on a ranch. Yet he is as handy with his pistol as with a lovely lady. To keep Mel from harm, he disguises himself and protects her. But his brazen masquerade can't hide his obvious desire. And when his deception is revealed, he will either face Mel's fierce wrath—or her fiery rapture.

_51970-4                                    $4.99 US/$5.99 CAN

# WEST WIND

## Linda Winstead

Annabelle St. Clair has the voice of an angel and the devil at her heels. On the run for a murder she didn't commit, the world-renowned opera diva is reduced to singing in saloons until she finds a handsome gunslinger willing to take her to safety in San Francisco.

A restless bounty hunter, Shelley is more at home on the range than in Annabelle's polite society. Yet on the rugged trail, he can't resist sharing with her a passion as vast and limitless as the Western sky.

But despite the ecstasy they find, Annabelle can trust no one, especially not a man with dangerous secrets—secrets that threaten to ruin their lives and destroy their love.

_3796-3                                     $4.99 US/$5.99 CAN